"*Double Indemnity* is another winner from Robert Whitlow, one of my favorite authors. The taut suspense builds until the likable pastor is falsely accused of murder, and his new girlfriend, an attorney, has to solve the case. Highly recommended!"

—COLLEEN COBLE, *USA TODAY* BESTSELLING AUTHOR OF *THE VIEW FROM RAINSHADOW BAY* AND THE ANNIE PEDERSON SERIES

"A rich and compelling story of family, faith, and friendship with just the right dose of legal thriller, *Relative Justice* is a winner."

—*SOUTHERN LITERARY REVIEW*

"Robert Whitlow's legal expertise shines in *Relative Justice*, a story of patent infringement and illegal gains, but it's his characters who will steal readers' hearts. Whitlow's fans are sure to enjoy going along for a memorable, roller-coaster ride."

—KELLY IRVIN, AUTHOR OF *TRUST ME*

"*Promised Land* is a book about coming home. Of becoming settled in your spirit and your relationships. With layers of intensity, thanks to international intrigue, moments of legal wrangling, and pages of sweet relationships, this book is rich and complex. A wonderful read."

—CARA PUTMAN, AUTHOR OF *LETHAL INTENT*

"This tense legal thriller from Whitlow boasts intriguing characters . . . One gripping chapter leads to the next . . . Readers will have a hard time putting this one down."

—*PUBLISHERS WEEKLY* ON *CHOSEN PEOPLE*

"If you're looking for a book with unexpected twists and turns that delves into the cultures of Palestine, Israel, and their peoples, you must check out this engaging novel."

—BOOKREPORTER.COM ON *CHOSEN PEOPLE*

"A legal thriller written from a contemporary evangelical Christian worldview, *Chosen People* presents intriguing, well-rounded characters, thought-provoking moral dilemmas, tense drama, and several surprising plot twists."

—*MYSTERY SCENE*

"Robert Whitlow's *Chosen People* is compelling, realistic, and inspiring. Robert combines the intensity of a legal battle against terrorists with a poignant depiction of Israel, with all of its tensions and grandeur. As a lawyer who handles cases for terrorism victims, I loved the realism of the novel and felt deeply the joys, disappointments, and triumphs of its characters. But the matters of the law were eclipsed by matters of the heart—faith, love, and hope in the midst of despair— this is where Whitlow truly shines."

—RANDY SINGER, BESTSELLING AUTHOR OF *RULE OF LAW*

"Whitlow writes a fast-paced legal suspense with amazing characters. There are twists and turns throughout, and a number of unexpected surprises to heighten the suspense. Whitlow is an amazing writer and he touches upon delicate topics with grit and respect."

—*RT BOOK REVIEWS*, 4 STARS, ON *A TIME TO STAND*

"Whitlow's timely story shines a spotlight on prejudice, race, and the pursuit of justice in a world bent on blind revenge. Fans of Greg Iles's *Natchez Burning* will find this just as compelling if not more so."

—*LIBRARY JOURNAL*, STARRED REVIEW, ON *A TIME TO STAND*

"Part mystery and part legal thriller . . . Definitely a must-read!"

—*RT BOOK REVIEWS*, 4 STARS, ON *THE WITNESSES*

"Whitlow's characters continuously prove that God loves the broken and that faith is a lot more than just showing up to church. [This] contemplative novel is a fine rumination on ethics, morality, and free will."

—*PUBLISHERS WEEKLY* ON *THE WITNESSES*

"Attorney and Christy Award–winning author Whitlow pens a character-driven story once again showcasing his legal expertise . . . Corbin is highly relatable, leaving readers rooting for his redemption even after family and friends have written him off."

—*PUBLISHERS WEEKLY* ON *A HOUSE DIVIDED*

"Christy Award winner Whitlow's experience in the law is apparent in this well-crafted legal thriller. Holt's spiritual growth as he discovers his faith and questions his motives for hiding his secret is inspiring. Fans of John Grisham will find much to like here."

—*LIBRARY JOURNAL* ON *THE CONFESSION*

DOUBLE INDEMNITY

ALSO BY ROBERT WHITLOW

Relative Justice
Trial and Error
A Time to Stand
The Witnesses
A House Divided
The Confession
The Living Room
The Choice
Water's Edge
Mountain Top
Jimmy
The Sacrifice
The Trial
The List

THE CHOSEN PEOPLE NOVELS
Chosen People
Promised Land

THE TIDES OF TRUTH NOVELS
Deeper Water
Higher Hope
Greater Love

THE ALEXIA LINDALE NOVELS
Life Support
Life Everlasting

DOUBLE INDEMNITY

ROBERT WHITLOW

THOMAS NELSON
Since 1798

Published in Nashville, Tennessee, by Thomas Nelson. Thomas Nelson is a registered trademark of HarperCollins Christian Publishing, Inc.

Thomas Nelson titles may be purchased in bulk for educational, business, fundraising, or sales promotional use. For information, please email SpecialMarkets@ThomasNelson.com.

Library of Congress Cataloging-in-Publication Data

Names: Whitlow, Robert, 1954- author.
Title: Double indemnity / Robert Whitlow.
Description: Nashville, Tennessee: Thomas Nelson, [2023] | Summary: "Matt and Elena Thompson present the picture of perfection. But their enviable life isn't all it seems. Their marriage is on the rocks, and financial disaster looms. Then Matt is killed in a hunting accident, and the questions and accusations begin to mount"-- Provided by publisher.
Identifiers: LCCN 2023001287 (print) | LCCN 2023001288 (ebook) | ISBN 9780785234739 (TP) | ISBN 9780785234746 (HC) | ISBN 9780785234753 (epub) | ISBN 9780785234760 (audio download)
Subjects: LCGFT: Christian fiction. | Novels.
Classification: LCC PS3573.H49837 D68 2023 (print) | LCC PS3573.H49837 (ebook) | DDC 813/.54--dc23/eng/20230203
LC record available at https://lccn.loc.gov/2023001287
LC ebook record available at https://lccn.loc.gov/2023001288

Printed in the United States of America

23 24 25 26 27 LBC 5 4 3 2 1

To those moving from religion to relationship. Enjoy the journey.

"You will seek me and find me when you seek me with all your heart."

JEREMIAH 26:13 NIV

PROLOGUE

CONNOR GRANTHAM MOVED SILENTLY THROUGH the woods. A cold mist hovered near the ground. Wearing olive-green pants and a light brown jacket, he'd slipped on a bright yellow vest to make sure no overeager deer hunters confused him for a white-tailed buck on the move at the height of the yearly rut. An orange cap covered his blond hair and provided additional warning to hunters. Every breath from his mouth released a tiny cloud of vapor that disappeared by the time it reached his blue eyes. Two months away from his thirtieth birthday, Connor was a shade over six feet tall and regularly walked many miles up and down the nearby hills.

A cold snap during the last week of September had brought a hard frost to the foothills of the Appalachian Mountains in north Georgia. Cool weather didn't keep Connor indoors. Up before dawn, he'd strapped on a headlamp and hiked two miles in the darkness to a familiar hilltop where he watched the sun rise above the tree line to the east. Many leaves had fallen from the trees, and the sun's appearance highlighted the hardy yellow, red, and gold stragglers that remained. Every season also had its own personality. In fall the trees celebrated a job well done with an explosion of color.

Connor wasn't a day hiker who reached a summit, took a few selfies on his phone, and quickly moved on. He liked to sit on a rock outcropping and savor each unfolding second that a sunrise brought into view. During the two years since moving to Bryson from Atlanta, Connor had discovered five local summits that he visited on a regular basis at various times and seasons.

When he reached the boundary for the property managed by the Burnt Pine Tree Hunting Lodge, he became extra vigilant. The company that owned the one-thousand-acre game preserve released two or three trophy bucks every year and fed them corn at designated spots in an effort to keep them on the property until they could breed with local does or be hunted by clients. Photos of this year's big bucks had been posted on the Burnt Pine Tree website the previous week. The magnificent specimens were imported from a much larger hunting preserve located in the Upper Peninsula of Michigan. Since he'd started hiking in the area, Connor had never seen one of the animals in the woods. Because they were targeted so heavily by hunters, the life expectancy of the bucks was usually days or weeks. Earlier he'd heard gunshots in the distance. It might have been a hunter bagging one of the trophy bucks, but the most likely target was one of the local white-tailed deer that were as plentiful as squirrels in a city park.

A graduate of the divinity school at Princeton, Connor obeyed the law, except when trespassing across private property during his hikes. Nailed to a nearby tree was a large white rectangular metal sign that warned: "Property of Burnt Pine Tree Hunting Lodge—No Trespassing—Hunting Prohibited Except by Registered Guests— Violators Will Be Prosecuted." One of the board of directors for Burnt Pine Tree attended the church where Connor served as minister. Reg Bullock had been one of Connor's strongest supporters at the church. If an employee of the preserve reported Connor to the sheriff's department as a trespasser, a quick phone call from Reg would take care of any problem.

The final quarter mile of the hike crossed the northwest corner of the hunting lodge's property. Beyond that was a short path to the dirt road where Connor had parked his vehicle. He heard a rustling in the leaves and out the corner of his eye caught sight of something brown moving through the woods. He froze and waited. Two large does, strolling toward the boundary line of the preserve, came into view. Connor positioned himself behind a large oak tree, pulled out his phone from the front pocket of his shirt, and took several photos. Female deer this large weren't common. He heard a loud snort. A few seconds later he caught sight of a massive buck with an enormous set of antlers trotting after the does. It had to be one of the recently released trophy animals. The male deer stepped down into a shallow gully about twenty-five yards from where Connor hid behind the oak tree. The buck paused to sniff the air. Puffs of vapor from the deer's nostrils floated up into the chilly air. Connor counted twelve antler points on the "atypical" rack. Muscles bulged in the buck's neck. Connor's heart was pounding. He shifted to video mode and started filming. After a few seconds, the majestic animal let out another loud snort and trotted off after the does with his nose in the air. Connor kept filming. If the deer continued in the same direction, he would soon leave the Burnt Pine Tree property.

A few seconds later, Connor heard an even louder commotion. Suspecting it was another buck chasing the does, he swung his phone in the direction of the sound and kept recording. To capture both bucks on video in the same day would be incredible. A flash of orange ended Connor's excitement. It was a hunter running through the woods. Generally, the only reason for a hunter to move that rapidly in this location would be to trail a wounded animal. The man was wearing an orange hunting jacket and a black toboggan hat. He stumbled into the gully and fell. Regaining his feet, the man brushed himself off. Connor stopped recording and lowered his phone as the man picked up his rifle.

"Are you okay?" Connor called out.

The man spun around toward Connor. The black toboggan almost covered his entire face.

"Yeah, I stepped in a hole."

The hunter sounded like he was from England, not north Georgia.

"No wounded deer came this way," Connor said. "But I just saw a big buck chasing two does. They may be off the Burnt Pine Tree property by now."

"Which way is the road, mate?"

"Northwest," Connor answered as he pointed. "I'm going there myself if you want me to show you."

Without replying, the hunter turned his back on Connor and started jogging again. He quickly disappeared in the trees. Connor leaned against the oak tree and rewatched the video of the big buck. It was definitely something he would have to show Reg after church the following day.

Ten minutes later Connor reached the dirt access road. There were no fresh tire tracks near his vehicle. The man he'd seen in the woods must have parked someplace else. Before starting his Jeep, Connor glanced down at his phone as a call came through. It was Michelle Cantrell, the church secretary.

"Did you hear about Matt Thompson?" she asked.

"No."

"He's been shot in a hunting accident."

CHAPTER 1

THREE WEEKS EARLIER

THE PHONE ON ELIZABETH ACOSTA'S DESK BUZZED.

"Liz, come to the big conference room," barked Harold Pollard, the senior partner in the law firm. "Mr. and Mrs. Rodriguez are here. And bring your laptop."

Twenty-six years old with straight black hair that fell below her shoulders, Liz grabbed her laptop and left the small office she occupied next to the break room. Five feet two inches tall, the young lawyer had piercing dark eyes passed down from her father. She walked briskly down the hallway and into the reception area. With five attorneys, Pollard and Associates was the largest firm in Bryson.

The main conference room was an impressive space. Harold believed it was important to send a message to both clients and opposing counsel that the law firm was successful and prosperous. The mahogany table was surrounded by twelve chairs and rested on an oversized oriental carpet on top of a shiny wooden floor. A built-in wooden cabinet concealed a media center. There were four pieces of original artwork on the walls and a sculpture incorporating local birdlife in one corner. Harold always sat at the head of the table. Liz entered through double doors.

Her fifty-eight-year-old boss was a short, slightly built man with thinning brown hair. To his right was a Latino man and woman. The man was wearing a neck brace. Harold slid an accident report across the table to Liz.

"Mr. and Mrs. Rodriguez were referred to us by Angel Santiago, the man we represented last year shortly after you came to work for the firm," Harold said. "Tell them you're going to obtain their information so we can help them."

Liz relayed this information in Spanish with an accent influenced by her paternal grandmother, who'd escaped from Cuba in a small boat to Miami. Liz had a large vocabulary. Mr. Rodriguez responded in a soft voice that revealed roots in rural Mexico.

"Explain that if they hire our firm, you'll be available to keep them up-to-date," Harold said. "I'll be back in fifteen or twenty minutes."

Liz knew the drill. Using her laptop, she opened the client intake template and obtained the facts from Luis and Maria Rodriguez. According to the accident report, their vehicle had been struck on the driver's side by a pickup truck that ran a stop sign and T-boned them. Maria only suffered cuts and bruises, but Luis's left wrist was shattered, a devastating injury for a carpenter. As Luis described his injuries, Maria started crying. Liz handed her a tissue from a box in the middle of the table.

"We don't want money," Maria said through her sniffles. "I want my husband to be healthy and strong for me and our children."

"How many children do you have?"

"Three," Maria answered. "Two boys and a girl."

"What are their names and ages?"

These types of personal questions weren't part of the standard intake process, but Liz liked to learn about a client's family. It helped keep clients from becoming just another file number. Liz provided Maria with the phone number for a local food bank that could assist them while Luis was out of work.

Harold returned to the conference room. "Almost finished?" he asked.

"Not much more," Liz replied.

"Have you gone over our fee agreement?"

"No."

Harold looked at his watch. "I have to leave in ten minutes for a motion hearing in front of Judge Godwin. Are they going to hire us? Mr. Santiago said they'd been talking to one of the big outfits that advertise on TV."

"Let me find out," Liz replied.

She asked Luis if he wanted them to represent him.

"Yes," Maria answered, then looked at her husband, who nodded his head.

"I understood that much," Harold said. "Sign them up. Standard contingency contract and medical release forms. Give everything to Jessica so she can send out our rep paperwork to the insurance company for the other driver."

"Based on what Mr. Rodriguez tells me about his injuries, this may be a policy limits case," Liz said.

"That's what we like to hear," Harold replied.

Smiling, he leaned over and shook Luis's hand.

"Gracias," the lawyer said.

The simple word represented twenty-five percent of Harold Pollard's Spanish vocabulary and was the reason he'd hired Liz as an associate attorney. Since her arrival, the number of the firm's

Spanish-speaking clients had increased significantly, mirroring the growing Latino population of north Georgia. More and more workers employed by local manufacturers came from Mexico or one of the Central American countries. Whether they were hurt on the job, charged with a crime, or injured in an auto accident like Luis Rodriguez, they needed legal representation, and Harold Pollard was an excellent trial lawyer. The first time Liz sat with her boss in the courtroom and watched him cross-examine a witness, she knew why he'd earned the reputation locally as the best trial lawyer in town. The seasoned attorney's ability to deftly obtain what he needed from a witness was impressive.

After graduating in the lower half of her class at Ave Maria School of Law in Naples, Liz received no job offers in Florida. She hoped that after two to three years of experience in north Georgia, she might be able to return home and land an entry-level job with a Florida firm. For now, Liz's role at the Pollard firm remained pedestrian. Often, she felt more like a Spanish language translator than a lawyer.

After ushering Mr. and Mrs. Rodriguez to the reception area, Liz handed the accident report to Jessica Thorpe, one of the firm's legal assistants. A year older than Liz, Jessica came to work for the law firm shortly after high school. Married with two elementary-school-age children, she and Liz quickly became friends.

"I'll forward my intake sheet," Liz said.

"I'm on it," Jessica replied in a twangy north Georgia drawl.

As soon as Liz was back in her office the phone buzzed.

"It's Raphael," the firm receptionist said.

Liz's boyfriend was scheduled to fly from Miami to Atlanta the following day. Their on-again, off-again relationship was close to its third anniversary. The time between visits had grown longer, and

Liz had considered cutting the tie. But dating options were scarce in Bryson, and Raphael provided a link to home and the lifestyle Liz eventually wanted.

"I'll take it," she said.

===

With a row of windows that offered a panoramic view of the foothills to the west, Connor's office was a wonderful place to meditate. But the outward beauty couldn't soften the ugly words bouncing off the walls during the contentious marital counseling session. Elena Thompson took a third tissue from her expensive purse and wiped her eyes. The thirty-two-year-old woman from Richmond, Virginia, with hazel eyes and an athletically trim figure, had started attending Rock Community Church six months earlier. Unlike most visitors, she sat toward the front of the sanctuary and always let Connor know how much she enjoyed the sermon. Matt, her husband, had only attended the church two times. They'd moved to Bryson upon the recommendation of Reg Bullock, who served on the board of directors for Matt's company, Daughbert Technology.

"I don't feel married," Elena said and sniffled. "The reason we came here was to get away from the rat race of Atlanta and be together."

"We spend all day together," her husband retorted.

"Matt, be honest," Elena shot back. "We may be under the same roof, but you're in your office on the phone and your computer at the opposite end of the house from six thirty in the morning until six thirty at night and then back again after supper."

Connor had visited the couple's custom-designed home that

sprawled across a prime hilltop. The marriage was the first for Elena and the second for Matt, who was ten years older. Although they'd not admitted it to Connor in their previous counseling session, he suspected Matt and Elena's relationship was the cause for Matt's divorce from Anne, his first wife. Anne had primary custody of their two girls.

"You wanted me working from home so you'd know where I was all day," Matt replied in frustration. "This is a critical time for the company. We're trying to go global, and whether that succeeds or fails is on me. I have to be available when our overseas partners can talk. Everything is coming to a head. This is a make-or-break time for the business."

"I'm glad you brought that up. Tell Connor what you told me last night," Elena replied.

"Which part?" Matt said. "You didn't let me say anything for half an hour."

Connor winced. Elena swiped her eyes again with her tissue.

Matt turned to Connor. "First, I appreciate you listening to us spill our guts," he said. "This is hard, but Elena and I agree that we need help."

"Get to what you said last night," Elena said.

"Okay, okay. I have an apartment in downtown Atlanta that I use when I have to spend the night in the city for meetings. I've only spent the night there a few times over the past twelve months, but that's going to change when people fly in for extended sessions with management and our technical staff. It doesn't make sense for me to stay in Bryson, fight rush-hour traffic, risk being late, and keep people waiting."

"How long will this last?" Connor asked.

"No idea!" Elena interjected, throwing up her hands.

"It's hard to predict," Matt added. "I don't want to make a promise to Elena that I can't keep."

"I hate being alone, and he knows it."

Given the couple's history, Connor was confident that trust was a huge issue between them. But instead of identifying the problem, he decided to suggest a practical solution.

"Would it work for both of you to stay in Atlanta part of the time when Matt's there?" he asked.

"Are you planning on inviting Anne and the kids over for dinner?" Elena asked her husband.

"I want to see the girls, but I'll be super busy."

Elena turned to Connor. "What do you think about him having regular dinners with his ex-wife at the apartment where they lived when they were first married?" she asked. "He's kept the lease for twelve years! I told him to let it and her go!"

"She's the mother of my children! We have to communicate."

"I only want you to be more passionate about us than you are about her."

"We're wasting Connor's time!" Matt replied in frustration. "I agreed to a civil conversation, not to listen to you repeat what we've been over and over and over. I'm looking for guidance, not a rehash of grievances."

"This is all new to me," Connor said in a calm voice. "It's helpful to learn about the practical and personal challenges you're facing."

Connor stopped. Both Elena and Matt were staring at him, waiting for a pearl of wisdom to drop from his lips now that he was more informed. He cleared his throat.

"Let me identify some resources that we can study together and use as a framework for moving forward. I'll send the information to both of you by the end of the day."

"You mean a book?" Matt asked.

"Or books," Connor replied. "I've found that studying the words on a page enables people to consider perspectives about a problem that's not possible in the emotion of verbal communication."

"I like that idea," Elena said. "I think it'll help me."

"I'd prefer audio," Matt said doubtfully. "That's how I best process and retain information."

"Okay, I'll get something that's available in both formats. Do you want to schedule a follow-up meeting now?"

"Yes," Elena quickly replied.

"I guess." Matt shrugged. "I want to give this my best shot."

"Let's make it in a couple of weeks," Connor suggested. "That will give you time to digest what I'll send you."

"Two weeks?" Elena responded. "I'd like to see you before then."

"That can be arranged if you're able to do the homework."

"Homework?" Matt grunted. "This is counseling, not school."

"It has a different meaning in this environment," Connor replied. "If it helps, think about it as research."

After the couple left, Connor closed his eyes, not to pray but to block out the image of the two angry people who'd dumped the garbage of their lives in his lap and expected him to sort through it and find hidden treasure. He then gazed at the splendor of the nearby mountains. Taking a pair of binoculars from a drawer in his desk, he focused on Caldwell's Knob, a prominent ridge. On a cloudless day, he could make out a massive poplar near the summit that grew from a base trunk, then divided and continued upward for over a hundred feet. The unique tree wasn't on an established trail, but Connor had figured out a way to get there.

He'd used a photo of the tree and projected it on a screen in the sanctuary as a sermon illustration when he spoke on marriage and told the congregation that a good marriage was like the tree. So long as each part stayed connected to the base trunk, it could survive and go higher and higher toward the heavens. He called it the "unity tree."

Because he'd never been married, Connor had lacked confidence when he stood behind the pulpit. He preferred expounding theological truth. Most of his sermons were drawn from seminary notes. Comparative analysis was his strong suit. But the marriage message birthed from his hikes to the overlook had become the most talked about sermon of his two-year ministry. People still mentioned the "tree sermon." Raising the binoculars to his eyes, Connor brought the tree, with its few remaining yellow leaves, into focus. A piece of the thickly ridged bark from the tree that he'd used as a visual aid during the sermon rested on the corner of his desk.

Turning to his computer, Connor spent forty-five minutes putting together resources to send to the Thompsons. He wondered what his mother, who was a PhD psychologist and professional counselor, would have suggested. Her death fifteen years earlier ended Connor's access to her wisdom, and the books that lined the shelves of her office were given away by his father before he remarried.

Because neither Elena nor Matt was present when Connor delivered the unity tree sermon, he included a link to the audio for them. After he pressed the send button, he swiveled in his chair so that he could again open his soul to the view of the mountains.

CHAPTER 2

LIZ CLOSED THE DOOR OF HER OFFICE BEFORE accepting the call from her boyfriend.

"Is this a good time to talk?" Raphael asked. "I don't want to drag you away from something important."

"No, it's fine. I just finished signing up a new client. According to Mr. Pollard, it's a good day when we settle a case, win a case, or take in a new case."

"Glad it's been a good one," Raphael said.

"How are you?"

"Okay, I guess. Mr. Garrison was in a terrible mood this morning. That puts everyone on edge."

Raphael sold residential real estate in Fort Lauderdale. Liz liked the Fort Lauderdale area and often scrolled through townhomes for sale and dreamed of finding the perfect one a short drive from the beach. She liked nothing better than the sand between her toes and the ocean breeze blowing against her face. Having unlimited options for dining and entertainment was a close second.

"Sorry about that," Liz said. "I'm looking forward to seeing you this weekend."

"About this weekend," Raphael said, clearing his throat. "I won't be coming. I canceled my flight."

Liz frowned. "Did something come up at work?"

"No, it's personal. I've met someone else."

"Who? When?" Liz asked in shock.

"Six weeks ago," Raphael replied and then began speaking rapidly. "Sophie and I ran into each other at a training event for the company. She works in the St. Petersburg office, and we really hit it off. I wasn't looking for someone else, but we sat next to each other at a luncheon followed by a dinner and a round of golf the following afternoon and—"

"I don't want to hear this!" Liz interrupted.

"I'm sorry," Raphael said after a few seconds of silence. "But it didn't seem right to fly to Atlanta just to end our relationship."

"Yeah, this phone call is much better."

"Liz, you're a great girl, and I really like you a lot—"

Liz slammed down the phone. The isolation she felt in Bryson suddenly tripled in size. Leaning forward, she buried her head in her hands.

She tried to work but was unable to concentrate. She checked Raphael's social media accounts. He'd already posted photos of himself and Sophie. Liz's replacement was tall, with light brown hair and eyes that, in Liz's opinion, were too widely spaced apart. Included was a picture of the couple on a putting green with Sophie posing next to the flagstick. Liz wasn't a golfer, and Raphael rarely played. In text beneath the photo, he wrote that he was getting a lesson from a "real pro." Her ex-boyfriend had certainly gone after someone different from her.

It was a five-minute drive from the office to the duplex where Liz lived. She rented the two-bedroom, two-bath dwelling from an older couple who'd built six units on property next door to their home. Each of the brick apartments had a fireplace in the main living area, a feature Liz didn't consider important when she moved in at the end of June but came to appreciate during the cool north Georgia winters. She enjoyed sitting in front of a crackling wood fire. It was something she'd liked doing with Raphael.

She parked her small white car in front of her unit. The leaves on the maple trees Mr. and Mrs. Devon had planted on the property had turned red. Her landlady, a white-haired woman in her late sixties, had a love of plants and lots of energy. Today, she was using an electric hedge trimmer to cut back the bushes that lined the front of the building. When she saw Liz, she turned off the trimmer and removed her goggles.

"You're home early," she said.

"Yeah, I wasn't getting much done."

Beverly Devon reached in the pocket of her jacket and put on her glasses. "Do you feel okay? There's a nasty cold virus going around. Two women in my bridge club have it."

"No, I'm fine."

Liz continued toward her unit. Her landlady's voice stopped her.

"Oh, I wanted to ask you something. Do you remember how much I enjoyed the Cuban stew you made? What did you call it? New clothes?"

"No, ropa vieja, which means 'old clothes.'"

"It was delicious. We're having a covered-dish luncheon after church this Sunday, and I wondered if you'd be interested in coming with Sam and me and bringing some of your stew? I know it's asking a lot, and if your young man is going to be in town, I don't want to interfere with your plans."

Cooking was therapy for Liz. And the stew made from shredded flank steak was one of her best dishes.

"He's not coming," she said, then paused. "And I need something to do on Sunday. What time?"

Beverly's eyes widened in surprise. "That's wonderful! I thought you'd say no. The church service starts at eleven, but we'd want to get there early to put our dishes in the fellowship hall. Would you like to ride with us? We'll leave about ten forty."

"Sure, thanks for inviting me."

=====

One of the main reasons Connor went to seminary was to satisfy his love of learning. He was happiest when he could read, think, and reflect. Diploma in hand, he tried to find a teaching position at a small Southern college, but nothing opened up. A friend in Atlanta mentioned the opportunity to serve as pastor of a church in Bryson, and Connor decided to check it out. The location in the foothills of the Appalachian Mountains ticked the box for another of his great loves—the outdoors.

While in seminary, Connor took a semester off and served a six-month stint as an intern in a large metropolitan church in Atlanta. His father, a successful cardiologist at Emory Healthcare, encouraged him to accept a permanent position. Connor rejected that advice and traveled two hours north to Bryson for an interview. A modest-size church in the mountains presented a totally different lifestyle rhythm from that of a large congregation with a staff of twenty-five. Connor liked the area and the people he met. Even though he was young and inexperienced, the search committee was thrilled with a candidate who had his academic qualifications. No other church in Etowah County could boast a pastor with Ivy League credentials. After a series of follow-up interviews, they offered him the position, and he accepted.

Following an initial burst of activity, Connor settled into a comfortable routine. When he told his office assistant not to disturb him, he could carve out a couple of hours without interruption. He would read. Or think. And make notes about what he read or thought. He studied a wide variety of topics: philosophy, human nature, history, science, political theory, the natural world, even sports.

The first year and a half at Rock Community Church proved to be everything Connor had hoped for. But then things began to change. More and more people like Elena and Matt Thompson showed up with problems that sapped his time and diverted his attention. Connor's sense of duty squelched open complaint, but in the privacy of his thoughts, he'd started wondering if it was time for him to consider moving on to something else. Since midsummer, he'd regularly checked on possible teaching positions at the college level, but nothing had come up. Today, he was reading an interesting article from a seminary in the Midwest when there was a knock on his door.

"Time's up," announced Michelle.

The church secretary, a sandy-haired woman in her forties, was a former high school English teacher. She worked part-time and did her best to protect Connor's routine. The busier he became, the more he came to rely on her. Michelle had a notepad in her hand.

"Elena Thompson called back less than ten minutes after you finished the session with her and her husband."

"What did she want?"

"She thinks it would be helpful to talk with you one-on-one before another session. She suggested you come to their house while Matt is in Atlanta for a few days."

"No," Connor said as he shook his head. "And you know why."

"Yes, I saw her grab your hand and pull you in for a tight hug as she was leaving church last Sunday. So far, I've not received any phone calls from anyone else who noticed."

"Good. No private meetings with Elena. I'm sending them homework."

"Do you want me to call her back?"

"No, she'll want to hear from me. I'll send her an email. What else?"

It took several minutes for Michelle to reach the bottom of her list. Connor sighed. One practical lesson he'd learned from his mentor at the large church in Atlanta was not to ignore emails and to promptly return phone calls, the same day if possible. Problems and questions didn't go away. Kicking them down the road wasn't an effective strategy. Connor received a lot of positive feedback from members of the congregation because he responded quickly. It made people feel important and valued.

"Don't forget to go by and see Lyle Hamilton on your way home," Michelle said.

"Right."

Connor didn't mind checking on the man in his thirties who'd suffered a terrible workplace injury that caused paralysis in both his legs. Lyle deserved any aid and comfort Connor could provide.

"And thanks for holding my calls earlier."

"I could tell you needed a break. Were you able to read something interesting?"

"Yes, there's so much written in the sixteenth century that makes as much sense now as it did then. And I'm not talking about the famous theologians. The way some of the Anabaptist writers describe their relationship with God really challenges me—"

Michelle raised her right index finger. Connor stopped.

"Be careful about coming across as anti-Baptist," she said. "A lot of our members have friends and family in Baptist churches. Duke and I went to a Baptist church before we came here."

"Anabaptist, not anti-Baptist," Connor replied with a smile. "And I wasn't preparing a sermon. This was for me. I'm not planning on preaching against anyone."

"Okay. Just trying to do my part to keep any fires from breaking out."

"Which I appreciate."

"Oh, when does your dad leave on his trip?"

Connor's father was traveling to Nepal to volunteer at a medical clinic in a remote region for two months. Most of that time he was going to be off the grid. Even in normal times, they communicated infrequently.

"Next week. We talked on the phone for a while last night."

―――――――――――

It was 5:30 p.m. when Connor locked the church door. He owned two vehicles, a hefty black four-wheel-drive Jeep with large knobby tires and a winch on the front bumper, and a small electric sedan that he drove around town. Gliding away from the church in his electric car, he drove across town to the Hamilton residence. Ten-year-old Josh Hamilton was in the front yard playing with a frisky brown puppy. The dog bounded over, and Connor lowered his hand for the animal to sniff.

"Is he new?" Connor asked.

"Yeah," Josh answered. "My dad says he's got some retriever in him so he should be good at chasing after a ball and bringing it back."

"Do you have a ball?"

Josh ran over, picked up a yellow tennis ball, and held it in front of the dog's nose. "Rascal, go get it!" he said, throwing the ball across the yard.

Yapping, the dog ignored the ball and jumped around Josh's feet and legs.

"I'm not sure he's going to learn how to fetch," Josh said sadly.

"He likes you more than the ball. Go inside the house and bring me a jar of peanut butter and a spoon."

Josh ran into the modest, ranch-style home. While he was gone, the front door opened, and Lyle rolled his wheelchair onto the front stoop and down a newly installed wooden ramp to the ground. Lyle was wearing a gray ball cap with the logo of a local industrial supply company on the front.

"Hey, Preacher!" he called out.

Connor raised his hand in greeting. He'd gotten used to being called "Preacher" by the locals. Eight months earlier, Lyle, a licensed electrician, fell from a roof at a manufacturing plant, rupturing a nerve in his back and rendering both legs useless. Before his injury, Lyle, a fix-it guy, had always been first on the scene for volunteer days at the church.

Josh came out of the house and jumped off the stoop. With big pushes to the wheels, Lyle rolled over to them. Lyle's arms were still muscular, but Connor had noticed worsening atrophy in the former electrician's legs.

"If you want a peanut butter sandwich, I'll fix you one," Lyle said to his son.

"This is bait," Connor replied.

Connor took the spoon from Josh and scooped out some peanut butter. He raised it to his lips for a taste.

"What kind of peanut butter is this?" he asked Josh.

"My mom buys the kind you have to stir," the boy said.

"She's into the natural, organic stuff," Lyle added. "Not that I'm complaining. I think it's better too."

"This is perfect," Connor said. "It has a strong smell."

Connor used his finger to smear peanut butter on the tennis ball, then held it down so Rascal could sniff it but didn't allow him to lick it. Connor gently tossed the ball about ten feet away.

"Fetch," he said.

The dog trotted over to the ball and began to chew it. Connor walked over with the spoon and waved it in front of the dog's nose. Rascal left the ball and became interested in the spoon. Connor picked up the ball and placed it on the spoon as he backed up. He repeated the process. By the fifth time, the dog was returning with the tennis ball.

"Your turn," Connor said to Josh. "Don't put the spoon back in the jar. Your mother won't appreciate that. Just use what's left and see if it works."

The dog retrieved the ball for the boy, who held it above his head in triumph as the dog pranced around at his feet.

"It works!" Josh proclaimed.

"Soon you won't have to use peanut butter," Connor said. "His retriever genes will kick in. Throw it farther."

Josh and the dog ran off together across the yard.

"Where did you learn that trick?" Lyle asked.

"One of my uncles was a duck hunter and raised hunting dogs."

"I've never gone duck hunting, but I shot skeet once and loved it." Lyle repositioned the wheelchair so he could watch Josh and the puppy.

Connor began thinking about where he could take Lyle to shoot clays. There was a facility south of Atlanta that he believed had wheelchair access. They watched Josh and Rascal for a few moments.

"Getting him a dog was a great idea," Connor said.

"Yeah, but it's hard to watch and not join in. Let's roll into the shade under that oak tree."

There were two large oak trees in the front yard. Connor followed Lyle, who positioned the chair so he could continue to watch Josh.

"How's your rehab going?" Connor asked.

"I've graduated from occupational therapy. I'm pretty good at operating the hand controls for my van and using the adaptive devices they gave me for around the house."

"How's Sarah coping?"

"Still believing for a miracle. She prays for me every night and anoints me with oil."

Sarah came from a different religious tradition than Connor. She attended Rock Community Church, but he suspected it was because the church was a place Lyle would go as well. Sarah's zeal was unsettling. Connor moved a leaf on the ground with the toe of his shoe.

"Sometimes, I think what's the use," Lyle continued. "But then I'd rather be married to a woman who prays for me to get better than one who spends her time complaining. And Sarah has stories about people in the church where she grew up who were healed of all kinds of sickness and illnesses."

"Any who were paralyzed?"

"One guy regained the use of his hand after it was torn up in a bushhog accident."

Connor didn't ask for details.

"I do have a favor to ask," Lyle said after a few moments passed.

"And feel free to say no. Would you be willing to take Josh with you sometimes for a hike in the woods? It's killing me that I can't do it."

"Of course," Connor replied immediately.

"Thanks, I was hoping you'd say yes."

"And I'd want to include you. There are wheelchair-accessible trails. The Bear Claw Trail is one that comes to mind."

"Maybe," Lyle replied doubtfully.

Before his accident, Lyle had joined Connor a few times for hikes in the woods. The Etowah County native had introduced him to several little-known, unnamed trails.

Josh returned with a clean spoon and a tennis ball that was dripping with dog saliva. "He's chasing the ball and bringing it back without peanut butter as a reward."

"I saw that," Connor replied. "It's bred in him to fetch. You just had to wake it up."

"Do you have a dog?" Josh asked Connor.

"My dog died a few years ago, and I'm still waiting for the right one to come along to replace her."

Josh held the ball close to Rascal's nose and then threw it. The brown animal dashed after it with the boy in pursuit.

"What kind of dog did you have?" Lyle asked.

"A German wirehaired pointer. It was fun taking her into the woods. I've mentioned Daisy a time or two in a sermon."

"I must have missed those Sundays. I'm sure I would have remembered it."

"I only brought her up to make a point."

Connor stopped and looked at Lyle, who chuckled and ruefully shook his head.

"I don't know, Preacher. I'm not sure I'd give that joke a passing grade."

"You laughed, didn't you?"

"Barely."

Connor lightly placed his hand on Lyle's shoulder. "Hang in there," he said.

"Thanks. I appreciate you stopping by. And let's talk more about a hike with Josh."

CHAPTER 3

THINKING ABOUT SOME OF THE GOOD TIMES SHE'D enjoyed with Raphael, Liz had trouble falling asleep. When she woke in the morning, she braced for a fresh wave of sadness to wash over her. Instead, all she felt was a twinge of regret. There would be a wound left by Raphael's departure from her life, but it wouldn't take long to heal.

Stretching her arms high in the air, Liz slipped out of bed and ate a breakfast of Cuban bread dipped into café con leche, a mixture of coffee and milk. There wasn't a place in Bryson to buy the long baguettes she liked so she baked the bread herself, using the recipe passed down from her grandmother. No matter where she might be, the meal made her feel at home. It was a bright, crisp day, and she drove to work with the car windows down.

"Good morning," Jessica said when Liz approached. "I checked your calendar and saw that your boyfriend is coming into town this weekend. Would the two of you like to come over for a cookout Saturday night? Max is going to cook ribs on the grill. There will be two other couples there. Once we put the kids to bed, we could have a game night."

"Raphael isn't coming," Liz replied. "He broke up with me yesterday afternoon. He met someone else a few weeks ago."

Jessica's face fell. "I'm sorry."

"It stings," Liz acknowledged. "But I'm relieved too."

"I totally get it." Jessica brightened. "The coolest thing about Raphael was his name. Otherwise, he was a dud. You can do a lot better."

"That's what you thought?" Liz asked in surprise.

"Yes, but it wasn't my place to offer an opinion. I was only around him a few times and thought maybe you saw something in him that I didn't. It's one reason I wanted to invite you over this weekend. To check him out a bit more."

"No ribs for Raphael." Liz shook her head.

"Double loss for him. But you can still come."

"No, thanks. I'll pass on showing up solo."

"Understood." Jessica paused for a moment. "Let me know when you're ready to meet the personal trainer I told you about a few weeks ago. He's the total package."

"I'll wait on that too."

"Of course. No rush."

Jessica picked up a stack of papers from the corner of the desk. "Harold came in last night and dictated a brief in the Braxton Properties case. Can you look it over and then take it to him at the courthouse? He's in a motion hearing in front of Judge Conklin at nine o'clock."

Liz had worked on the case and knew it inside and out. Ten minutes later she returned the brief after making four corrections. She showed Jessica what she'd changed.

"Glad you caught that," Jessica replied. "I wasn't sure about that one word. Harold was spitting it out like a machine gun. Let me make the copies."

The Etowah County Courthouse was located in the middle of

town. Surrounded by intersecting streets, the original two-story building was constructed in the 1950s with an annex added fifty years later. There were two courtrooms. A small one downstairs near the clerk's office, and a larger one on the second floor. After stopping by the clerk's office to have one of the copies of the brief stamped, Liz walked up the stone staircase whose steps were visibly worn by everything from women's heels to men's rough work boots.

She entered the courtroom from the rear. Harold Pollard was sitting in the front row. Judge Conklin, a perpetual scowl on his face, presided from his elevated seat behind a dark wooden barrier. This morning, he was hearing pleas in criminal cases. Liz had learned the judge's scowl didn't signify a bad mood. It was how the gangly man looked when he was concentrating. She slipped in behind her boss and handed him three copies of the brief. Their client was seated beside him.

"Stay," Harold said. "This should be fun."

———

Connor lived in a compact one-story wooden cottage built in the 1940s. On one wall of the living room was a framed calligraphy of Psalm 78:72: *And David shepherded them with integrity of heart; with skillful hands he led them.* The verse was a seminary graduation gift from a friend of his mother.

Finishing a light breakfast, he went into the living room. Tablet in hand, he was going to practice his Sunday sermon by reading it out loud. After writing, revising, rewriting, and again revising the message, he rarely strayed from his notes. Each sermon lasted between thirty and thirty-two minutes. He scrupulously avoided plagiarism and gave credit when he quoted another theologian or scholar. By studying the style of well-known orators like Abraham Lincoln, Winston Churchill, Martin Luther King Jr., John F. Kennedy, and Ronald Reagan, Connor hoped to make the leap from an essayist whose papers received high marks from professors to an effective oral communicator.

Connor took a sip of coffee and turned on his tablet. It was going to be "Homecoming Sunday." Former church members who no longer lived in the area would be present, and a covered-dish luncheon would boost attendance. The title of Connor's sermon was "A Place Called Home." Connor considered it a feel-good message with an equal mix of sentimentality and substance.

The brass knocker on the front door sounded. Laying his tablet on a coffee table, he went into the small foyer. Through a window sidelight he recognized the man wearing a lightweight green jacket and jeans standing on the front porch. It was Matt Thompson.

"Good morning," Connor said without inviting Matt inside.

"I want to talk."

"I'll be glad to set up an appointment for you at the church. That's where I usually meet with people."

"Now."

Matt stepped forward, forcing Connor to move aside. They ended up standing awkwardly close to each other in the foyer. Connor wasn't ready to surrender protocol.

"Is there a time that would work for you later today?" he asked. "I normally don't have counseling sessions on Fridays and take half a day off. But I could make an exception."

"Please," Matt replied in a humbler tone of voice. "I won't take up too much of your time."

Connor relented. "Okay, come into the living room."

The living room had a short upholstered couch and two side

chairs picked out by one of Connor's aunts who oversaw the decoration of the house. An antler he'd found in the woods the previous summer rested on the mantel to the right of the mirror.

"Do you have any more coffee?" Matt asked. "I left the house in a hurry and didn't have any."

"How do you take it?"

"Cream and one teaspoon of sugar."

Connor went into the kitchen, a rectangular room with black-and-white floor tiles and a single window over the sink. When he returned to the living room, Matt was inspecting the antler. Connor handed him the coffee. He'd prepared one for himself too.

"Do you hunt?" Matt asked.

"Mostly with the camera on my phone. I may harvest a doe for meat. I've been to Montana and Idaho with my father a few times to hunt elk. I'm more into hiking and climbing."

Matt took a sip of coffee. "I have a deer hunt coming up in a few weeks at Burnt Pine Tree. It's a company-sponsored event with people coming in from all over. Reg suggested it. He says they're bringing in some big bucks from out of state and releasing them right before our weekend."

"Yes, that's part of their annual program."

Connor motioned for Matt to sit in one of the side chairs. "What's on your mind?"

Matt clasped his hands in front of him before he spoke. "You've got to know something before Elena and I have any more meetings with you. I'm in love with two women, and I've been married to both of them. Even though I'm divorced from Anne, I'm still connected to her, not just because of the girls but because of my feelings for her. She stuck with me through the tough early years of beginning the company, and now that we've had this time apart, I realize the problems that caused the divorce weren't bad enough to justify a split."

"But you're divorced now."

"And I love Elena too," Matt continued. "She's different from Anne in just about every way, but I like being married to her. I'm never bored with Elena, and you have to admit she's gorgeous. What she said the other day about not spending time together was an exaggeration. We enjoy hanging out on our deck with a glass of wine in the evenings and traveling together, which happened a lot the first few years of our marriage but not very much since. Now I'm in a super busy season at work. We're in a bit of a tight spot, and my main business partner wants to sell the company. I disagree. I think the timing isn't right, and we should keep building what we have. It's caused a huge rift."

Connor wasn't thinking about Matt's problem with his business partner. He was stuck on the "I'm in love with two women" comment. Polygamy wasn't an option he could recommend.

"What are you asking me to do?"

"Elena really likes you and thinks you can help us sort through our issues. I'm willing to go along but want you to include Anne too."

"How?"

"Maybe the three of us should meet. I've wondered about inviting her to a joint meeting with Elena."

"All four of us?"

"Yeah."

"Is Elena willing to do that?" Connor asked skeptically.

"I don't know. I thought I'd ask Anne first. If she says no, that's the end of it. When I leave here, I'm driving to Atlanta. I'll see Anne and the girls this weekend and suggest she join us."

"What would be the goal of including both women? And how do you think they would react to each other?"

"I know it's tricky, but if I stay married to Elena, there's got to be a way to have an ongoing relationship with Anne that Elena can accept. I thought it over after our meeting yesterday and realized we need a third party to step in and mediate."

"Are you thinking about divorcing Elena?"

"That thought crossed my mind, but I'd rather learn from the mistakes I made with Anne."

Connor had run out of questions to ask. "Matt, what you're suggesting is way outside the grid of anything I've done or studied. I have so many ethical and moral questions I'm not sure where to start."

Matt's countenance darkened. "I thought your job was to help. That's what Elena told me when she convinced me to come see you in the first place. When I'm in a business dispute, we get everyone involved in a room and either sort it out or end up in litigation."

"This isn't the same."

"But it's analogous. If there's a problem, I'm not afraid to think outside the box. Would you at least be willing to talk to Anne on the phone if she agrees to it?"

"Does she attend a church in Atlanta? I'd rather work with her pastor or counselor."

Matt shook his head. "Church wasn't part of our life together, but she's not opposed to religion."

Connor leaned forward. "Look," he said. "My goal is to help you and Elena. The only way I'd bring Anne into the mix is with Elena's permission and an understanding by all of you that my main goal is to save your current marriage and, secondarily, foster a healthy relationship for you with your children."

Matt nodded. "I'm good with that approach if Elena convinces me she wants to stay married. I can tell she's considering an exit strategy."

"Why do you say that?"

"Oh, she's sneaking around collecting information about our finances. And I know she hired a private detective a few months ago to spy on me while I'm in Atlanta. I spotted him right off. I suspect she located the outfit he works for because our company has used them in the past."

"And you've not confronted her about any of this?"

"Why should I? I already know what she's doing without asking her to admit it. What's the point of making her lie?"

Connor paused for a moment. "Does Anne know you still have feelings for her?"

"Probably. Women have a way of figuring stuff out. When you get married that's one of the first things you'll realize."

Matt checked his phone and took a final drink of coffee. He handed the cup to Connor.

"I gotta go," he said. "You brew a decent cup of coffee. It's got punch to it. Thanks for breaking protocol to talk with me."

"Yeah," Connor managed as he rose from the chair.

He led Matt to the front door.

"I'll be in touch," Matt said as he left.

Connor returned to the living room and picked up his tablet. But he didn't practice his sermon. Instead, he entered a summary of his conversation with Matt into an existing file labeled "Thompson Marital Counseling."

CHAPTER 4

HAROLD'S OPPONENT WAS A SEASONED LAWYER NAMED Marvin Stancill. Stancill was a large man in his fifties with an ample belly. He and Harold had crossed legal swords for years. Today, Liz listened with admiration as her boss parried every thrust and deftly counterattacked. Harold included information contained in the brief, but also implications prompted by the other lawyer's claims.

Stancill became more and more frustrated. Finally, he blew up. "Judge, Mr. Pollard is twisting everything I'm saying!"

"He's arguing his case," the judge replied dryly. "You're free to do the same."

After several more minutes of rapid back-and-forth passed, the judge raised his right hand. "Enough," he said. "Both of you will keep talking just to make sure you get in the last word. That's my job. Mr. Pollard, prepare an order granting your client a temporary restraining order against sale of the property. I'm going to place this on the next trial calendar. And I don't want to receive a request for continuance from either one of you. When you file something in my court, you'd better be ready to proceed."

"Thank you, Your Honor," Harold said.

Stancill quickly exited the courtroom. Liz, Harold, and the

client, a man named Lamar Braxton, followed a couple of minutes later.

Once in the hallway, they stopped. Braxton spoke. "Good job, Harold. By putting the brakes on the deal, we'll be able to negotiate a solution I can live with."

"I hope so."

Braxton eyed Liz for a moment.

"Sorry, I should have introduced you to Ms. Acosta," Harold said.

Liz shook the client's hand.

"I've noticed your name on my bills from the firm," Braxton said. "Your hourly rate is a lot less than what Harold charges me. Are you the one who speaks Spanish?"

"Yes."

"Would you be available to help me obtain dispossessory warrants for tenants who don't pay their rent?"

"It's up to Mr. Pollard to oversee my caseload," she said, glancing at her boss.

"We'll discuss it and let you know," Harold replied.

The client left.

"Why didn't you jump in sooner about the new work?" Liz asked. "Mr. Braxton should have asked you that question, not me."

"Because soon you'll be making those choices on your own," Harold said. "In fact, that's what we're going to do with this request. Talk it over with Lamar and let me know your decision about representing him."

━━━━━━━━

Early Saturday morning Liz went to the grocery store to buy the ingredients for ropa vieja. The influx of residents to north Georgia from Latin America had motivated the local grocery stores to expand their inventories, and she didn't have a problem locating the spices needed. Like many stews, ropa vieja tasted better the second day, after the ingredients had an opportunity to meld, and would be at peak flavor by noon on Sunday. The combination of cooking and music got Liz's feet moving in the small kitchen. She was an excellent dancer. One of her ex-boyfriend's failings was clumsiness on the dance floor. When the stew was done, she sampled some for supper. It was tasty.

———

Liz woke up regretting that she'd accepted Beverly Devon's invitation. Sunday was a day to relax or clean house, and unless she had someplace to go, Liz liked to stay in her pajamas. But she'd promised, and there was way too much ropa vieja prepared for her to eat alone. Around 10:15 a.m. there was a knock on her door. It was her landlady, who was wearing a nice dress and low-heeled shoes.

"I don't want to bother you, but I wanted to make sure you're still coming to the church," Beverly said.

"Yes. I just need to pack up my food. If it's okay, I'd like to bring it in a slow cooker to keep it warm."

"Wonderful! You're still welcome to ride with us."

Liz had agreed to come to the church but decided she didn't want to take a chance of getting trapped there.

"No, thanks," she said. "I'll see you there."

"We'll save a place for you. We always sit in the fifth row from the front on the right-hand side of the church."

Liz nodded. "I'll look for you."

One of the first things Liz had noticed about Bryson was the large number of Christian congregations for such a small town. There were more varieties of churches than selections at a candy store. It was clear how the Bible Belt earned its name.

She was familiar with Rock Community Church, whose stone-and-glass exterior made it one of the more beautiful sanctuaries in the area. She turned off the main highway and drove a short distance up a hill. She saw Becky Carrington, the law firm receptionist, get out of her car with a baking dish in her hands.

"Becky!" Liz called out.

The young woman turned around and looked at her in surprise. Liz told her about the invitation from Bev Devon.

"Follow me to the fellowship hall," Becky said. "That's where we leave the food."

Becky eyed the cooking pot. "What did you bring?"

Liz told her about the dish.

"I want some of that," Becky replied. "It sounds way more exciting than my broccoli chicken casserole."

Connor knew there would be a big crowd for the homecoming service and the meal to follow. He stayed in his office until right before the service started. Even after two years of experience and with extensive preparation each week, he still got butterflies in his stomach when he was about to speak in public. He entered the sanctuary and stood behind the pulpit with the twenty-member choir arrayed behind him. There were quite a few unfamiliar faces present.

At precisely 11:28 a.m., Connor began to speak. As he talked, he was pleased with the visible reactions from the people in the pews to "A Place Called Home." Except for the tragedy of his mother's illness and death, most of his childhood memories of home were positive. His estrangement from his father came later. Even in the midst of her sickness, Connor's mother maintained an inspiring grace. Someday, he'd talk about her publicly. But not yet.

Because so many people didn't come from a positive family environment, Connor was sensitive in the way he addressed the "places we came from." Contrary to her usual rapt attention, Elena avoided eye contact with him as he spoke.

Twenty-two minutes passed before he reached the closing section of the sermon about the Christian's "future home." In seminary, theological debates and controversies about the reality and nature of heaven left him with a tangled web of unsatisfying thoughts. What energized his thinking about heaven was his love of nature and the realization that the Garden of Eden was a picture of how God intended people to live in his presence.

"So don't think about having to spend eternity practicing a harp while sitting on a cloud. Look forward to enjoying a place of incredible beauty and fruitfulness where we will once again walk with God in the cool of the evening."

It was quiet when Connor finished. More quiet than normal. Connor wasn't sure why. He cleared his throat. "The benediction will also serve as a blessing for the wonderful meal we're going to enjoy in the fellowship hall. Even if you didn't bring anything, please come. There will be plenty for all."

As soon as he stepped down from the pulpit, Connor was surrounded by people asking questions about the last portion of the message. Was the Garden of Eden a real place? Do animals go to heaven? Why did he talk about heaven but didn't mention hell? What language is spoken in heaven? Do people only wear white robes or is there an option for colorful clothes? What happens to people in parts of the world who die without ever hearing about Jesus?

No topic had ever elicited such a vigorous and varied response. Connor was more used to people shaking his hand on their way out the door than being mobbed. He was stunned. Giving brief answers or promising to think about the question, he made his way to the fellowship hall. Reg Bullock came up to him. The lean man in his early sixties with thinning gray hair and slightly red cheeks had been one of Connor's strongest supporters at the church and a surrogate father figure. He gave Connor a big thumbs-up.

"Way to go," he said.

"I had no idea that last point was going to cause such a reaction."

"That's what you want, isn't it? For people to listen and care about what you say?"

"Yeah, but I'm not ready for all the questions."

"Don't send anyone to me." Reg smiled. "I'm trying to figure out how to navigate this life before I focus on the one to come."

"That's what I emphasize too."

Reg patted him on the shoulder. "And my immediate goal is not to be stuck at the end of the food line."

After Reg left, Elena approached Connor and brushed against his right arm. "I'll save a place for you," she said.

"Thanks, but go ahead and eat. I need to greet some of the visitors who came this morning."

"That's sad," Elena said with a pout. "But I understand."

Instead of joining Reg in the queue for food, Connor sought out unfamiliar faces. He saw Beverly Devon standing beside a petite young woman with long dark hair. He headed their way.

"This is Elizabeth Acosta," Beverly said when Connor joined them. "She's a lawyer who lives in one of my duplexes and brought the most amazing stew dish you've ever eaten. I'm going to grab a bowl and get some so you can taste it. We're going to sit together and would love for you to join us."

Without waiting for an answer, Bev hurriedly left on her mission. Connor extended his hand to the young woman.

"I'm Connor Grantham," he said. "Thanks for coming."

"Elizabeth Acosta."

"How long have you lived in Bryson?"

"Around eighteen months. I'm an associate at the Pollard firm."

Debating whether to accept Bev's invitation, Connor hesitated. Out the corner of his eye he saw Elena placing her purse on an open seat beside her.

"Please tell Bev that I'll join your table," he said.

By the time Connor was ready to enter the food line it had shrunk considerably. So, too, had the offerings. Quite a few casserole dishes were empty, as were multiple vegetable containers. Veteran churchgoers knew the best items and abandoned any effort at Christian charity in the scramble for the most popular selections. Connor collected a hodgepodge and joined the group at a table for eight.

"That's an interesting plate," Bev observed when he sat down. "Two different kinds of congealed salad, a roll, corn bread, and nothing green."

"I'm just grateful for God's provision," Connor replied wryly.

Liz smiled.

"But you have this," Bev said as she slid a bowl of stew over to him. "I saved it from the ravenous horde."

"What is it?" Connor asked, picking up a spoon.

"Ropa vieja," Liz answered.

Connor took a bite. It was hearty with a rich flavor. "This is delicious," he said.

"Tell him what it means in Spanish," Beverly said.

Before Liz could answer, Connor spoke. "'Old clothes,' because the meat is shredded like torn fabric and the peppers and tomato are like multicolored garments. Just like Joseph's coat of many colors."

"Whose coat?" Liz asked with a puzzled expression on her face.

"A man in the Bible," Connor said. "I've heard of this dish. It's from Cuba, right?"

"Yes. My paternal grandmother immigrated to the US from Cuba in the 1960s. I grew up in south Florida."

Connor took another bite of the stew. He pushed his other plate to the side.

"I hope neither one of you brought the congealed salad," he said to Bev and another woman at the table. "Ropa vieja is all I'm going to eat."

=====

The church was different than Liz expected. Except for Easter Sunday and Christmas Eve, she rarely attended any type of religious service. And she'd never read the Bible. There wasn't any kneeling or reading from religious books. And the minister's sermon reminded her of a college lecture. The parts about family she found interesting. Liz didn't have any settled beliefs about life after death.

"You mentioned spending time in the woods," she said to Connor as he ate. "What do you like to do?"

"Hike and climb, usually by myself early in the morning. Every so often, I'll camp overnight if it's too far to travel in and out in one day."

The only time Liz had ventured into the woods since moving

to Georgia was an afternoon drive with Raphael to a parking lot followed by an easy ten-minute hike to an overlook. Going for walks anywhere had never been part of their relationship. She exercised while watching videos at home.

"Like Thoreau?" she asked. "Or Wendell Berry?"

Connor stopped and smiled. "Maybe a little. I certainly don't mind the comparisons. Do you like the outdoors?"

"It's the beach for me," Liz replied. "I've not explored the mountains since I moved here."

"Connor, you should show her around," Bev suggested. "Our daughter and son-in-law really like the hike to Cloudland Canyon Falls. It's not too strenuous. That's where he proposed to Mary."

"That's okay." Liz squelched her landlady's matchmaking efforts. "I'll hold out for the ocean."

An elderly man came up and began asking Connor about the sermon. The man had been married and widowed three times and was concerned about his marital status in eternity. To Liz, it sounded like a law-school exam question.

"There's no marriage in heaven," Connor said. "Jesus was clear about that in the gospel of Matthew. You and your former wives will be friends but nothing more."

"That's hard to imagine," the man began as he shook his head. "My first wife and second wife were really close. My first wife even told me to marry Gladys if she died before I did. But my third wife didn't like either one of them."

"Whatever bad feelings there were among them won't survive the trip to the other side," Connor replied.

"But who will I live with?" the man persisted. "I guess I could spend a week with each one followed by a week by myself."

"The sorts of problems we have here won't exist in our heavenly home. There are going to be many mansions. Visits will be optional. Try not to worry about it."

Bev sighed after the man left. "I really liked Gladys. She was a sweetheart. Ronald was only married to his third wife for about a year."

They ate in silence for a few moments before Bev spoke again. "Pastor, I've read the verse you just mentioned in Matthew, but why wouldn't there be marriage in heaven? I mean, if two people really love each other, they should have the option to continue the relationship. Sam and I feel that way, right?"

Sam Devon was one of the quietest men Liz knew. The short, slightly overweight man with wispy white hair had retired as the manager of a local home improvement store. He enjoyed working in his vegetable garden, riding his mower, and doing minor improvements on the couple's rental properties. He would raise his hand in greeting when he saw Liz but rarely spoke.

"Yes," Sam replied and took a drink of sweet tea.

"That's what he has to say." Another woman at the table chuckled. "I wouldn't put Donny on the spot by asking him that question in front of the preacher and a bunch of other people."

"Tell her why," Bev prompted her husband.

"So you can wash and fold my clothes," Sam replied matter-of-factly.

Liz burst out laughing, then, not sure if her landlord was joking, clamped her hand over her mouth. Connor chuckled. Bev stared open-mouthed at her husband.

"You're the only one who could get my robe as white as it ought to be," Sam continued with a grin.

"Quit it," Bev replied, giving her husband a playful tap on the arm.

Sam leaned over and gave his wife a quick kiss on the cheek.

"Preacher, I don't know how it all works in the hereafter," Sam said, looking at Connor, "but forty-eight years isn't near long enough for me to learn all the ways I love and appreciate Bev."

Bev beamed. Liz got up and went to the dessert table. Connor appeared at her elbow.

"I've never seen that side of Sam," she said.

"He keeps quiet, but Sam has a dry wit. He's both a comic and a romantic. And Bev is a saint who does a lot of good without seeking recognition or thanks. We should all be more like her."

"They've been nice to me," Liz said, eyeing the dessert table offerings. "What do you recommend?"

"This is picked over. The really good stuff—peach cobbler, chocolate pecan pie, and Prissy Henry's banana pudding—is all gone. The safest bet is a fudge brownie."

"I only want half of one."

"Me too. We can share."

As she nibbled her brownie, Liz enjoyed the friendly atmosphere in the room. She walked out of the fellowship hall with Sam and Bev.

"What did you think?" her landlady asked as soon as they were in the parking lot.

"I enjoyed all of it," Liz replied.

"That makes me so happy. Which part was your favorite?"

"The luncheon."

"I knew you'd like Connor. He had a chance to go to law school but turned it down and graduated from Princeton Seminary. He's very smart."

"I could tell."

"And I promise not to try to pair you two up."

"It's too late to promise that," Liz teased.

"Oh, that was nothing."

"When I was at the dessert table with Connor, he told me you were a saint who does a lot of good and all of us should be more like you."

"He did?" Bev replied in surprise.

"Those were his exact words."

CHAPTER 5

CONNOR WASN'T ENERGIZED BY BEING AROUND A lot of people. Once he got through the intense social interaction required of a minister on Sunday mornings, he went home, propped up his feet, and read. He'd just started reading a new book when his phone vibrated. It was Matt Thompson. The technology entrepreneur was mastering the art of interruption. Connor answered the call on the last ring before it went to voice mail.

"Matt, here. Do you have a few minutes to talk? I'm at the apartment, and Anne is in the other room."

Connor glanced up at the ceiling for a moment. There was no escape hatch in the cream-colored drywall.

"Okay, I'm listening," he said, swinging his feet off an ottoman and onto the floor.

"Anne is on board with letting you help navigate the situation with Elena. We believe it would be best for you to bring it up. Like I said, Elena will be much more open to a suggestion coming from you rather than me."

"Even if I mention it, she's going to know it was your idea."

"Trust me, it will make a difference. You and I could say the exact same sentence and get two totally different responses."

"What do you suggest I say?"

"Including Anne in the mix is a way to comprehensively address our problems. Anne is willing to work with your schedule and come to Bryson. It might not be good to start out with all three of us in the same room, but that's where I hope we end up."

While Matt talked, Connor strategized.

"Here's what I want you to do," he said. "Remember the list of marital issues I asked you and Elena to prepare before our first meeting?"

"Yeah."

"Elena wrote three pages. You jotted down a few items on a quarter of a page. Go back and put some more work into that and add what should be addressed if Anne is going to be involved."

"Okay."

"Then listen to the podcasts and sermon I sent after our meeting last week. Make a note of anything that applies or gives you any insight."

"I already listened to the sermon about the two tree trunks on my way to Atlanta. It was good. And the podcast by the guy explaining the differences between men and women was helpful. I realize a lot of what he said included generalizations, but I could see how Elena, Anne, and I are wired."

Connor was impressed by Matt's unexpected compliance. "Okay, I'll talk to Elena. When are you returning to Bryson?"

"Not until Wednesday evening. The next three days are packed with business meetings."

"Honey!" a woman's voice called out in the background. "Abby needs your help!"

"Just a sec!" Matt replied.

A few moments of silence followed. While Connor waited,

Anne's term of endearment for Matt bounced around inside his head. If that's how Matt's ex-wife felt about him, it would be foolish to put her in the same room with Elena. Connor might talk to Anne privately but with very limited goals.

"I have to go," Matt said. "One of my daughters has a question about her math homework. We'll talk soon."

———

It was a clear, crisp fall morning, unlike any weather Liz experienced in Florida. As soon as she arrived at the office, Jessica Thorpe cornered her at the coffeepot in the break room.

"Confidential sources inform me you went to church, and the preacher hit on you."

Liz immediately guessed the identity of the informant. "Becky was sitting at the next table. I doubt she heard anything that went on."

"Not true. She's an expert lip-reader. And she says you and the tall, good-looking preacher man shared a brownie."

Liz moved toward the door. "Let's bring in the witness so I can cross-examine her."

"No, no," Jessica said quickly. "That'll terrify her. After all, you're one of the lawyers."

"Please." Liz shook her head.

"I'm exaggerating," Jessica replied. "But I would have lost a bet that you'd be at church on Sunday morning."

"My landlady invited me and asked me to bring one of the Cuban dishes I like to cook."

"I'm sure that was a huge success. Did you have a good time? Max and I occasionally go to church with his folks and the kids attend Vacation Bible School in the summer. It's a social connector, just not one I had on the radar for you."

Liz prepared to leave with her coffee.

"Do you think you'll go back to the church?" Jessica asked as Harold entered the room.

"Hold on," Harold said, raising his right hand. "No proselytizing at the office. Jessica, you know that's our policy."

"She wasn't proselytizing," Liz responded. "I visited Rock Community Church yesterday and we were talking about it. It's all voluntary."

"We stay away from religion and politics around here," Harold said. "Those things can be a big distraction. That's what cost Jeff Layers his job."

"Politics weren't off the table when Judge Conklin was up for reelection," Liz said and immediately regretted her words.

Harold stared at her for a second, then chuckled. "Touché," he replied. "But no employee has to contribute or attend any fundraiser that the law firm sponsors. Swing by my office in half an hour. I have a new case that I want to talk over with you."

"That was gutsy," Jessica said in a soft voice when Harold left.

"It just popped out."

"It's a good thing he likes you."

"You're sure about that?"

"Yeah," Jessica said seriously and nodded. "He thinks you're entertaining."

———

Liz scrolled through her emails. Before coming to the law firm, she'd struggled at times with procrastination, especially when it required her to write. She often turned in papers at the last minute or even late. Putting anything off when it could be dealt with immediately was anathema to Harold Pollard. To compensate for her natural tendency, Liz had adopted a system of preprogrammed reminders on her computer that forced her not to delay. She took care of several items and copied her boss on the responses before going to his office.

"Glad you took care of Tom Fahey's issue," Harold said. "He's like me and appreciates promptness."

"Yes, sir."

Harold picked up some papers from his credenza. "I received a call on Friday afternoon from a woman with a possible divorce case that would involve a lot of money."

The state of Georgia had a quickie divorce law, and there were lawyers in town who fought over the run-of-the-mill cases that could be wrapped up in sixty to ninety days. Earlier in his career, Harold practiced a lot of domestic relations law but now limited himself to more complicated divorces that justified large fees. Liz had helped him with several of them. She found the work emotionally exhausting, especially if the care and custody of minor children was an issue.

"The woman is married to the CEO of a tech company called Daughbert Technology based in Atlanta. They live in a big house on Morgan Drive. She's kicking the tires for a lawyer. I'm not sure she even wants a divorce, but if she decides to file, I don't want her to run off and hire a big firm in Atlanta. At this point, she wants to know how to protect herself financially and asked if we had a female lawyer she could work with. I told her yes."

Liz swallowed. "If it's a complicated situation, I'm not sure I know enough to advise her."

"Don't worry. Your main role will be hand-holder and

information-gatherer. I'll jump in if it gets technical from a financial or legal standpoint. But I want you to call and set up an appointment for her to come into the office. Sync it with my calendar."

"How soon?"

"ASAP. You know how it works."

In a law practice that heavily relied on representing individuals, making quick contact with people who needed help was vital. Often, they would be calling multiple lawyers.

"Okay, I'll do it this morning."

Harold handed her his notes. Liz took her boss's mix of scribble and shorthand straight to Jessica for deciphering.

The legal assistant started reading and shook her head. "Oh, I've heard about this couple. Max did the stonework on their house. He said the wife was high-maintenance."

"Do they have any kids?"

"I don't know."

Jessica glanced down at Harold's notes and pointed to some lines of text that Liz couldn't read. "They don't have children together, but the husband has two children from a previous marriage. I'll transcribe Harold's notes. It took me two years to learn to untangle his personal shorthand."

"Thanks."

Relieved that there weren't any children to fight over, Liz returned to her office. Fifteen minutes later, Jessica appeared with the typed information and placed the sheets on Liz's desk.

"They've been receiving marital counseling from Connor Grantham," she said. "Any idea who that might be?"

"He's the minister," Liz started, then stopped. "You know who he is."

"Just checking to make sure you hadn't forgotten him already,"

Jessica quipped. "Do you want me to call Mrs. Thompson and set up the appointment? Harold wants her to meet with both of you."

"No, he told me to do it."

After Jessica left, Liz read over the notes. They didn't contain a litany of Matthew Thompson's faults. The greater focus of Elena Thompson's phone call with Harold had to do with the couple's financial status and what Mrs. Thompson might expect to receive in a divorce after five years of marriage.

———

Connor arrived early at the church. Unlike the rest of the working world, Monday was his favorite day of the week. He rarely scheduled appointments and used the day to be by himself to read, study, and think. Today, he had an unusual number of phone calls and emails about his sermon. All of them had to do with heaven. One person even called the message "A Place Called Heaven," not "A Place Called Home." Connor knit his brow and stared at his computer screen for several seconds after reading a particularly thorny question. He did the best he could to address the questions on a topic he'd not figured out himself. He then started in on the phone calls. It was 11:00 a.m. before he reached the final two. Michelle knocked on his door and entered.

"You've been busy," she said.

"I'd like to say I've been in heaven, but it wouldn't be true."

"I'm not surprised. I can't remember a sermon that stirred up more interest. Usually during church luncheons the conversation around the table focuses on local events or family activities outside the church. Yesterday, everyone wanted me to pretend I was you and talk some more about heaven. It was exhausting."

Connor laughed. "Maybe I'll talk about heaven again after I figure out more what I believe," he said.

"I barged in because Elena Thompson has called twice this morning and didn't want to leave a message. I don't think she wants to talk to you about heaven. She sounded upset."

"I'll wait to call until later this afternoon."

"If she wants to come in to see you, remember that I have a dentist appointment this afternoon and will be gone after three o'clock."

Connor never met alone with a woman unless Michelle was at her workstation, and he always left the door cracked open. Elena Thompson had pushed the limits. A couple of times she'd shown up when Michelle was running errands and not at her desk. When that happened, Connor left his office door wide open.

"Okay. That's not happening anyway until she and Matt complete the homework that I gave them."

Michelle was gone by the time Connor called Elena. Before doing so, he jotted down a few notes. The first part of the conversation wouldn't require anything from him except to listen. The phone rang several times, and he relaxed as he anticipated leaving a message.

"Connor, is that you?" a breathless Elena said.

"Yes, sorry it's taken me so long to get back to you."

"Matt is in Atlanta until Thursday. I've cooked dinner, and there's nobody to share it with me. Would you like to come over?"

Elena's husband had evidently added an additional day in Atlanta since talking to Connor.

"Thanks, but I have another commitment."

"Oh," Elena said with disappointment in her voice. "I've been studying the information you recommended and would like to discuss it. Matt claims he'll be ready to meet again on Friday, which may be a good idea because we won't have been together enough this week to get on each other's nerves. Do you work on Friday or is that your day off?"

"It depends."

Connor checked his calendar. He'd planned on going for a hike in the morning. There was a chance of rain later in the day.

"We could meet Friday afternoon at three o'clock if that works for you."

"Yes. Would you contact Matt about it?"

"Okay." Connor cleared his throat. "What would you think about including Anne in some of our discussions?"

"In the room with us?" Elena asked sharply.

"Not unless you agreed and thought it would help. But it might be beneficial if I talked with her."

"Half the time, I feel like she's already sitting in the room whispering into Matt's ear," Elena grumbled. "He put you up to this, didn't he?"

"Yes, he mentioned it."

Elena was silent for a few moments. "Do you think there's a chance Matt is thinking about leaving me and returning to Anne?"

Connor felt trapped. He took a deep breath. "My opinion isn't what's important, and my only goal is to help save your marriage."

"I wish that's what Matt wanted. I was convinced that he made his choice when he married me, but now I know he's about to dump me and leave me with nothing."

"Don't give up—"

"Oh, I'm not giving up. Not without a fight. Maybe getting to know Anne will help you see why Matt should stick with me. She's a master manipulator."

CHAPTER 6

LIZ MET WITH LAMAR BRAXTON IN HER OFFICE. He finished explaining what he wanted her to do as the attorney for his rental property business.

"I'll agree to represent you only if as a first step I can try to negotiate reasonable terms that allow people to stay in their apartments and cure any default," Liz said. "Otherwise, I'm not interested."

"How much time will that take?" Braxton frowned. "I don't want a big legal bill on top of losing rent."

"We'll cap that part of the representation at three hours per case. I believe you'll come out better with long-term tenants than a lot of turnover and empty houses."

"What kind of proposals would you recommend? I don't want to have to mess around with this sort of thing."

Liz was ready. "No payouts of more than six months to catch up any rent in arrears. And if the tenant misses a payment, the arrangement is void, and we proceed with eviction, which the magistrate is more likely to grant if you've tried to work with the lessee."

Braxton was silent for a moment.

"Okay," he said with a shrug. "Let's give it a try. It can't be worse than what's already happening. I'll have the girl in my office that keeps up with the rentals get in touch with you. She's been stressed out over it and hates going over to the courthouse."

"And I'll send over a contract for this aspect of our representation," Liz said.

As soon as Braxton left, Liz reported the result to her boss.

"I like that," Harold mused. "Who says you can't be a lawyer and a human being at the same time?"

The phone on Harold's desk buzzed. He pressed the speaker button.

"Elena Thompson is here to see you and Liz," Becky said.

"She's early. Put her in the main conference room and let her know we'll be there shortly."

Harold looked up at Liz. "Any questions before we start?"

"I'm not sure what to ask."

"Our job is to listen, not jump in with advice."

Harold let Liz enter before him. Elena Thompson was wearing a blue sweater and beige slacks. She placed an expensive-looking handbag on the table in front of her.

"You look familiar," Elena said, cocking her head to the side. "Where have I seen you before?"

"I visited Rock Community Church yesterday with Beverly and Sam Devon."

"Did you stay for lunch?"

"Yes."

"Yeah." Elena nodded and seemed to inspect Liz more closely. "You sat at the table with Connor Grantham."

"That's right," Liz replied, wondering where the conversation might go next.

Harold spoke. "And what is discussed in these walls stays here. It's not discussed at church, the country club, or on the sidewalk.

Preserving client confidentiality in a community as small as Bryson is an obligation we take seriously."

"That's good to know," Elena said, directing her attention to Harold. "And thanks for agreeing to meet with me on such short notice. I thought I'd have to wait a week or two to see an attorney."

Harold took his customary seat with Liz to his left, and Elena across from her.

"Oh, there's no need for you to stay, Mr. Pollard," Elena said. "I wanted to meet with one of the firm's female attorneys."

Harold cleared his throat and spoke. "If the firm represents you, any of our attorneys may be involved at one time or another based on their particular area of expertise and experience."

"But for now, I'm more comfortable discussing the situation with another woman."

Harold was about to speak, but after a quick glance at Liz, he shut his mouth.

"Fine, I'll leave you two to go over the situation."

Harold left the room. Every client was different and surprises were common. But this was a first for Liz.

Elena looked across the table at her. "I know that probably violated your protocol, but I've had terrible experiences with older male attorneys in the past. Mr. Pollard may be a nice man, but I'm more comfortable talking about my marital situation with another woman. You're not married?"

"No."

"Divorced?"

"Never married."

"Okay."

Elena opened her purse and took out several sheets of paper that were folded in half. "This is background information about

Matt and me along with the questions I want answered. I'd like your responses to be in writing. I've opened a new email account that he doesn't know about and rented a post office box in my own name."

"What about a separate bank account?" Liz asked.

"Done months ago. I've built it up so that I have what I need if we go to war."

"Understood. May I take a few moments to read what you've written? I might have follow-up questions."

"Go ahead."

The summary was organized and detailed, the financial information set forth in a spreadsheet format. There was a lot of background information and a list of more than twenty questions. Both Elena and Matt had been married before. He had children; she did not.

"This is impressive," Liz said. "How did you come up with this?"

"A friend who went through a divorce two years ago gave me a template her attorneys used. I assumed this was the most efficient way to proceed."

"It is," Liz agreed. "I'll get to work. But first, you need to sign a contract for representation. It will include the hourly rate for all the attorneys at the firm who may work on the case."

"I don't want to get shuffled off to someone else."

"Understood."

Liz left and went to Jessica's desk. "I need a standard domestic relations contract for Elena Thompson to sign."

Jessica pulled up the form and began typing.

"How much deposit?" the assistant asked. "Based on Harold's phone call with her, there's a lot of money up for grabs."

"I didn't check with him. She's not asking us to file a complaint for divorce, just research a bunch of questions. It's all preliminary so she can be ready if they split up. What do you think is fair?"

"Twenty-five thousand," Jessica responded. "No matter what the client says at the beginning of a case, it always ends up more complicated than they let on."

The contract and letter of representation exited the printer, and Jessica handed the papers to Liz, who returned to the conference room. Elena was talking on the phone but immediately ended the call.

Liz handed her the documents. "Please read this, and let me know if you have any questions. Given the amount of the marital assets and the complexity of the situation, we'll require a twenty-five-thousand-dollar deposit."

"That's reasonable compared to what a few of my friends had to pay." Elena signed the contract. "Email the wiring information for the firm bank account, and I'll authorize a transfer. How soon will you be able to respond to my questions?"

Liz knew Harold would want her to prioritize the case at the top of her work queue.

"Is Friday soon enough?"

"Make it Friday morning before ten. I'd like to have the information before Matt and I have another counseling session with Connor Grantham. Matt's ex-wife is going to be involved either in person or on the phone. It's not enough that Matt spends as much time with her in Atlanta as he does with me here in Bryson. Now he wants her to be a part of our meetings with Connor."

"His ex-wife?" Liz asked in a puzzled voice.

"Yeah, we'll see how it goes. I was just on the phone with a private detective. He's been following Matt around for several months and is on duty now in Atlanta."

"What has he uncovered?"

"Enough, but I want more," Elena replied cryptically. "I'm tired of being dangled on a string at the end of a rotten branch."

Elena left, and Liz went directly to Harold's office. He listened to her summary of the meeting and read the document Elena prepared.

"Was twenty-five thousand enough for a deposit?" she asked.

"That's fine. And you'll put a significant dent in it answering all her questions in written form. The danger in that method is she'll have our opinions in writing. Make sure you include plenty of disclaimers. Results in divorce cases are hard to guarantee."

Anxiety welled up inside Liz.

"This is a great learning opportunity for you," Harold continued. "The trial notebook for domestic cases I put together a couple of years ago will help a lot. Also, quote from appellate decisions in your answers and include conflicting lines of authority. That will help her realize domestic relations law is a mix of science and art."

"Yes, sir."

Harold smiled. "I'm excited for you. You generated this business, not me. This is a great opportunity."

"Generated the business? She called you, not me."

"Only because she saw that a female attorney worked here."

<hr>

Midweek, Connor called Lyle Hamilton. "Do you and Sarah have any plans for Josh on Friday? I understand it's a teacher workday at school."

"No, he was going to just hang out here with me."

"What if the three of us head to the woods for a few hours? We could hike the Bear Claw Trail I mentioned the other day."

"I've fished in that area many times, but it gets steep on the way out."

"I can help you."

Lyle was silent for a moment before he spoke. "I'll talk to Josh and let you know as soon as he gets home from school."

Connor spent the rest of the afternoon working on his sermon for Sunday morning. Ignoring requests for another Sunday focused on heaven, he decided to speak about the differences between secular and biblical wisdom. He'd written a paper in seminary about the etymology of the word "wisdom" in both Hebrew and Greek and drew from his previous research. It was a subject that excited him much more than speculation about the afterlife. Time flew by while he wrote. Before leaving the church, he received a text from Lyle confirming the hike.

Connor quickly replied:

That's super!

———————

Friday morning, Connor arrived at the Hamilton house shortly after 7:00 a.m. Josh opened the door when he knocked. The boy was holding a leash attached to his puppy, who was straining to get to Connor.

"Ready to go?" Connor asked.

"Mr. Connor, can we take Rascal? My dad said yes, but it's okay if you say no."

"Sure. Dogs make everything better."

Lyle rolled into view behind his son. Sarah Hamilton was behind him. Sarah was a slender woman with long brown hair and intense green eyes.

"Want a cup of coffee to go?" she asked.

"Thanks, but I have one in the car."

"I enjoyed your sermon about heaven," she continued. "I'd never heard it compared to the Garden of Eden, but it made a lot of sense."

"Glad you liked it. I've received tons of feedback."

"I'm not surprised."

"I have water and snacks for both me and my dad," Josh said, holding up his daypack. "We both like smoked-meat sticks. Do you want some too?"

One of Connor's uncles made beef jerky every Christmas using flank steak. It was so much better than anything bought at a store that it had ruined Connor's taste buds for manufactured substitutes. He'd rather eat an energy bar.

"No, but I could use an extra bottle of water."

It was a cloudy morning, and Connor hoped the forecast was accurate that the rain would hold off until the middle of the day. All three of them were wearing jackets. Connor's coat was weatherproof.

"I packed ponchos in case it rains," Josh said as they put their gear in the back of the van.

There was a motorized lift on the vehicle's side door. Lyle maneuvered the wheelchair into position and let Josh press the button to raise it. The chair occupied an open space behind the passenger seat. Josh sat up front with Connor with Rascal at Josh's feet. The van was several years old and sparkling clean.

"Your van is in great shape," Connor said as he started the engine.

"It's been an ongoing project for Josh and me. I do some of the work and supervise him on the rest. Sarah likes a clean vehicle."

Connor looked over at Josh. "Could I hire you to detail my Jeep? It could use a thorough cleaning."

Josh turned in his seat and looked at his father. "Can I?" he asked.

"If you're willing to do the work."

It took them half an hour to reach the road that led to the trail-head. They made their way past new-growth pines and hardwoods. It had been about thirty years since the area was logged. A few rays of sun streaked through the branches.

"Maybe we'll miss the rain," Connor said, leaning forward to look up through the windshield.

They reached the parking area. Connor pulled in beside an old white pickup truck that was covered with stickers, including one that read "Eat More Possum."

Connor pointed out the sticker after they got out of the van. "Josh, how often does your mother cook possum?"

"Never," the boy replied. "That sticker's not serious."

"You're not going to get much past him," Lyle said as he propelled the wheelchair off the lift onto the gravel. "I've given up."

"But you can still try," Josh added.

Connor laughed. "I'll take that as a challenge."

Both Connor and Josh had small daypacks. Lyle insisted on putting some of their items in a bag attached to the back of his wheelchair. Even though it was a chilly morning, Lyle took off his jacket and stowed it as well.

"I'll heat up rolling this thing even if it's downhill," he said. "Coming back up will be the challenge."

The wheelchair had thick, wide tires, and Lyle's arms were strong. Within a few hundred feet of the parking lot the trail introduced a series of switchbacks as they descended toward the stream. Scampering from one side of the path to the other, Rascal covered three times as much real estate as the others. Connor led the way with Josh following and Lyle in the rear.

"It's odd seeing the trail from a chair," Lyle said when they stopped for a drink of water. "I remember the last time I came here. It was about three years ago. I brought my three-weight fly rod and hiked up to a little waterfall. There was a pool at the base of the falls, and I pulled a pair of beautiful little brookies from it."

Connor glanced at Josh, who was staring at the ground and kicking the dirt with his toe.

Lyle turned toward Josh. "It's time I started teaching you to cast with a fly rod," he said. "We'll start out in the front yard. I can show you the basics, even from my wheelchair."

"I don't know," Josh replied in a subdued voice. "If you can't take me fishing, I don't want to go."

They moved at a slow pace, and the sun was climbing up in the morning sky when they reached the stream. The threat of unexpected rain retreated. No one else was in sight. There was a grassy clearing with a wooden picnic table. The park service had placed a row of large rocks in the shallow stream so it could be easily crossed. Connor sat on a bench with Lyle at the end of the table. Josh took Rascal to the stream and began coaxing the puppy to leap from rock to rock.

"Thanks for doing this," Lyle said to Connor.

"Hey, this is fun for me."

Lyle was silent for a few moments. "You saw how Josh reacted when I brought up fishing. Before the accident, he was all in on learning how to fly-fish."

"Don't quit suggesting it. Eventually, I believe he'll want to give it a try."

Connor leaned forward, rested his arms on the table, and watched

Josh and Rascal. The dog slipped from a rock into the water that was less than a foot deep. Josh scooped him out and positioned him on a bigger slab. The puppy shook his body and sent cool water flying onto the boy. Josh held out his hands to shield himself and laughed.

"Hearing him laugh is worth a lot," Lyle said.

They spent over an hour alongside the stream, followed by a midmorning snack. Connor helped Lyle out of the wheelchair so he could put his hands in the water. Father and son then started throwing small river rocks at a decaying tree stump. Lyle was surprisingly accurate, and Connor saw Josh's competitive side emerge.

"I was a pitcher in high school," Lyle said when Connor commented on one throw.

"He pitched a no-hitter when he was a junior and another when he was a senior!" Josh added. "I have the game balls with the dates and scores written on them in my room. Did you play baseball?"

"Lacrosse was my main sport in high school."

"What's that?" Josh asked.

"Originally, it was a Native American sport," Connor replied and gave a brief explanation.

"I'd rather play baseball," Josh said when he finished.

When it was time to leave, Lyle ate an energy bar. "Ready for Everest," he said.

Josh and Rascal led the way with Lyle behind and Connor in the rear. Josh went too far ahead and disappeared around a corner. Lyle called him back. When the boy didn't immediately appear, Connor jogged up the trail. He found Josh squatting down and looking at an enormous dragonfly perched on a fern.

"Can we catch it and keep it?" he asked.

"Leave it alone. It's a male blue dasher. They kill a lot of insect pests."

Huffing and puffing, Lyle rounded the corner. "Why didn't you come when I called?" he asked Josh.

"Sorry, I was looking at this bug."

Lyle joined them. "That's one of the biggest ones I've ever seen," he said.

Rascal, who was at the end of the leash, joined them, and the dragonfly took off.

"Stay in sight if you want to be in the lead," Lyle said to Josh as they started forward. "And that rule applies if you're ever in the woods with Mr. Connor."

Josh and Rascal continued in the front. As they climbed higher, Connor increasingly appreciated Lyle's physical effort. Rolling the wheelchair uphill was tough. He could hear Lyle breathing heavily.

"Do you want me to push and give you a break?" Connor asked, coming up beside him.

"No, this is a challenge I've set for myself today. I want to see if I can do it on my own."

Connor backed off. Ten minutes later they crested the final climb. It was a short, gradual descent to the parking lot. Opening the side door of the van, Josh took out a metal bowl and walked over to a faucet to fill it with water for Rascal.

Lyle wiped his forehead with a red bandanna.

"You did it," Connor said to Lyle. "That was impressive."

"Harder than I imagined," Lyle replied. "Do you know one thing I thought about?"

"What?"

"There won't be any wheelchairs in heaven. My disability is temporary. Your sermon the other day reminded me of that."

"That's the best feedback I've received."

CHAPTER 7

FACING THE FRIDAY MORNING DEADLINE, LIZ WAS putting the finishing touches on her responses to the questions posed by Elena. She'd placed her phone on do not disturb to prevent interruptions.

Jessica appeared in the doorway of Liz's office. "Elena Thompson has called twice in the past hour," the assistant said. "Becky sent the second call to me. How are you coming with the memo?"

"Almost done. That's why I'm not taking calls. Where's Harold? I want him to review the memo before I send it."

"Out at a deposition."

"I checked his calendar and thought he was here until this afternoon."

"Let me read it," Jessica suggested. "It's always good to have a second set of eyes that might spot an error."

Ten minutes later, Jessica returned. "I'm finished," she said with a deadpan expression on her face.

"And?" Liz asked.

"I'd say it's your best work since you joined the firm."

"Really?"

"Yeah. I corrected one misspelled word and added a comma or two. I was impressed."

Liz forwarded the memo to Elena, then called her. "Sorry I wasn't available earlier. I was completing your memo. It should be in your inbox shortly."

"I need it now," Elena said curtly.

"Check."

Liz waited.

"Got it. Stay available in case I have any follow-up questions."

Liz went to Jessica's desk and told her the client's response.

"That's not surprising," Jessica said with a slight shake of her head. "Rich folks are always the most demanding. The poor people we represent are much more appreciative."

"I appreciate you," Liz said.

"That's nice." Jessica smiled. "And you can always count on me to tell you the truth about your memos, outfits, dating choices, baby care. Anything."

Liz laughed. "What's your favorite dessert?"

"That's a hard one," Jessica said. "It depends on my mood and the time of the day. I like éclairs in the morning if they're fresh and the filling is extra rich and creamy. For lunch, a coconut pie hits the spot, but only when the meringue is covered with toasted coconut flakes. And after supper there's nothing better than a fresh fruit pie and homemade vanilla ice cream. The type of fruit is seasonal. I like them all: peach, apple, cherry, blackberry, blueberry. Why do you want to know?"

"I want to either bake or buy you a dessert for helping me so much."

"Surprise me."

Liz stepped out for a quick lunch. On her way back to the office, she went to a local bakery and bought a coconut cream pie. Jessica wasn't at her desk when she returned. Liz placed the whole pie next to the assistant's keyboard.

Jessica entered her office soon after and a few minutes later burst into Liz's office. "Thank you!"

"You're welcome. Did it have enough coconut flakes?"

"Yeah, I cut a huge slice that had the most coconut on top for me and put the rest of the pie in the break room for others to share."

"Have you tasted it?"

"Delicious. I'm going to savor it for the rest of the afternoon." Jessica paused before continuing, "Unless my willpower evaporates and I devour it in the next five minutes."

Liz avoided the break room. Trying to anticipate Elena's follow-up questions, she continued to study the issues raised by the new client. She found several points that needed clarification.

Around 1:30 p.m., Becky buzzed her phone. "Elena Thompson is on line 3."

"Thanks for the memo," Elena said when Liz answered. "It really gives me confidence going into the meeting this afternoon with Matt."

"Good."

"But I didn't like your answer about Matt's obligation under the divorce decree to keep paying the premiums on the big life insurance policy for Anne. She bled him dry at the time of their split, and I hate the thought of her profiting from his death. Two million dollars is a lot for her to receive if he dies. Of course, she'd burn through that money and wonder where it went."

"He's only required to keep the insurance in effect until their youngest child reaches age twenty-one. Matt is in good health, isn't he?"

"Yeah."

"And I assume he has an insurance policy payable to you."

"But until recently it was half as much as hers. Matt argued that Anne needed a bigger policy because of the kids, but to me it was another way he showed that he loved her more than he does me."

Liz had never considered the size of an insurance policy an indicator of love. To her, it was merely a practical part of a financial plan.

"Was I clear about the ways the value of the business might be calculated in case of a divorce?" Liz asked. "That's the most complex part of the situation."

"Yes, that was an issue with Anne too. But back then the business was just getting started, and he quickly paid her off. Now it's going to be worth millions if things work out the way he believes they will."

In most high-dollar divorces, legal wars were waged between competing business valuation experts and accountants.

"Anything else?" Liz asked.

"That's it for now. I'll call you after our counseling session."

———

Connor arrived at the church half an hour before the meeting with Elena and Matt. While he waited, he reviewed his notes from the previous sessions and what he'd added since then. He went through Matt's updated responses and compared them with Elena's previous submission. There was a lot to discuss.

Michelle cracked open his door. "They're here," she said in a soft voice. "Do you want me to stay?"

The church secretary usually left early on Friday.

"No."

Connor stepped into the waiting area. Matt Thompson was sitting on one side of the room with Elena on the other.

"Anne is available to join on a conference call," Matt said before Connor said anything.

Elena's face was a dark cloud.

"The three of us will meet first," Connor said.

Connor held open the door for Matt and Elena. Three chairs were arranged in a circle in the open space in front of his desk. The tension in the room was palpable. Connor opened a sheet of paper he was holding in his left hand. He'd written out a prayer that he intended to read.

"Let me hold on to this prayer," he said and faced Elena. "I know we talked the other day about Anne possibly joining us in some fashion, but I want to make sure you're completely on board with it. If so, there may be times when I speak with one or all of you privately or as a group."

"I don't want to be left alone in a room while you talk to Anne and Matt," Elena said.

"She's not a threat to you," Matt replied brusquely. "Not in any way. Anne is the mother of my children, nothing more."

"Don't be ridiculous," Elena shot back. "Her interference in our lives is the main reason we're here. I hope Connor can convince you to see what's really going on and let Anne know that our marriage is off-limits."

Matt looked at Connor. "Ultimatums are Elena's specialty."

"I'll ignore the insult," Elena said. "And I'd like to know what you identified as the issues for discussion today. I sent both you and Connor a copy of what I provided before our first meeting and the additional information before this one. I've never received anything from you except a few bullet points, and I don't want to be ambushed."

"Ambushed!" Matt exploded. "We're in a counseling session with a minister, not a courtroom for a divorce case."

"And it's up to you to decide if it stays that way," Elena replied coldly.

While the exchange took place, Connor tried to remember if there were any incendiary comments in what Matt sent him. Nothing came to mind.

"Show it to her," Matt said with a wave of his hand. "I'm not hiding anything, and I hope she isn't either."

Connor retrieved the folder from the top of his desk. It was considerably thicker than at their last meeting. He handed two sheets of paper to Elena and watched her facial expression while she read. Her eyes moved rapidly back and forth. Her face revealed nothing.

"That's very helpful," she said. "It's good to see that both of us realize some of the things we need to work on."

Connor sighed in relief.

Elena faced Matt and held the sheets of paper up in the air. "I have one question. Why did you ask Anne to help you come up with the issues and why they're important? You didn't write this."

Matt's face reddened. "Look, I came today to apologize for some things and try to make progress," he said. "If you don't want to listen to me, we can leave now."

"I think Elena should hear what you have to say," Connor suggested.

"Go ahead," Elena said grudgingly.

Matt leaned forward with his hands together in front of him. "I'm sorry for making you feel insecure in our relationship. I want to spend more time with you and will set aside time on my business calendar just for the two of us. Those times will have a higher priority than anything else. Period. We're also going to plan three vacations, each at least seven to ten days long, during the next year. You get to pick two destinations; I get to pick one. And I promise not to make one of them Cozumel." Matt turned to Connor. "We both got food poisoning there a couple of years ago."

"I agree. No to Cozumel," Elena said in a softer tone of voice.

"And in the future my interactions with Anne are going to be focused on the girls."

"Are you serious?" Elena asked.

"One hundred percent. And I'm going to start attending church with you on a regular basis."

"But you thought it was boring," Elena blurted out, then looked apologetically at Connor. "It's what he told me."

"That's true," Matt admitted. "But I think my attitude can change."

He proceeded to address other issues. "I believe it's time you received professional counseling to help you deal with what happened from the time you were four until you turned eight. I've thought there's no reason to bring up bad stuff from the past, but I may be wrong."

"That's Anne talking," Elena said to Connor. "She thinks I'm psychotic because my mother dropped me off with an aunt who didn't want me and turned me over to the Virginia Department of Social Services. I spent three years in the foster care system before I was placed in a home and eventually adopted. The experience made me stronger, not crazy."

"You're listening to Matt. Let him finish. You can respond in a few minutes."

Matt looked down at the sheets of paper in his hands. "Let me check the information we sent you before the meeting," he said to Connor.

"'We'?" Elena cut in. "So Anne did help you write it!"

"No; well, partly. She knows we're in marital counseling and wants the girls to have a good environment when they visit. But I put this together myself with a few notes she provided about stuff that's important to her."

"Important to her? I already know she's behind the recommendation that I see a psychiatrist. She wants to be able to prove that I'm not fit to be in the home when the girls come for a visit."

"They've not been to our house in over three months."

"Because you exercise all your visitation rights with Anne at the apartment in Atlanta."

"Anne doesn't spend the night at the apartment."

"What time does she go home?"

Matt pressed his lips tightly together.

Connor jumped in. "Matt, is there anything else you want to say about what you prepared?"

Matt leaned back in his chair. "No, I'm done."

"Let me talk one-on-one with Elena for a few minutes," Connor said.

"Sure," Matt replied. "Do you want me to wait in the reception area?"

"Go to the sanctuary," Elena said. "That way I'll know my conversation with Connor will be private."

As soon as they were alone, Connor spoke. "Matt is really trying. This is a great chance to make progress."

"Trying to do what? Lure me into a false sense of security before he tries to destroy me? Matt is a great salesman. He knows how to make someone feel comfortable right before he takes a bunch of their money."

"But he made some apologies and promised positive steps."

"I heard him," Elena replied. "But so much of my trust has been destroyed that it's going to take time to build it up again."

"That's understandable." Connor paused. "What would you say to encourage him? Could you apologize for something that's happened or you've said to him when you were upset?"

"Why would I apologize to Matt?" Elena asked. "He's the one who's put me through torment. If I'm having mental issues, it's because he's abandoned me and focused on his relationship with Anne. He hides behind the girls, but I know what's really going on."

Based on his conversation with Matt, Connor couldn't contradict Elena. But he wasn't willing to completely retreat.

"Could you at least thank Matt for what he's shared?"

"Yeah, I can do that."

"Good. Is there anything else you could mention that might be positive?"

Elena stared directly into Connor's eyes. "I'm positive that what you're hearing today is part of a strategy he's worked out with Anne. This is new to you, but I've seen it before."

Frustrated, Connor asked, "Then why thank him?"

"Because you want me to do it, and I'm here to take your advice."

"Anything else before I bring him back in?"

"Yes. I've talked with Liz Acosta about my legal rights," she said. "She's the young lawyer who visited the church last Sunday."

"I remember."

"I hired her not because I want to get a divorce, but because I can't afford to get blindsided. I've been one hundred percent committed to my marriage since day one."

Connor grimaced. In his limited marital counseling experience, bringing in lawyers had never helped reconciliation between the parties. But it wasn't his role to discourage someone from seeking legal advice. He left the room and escorted Matt back to the office.

"Thanks for what you said," Elena said as soon as Matt was

seated. "I want to plan some vacations but not until you finalize what's going to happen with the business. As hard as you might try not to, you'd be thinking about it when we were away."

"Okay," Matt replied.

Elena didn't say anything else.

"That's it?" Matt asked.

"For today," Connor said. "I'll close our time with a prayer."

In the prayer, he included a request that God work in all their lives.

"Would you like to schedule another session?" he asked. "And given what Matt's shared today, is it necessary for Anne to join us?"

"Not for me," Elena replied.

"Let me think about it," Matt said more slowly.

Elena gave Connor an "I told you so" look.

They all stood.

"I have something else I'd like to discuss with Connor," Matt said. "It's about me, not us."

"I'm fine with that so long as you're telling the truth. If not, I'll expect Connor to keep you honest."

"Don't worry," Matt replied. "Go home and get ready for our date tonight."

"Date?"

"To the new seafood place in north Atlanta you mentioned last week. I made reservations."

Elena paused. "That sounds nice."

CHAPTER 8

IN LIZ'S INBOX WERE THE FIRST TWO TENANT EVIC-
tion cases from Lamar Braxton. One of the rental properties was an
older apartment building with eight units in an area of town largely
populated by recently arrived Latinos. It was next door to a small
restaurant that served the best tamales in Etowah County. Liz tried
to reach the tenants by phone. No one answered at one number, and
the other number was no longer in service. Having skipped lunch
to work on the memo for Elena Thompson, she was hungry and
decided to see if she could personally contact the tenants. Stopping
by Becky's desk on her way out of the office, she told the receptionist
what she was going to do.

"But first, I'm going to swing by Manuel's Taqueria on Kenilworth
Avenue and grab a late lunch," she said.

"Is that the little place painted bright blue?" the receptionist
asked.

"Yes. They serve the best tamales in town. Very authentic."

"I've always wanted to try it."

"Would you like me to bring you some?"

"That would be so sweet," Becky replied brightly. "Just pick out a variety and let me know how much it costs. My boyfriend is coming over for supper, and I can surprise him."

The changing ethnic demographic of Bryson became apparent as soon as Liz turned onto Kenilworth Avenue. Dark-haired boys were kicking a soccer ball in a scruffy vacant lot. A commercial center with several retail businesses had signs out front in both English and Spanish. Over half the vehicles parked in front of the houses and along the street were pickup trucks. There wasn't much similarity between the area and the affluent neighborhood in south Florida where Liz grew up. Her father had started and sold two companies, and her mother's family owned a large orange grove. Liz's father made an effort to expose her to Cuban culture, but he was half Anglo himself. Only with her grandmother did Liz feel a connection to that aspect of her roots.

She pulled into the parking area for the restaurant. Midafternoon on Friday there were only a couple of cars in the parking lot. She went inside.

"Greetings, senorita!" said Manuel Domingo from his place on a stool beside the cash register.

Behind the owner and in partial view was the kitchen. Liz could see a couple of large pots on the stovetop.

She spoke Spanish when she visited the restaurant.

"You know what I want," she said. "It's only a question of how many. Two now, and two to take home for later. Also, I want to order a to-go meal for the receptionist at the law firm. She's going to surprise her boyfriend for supper, so make it fancy."

Manuel opened his arms to encompass the interior of the small restaurant with limited seating at six tables for four. "Everything about this place is fancy."

Manuel barked orders to the kitchen. Liz sat down. A few

minutes later, the proprietor placed a couple of tamales, one filled with red chili and the other with seasoned chicken, on the table. The golden corn husks were each neatly tied with a string and a bow. Beside the tamales was fresh salsa and avocado. Liz untied the string, removed the husk, and took a bite of the chili tamale.

"Perfection," she said. "Your masa is the best."

Manuel smiled. "What brings you here in the middle of the afternoon?" he asked. "You should be taking a siesta."

"Siestas aren't part of the routine at the law office," Liz said after she'd wiped her mouth with a small paper napkin. "I need to talk to some tenants who live in the apartment building next door. I tried to call but couldn't reach them."

"Who is it?"

The paperwork was in her car, but Liz pulled up the basic information on her phone. When she mentioned the first name, Manuel held up his hand and stopped her.

"No," he said with an alarmed look on his face. "You should not knock on his door. Too dangerous."

"His phone is disconnected."

"I'm not surprised. Wait a minute. Let me talk to Jose."

Manuel went into the kitchen for a minute, then returned. "The man you're looking for is in jail, which is a good thing."

"Was he living there with his family? Does he have a wife or kids?"

"No, there was some bad stuff going on in that apartment. Troublemakers coming and going. Whoever is living there is not someone you want to meet, whether during the day or at night."

"Thanks," Liz replied.

She mentioned the other name.

Manuel nodded as he said, "Yes, I know that family too. The

husband lost his job at the chicken plant. I'm not sure why. The wife works as a custodian at the hospital. They have three or four kids. Are they in trouble?"

"I can't tell you, but I'd like to talk to them."

Manuel was silent for a moment. "They are behind on their rent," he guessed. "Does your law firm represent the man who owns the building?"

"Manuel, you could get a second job as a detective," Liz said. "If they promise to catch up on the rent, will they follow through?"

"If it's possible. They are good people."

Forty-five minutes later, Liz was on her way back to the office with a signed, modified rent agreement on the car seat beside her.

━━━━━━

Curious, Connor sat down with Matt across from him.

"That was hard," Matt said. "But I think it was the right thing to do."

"I agree. Admitting the need to change is tough. I commend you."

Matt cleared his throat. "One of the podcasts that you recommended really shook me up. And not about my marriage. It was like a punch in the gut."

"Which one?"

"About the story in the Bible of the successful farmer who built a bigger barn so he could retire and enjoy all his crops right before he died. The story perfectly described my mindset and goal for the past twenty years."

"What podcast are you talking about?"

Matt told him the name of the speaker.

"That's not the one I sent."

"Yes, it is." Matt opened his phone, found the email with attached links, and handed it to Connor, who recognized the speaker but not the subject matter.

"You're right," he said, handing the phone back to Matt. "I meant to link you to his talk about the keys to building successful relationships."

"Anyway, it caused me to reevaluate where I am in my life. With Elena, Anne, my business, what I believe. Everything. Elena doesn't know the details, but the business has taken on a ton of debt over the past two years as we've tried to expand into foreign markets and compete with some of the big boys. It's a big gamble with a huge reward if we're able to pull it off. If that happens, I'll need huge barns. But my main business partner, a guy named Winston Boone, who's been with me since the beginning, is nervous and wants to sell to a competitor and get out now. I'm working hard to keep him on board with my plans. Anyway, there was a challenge at the end of the podcast. Would you like to hear it?"

"Sure," Connor replied.

"I know exactly where it is," Matt said. "It's forty-two minutes in."

Connor watched Matt's face as he located the section of the podcast.

"It's not long," Matt said as he pressed the play symbol.

Connor recognized the speaker's voice: "This parable isn't just about finances. Money is just one indicator of what's important in a person's life. The real message is whether you want God to be in charge of everything, no limits, no boundaries, nothing held back. That's what it really means to follow Jesus Christ, to be a true disciple."

Matt stopped the recording, looked at Connor, and asked, "Do you believe that?"

It was a simple yet orthodox message.

"Yes."

"This absolutely blows my mind," Matt said, shaking his head from side to side. "If I want to do this, what should I do?"

"If you want to do what?"

"Become a true disciple of Jesus Christ. Even saying this to you, I'm trembling on the inside because I don't know what's going to happen. Do I sound crazy?"

Connor had read about enough different expressions of Christianity to have a broad-minded view of what fit under the faith tent.

"If that's what you believe, then it's not crazy."

"Great," Matt said with relief. "I listened to another podcast by the same guy, and he recommended praying out loud with someone if you want to become a disciple of Jesus. Do you do that with people?"

"Yes, but only if you don't feel pressured. I hate manipulation."

"'Pressured'?" Matt tilted his head to one side. "The guy was talking through the speakers in my car, not sitting beside me in the passenger seat. But I know what you're driving at. I'm a salesman; I know a sales pitch when I hear it. The only pressure I felt was on the inside. And it comes back every time I listen to what I just played for you."

"Okay," Connor replied. "I'll be glad to pray with you."

"Thanks. This is your area of expertise, so you go first."

Connor cleared his throat and offered up a brief prayer of thanks acknowledging God's desire to call Matt Thompson as a disciple. Still keeping his head bowed and eyes closed, he stopped to figure out what to say next. Matt didn't wait on him.

"Yes, God, I believe that's what you're doing, and I want to say yes to putting you in control of my life so that I can be a true disciple of Jesus Christ. Amen."

Connor opened his eyes and found Matt looking directly at him. Matt wasn't emotional. "Was that good enough?" he asked.

"That's not for me to say. What do you think?"

"I'm satisfied."

"Does Elena know about the podcast and its impact on you?"

"No, I was going to tell her at dinner tonight."

"How do you think she'll respond?"

"I have no idea. Any advice on how to do that?"

"The same way you did with me."

"Okay." Matt paused. "Anne was positive when I told her."

"You told her first?"

"Yeah, it came up out of the blue when we were talking yesterday. She and the girls were at the apartment for a few hours."

"If possible, I wouldn't tell Elena she's getting the news later than Anne."

"Right. I already thought about that." Matt ran his fingers through his hair. "One other thing. This is changing my perspective about the business. Our company is going to have a retreat with top management at the Burnt Pine Tree Lodge next weekend. We're going to hunt on Saturday, but Friday evening at dinner, I was thinking about telling the guys about the podcast."

"That's bold. Will it offend anyone?"

"I'm not sure. But I'm considering it. Most of them are like me. All their focus is on building bigger barns."

"Will Reg Bullock be there?"

"Yeah, several members of the board are coming, and he helped coordinate the event."

"Reg will be an ally. He's a good man."

"Yes, our company CPA recommended him for the board two years ago. I'm glad he accepted."

After Matt left, Connor remained in his office. He'd never been present when a person made such a dramatic shift in their religious beliefs. Matt Thompson had become a disciple of Jesus Christ, and Connor had played a minor role in the process. He offered up a prayer of thanksgiving.

CHAPTER 9

BOUNCING AROUND IN HER LIVING ROOM, LIZ finished an intense exercise routine. Saturday was the one day of the week when her workout wasn't limited by her schedule, and she'd pushed the limits of her endurance. Grabbing a sports drink, she went outside her apartment and sat in a white Adirondack chair positioned in the shade. The stirring of the cool morning air felt good against her hot face. The refreshing breeze was an advantage of north Georgia over the perpetual humid heat in Florida.

Bev Devon came out the front door of her house and waved. Liz lifted a weary arm. The workout had focused a lot on her shoulders. They were burned out.

"Did you go for a run?" her landlady asked.

"No, I was watching an exercise routine on YouTube."

"It looks like you did more than watch."

"My body agrees," Liz said.

"I need more of that," Bev said. "One of my friends does Zumba. She's invited me to come over and join her, but I'm not sure about it. She says it's like salsa dancing."

Liz smiled at the thought of two older women dancing in front of a computer screen.

"You should give it a try. Is Sam a dancer?"

Bev's eyes widened. "How did you guess? That's how we met. At a high school dance. We'd both arrived with someone else and left with each other."

"That must have been dramatic."

"The other boy and girl were our friends. Anyway, Sam and I would go anyplace we could if there was dancing."

Liz took a long swallow of her sports drink.

"Do you have any interest in coming back to the church tomorrow?" Bev asked. "You seemed to enjoy it."

"I did."

Liz's reservations about attending another church service focused more on seeing Elena and keeping their interaction professional and confidential than anything else. But in a small town like Bryson, the chance of running into a client or opposing party in a social setting wasn't unusual. It happened all the time to Harold and the other lawyers at the firm. She'd been with them at lunch when people they'd either represented or sued walked into a diner. They'd simply continue eating. Harold claimed people had to adapt to him, not the other way around. Liz wasn't quite there yet.

"Of course, there won't be lunch afterward," Bev continued. "More people come to church when there's going to be a big spread of food. By the way, your stew was a huge hit. Three of my friends called me and asked if you'd given me the recipe."

"I'll come," Liz said, making up her mind. "And I'll bring copies of the recipe for your friends."

"Wonderful!" Bev said, clearly pleased. "Would you like to ride with Sam and me?"

"No, but thanks. I'll drive."

As she got ready the following morning, Liz stood in front of her closet. The women at the church wore a wide variety of clothes. Liz decided to be a little fancy and selected a fall-themed outfit featuring a harvest yellow dress. She parked beside the Devons' vehicle. Inside, it wasn't quite time for the service to start. People were milling about and talking. Liz sat down beside Bev.

"I'm so glad you made it," she said. "You look fabulous."

"Thanks, Bev."

"Oh, there's Pam Forsett. She wants the recipe."

Bev motioned to a well-dressed woman in her sixties with dark brown hair. Bev introduced her to Liz, who handed her a copy of the recipe along with her phone number and email at the bottom of the sheet.

"Thanks so much," Pam said in a silky Southern voice. "Curtis loved your dish. Next Saturday is his birthday. I'm going to surprise him and make it."

After she left, Liz turned to Bev and commented, "That's a lot of pressure to get it right the first time."

"Don't worry about Pam," Bev replied. "She could be a professional chef."

Shortly before the service started, Elena arrived, accompanied by a man.

"Is that Elena Thompson's husband?" Liz asked Bev in a soft voice.

"Yes, but he usually doesn't come with her. Why?"

"Just asking."

The service followed the same format as before. Now that it wasn't all new, Liz felt more comfortable. After the choir sang a song, Connor Grantham spoke from a passage in the book of

Matthew about seeking first the kingdom of God, a concept that wasn't familiar to her. It all struck Liz as more theoretical than practical. According to the minister, intention led to actions. But how to determine if individual conduct was consistent with seeking God's kingdom was unclear to her.

The service ended. Another woman who wanted the recipe for ropa vieja came up to them. After giving her a copy, Liz said goodbye to Bev and made her way to the rear of the sanctuary. Connor was standing in front of the door shaking hands with people as they passed by on their way out. Liz considered dodging the line but decided it would appear rude.

"Glad to see you again," Connor said when she reached him. "Would you be able to stay for a few minutes? I have a question for you."

"Okay."

Liz stood to the side in the foyer as people continued to stream by. The minister had a nice smile. Elena and Matt appeared. Liz nodded at Elena, who quickly shook her head. The couple lingered in front of Connor before moving on. Soon there was a gap in the line.

Connor came over to her. "Are you free for lunch?" he asked.

Surprised, she said, "Right now?"

"I often invite people who've visited the church a couple of times to lunch. There is a husband and wife still in the sanctuary who said they could join us. We'd go someplace in town. The church would pay."

Liz had no plans except a sandwich. The church was proving to be a place to meet people.

"I'd like that," she said.

Another cluster of people, including Bev and Sam, emerged from the sanctuary. When Bev saw Liz talking with Connor, she smiled broadly. The minister resumed his place near the exit. A young couple approached. Connor spoke to them and motioned to Liz. A moment later they moved on, and the minister came over to her.

"Turns out they aren't going to be able to come," he said. "We can connect another day or time."

"Today is good," Liz answered.

Connor hesitated for a second. "Okay. I'll meet you in the parking lot. I have to go to my office for a minute."

=====

Connor had changed his sermon after the Friday meeting with Matt Thompson. Switching topics that late in the week was rare. And the attention Matt gave during the message was Connor's reward. It was hard for Connor to make eye contact with anyone else. He kept coming back to Matt. On the way out the door, Matt firmly shook his hand.

"What you talked about this morning made a lot of sense," Matt said.

"I always love what you say," Elena added with a smile.

Connor went to his office to grab the packet of information he gave people who visited the church. He usually took prospects to a popular local restaurant. Connor enjoyed the food, especially the fried chicken, which reminded him of how his grandmother prepared it. Liz Acosta was in the parking lot leaning against a small sedan.

"I thought we could go to Parker's Restaurant," he said. "They have a good Sunday buffet."

Liz wrinkled her nose. "I ate there this week with people from work. Would you be okay with the Olive Tree?"

"Never heard of it. Is it new?"

"Open for a couple of months. It's in a renovated house on Poplar Street right before the area turns residential. They serve Mediterranean-style food. I've been once and liked it."

"Sure, I'll follow you."

Connor drove his electric car to the restaurant. During the short drive, he resolved not to ask the lawyer anything about Elena Thompson. At a stoplight, he saw Liz's head bobbing back and forth as she listened to music.

The restaurant was on a tree-shaded street. They parked along the curb in front. Inside, the former residence had been opened up into a large room that likely combined the former living and dining areas. There were tables for four and two.

"Sit where you'd like," called out a young woman with dark hair who was carrying food on a tray.

Without asking Connor, Liz walked over to the table for two and sat down. There were live plants placed around the room and Mediterranean-themed art on the walls. They scanned the menu on their phones.

"What did you order when you came before?" Connor asked.

"I built my own rice bowl with lamb as the protein. I've not found anyplace else in town that serves lamb, and I love it."

The waitress who'd greeted them placed two glasses of water on the table. "Anything else to drink?" she asked.

"Water is fine," Liz said.

"Mint limonada," Connor said.

"I didn't see that," Liz commented.

"You should try it," the waitress said.

"You can sample mine," Connor offered.

"It's good if you like lemons and mint," Connor said after the waitress left. "The first time I tried it was on a Greek island. When I was twelve years old, my family spent three weeks on a chartered sailboat cruising the islands in the Aegean."

"Tell me more."

Connor gave Liz a quick travelogue. "My older brother didn't like it that much. He wanted to be at home spending the time with his friends, but my older sister and I loved it."

"That sounds like a fantastic trip," Liz replied.

"It was my mother's dream. My dad planned it for her, down to the last detail. She passed away from cancer about a year after we came home."

"I'm sorry."

The waitress returned with Connor's drink. It was light green with a sprig of mint floating on top.

"You first," he said to Liz.

She took a sip and pursed her lips together. "It's tart."

Connor sampled it. "That's the way I like it. Not too much sugar."

They ordered their food. Both chose lamb.

"Do you have any questions about the church?" Connor asked.

"Even if I did, I'd rather hear you talk about sailing around the Greek islands," Liz said.

Connor told her more about the trip with his family. "The sky and the water were so beautiful," he said. "If I close my eyes, I can still bring back scenes."

"Do you have any photos?"

"Actually, I do."

Connor found the album and handed his phone to Liz. He ate while she scrolled through the pictures.

"I can see the family resemblance with your mom," she said.

"Yeah, everyone says that. My siblings look more like my dad. My brother is an anesthesiologist who lives in Boston with his wife and two kids. My sister is married and works as the CFO for a company that sells designer clothes. She and her husband live in Charleston, South Carolina." Connor paused. "My father is a cardiologist in Atlanta. He's on a short sabbatical and about to leave for a two-month volunteer stint at a clinic in Nepal."

"That's a lot of brainpower." Liz returned the phone to him.

"What about you and your family?" Connor asked.

"Everybody lives in the Miami area. My father is a businessman, and my mother's family has owned orange groves for generations. My father's mother came to America when she was a teenager as a refugee from Cuba. She married a man who made a career as a civilian worker on Air Force bases in Florida."

"You learned about Cuban food from your grandmother."

"Partly. It's everywhere in Miami. I just like it."

"Are you fluent in Spanish?" Connor asked in the same language.

Liz rattled off a rapid reply that caused Connor to raise his hand after a few seconds. "No need to show off," he said. "That's more than enough. You lost me after the second sentence."

"My language ability is the reason I received an offer from the law firm here in Bryson."

"That makes sense. Siblings?"

"Two younger sisters. One is in college and the other a senior in high school." Liz took a bite of food. "Have you traveled a lot?"

"Yeah, but not much recently."

"Where have you been?"

"All over Europe, twice, Turkey, Egypt, Israel, India, Japan, China, Tanzania, and you already know about Greece."

Liz's eyes widened. "And you can prove it with pictures on your phone?"

Connor smiled. "You can put me under oath and cross-examine me if you like."

"And now you're living in Etowah County, Georgia." Liz shook her head. "You have to admit that seems odd."

"Why?"

"How many people in this restaurant have visited more than a few states? Much less gone all over the world."

"You're the first person who has asked me about that sort of thing in a long time."

"Which doesn't answer my question."

Connor paused. "More than travel, I value solitude and study. I love going off by myself in the mountains. Living here gives me the chance to do both things."

"Fair enough," Liz replied slowly. "I know you invited me to lunch because I visited the church two Sundays in a row. If you were sitting where I am, what should I ask about it?"

"It depends on what interests you."

"I want to meet more people. You may like isolation but that doesn't work for me. I'm friends with a woman who works at the law firm, but she's married with children. And I work long hours, though that's not a good reason for not getting out more."

"There are several single women around your age who attend. One that comes to mind is an accountant who works for one of the local banks. Her name is Cynthia Jones. I'll introduce you to her."

"Does that mean I have to come back to the church?"

"Yep," Connor confirmed.

Outside the restaurant, Liz and Connor walked to his car where he gave her a packet of information about the church.

"When will there be another of those big dinners after the service?" she asked. "It reminded me of a family reunion."

"We only have three or four of those a year."

"You should do it more often. People like that sort of thing."

"If we did, what would you bring?"

"Picadillo à la habanera. Are you familiar with it?"

Connor paused for a moment. "A stew that sings?"

"Pretty good translation. It's made with ground beef, tomato sauce, olives, and seasonings."

"We'll have another church dinner around Thanksgiving. Maybe you can bring it then."

Driving home, Liz thought about how magical it would be to visit the Greek isles.

Thirty minutes later there was a knock on her door. It was Bev Devon with a small plate in her hands.

"I brought you some date bars," she said, handing Liz the plate. "Do you like dates?"

"Yes."

"I didn't get a chance to ask you about the service," Bev continued. "Doesn't Reverend Grantham do a good job? He's so smart. It's like every sentence comes out so polished it could be written in a book."

"I think he reads his sermons."

"Maybe. I'm not sure. I saw you talking to him in the foyer."

"He invited me to lunch."

The excited look on Bev's face brought a smile to Liz's face. She motioned for her landlady to step inside.

"It wasn't supposed to be the two of us, but the other couple he invited had to cancel," Liz said. "You probably know this, but he takes visitors to lunch so he can get to know them, and so they can ask questions about the church."

"Where did you eat?" Bev asked.

Bev was unfamiliar with the Olive Tree, but she nodded and said, "That sounds perfect for two young people. I'm so glad you had that time together."

"It was nice. Connor is an interesting man. We talked about—"

Bev held up her hand. "Oh, I won't ask you what you discussed."

"Mostly about family and what we're interested in," Liz continued.

"That's great," Bev said enthusiastically.

"He's going to introduce me to a woman named Cynthia Jones. He thinks we might become friends."

"You'll love Cynthia. She's a huge sports fan. And I know you like to exercise."

Liz didn't see the correlation. "Thanks again for the dessert," she said.

When Liz arrived at the office Monday morning, there was a thank-you card on her desk from Becky. She and her boyfriend had enjoyed their meal from the taqueria. Also on her desk was a file with a message on top from Harold: "See me ASAP."

"Sit," Harold ordered when Liz entered the senior partner's office. "I woke up at four this morning thinking about the Simmons Company fire claim and couldn't go back to sleep, so I came into the office. A detective with the sheriff's department questioned some of the workers, but I can't get a summary of the report from one of my contacts because it's an ongoing investigation. I want you to interview three of the Latino workers who were there that day and find out if they know anything about the fire."

"How soon do you need this?"

"As soon as possible. Depositions start next month."

Liz hesitated. "Is someone going to interview the English-speaking workers?"

"Of course!" Harold barked. "A private detective firm is doing that, but they don't have a Spanish speaker available."

"Yes, sir."

Late that afternoon, an exhausted Liz returned to the office. Becky greeted her.

"Where have you been all day?" the receptionist asked.

"Going into sketchy parts of town to track down people who are hard to find. After today there are a lot more folks in Etowah County who know that I'm a lawyer. I handed out a lot of cards. Is Harold here? I didn't see his car."

"Yes, his Mercedes is in the shop again." Becky glanced down at her phone. "He just finished a call."

Liz returned to the senior partner's office. For someone who'd been up since before dawn, he looked surprisingly chipper.

"Any luck?" he asked.

"Not sure about luck, but I found all three of them. I'll put everything in a memo but can give you a verbal report now if you have a few minutes."

"Go ahead."

Liz held up her phone. "I obtained recorded statements that are in Spanish."

"Anything relevant?"

"I think so."

Liz summarized her findings. One worker provided information that was very helpful to their theory of the case.

Harold perked up. "Did you get this fellow's home address?"

"Yes."

"Transcribe his statement and get him to sign it tomorrow."

"Yes, sir," Liz said.

She turned to leave. Harold's voice stopped her.

"Liz," he said.

She faced him again.

"Good job."

———

It was dark when Liz finally arrived at home. She kicked off her shoes and sat down in her tiny living room. Her phone vibrated, and she reluctantly took it from her purse. It was Elena Thompson. She let it go to voice mail.

CHAPTER 10

CONNOR WAS OUT OF BREATH WHEN HE REACHED the summit and scrambled onto a rock outcropping. Spread out before him was Bryson. From this vantage point the downtown area was visible, but much of the residential sections of town were obscured by trees along the streets and in the yards. He could see the roof and part of the parking lot for Rock Community Church.

Few people visited the overlook where Connor sat because it required a thirty-five-foot technical climb up a steep rock face. Scaling the summit was by far the most dangerous thing Connor had attempted on his local treks. Going down safely was tougher than climbing up. Today, he'd decided to work to reduce the risk in the future and brought some heavy-duty climbing rope that he was going to attach to a tree at the top. So long as the ropes were secure, climbing up and going down would be much simpler. Trusting the integrity of a rope required a different kind of faith than using only his hands, feet, and strength.

Taking a thermos of coffee from his daypack, Connor took a drink and tried to figure out how to work the climb into a sermon. If he talked about scaling the rock wall unaided, there would be men and boys in the congregation who would want to give it a try, and their wives and mothers would be upset with Connor for mentioning it.

On the drive to the trailhead, Connor had listened to the podcast he'd mistakenly forwarded to Matt Thompson about the parable of the rich man and his bigger barns. It was a confrontational message. Connor couldn't imagine the senior minister at his father's church in Atlanta basing a sermon on the passage. Many of the people in the affluent congregation had massive virtual barns, with more under construction.

Connor took another drink of coffee and stared out across the valley. The previous afternoon, he'd learned about an opening for an assistant professor of philosophy and religion at a small, prestigious college in Virginia. It was exactly what he'd been hoping to find. The school was located within reasonable driving distance of the mountains. And the wooded campus was perfect. It was easy to imagine himself sitting in an office in the liberal arts building with a view of the quad through a window. The record of his qualifications and recommendations were already in place. All Connor had to do was update his résumé and press the send button. But if he wanted to be considered for the job, he couldn't delay. He pressed his lips together and prayed silently for guidance.

Two hours later, he stopped by Michelle's desk. "Any fires to put out?" he asked.

"The phone has been a lot quieter than usual after you preached the sermon about heaven," she said.

"Is that good or bad?"

"You'd have to ask God or the church board the answer to that question."

Connor reached into the front pocket of his shirt and gave her the receipt for the meal at the Olive Tree. "This is for the visitor lunch," he said.

"Why not Parker's?" Michelle asked. "That's where you always go."

"Liz Acosta suggested the Olive Tree. It's a new place on Poplar Avenue."

"Just the two of you?"

"Without a chaperone," Connor replied with a smile. "We were in a public place. Liz and I had a good conversation. I think she'll be back. She wants to meet people, and I suggested Cynthia Jones."

"That's a great idea, except Cynthia moved to Greenville, South Carolina, last week to be closer to her family. I think her mom has some health issues. And Cynthia will love being closer to Clemson so she can go to the football games."

"I didn't know about her mother."

"It came up all of a sudden."

"Send me Cynthia's cell number, and I'll give her a call."

"Will do." Michelle paused. "Do you want me to see what I can find out about Liz Acosta?"

"Why?"

"She's cute, and as a lawyer has to be smart. I could see you getting to know her better, that's all."

"That will happen naturally if she keeps coming. And I'd rather conduct my own reconnaissance. I've not dated anyone in the church since I came here. As a general rule, that's not a good idea. If I go out with a woman in the church and it doesn't go well, it could be a problem."

"Maybe, but have you dated anyone at all?" Michelle asked, then immediately continued, "Sorry, that's none of my business."

"I've spent time with a woman in Atlanta who I've known since high school, but it's not been regular."

"You're smart to be careful about women in the church," Michelle said. "And once word got out, there would be a ton of interest. People would jump to all kinds of conclusions and opinions. Just stick to internet dating sites in your search for a mate."

"I'm not on any dating sites, but if I decide to sign up, should I come to you for advice?"

"Absolutely. I can help edit your profile. A nice picture of you standing behind the pulpit on Sunday morning would set you apart from the crowd."

Connor went into his office. Pulling up the portal for online submission of his application for the assistant professorship, he stared at it for a couple of seconds. It just didn't feel like the right time to apply for a teaching job. Connor closed the portal. He rarely made a decision based on feelings, but this time he did.

———

There was an envelope on Liz's desk when she arrived at work the following morning. Inside was a gift card. When she saw the amount, Liz dropped the card in surprise. It was for one thousand dollars. Jessica appeared in her doorway.

"How's your day going?" the assistant asked with a smile on her face.

Liz held up the card. "Did you know about this? Where did it come from?"

"Harold called me first thing this morning and sent me out to get it. He said you hit a home run for him in the Simmons case."

"I hope so."

"Harold must think you did."

"Is he here?"

"No, he's coming in later but wanted that on your desk first thing. It was the kind of errand I prefer to typing the responses to interrogatories."

"I was just doing my job."

Jessica stepped into the office and lowered her voice. "Harold is an odd guy. Sometimes that's good; other times not so much. He can be randomly generous. I've seen that in operation. Today was your day."

Liz looked again at the card. "I'm not sure what to spend it on."

Jessica held up her right hand, which glistened with three different rings. "You'll think of something," she said.

Liz put the gift card in her purse. Instead of sending Harold an email, she handwrote a thank-you note. Swiveling in her chair, she listened to her voice-mail messages. There was another one from Elena. The tone of voice was firm. Liz returned her calls in the order received. It was close to 10:00 a.m. before she dialed Elena's number.

"I'm not sure what's going on with Matt," Elena said as soon as she answered the phone. "He's acting strange. Did Connor Grantham say anything about him when the two of you went to lunch on Sunday?"

"Uh, no. How did you know I went to lunch with Connor?" Liz asked.

"That's what I heard. Did you and Connor discuss Matt and me?"

"No. Connor invites people who've visited the church out to eat so they can ask him questions."

"He never did that with me."

Liz didn't know what to say so kept quiet.

Elena continued, "And you're sure that you've not talked to Connor about Matt and me in the past twenty-four hours?"

"No, he doesn't even know you've retained the law firm. Why are you asking me this?"

"I let it slip that I've hired you during a private conversation with Connor during a counseling session last Friday. I also believe Matt found out that I've consulted a lawyer."

"What makes you think that?"

"The way he's been acting for the past few days. He was so agreeable during our session with Connor that I realized he was manipulating the situation, but I can't figure out his angle. He took me out to a nice dinner on Friday and told me that he's going to get serious about God. Then, he only worked a couple of hours on Saturday and came to church on Sunday without being asked. He's setting me up for something. What could it be?"

"What makes you think he's insincere?"

"You don't know him like I do. Matt is a top-notch salesman who knows how to convince people to do things they'd never consider otherwise. That's one reason he's been so successful in business and how he swept me off my feet when we started dating. But once he closes a deal, Matt moves on to the next challenge."

The way Elena described the foundation of her relationship with her husband and how she viewed him now made the possibility of future marital bliss unlikely.

"Did he ask you to change anything about your finances or living arrangements?"

"Not yet, but I can feel it coming."

"That's what you should be on guard against. Also, any suggestions about interaction with his ex-wife or the kids. You're hypervigilant, so it's going to be hard for you to be taken advantage of."

"He claims he's going to cut back his personal interaction with his ex, and I'm checking the bank balances every day to see if there are any odd transactions."

Liz thought about Elena's secret stash. It wouldn't be surprising if Matt had done the same thing.

"What could he do that I wouldn't know about until it was too late?" Elena continued.

"That's covered in the memo I prepared for you. For someone as sophisticated as Matt, transferring funds offshore so we can't trace them would be a possibility. Another area would be modifications to his estate plan or life insurance program. You have the original wills and copies of the insurance policies, but he could secretly sign a new will and make a change in a life insurance beneficiary, which you wouldn't know about until he had to reveal it in discovery."

"Or if he died," Elena said. "Remember, Matt's divorce papers from Anne require him to keep life insurance in place for her and the kids. I don't have that protection."

"That's legally correct."

"It seems like the only way a woman can guarantee the future is if she's divorced and her husband is under some kind of court order."

Liz had never considered that point of view and wasn't ready to believe it was true. She glanced at her computer. She was scheduled to be on a conference call in five minutes.

"Anything else?" she asked.

"I guess not. Oh, there is one more thing," Elena added quickly. "If I call the law firm that prepared our wills, does the attorney have to tell me if Matt has modified anything?"

"No. Any conversations Matt has or actions taken are protected by attorney-client confidentiality."

"What about the insurance agent Matt uses? They've been

friends for years. Does he have to tell me if there's been a change in the life insurance policies?"

"There are rules, but I'm not sure about the details. Do you want me to research it?"

"No, I'm friendly with the guy's assistant. If I call and ask her to send me copies of our policies, she'll do it."

After the call ended, Liz quickly entered her time. True to Harold's prediction, Elena was burning through her deposit.

CHAPTER 11

Tuesday morning, Connor received a text from Matt Thompson requesting a day they could meet for lunch. Connor suggested Wednesday of the following week. Matt gave him a thumbs-up. But instead of moving on to something else, Connor decided to call him.

"Hope this isn't a bad time to talk," he said.

"No, I just came out of a meeting going over final details for the company retreat this weekend at Burnt Pine Tree."

"Are you still planning on talking Friday evening about what we discussed the other day?"

"Yeah, and it's going to be different from any boardroom speech I've ever given. I'm both excited and nervous."

"What are you going to say?"

"I'm going to read the story in the Bible without telling them where it's from, then ask them what they think. Once that's done, I'm going to tell them how it's changed my perspective on life. And if it's okay with you, I'm going to recommend they listen to what you said at church this past Sunday."

"I wish I could be there, and I'm honored that you're recommending my sermon."

Matt was silent for a moment. "Would you pray for me?" he asked.

"Absolutely." Connor closed his eyes. "God, I ask you to be with Matt this weekend. Help him to speak clearly and persuasively. May the people in the room really listen to what he has to say." Connor paused. "And I thank you for the influence that Matt has had on my life. Amen."

"Thanks, but what are you talking about? How have I influenced your life?"

"Every minister wants to have conversations with someone like you. It's been a highlight of my time in Bryson. I look forward to getting together next Wednesday and finding out about the weekend."

———

Midafternoon on Friday, Connor and Michelle were talking in his office. He glanced out the window. It was a gray day with clouds over the mountains. The weather forecast called for a windy night with a steep drop in temperature.

"It's supposed to be clear and chilly in the morning," he said. "If I finish my sermon this evening, I'm going for an early morning hike to Caldwell's Knob."

"Have fun. I'll be sleeping. What are you going to talk about on Sunday?"

"The parable in Luke 12:16–21 about the rich man who had an abundant harvest, then decided to build bigger barns and take life easy, only to die before the next morning."

"That's intense."

"It fits with what I shared last Sunday about seeking first the kingdom of God."

"I guess so," Michelle replied skeptically. "I'd like to say I'm looking forward to hearing what you have to say, but I'm not sure that's true. Are you going to talk about giving to the church? You usually don't do that except on pledge Sunday."

"There are all kinds of giving. The biggest is giving up control of our lives to God."

———

Connor slept fitfully that night. The sound of the wind blowing against the house woke him a couple of times. In the predawn morning, the air was still, the clouds were gone, and the cold had arrived. He layered up for his hike. As soon as the sun crested the treetops, the temperatures would quickly rise. It was hazy dark when he parked his Jeep on an access road that ran along the edge of the Burnt Pine Tree property. Taking a final sip of coffee, he left his vehicle and walked rapidly across a corner of the private preserve to avoid any contact with hunters. All the tree stands were hundreds of yards from where he made his way through the stretch of woods.

He reached the mountaintop moments before sunrise. There was an exposed rock where he could sit and enjoy the view. The gap in the trees at the top of the "knob" rewarded him with a panorama to the east. Connor leaned back on his hands as the sun peeked into view and rose with a burst of speed that always amazed him. An hour passed before he began the descent to his vehicle and saw the big buck majestically making his way through the woods. After encountering the lost hunter, he made his way to his Jeep and received the phone call from Michelle that Matt Thompson had been shot.

"I just crossed a corner of the Burnt Pine Tree property," Connor said.

"I don't know any details, but that's where they sent the ambulance," Michelle responded, her voice trembling. "A friend whose husband works at the sheriff's office called me."

In shock, Connor gripped the steering wheel tightly. "I didn't see or hear anything," he said. "Let me know if there's any additional news."

Connor felt sick. He knew the devastation a bullet from a deer rifle could inflict on a large animal. He grabbed his cell phone and called Reg Bullock's number.

"Did you hear that Matt Thompson's been shot?" he asked.

"Yes, I'm at the lodge."

"How bad is it?"

"I didn't see him before they loaded him into the ambulance, but I understand it's life-threatening. I was half a mile away from Matt on the hunt. His group was not far from the big clearing where we throw out a bunch of field corn. Andy McNamara called me on the radio and told me about it."

Andy was in charge of hunting activities at the preserve. Connor knew the field. The church had used the clearing for a picnic the previous spring. He reached the paved road and turned toward town.

"Do you know what happened?" he asked.

"No, he was alone. The guide assigned to their group found him."

"I crossed the northwest corner of the Burnt Pine Tree property a few minutes ago on my way back from Caldwell's Knob. Now I'm on Route 231 on my way to the hospital," Connor said. "I'll call you later."

Upon arriving at the hospital, Connor identified himself as a minister and was granted access to the surgery waiting area.

Walking hurriedly through the door, he saw Elena with her back to him talking to a doctor dressed in scrubs. The doctor left. Elena turned around, saw Connor, and burst into tears. Rushing over, she fell into his arms. While Connor held her, Elena tried to speak between sobs.

"Don't try to say anything," he said softly.

Elena buried her face in his shoulder. When she finally raised her head, her face was streaked with tears, her eyes red. She continued to struggle to catch her breath.

"Hunting accident," she managed in between breaths.

"I know."

Elena pulled back, pointed to her abdomen, and made a circle. "He was hit here," she said.

Connor paled. His hope during the drive to the hospital had been that Matt might have shot himself in the foot or arm. This was dire news.

"They're going to operate," Elena continued, then stopped as more tears flowed. "To try to stop the bleeding and save him."

Elena again clung to Connor, who gently patted her on the back.

"Sit down," he said, extracting himself from her embrace.

The door opened, and a nurse entered with a clipboard in her hand.

"Mrs. Thompson," the woman said. "Please come with me. We need your signature on the consent forms."

"Will you stay here?" Elena asked Connor.

"Yes. I'll be here or in the chapel down the hall."

"Don't leave me," Elena said, gripping his right arm tightly.

"I won't."

Two-and-a-half hours passed with no word on Matt's status. Connor wasn't sure where they'd taken Elena to wait. Finding it hard to sit still, he went back and forth between the tiny chapel and the surgery waiting room. Connor prayed in the chapel and checked his phone in the waiting room. As news of Matt's injury became known across the community, so did the rumors and questions that popped up on Connor's phone. Some people claimed Matt was dead. Others said he'd suffered a major wound. Connor kept his answers brief, advising those seeking information to pray for Matt, who remained in surgery. He was sitting with his head bowed in one of the short pews in the chapel when the door opened. It was Elena, her face ashen.

"He didn't make it," she said flatly. "Severe damage to his liver, and he lost too much blood."

"I'm so sorry."

"They let me tell him bye." Elena paused. "But he was unconscious."

Connor scooted over on the pew to make room for Elena. "Would you like to sit down?"

"No." Elena shook her head. "I'm going home. They're taking his body to the funeral home."

"Call me if you need anything. Day or night."

"Will you hold a service for him at the church?"

"Of course."

After Elena left, Connor stayed in the chapel. Even though he'd only been with Matt a handful of times, the connection he'd developed with him was significant. Connor looked up at the ceiling and closed his eyes. He'd exhausted his reservoir of prayer pleading for Matt's life. Now he had nothing else to say to God or anyone else.

Liz put on her running shoes. She didn't run often, but occasionally she'd go out for a slow-paced jog. There was a nature trail that began in the center of town. Because of the overnight drop in temperature, she put on her warmest exercise outfit. It was an eight-minute drive to the park. Afterward, she planned on stopping by the office for a few hours' work. As she walked toward her car, she saw Bev rapidly approaching with a concerned look on her face.

Raising her hand, Bev called out, "Wait!"

Puzzled, Liz stopped. Her first thought was that something might be wrong with Sam.

"Have you heard the terrible news about Matt Thompson?" Bev asked breathlessly.

"No."

"He was in a hunting accident this morning. They've taken him to the hospital."

"How serious is it?" Liz asked.

"I'm not sure. The friend who called me didn't know. She heard about it from Michelle Cantrell, the church secretary. Connor is at the hospital."

Liz took her phone from the pocket of her running pants and checked to see if she'd received anything from Elena. No texts or emails.

"Where did it happen?" she asked.

"At Burnt Pine Tree. Matt's company rented the whole place for the weekend, and they went hunting early this morning." Bev shook her head. "Sam used to go deer hunting every fall. It always made me nervous because there can be so many people tramping through the woods that it's easy to make a mistake, even if you're wearing one of those orange vests."

"That's terrible," Liz said as she absorbed the news.

"All of us must pray for Matt," Bev said, fighting back tears.

Liz drove to the hospital. Upon entering the parking lot, she saw Elena's light blue BMW convertible in a spot close to the emergency room entrance. Liz slowed. Elena, her head bowed, exited through the emergency room doors. Liz pulled into a parking space and got out of her car. Elena saw her. The client wasn't wearing any makeup, and the strain on her face was obvious.

"I just heard about Matt," Liz said. "How is he?"

"Dead," Elena said flatly.

Liz felt speechless. "I'm sorry," she managed after a few seconds passed.

Elena shook her head from side to side. "I just can't believe it," she said, her voice cracking. "Even though I saw his body."

Liz reached out and put her hand on Elena's shoulder. They stood in silence for several moments. Liz had never been with someone who'd suddenly lost a loved one. After a few more seconds, she removed her hand from Elena's shoulder.

"Is there anything I can do for you?" she asked.

Elena looked up. "Call his ex-wife and let her know. I can't do it. She can tell the girls. I'll send you Anne's number."

Liz wanted to say no but felt trapped because she didn't have an alternate suggestion. She waited while Elena forwarded the information.

"What should I tell her?" Liz asked.

"That Matt was killed in a hunting accident. If she wants details, she can ask some of the men from the company or call the sheriff's department."

"Anything else?"

"I don't want to go home to an empty house." Elena sighed. "But

I don't have any place else to go. Could you come over this afternoon? I know there are legal matters we have to go over."

"That can wait for a few days."

"No," Elena replied. "There's no use putting it off. I'll get everything out of the lockbox in Matt's home office."

"Are you sure?" Liz asked in surprise.

"Yes, it will give me something else to think about." Elena stopped. "Besides him lying dead on an operating table."

"Okay," Liz said.

"Two or three o'clock," Elena said as she moved on. "It doesn't really matter."

"All right, but if you change your mind, let me know."

"I won't."

Elena took out her key fob and pressed the button to unlock her car. Even though it was a cool morning, Elena lowered the convertible roof as she left the parking lot.

Sitting in her car, Liz called Anne Thompson. When the call went to voice mail, she simply hung up without leaving a message. Another familiar face exited through the ER doors. It was Connor Grantham. Liz opened the door of her car and caught his attention.

CHAPTER 12

"DID YOU HEAR ABOUT MATT THOMPSON?" CONNOR asked when he reached Liz.

"Yes, I ran into Elena as she was leaving. She asked me to call his ex-wife and break the news to her."

"No, as Matt's pastor, I should do it."

"Are you sure?"

"Absolutely."

"Thanks," Liz said with obvious relief. "I tried to call, but Anne didn't answer. I didn't leave a voice mail."

Connor stared at the pavement. "I barely knew Matt, but over the past couple of weeks, we'd spent more and more time together."

Liz didn't say anything.

Connor looked up. "How was Elena when you talked to her?"

"Scattered, which is understandable. She asked me to come over to her house later today so that she wouldn't be alone."

"That's good. She needs someone to be with her. I'm not sure, but I believe she has a sister who lives in Richmond. Hopefully, she can come."

Connor stepped away.

"Thanks again for agreeing to call Matt's ex," Liz said.

Connor waited until he was at home to call Anne Thompson. She answered on the third ring. He identified himself.

"I already know," Anne interrupted him. "One of his coworkers called me as soon as it happened and then let me know that Matt didn't make it through surgery."

"I'm so sorry," Connor said.

"I'm devastated and not sure what to tell the girls. They spent the night with friends. I pick them up in an hour."

"They don't know anything?"

"No. I've been pacing back and forth through the house either wringing my hands or crying my eyes out. There was no use laying the uncertainty on them. Any suggestions?"

The question caught Connor off guard. It wasn't the sort of situation that could be quickly addressed by a podcast. Then, he remembered.

"My mother died of cancer when I was about the same age as your older daughter," he said. "It wasn't a complete shock, but it came faster than we expected. My father sat me down in the living room of our house and broke the news. The thing I remember was that he grabbed my hand when he told me that she was gone. That physical contact meant a lot."

"I'm going to do more than hold their hands," Anne replied, her voice cracking. "I'm going to wrap my arms around them."

Connor could hear Anne begin to cry.

"They know their daddy loved them," she managed. "And the truth is, Matt and I still loved each other too."

Connor didn't respond. Anne sniffled for a few moments, then regained her composure.

"Thank you for calling," she said. "Are you going to have a funeral service for Matt at your church?"

"Yes, that's what Elena wants."

"Will I have any input into what you do?"

"Yes," Connor replied without hesitation.

Shortly after finishing the phone call with Anne, there was a knock on Connor's front door. Reg Bullock was standing on the front stoop with a somber expression on his face. On his head was a cap with the Burnt Pine Tree logo on the front. He followed Connor into the living room.

"Did you see Matt at the hospital?" Reg asked.

"Only Elena. I stayed until she got the bad news."

The two men stood in silence for a moment.

Reg let out a big sigh. "Matt was using hollow-point ammo, and we both know what that can do."

Connor motioned for Reg to sit. "I saw Elena briefly before Matt went into surgery but not again until after they came out and told her that he didn't make it."

"Thanks for being there. I know it's got to be one of the worst parts of your job."

"Yeah. This was so sudden and unexpected. And Matt was young—" Connor stopped.

Reg leaned toward Connor and took a deep breath. "You should know that Matt spoke to the group from the company after dinner on Friday night. No one expected what came out of his mouth. He indicated his priorities would be changing based on a podcast he'd listened to and conversations with you."

"Yes," Connor confirmed. "I've spent time with him over the past few weeks but can't take any credit. Matt encountered the Lord in a way I've never seen since becoming a minister."

"That came across in his remarks." Reg paused. "Which made some folks on the corporate team uncomfortable."

"Why?"

"There was already a strong difference of opinion about the direction of the company between Matt and Winston Boone, who cofounded Daughbert Technology with him. Winston came up to me after Matt shared about his change in perspective and wanted to know what was going on. He knew I'd been the one who suggested Matt move to the mountains to get a fresh start in his personal life."

"Why was Winston uncomfortable?"

"Corporate boards value stability. Winston wants to sell the company, and he interpreted Matt's remarks as a lack of commitment to either making the company more attractive to a buyer or taking it to the next level as a stand-alone entity. It's all irrelevant now."

Connor stood. "Would you like a bottle of water?" he asked.

"Yeah."

Connor grabbed a couple of bottles of water from the refrigerator. Reg took a drink and stared across the room.

"It's hard to figure out how Matt shot himself in the abdomen," Reg said. "A foot, a leg, I could understand. The man who was guiding the group thinks he must have tripped and discharged the gun. Even that's tough to piece together. Think about it. How did Matt's hand hit the trigger? Or could it have been a stick that struck it? Why was his safety off? I could go crazy trying to unravel it."

"Who was the guide?"

"Stan Maxwell. He's a young guy who works part-time when we have a big group. Stan heard the gunshot and came over to see whether Matt had taken a deer. When he saw Matt lying on the ground, he called 911 and immediately started trying to stop the bleeding."

"Was Matt conscious at that point?"

"I don't know. I've not talked in person with Stan. This all came from Andy. The sheriff's department is investigating. They're in the process of taking statements from everybody who was on the property."

"Have they interviewed you?"

"Not yet, but it's coming."

Connor picked up his phone from the coffee table. "I saw one of the hunters at the northwest corner of the property. What was he doing that close to the boundary line?"

"They spread out to avoid getting in one another's way."

"I took a video. I was going to show it to you tomorrow at church. It seems pointless now, but one of the big bucks released on the property passed right in front of me. Maybe the hunter was tracking him, although he was making so much noise that he didn't have a chance of sneaking up on him."

Connor queued up the video and handed the phone to Reg.

He nodded as he looked at the phone screen. "Yep, that's one of the males we brought in from Michigan. And based on where you were standing, the does are leading him right off the property."

"The hunter shows up at the very end. He tripped and fell to the ground, but I'm not sure I caught that part."

"I kind of see him. It looks like he's wearing one of the vests we hand out to guests, but I can't be sure."

"You can't see it in the video, but he was running pretty fast and wanted to know the direction for the logging road. I thought he might have parked there but didn't see any fresh tire tracks except those from my Jeep."

"We tell the hunters that if they get turned around or lost to head north and use that old road to bring them back to the lodge."

Connor leaned back in his chair. "There may be some issues with the funeral. I've already talked with Matt's first wife. She wants to be involved in what we do."

"I've never met Anne. She and Matt were divorced long before I came onto the board. But Elena is his widow, so what she wants for the service is more important."

===

Liz called Harold. He'd not heard about Matt Thompson's death.

"That's awful," Harold said. "I've been trout fishing all morning and left my phone in the truck. Any more details on exactly what happened?"

"No, but Elena wants me to come over to her house."

"Today?"

"Yes. I think she has legal questions."

"The fact that she's asked you to be with her is a big deal. It means she trusts you. Listen and take notes. As long as she knows you're empathetic, it'll be okay that you don't have a lot of answers. We can handle that later. Maybe she just wants someone to be in the house with her."

"I'm dreading it," Liz said.

"I don't want to be cynical, and I've only met Elena once, but remember why she contacted us in the first place. She saw her marriage heading toward the rocks and wanted to have a lifeboat on hand so she could escape. The marriage ended, just not in the way she suspected. She's still going to be looking for financial security."

"Yes, she asked me more questions the other day about whether

Matt could secretly change his will or switch beneficiaries on his life insurance policies. It bothered her a lot that Matt's ex-wife is more protected than she is."

"Whatever Thompson did or didn't do is set. We need to review the insurance policies in case there are special provisions for accidental death. That could double the payout. Assuming he didn't change anything recently, do you know how much insurance he had in place?"

"Not exactly. Elena gave us copies of the policies."

"Where are you now?"

"At home, but Jessica and I scanned all the documents into the s-drive."

"Check the insurance policies and carefully read the will before you go to Elena's house. But like I said earlier, do more listening than talking. Whatever she feels about her husband's death, she's in shock and may not remember clearly what you say."

"Thanks," Liz said. "And I appreciate the generous gift card."

"Save it. The best thanks you can give me is to continue to produce results at the law firm."

After the call ended, Liz accessed the electronic file and located the insurance policies. They'd been entered in chronological order from the oldest to the most recent. In the first policy, Matt Thompson left two million dollars to fund a trust administered by his ex-wife, Anne K. Thompson, for the benefit of their children. There was no double indemnity provision for that policy, which was issued while he and Anne were still married.

Next, there was also a postdivorce policy, payable directly to Anne for one million. Liz found a clause in the policy stating that the death benefit would be "doubled in the event the insured's death is ruled to be accidental." Thus, if Matt died in a hunting accident,

Anne would be paid two million dollars under that policy. It was puzzling why Matt purchased a policy payable to his ex-wife after their divorce. Sometimes, a spouse would agree in a settlement to do so, which then became a part of the divorce decree. Liz read over the divorce paperwork. The order signed by the judge required Matt to keep the first policy in effect but made no mention of a requirement to purchase a second one.

Matt purchased a policy naming Elena as beneficiary shortly after they married. When Liz checked the date of the policy, her mouth dropped open. It was issued at the same time as the post-divorce policy for Anne and contained exactly the same terms except it had a face value of two million dollars. If Matt's death was ruled accidental, Elena would receive four million. A final policy, payable to Matt's estate in the amount of one million dollars with a double indemnity provision, had been issued less than a year ago.

In his last will and testament, Matt included a list of specific bequests, then left everything else to Elena, which would include his ownership interest in Daughbert Technology and the proceeds of any life insurance policies payable to his estate. Assuming there were no more insurance policies, an accidental death would swell the amount received by Elena from three million dollars to six million. The value of Matt's interest in the company could be much more.

Shortly before 2:00 p.m., Liz turned into the driveway for the Thompson home. The house wasn't visible from the street, and the access road twisted back and forth before bursting into the open at the top of a hill. The wood-and-stone house wrapped itself around the scenic hilltop. The front yard was small but the grass was startlingly green. There were multiple beds highlighting bushes, shrubs, and small trees. The main landscape feature was a waterway that originated somewhere behind the house and cascaded across rocks and down a two-foot-high waterfall. There was a little wooden bridge that spanned the water on the walkway to the front door. Massive picture windows were strategically placed in all the walls. Liz parked in front of the house. Before going inside, she called Connor.

"I'm at Elena's house. Are you still available to come if she thinks it's a good idea?"

"Yes. I can be there in ten minutes or less. Just make sure that's what Elena wants."

"I think she needs a minister more than a lawyer."

Liz crossed the wooden bridge and rang the door chime. The door opened. Elena was wearing jeans and a peach-colored sweater. She'd put on makeup and looked as normal as when she came to the law firm.

"We can talk in the office," she said.

There was a stone floor in the foyer that transitioned to dark-colored wood as they passed through the den and down a short hallway. Matt's office was on the west side of the house, and the afternoon sun could be seen above the distant mountains. It was a rustic space with a large wooden desk, comfortable leather chairs, and a computer setup with three large monitors. There was a woodland scent in the air.

Elena pointed to the monitors. "Matt could jump from meeting to meeting so fast it would make your head spin. I think his ability to multitask was one key to his success."

On the lower shelf of a built-in bookcase behind the desk, Liz saw several photos of Matt and Elena at various vacation sites: snow skiing, the beach, sailing on a yacht, in front of the Eiffel Tower. There were also photos of Matt's daughters but none including Anne. Seeing the children made Liz sad. They'd lost their father at such a young age.

Several stacks of papers and documents were neatly arranged on the desk. A portion of the bookcase concealed a safe that was open. Elena tapped the top of one stack with her index finger.

"I've double-checked all the contents of the safe since coming home from the hospital and don't see anything different from what I brought to your office. I'd put everything back carefully so Matt wouldn't know I'd taken anything out to look it over. Of course, like you told me the other day, he could have made some changes in secret and not told me about it."

The way Elena talked about her husband, who'd only been dead for a few hours, made Liz uncomfortable. She shifted in her chair.

"I have to do something to keep my mind occupied," Elena continued. "If I just sit and stare out the window, I'll lose it. I'm dreading when it's time to go to bed later tonight, and the walls of this house that have heard Matt's voice begin to shout in my ears. At least I have a bottle of high-powered sleeping pills. My fear is that I'll be tempted to take too many."

Liz sat up in alarm. "If that's on your mind, you need to—"

"I know that's not the answer. I'm going to call Connor Grantham as soon as you and I finish."

"Would you like Connor to come over now?"

Elena hesitated. "Yes, but I don't think he'll stay if you go. He's only been to the house once when it was just the two of us, and he wouldn't leave the foyer."

"I'll hang around."

"Let me think about that," Elena said. "But first let's talk about Matt's estate. Should I be worried about Anne barging in and trying to take over? If she sees any chance to take charge, she'll pounce."

"Not if the last will and testament you gave me is current. You're named as the executrix, which means you're the legal representative.

And because Matt was a resident of Etowah County at the time of his death, the local probate court, not the one in Atlanta where Anne lives, will have jurisdiction. I spoke with Harold Pollard, and he says our law firm can help with anything you need." Liz reached into her purse. "I prepared a memo for you after I reviewed the life insurance policies. We'd not talked about that much because it wasn't pertinent to our previous conversations and wouldn't become so unless you and Matt split up."

"Right, which is the reason it may turn out that Anne is taken care of and I'm not."

Liz handed Elena the memo. "Let's hope that's not true. This is what I put together."

Liz watched Elena's face as she read. Perhaps it was some type of emotional defense mechanism, but Elena Thompson showed no more sign of emotion than if she were checking a grocery list.

"I remember when he bought that extra policy for Anne," Elena said. "It made me really mad, but he did it anyway. I always suspected there was something she had hanging over him but never could find out. Whatever it was, she can't hurt him now."

"No, she can't."

Elena laid the memo on the corner of the desk. "I didn't know what double indemnity meant, but it seems simple enough. If Matt's death was accidental, I receive twice as much from the insurance companies."

"Correct."

"That will help a lot," Elena said. "There's a big difference between three million dollars and six million."

"Yes, it's twice as much money."

"Plus, the value of the company," Elena continued.

"If we have the correct last will and testament, Matt's ownership interest in Daughbert Technology will be included in the residuary estate that passes to you. Determining the value of the company would have been a huge part of any divorce case. Now, it will require a different analysis since he's no longer there to help make it profitable. There will still be experts and accountants involved."

"Which will cost a lot of money that should go to me." Elena frowned. "Matt always claimed the company would go under within a year if he resigned. The other men who own a piece of the corporation have been putting a lot of pressure on him to sell. He'd been the only holdout."

"I believe there are four partners, including Matt."

"Right, but Matt and Winston Boone controlled things. Matt was the visionary and salesman and Winston was the nerdy accountant type who ran the office. He was glad when Matt and I moved here because that meant Matt wasn't in the office as much. Winston was always worrying about the future. Matt was the brave one. He built the company and made it what it is."

Some of the tension in Liz's shoulders released at Elena's more human tone.

"Anything else to discuss today? There will be a lot to do later."

Elena pressed her lips together. Liz waited for the inevitable follow-up questions.

"No," Elena said slowly. "I'm sure I'll think of something and send you a text or email. I want you involved even if other lawyers in the firm help out."

"Of course. I've already cleared that with Mr. Pollard."

"Good." Elena rubbed her temples with the tips of her fingers. "If you can stay longer, I'm going to call Connor and ask him to come now."

"Okay."

CHAPTER 13

AFTER REG BULLOCK LEFT, CONNOR WENT FOR A long walk in his neighborhood. He couldn't get his last conversations with Matt Thompson out of his mind. His heart ached over a life so brutally cut short. He turned a corner and saw a red maple tree with only a few stubborn leaves clinging to the tips of its branches. Connor realized that death came for all living things, but never had the fragility of a person's time on earth been thrust so forcibly upon his soul.

Returning home, he sat in the living room with his tablet in hand. He opened his sermon notes and read what he'd written about the parable of the rich man and his bigger barns. In a way, everything had changed since he'd hiked to the top of Caldwell's Knob and finished the message. But in another way, nothing had changed. Matt Thompson, the person who inspired the sermon, was gone. The vanity of trusting in riches stood out even more starkly.

Connor turned off his tablet. There was no way he could deliver the sermon. The congregation would immediately identify Matt as sharing the fate of the rich man. To explain otherwise would be an impossible hurdle to overcome. None of that altered reality. What Connor had witnessed in Matt Thompson's life was the most dramatic expression of God's desire to reach a person that he'd ever seen. The almighty God, who knows the end from the beginning, reached out when no one suspected how short the forty-two-year-old's time on earth would be. Connor might not get a chance to preach the sermon about the rich man to others, but that didn't stop him from preaching it to himself. His phone vibrated. It was Elena.

"Can you come over, please?" she asked. "Liz Acosta is here."

"I'm on my way."

———

Connor parked behind Liz's vehicle. Walking to the door, he received a phone call from an unknown number. Usually, Connor let that type of call go to voice mail, but standing on the front porch, he decided to answer.

"Is this Reverend Connor Grantham?" a male voice asked.

"Who's calling?"

"This is Detective Norman with the Etowah County Sheriff's Department. I'm at the Burnt Pine Tree Lodge and just finished talking with Reg Bullock. He told me you were on the property this morning around the time of the incident involving Matt Thompson."

"Yes, I crossed the northwest corner of the preserve on my way up and back from Caldwell's Knob."

"Could you come to the lodge and give a statement?"

"Now?"

"Yes, and make sure you bring your phone. Mr. Bullock says you took a video of one of the hunters."

While the detective was talking Elena opened the door. Connor could see Liz behind her. He raised his index finger to his lips.

"I'm on my way," he said. "It should take me about thirty to forty minutes to get there."

"I'll be here."

The call ended. Liz joined Elena in the doorway.

"What's going on?" Elena asked.

"It was a detective from the sheriff's department. He wants me to come to the lodge at Burnt Pine Tree so he can ask me a few questions."

"Why would he have questions for you?" Elena asked.

"I took an early hike in the area this morning. My route cut across a corner of the property owned by the hunting preserve."

"Did you see or hear anything?" Liz asked.

Connor entered the foyer and told them about the video.

"I want to see it," Elena demanded.

As soon as Connor pulled up the video, Elena grabbed his phone and stared at the screen. Liz looked over Elena's shoulder. Even to a nonhunter, Liz could appreciate the fact that the big buck had huge antlers. The brief snippet of the video that featured the hunter only lasted a few seconds. Liz didn't see much of the man beyond a flash of orange.

"That's it?" Elena asked.

"Yes."

"Did you say anything else to the man?" she asked.

"Other than to offer directions, no."

"Did he say anything else to you?"

"No. He was in a hurry."

Elena returned the phone to Connor. "I don't understand why the sheriff's department wants to talk to you," she said. "Don't they have anything important to do? It was a terrible accident! And Matt's dead!"

Neither Connor nor Liz responded. Elena glanced down at the floor for a moment and then looked up at Connor.

"I wish you hadn't told the detective you would come," she said. "I need you here with me."

"It shouldn't take too long. As soon as I'm finished, I'll check in with you."

"Liz should go with you," Elena said.

"Why?" Liz asked.

"You're my lawyer, and I want to know exactly what's going on."

"Do you mind?" Liz asked Connor.

"No."

"That makes me feel better," Elena said in a less agitated voice. "Let me know how it goes."

Liz followed Connor down the walkway.

"Want to ride with me?" he asked. "I'll bring you back when we finish."

As soon as they were inside the car, Liz spoke. "I feel sorry for Elena, but I'm not sure how I'm supposed to help by doing this."

"Me either, but Elena is going to need a lot of help from as many people as possible."

"When we talk to the detective, I'll make it clear that I'm not representing you but Elena," she said.

"Of course. I don't need a lawyer."

They turned onto the main road leading away from the house. Liz stared out the window as the countryside flashed by.

"I thought about going to law school," Connor said. "I even took the LSAT and applied. My father would have liked that."

"What schools did you consider?"

"Columbia, Virginia, and Michigan, along with a few others."

"Were you accepted?"

"Yes."

Liz was impressed. All three of the schools Connor mentioned were in the top tier of the entire country. "Not Harvard or Yale?"

"Wait-listed, but it didn't matter. I wouldn't have gone."

"If you had, you would have probably ended up as a partner in a massive law firm."

"Then I'm glad I didn't."

They reached a large sign that read "Burnt Pine Tree Hunting Lodge—Members and Guests Only."

"Have you ever been here?" Connor asked as they turned onto a gravel road.

"No. It sounds like a good old boys' club to me."

"Actually, that's not true. Women are welcome."

"Do you hunt here?"

"No, I'll harvest a doe a year on public land because I like the meat. Trying to score a big buck isn't that interesting to me. A properly seasoned backstrap on the grill is what gets my attention."

"'Backstrap'?"

"A cut of meat along the side of the animal's spine. Very tender. I bet you could substitute venison in some of your Cuban dishes."

They drove half a mile to a clearing in the woods. The lodge was a rambling cedar-sided building with a long front porch, three chimneys, and six pop-out dormers in the roof. A pair of sheriff's department vehicles were parked in front along with several other cars and trucks.

"Reg Bullock, a member of the church, is still here," Connor said, pointing. "That's his blue truck. He's the one I showed the video to."

Connor had visited the lodge several times for catered dinners. The facility was a favorite location for high-end fundraisers. He and

Liz walked up three steps to the porch. The large front door was constructed with broad planks from old-growth trees. The iron door handle was crafted by a blacksmith in the shape of a small antler.

"You could hurt yourself on that thing," Liz said when Connor grabbed the handle to open the door for her.

"It's unique."

They entered directly into the lodge's great room. The floors were pine planks. The furniture was a mix of wood and leather. Across from the front door was a massive fireplace large enough to accommodate logs at least eight feet in length. No fire was burning. The only people in the room were Reg and a sheriff's deputy. Reg introduced Connor to the deputy.

"And I'm Elizabeth Acosta, an attorney who represents Matt Thompson's wife."

"I've seen you at the church," Reg said.

"I'll see if Detective Norman is ready to talk with you," the deputy said.

"They're set up in the boardroom," Reg said. "The last of the folks from Matt's company left about ten minutes ago."

"Was Winston Boone one of them?" Liz asked.

"Yes," Reg replied, glancing over his shoulder at Connor. "Sorry to drag you into this, but when Detective Norman was asking me questions, I simply answered them without thinking that he'd want to talk to you too."

The deputy returned. "Come with me," he said.

Connor and Liz followed the deputy down a carpeted hallway. On the right were double doors that led to a conference room with a long wooden table surrounded by ten leather chairs. Seated at one end of the table was a stocky man in his thirties with an old-fashioned flattop haircut. He was wearing a white shirt with his black tie loosened and pulled away from his neck. There was a small recording device, a tablet, and a manila folder on the table in front of him. Norman was making notes on the tablet. He stopped and looked up when they entered but didn't stand.

"Reverend Grantham?"

"Yes, and this is Ms. Acosta."

"We've not met," Liz said, stepping forward to shake the detective's hand. "I'm an attorney at Pollard and Associates."

"Do you want an attorney present while I speak with you?"

"Ms. Acosta isn't my attorney. She represents Elena Thompson."

"And I'm here at her request to find out what you've determined about her husband's death."

The detective pushed his chair away from the table. "It's an ongoing investigation. Once we finish, I'll speak with Mrs. Thompson directly, or if she prefers, to you. Unless you're here to represent Reverend Grantham, please wait in the great room."

For a split second, Connor wanted to ask Liz to stay. The only time he'd ever been interviewed by the police occurred when he was pulled over late one night in Maryland for driving fifteen miles per hour over the speed limit. His attempt to talk his way out of a ticket completely failed.

Liz left, and Connor sat in a chair to the detective's right.

"Do you have any objections to me recording the interview?" Norman asked.

"No."

"Did you bring your phone?"

"Yes."

"Do you still have the video you mentioned to Mr. Bullock?"

"Yes."

"We'll get to that in a minute. Ready to go?"

Connor nodded. The detective pressed a button on the machine and asked Connor to state his name, age, and address. Norman then went through an obviously canned introduction to the interview process. Connor felt like he was in a movie or on a TV crime show.

"Do you agree to continue with the recording?" Norman asked.

"Yes."

"Begin with when you left your house this morning and tell me everything you remember."

Connor hadn't expected such a broad question. He took a deep breath and verbally relived his day. While he talked, Detective Norman occasionally scribbled on his tablet with a stylus. From where he sat, Connor couldn't make out anything the detective was writing. Norman didn't interrupt until Connor came to the part when he returned to his Jeep and drove to the hospital.

"Show me the video you took on your phone," the detective said.

Connor pulled it up and handed his phone to the officer.

"Did you take any other videos or photos?" Norman asked.

"No videos, but I took a few photos earlier in the hike. They're all nature shots. There was frost on some ferns that I thought looked interesting."

"May I look at your album?"

"Go ahead."

Moments later the detective returned Connor's phone. "Do you mind if I take your picture?" he asked.

The idea of a mug shot flashed through Connor's mind. "No."

The detective pulled out his phone, took a picture, then handed his phone to Connor.

"Scroll through the photos of the other people I've interviewed today and tell me if you can identify the man you saw running through the woods."

"You saw the video," Connor replied. "The hunter never faced me while I was recording and when he turned toward me, it was hard to see much of his face because the black toboggan hat was pulled down low. Has anyone told you they were in the same area?"

"Just look. Take your time."

All the pictures were taken in the conference room. Reg Bullock was the only person Connor knew.

"I don't recognize anyone except for Reg Bullock," he said, sliding the phone across the table.

"Check again."

Connor repeated the process. All the photos were of white males from their twenties through sixties in age. Four of the men had darker hair. Connor studied them more closely. He enlarged one of the pictures so he could compare the man's clothes and then watched the video again on his phone, freezing the frame when the man came into view.

"This one is a possibility," Connor said, handing the phone to the detective. "But I can't make out if the shirt he's wearing beneath the hunting vest is the same or not."

Norman looked down at his phone. "That's what I thought too," he said.

"Who is he?"

The detective tapped the screen on his tablet. "Jerome Rossi. He's a new hire in the IT department at Daughbert Technology. His father was in the military, and Rossi lived in the UK for a while when he was a kid. When you mentioned that the man you encountered spoke with a British accent, I thought about Rossi."

"Was he in the area where I crossed the preserve property?"

Norman, who was making notes on his tablet, didn't answer.

"Tell me about your relationship with Mr. and Mrs. Thompson," the detective said.

"They attend Rock Community Church. They've seen me several times for marital counseling."

"What sort of trouble were they having in their marriage?"

Connor hesitated. "That's confidential."

Norman ignored Connor's response. "Any indication of domestic violence or abuse?" he asked.

"No."

The detective moved his finger across his tablet. "Was Mr. Thompson depressed?"

"Not that I'm aware of. Based on my most recent interaction with him, Mr. Thompson was in a good frame of mind."

Norman grunted slightly. "Mr. Bullock says you spoke with Mrs. Thompson at the hospital," he said. "Tell me about that."

Connor related their brief encounter before Matt was taken into surgery and a few hours later after Elena learned her husband had died.

"Have you seen or talked with Mrs. Thompson since then?"

"I'd just arrived at her house when I received the call to meet with you. Ms. Acosta was with her."

"Had you been there previously?"

"Once."

"For counseling sessions?"

"No, we did that at the church."

"Did anyone from Daughbert Technology come to the hospital?"

"I'm not sure. I spent most of my time waiting and praying in the chapel."

"Do you know of anyone with a reason to kill Mr. Thompson?" the detective asked without looking up from his tablet.

The casual way the detective asked the question startled Connor. "Uh, no," he managed.

"Without violating clergy-parishioner confidentiality, is that still your answer?"

"Yes. It sounds like a tragic accident to me."

"What evidence do you have that you weren't in the area where Mr. Thompson was found?"

"I'm telling you the truth," Connor protested. "I didn't see or hear anything except what I've told you."

"Anything else to add before I turn off the machine?"

"Why did you ask me that last question? Did someone claim they saw me?"

"Thanks for meeting with me," the detective said, rising to his feet. "I'll be in touch if I have any additional questions. Will you let me know if you think of anything you may have forgotten to mention?"

"Yes."

———

During the time Connor spent with the detective, Reg gave Liz a tour of the lodge: the dining room, the kitchen, and the trophy room adjacent to the great room. Small metal plaques beneath each animal identified the name of the hunter, date of the kill, and what Reg explained was the Boone and Crockett measuring score for the antler rack. He proudly pointed out one deer with his name as hunter on the plaque.

"That's the only buck I killed that made it in here. And his stay may be temporary. As bigger ones are harvested, the smaller deer are moved out. But my trophy won't go homeless. I have a place reserved for it in the den at my house."

"Good to know it has such a bright future."

"Are you anti-hunting?" Reg asked apologetically. "If I'd known that, I wouldn't have dragged you in here."

"No, it's just a lot of death in one place. I'm not opposed to the sport. Because deer have no natural predators, I know it's necessary to cull the population."

They returned to the great room. Liz saw Reg glance at his watch.

"You don't have to stay on my account," she said.

"I want to make sure everything went okay for Connor. It's intimidating to be dragged in for questioning by a detective, especially since Matt and Connor recently struck up a friendship."

"They did? I wasn't aware of that."

"They had some good talks about life and faith."

They sat in silence.

Liz tapped her foot against the floor. "Was Matt conscious when they found him?" she asked.

"No," Reg said and shook his head. "I spoke earlier with Stan Maxwell, the guide who was the first on the scene. Matt was alive but nonresponsive."

Reg checked his watch again. "I've got to go. Will you ask Connor to give me a call?"

"Certainly."

Reg left. Another fifteen minutes passed before Connor finally reappeared. He looked distressed.

"Are you okay?" Liz asked.

"Not really, and I'm ready to leave."

"What happened?"

"We'll talk in the car."

Liz followed Connor as he walked rapidly down the steps and toward his vehicle.

The minister put both hands on the steering wheel once inside. "I need to tell myself that I'm not under suspicion for doing anything wrong," he said.

"Did he accuse you?"

"Not directly; it was just the way he talked and what he implied without saying it."

"That's not uncommon," Liz replied. "I saw that when I worked as a law school intern in the public defender's office in Naples. People in law enforcement attend a secret school that teaches them how to make people feel guilty when answering questions about the weather."

Connor glanced over at Liz. "This isn't funny."

"I'm not joking. There's no secret school, but making a person uncomfortable is a common interrogation technique."

"It worked on me."

They rode in silence for a moment.

"Reg Bullock told me that Matt wasn't able to communicate when they found him," Liz said.

"Yes, he mentioned that to me."

"I guess we'll never know from him what happened. Tell me what Detective Norman asked you so we can figure out the best way to summarize it for Elena and lessen the chance that she's going to get upset."

While Connor talked, Liz could understand why he'd been uncomfortable.

"The cause of Matt's death is an open investigation," she said. "That's why Norman left you hanging and didn't answer your questions. But you know where you were this morning and why you were there."

"But I don't have any proof except for a man I don't know who I saw for fifteen or twenty seconds."

"He's the one who should be nervous," Liz responded. "Do you think he got a better view of you than you did of him?"

"I have no idea. He was in a hurry to keep moving. He looked a little like an IT guy who works for Matt's company, but I can't be sure."

Connor turned onto another road.

"There's a reason why the detective asked if Matt was depressed," Liz said. "Did he give any indication that he thinks Matt could have committed suicide?"

"No, and Matt wasn't depressed. I mean, he was upset about his domestic problems, but he wanted to work on them, not escape by killing himself. I've known Matt only for a short time, but during the past few days he had one of the most remarkable experiences with God I've ever witnessed."

"Reg alluded to that. Did you tell the detective?"

"Not specifically. I'm not sure he would have understood."

"Do you want to tell me?"

"Maybe another time."

Liz didn't press him. Connor seemed preoccupied with his own thoughts. They reached the driveway for the Thompson home.

"Get ready to be questioned again," Liz said.

"I know. I've been going over in my mind what to say."

CHAPTER 14

Elena reacted immediately when Liz mentioned asking Reg Bullock if Matt said anything after he was discovered.

"What did Reg tell you?" she said sharply.

"Matt was unconscious when one of the guides found him."

"And you're sure Matt didn't say anything to anyone after the accident?" Elena persisted.

"That's what Reg told me."

Elena nodded. "Okay. And the EMTs at the hospital said he didn't speak to them during the ride in the ambulance."

"The police wanted to see the video I took on my phone," Connor said. "Then the detective made me look at a bunch of photos of people who work for Matt's company. The only one who looked vaguely similar was a guy with dark hair who works in the IT department named Jerome Rossi."

"I've met Jerome," Elena replied. "Matt liked him. Let me see the video again."

Connor handed her his phone. She stopped the video when the man appeared and enlarged the image. "I don't know who that is because you can't see his facial features, but it's not Jerome. He's a lot smaller than the guy you ran into. Jerome is really short and probably doesn't weigh more than a hundred and forty-five pounds."

"The man in the video was definitely bigger than that."

Elena turned to Liz and continued asking her legal questions. Several minutes passed.

"Should I step outside?" Connor asked. "This sort of information should be confidential."

"It's fine with me," Elena responded. "I don't have anything to hide from you."

"Your call," Liz said to her client.

"I want you to stay," Elena replied.

Connor remained in the room. Some of the discussion about Daughbert Technology was different from what Matt had told him, but Connor didn't comment. Finally, there was a lull in the conversation.

"Would you like to discuss the memorial service?" he asked Elena.

"You come up with something," she said as she raised and lowered her shoulders. "That's your area of expertise."

"I'll make sure you approve my ideas."

"Okay," Elena said. "While you were talking to the detective, I called the funeral home and picked out a casket online and bought a burial plot in a cemetery they own. I can't deal with any of this."

"Should I ask Anne what she'd like to include?"

"I'd forgotten about her." Elena frowned, then turned to Liz. "Did you tell her about Matt's death?"

"No, Connor did it."

"How did she react?" Elena asked him.

"She already knew from someone with Matt's company," Connor replied. "Like all of us, she was shocked."

"I know she'll show up with the girls," Elena said, pressing her lips together. "But I don't want her doing anything except sitting in the sanctuary."

"What about your mother in California?" Liz asked Elena. "Were you able to reach her?"

"No, she's off somewhere on an island with her new boyfriend, but I talked to my sister. She's getting a babysitter for her kids and coming down tomorrow from Virginia. She can only stay for a couple of days."

Connor, who knew less about Elena's family than Liz, was relieved there was at least some family support on the way.

"Tracy never liked Matt," Elena continued. "She thought I should marry a friend of her husband after my divorce from Franklin."

Connor's mouth dropped open. Elena hadn't revealed the presence of a previous marriage on the form she filled out prior to their first counseling meeting.

Liz and Elena continued to talk about next steps in the investigation.

"I'll arrange the meeting with the detective and inform him that he'll only talk to you with me present," Liz said.

"And not for at least a week," Elena said. "These people need to give me space. Find out what you can. I don't want to have any big surprises."

"Mr. Pollard has connections inside the sheriff's department, but I can't promise anything."

"Try hard." Elena held her hands to her face for a moment. "I'm exhausted."

"We'd better go," Connor quickly replied. "But I'll check on you after church in the morning."

"What time will you come by?" Elena asked.

"I'll call. Maybe I can meet with you and your sister."

Once they were away from the house, Liz turned to Connor.

"Thank you," she said. "It takes more than one person to help Elena. And you're the one making the biggest sacrifice of time and energy. I'm getting paid by the hour. Focusing on her legal situation seems to be Elena's way of dealing with the loss."

"I could tell that she's putting a lot of pressure on you to make everything work out the way she wants it to."

"And the thought of Detective Norman asking her questions freaks her out. Elena has never felt secure or in control of her life either as an individual or in her marriage to Matt. Does that make sense to you?"

"Maybe."

"That's what I was thinking during our meeting. In some ways, she's very organized. Then, her mind seems to be all over the place. It's like dealing with two different people."

"You're right about that," Connor replied.

"Did you know Elena was married to someone before Matt? I saw the look on your face when she mentioned it."

"She didn't share that with me."

"I wonder what she's not shared with either one of us," Liz said. "Hopefully, nothing too important in light of what she's facing."

"What are you going to do now?"

"Go home, fix a sandwich, and stare at the TV. And you?"

"I have to figure out what I'm going to say to the congregation in the morning. I had a sermon prepared, but it was inspired by Matt's life, not his death."

Liz ate her sandwich but had trouble finding anything on TV that could hold her interest. Fatigue from the emotional events of the day set in, and she went to bed. When she awoke in the morning, a split second passed before she remembered all that had happened. She rolled over and picked up her phone from the nightstand. There were no text messages or emails from Elena. Liz wasn't sure if that was a good sign or not. Yawning, she closed her eyes and didn't wake up for another thirty minutes. This time, she forced herself to get out of bed.

Because she'd slept so much, Liz got up and started cleaning her apartment. She was leaning over scrubbing the tub when she thought about how Connor spent early Sunday morning. It certainly wasn't cleaning his bathroom or vacuuming the floors. She'd not planned on attending the church, but after finishing the bathroom she decided to take a shower and go.

The church parking lot was almost totally full. Bev and Sam were in their usual pew, but there wasn't any space beside them. Liz squeezed into a spot at the rear of the sanctuary beside a well-dressed couple in their forties. Connor and the choir entered at the front.

The service proceeded in typical fashion. There was no mention of Matt's death during Connor's opening remarks and brief prayer. When it came time for the sermon, Connor looked down at his tablet for several moments before saying anything. He cleared his throat.

"I want to dedicate the message today to Matthew Thompson, who, as many of you know, died yesterday in a tragic hunting accident. Please be praying for his wife, Elena, and the rest of his family. There will be a memorial service celebrating his life. The day and time will be posted on the church website."

A smattering of low conversation rippled across the room. Connor waited until it died down.

"Usually, I start preparing my sermons early in the week. The message I intended to deliver this morning is finished." Connor paused. "But I'm not going to give it. What's on my heart is so heavy that I can't push it aside. Some of you may not be able to attend Matt's service, so I don't want you to miss what I intend to share at that time. My text today is John 6:44. This is Jesus talking."

Connor didn't look down to read but continued to face the congregation. He spoke from memory: "'No one can come to me unless the Father who sent me draws them, and I will raise them up at the last day.'"

Connor let the words linger in the air, then spoke them again, slower and with greater emphasis.

"Over the past few days, I've seen this happen in Matt Thompson's life and want to tell you about it. Not just because of the impact on him but because of what it can mean to each of us."

What followed wasn't as polished as the sermons Liz had heard before. Instead of reading his notes, Connor spoke extemporaneously. He described how God influenced Matt Thompson through a podcast. He didn't say much about the podcast except that it had changed the dead man's perspective on life. There was no denying the passion in Connor's voice as he took the congregation on a journey into Matt Thompson's soul. It made Liz wish she'd had the opportunity to get to know Elena's husband.

"I regret more than I can express that I didn't get to spend more time with Matt," Connor said. "But I'm also extremely thankful for the amazing few days I spent with him before his life so tragically ended."

Connor paused and fought to maintain his composure before continuing.

"I don't normally talk like this because it's so subjective," he said. "I believe we have a brain and are expected to use it. But if you sense God calling you like he did Matt, I suggest you respond."

Connor stopped, stared at the congregation, and didn't speak for several moments. The silence became uncomfortable, and the woman sitting next to Liz shifted in the pew. Connor glanced down at his tablet, then looked up. It seemed like he was searching for the next thing to say.

"Let us pray," he said.

Liz bowed her head and tightly closed her eyes.

———————

Connor stood in the narthex, unsure how the sermon might have been received. Never before had Connor poured out his heart so intensely in public. After he gave the benediction, he wished he could avoid going to the rear of the sanctuary but knew he couldn't. Most people thanked him for the message. Some simply shook his hand. Even though he'd said the day and time for Matt's funeral service hadn't been set, people still asked him that question. Connor kept his responses short.

"I know that was hard, and you did a good job," Reg Bullock said, gripping Connor's hand firmly. Then he continued in a low voice, "Call me sometime later this week about your interview with Detective Norman. More information is coming out."

Connor wanted to ask what Reg meant, but the businessman moved on out the door.

Liz appeared and extended her hand. "I'd like to talk to you about your sermon," she said.

Connor considered inviting her to lunch. He'd already decided not to set up anything with visitors because he really wanted to be alone.

"But not today," Liz continued.

As soon as he could, Connor left the church and drove home. Turning down his street, his phone vibrated. Lyle Hamilton's name appeared. The Hamilton family had been in their usual spot in the sanctuary, which gave the best wheelchair access.

"I know this is off the wall," Lyle said when Connor answered, "but Sarah made a big pot of chili last night, and we'd like to bring some over. We won't stay long."

"That sounds great."

"Give us fifteen minutes."

Connor changed clothes, putting on a pair of jeans and a flannel shirt. He brewed a cup of tea while he waited. There was a knock on the door. Josh was standing on the front porch with a round plastic container in his hands. Lyle and Sarah were in their van parked alongside the curb. Josh handed him the container.

"Here you are, Mr. Connor," Josh said.

"Thanks. Let me put this in the kitchen, then I'll come out for a minute to speak to your folks. Tell them not to leave."

After a quick trip to the kitchen, Connor walked across the front yard. Sarah was behind the wheel. She lowered the window.

"How did you know I needed chili?" he asked.

"The Lord told me," she replied.

"And I agreed," Lyle added from the passenger seat. "I didn't say anything to you on my way out of the sanctuary, but I've never heard you speak like you did today."

"That's because you spoke from your heart, not your head," Sarah added. "I bore witness to it."

Connor had never received a compliment from Sarah Hamilton about a sermon. Her intense gaze intimidated him.

"Thank you," he said.

"No, thank you," Sarah responded. "I was deeply touched by the Lord as you spoke."

Connor wasn't sure what else to say. "Thanks for the chili," he managed.

As he stood in the kitchen, Connor mulled over Sarah's words. Perhaps it was less a compliment about the morning's sermon and more an indictment of every other message he'd preached. But he knew she wanted to encourage him. Connor had definitely spoken from the heart. How that might impact his future ministry was beyond figuring out today. He opened the refrigerator and got some grated cheese to sprinkle on top of his bowl of chili.

CHAPTER 15

EARLY MONDAY MORNING LIZ ARRIVED AT THE office and stopped by Jessica's desk. The legal assistant already knew about Matt Thompson's demise.

"How did you find out?" Jessica asked her.

Liz gave an abbreviated summary of what happened on Saturday. She decided not to say anything about the video Connor filmed on his camera but mentioned the trip to Burnt Pine Tree Lodge and the interview by Detective Norman.

"It sounds like Bobby Norman was being his usual self."

"You know him?"

"Yeah, he went to high school with my older brother and used to hang out at our house. Bobby is an odd guy."

"What do you mean by 'odd'?"

"Rubs people the wrong way without even trying. I wouldn't take the way he treated you and Connor personally. His parents split up when he was a kid, and he was raised by his father. Bobby's social skills never developed. But he's smart. He was salutatorian of our graduating class. He took one of my friends to prom when he was a senior. Bob Sr. worked for the sheriff's department, so it wasn't a surprise that's where Bobby ended up."

"How long did he date your friend?"

"Once was enough." Jessica smiled. "Valerie just needed someone to escort her through the door. She danced with a bunch of guys that night."

"Did that make Norman mad?"

"No, he just hung out with his football pals."

"What would it take to convince him to talk to me? Elena is putting a lot of pressure on me to find out what he knows about Matt's death."

"It's been awhile since Bobby and I talked. Do you want me to give him a call?"

"Let me ask Harold. He may have an inroad with someone at the sheriff's department. Do you know when he's coming in?"

Jessica checked her computer monitor. "Not until this afternoon. He has a motion hearing in Bartow County this morning."

Shortly before noon, Becky buzzed Liz.

"Elena Thompson is on the phone," she said. "Says it's important."

Liz took a second to prepare herself, then picked up the receiver and said hello.

"Have you found out anything?" Elena asked.

"Not yet. Mr. Pollard is out of town until this afternoon. He may be able to get an update about the investigation. But it's so soon—"

Elena interrupted her. "I talked with a secretary at Matt's company. The bosses are scrambling around this morning like a bunch of crazy men."

"As Matt's widow you have a legal right to know the status of the company."

"I want someone loyal to me on the inside. Donna prepares the minutes of the corporate meetings and memos for the owners."

Elena said something to someone else that Liz couldn't hear.

"Sorry, that was my sister," Elena said. "I'm meeting Connor for lunch to plan the funeral."

"He really honored Matt in his sermon yesterday. It was very well-done."

"That's what I heard. Maybe I'll listen to it later. Gotta go."

As soon as Harold arrived, Liz went to his office. The senior partner was opening his mail.

"Do you have time for an update about Elena Thompson?" Liz asked.

"Talk while I do this," he replied. "I can multitask."

Liz shut the door and gave a much more detailed report than she'd provided Jessica. Harold kept opening and reading his mail while she spoke. When she mentioned Connor's video and Detective Norman's interest in it, Harold stopped and placed his sterling silver letter opener on his desk.

"Do you have a copy of the video?" he asked.

"No. It's on Connor's phone."

"Get him to send you one as soon as possible. I want it in our file so we can have it analyzed."

"Because of the language in the insurance policies?"

"Yes. Once the companies find out there is even the hint of a criminal investigation, they're going to resist payment under the double indemnity provisions. And it won't stop there if they can craft an argument that a beneficiary had Matt Thompson murdered."

"Murdered?" Liz asked in shock.

"Even if there's no basis for it, that's how insurance companies think, especially when there's this much money on the line. We're talking millions."

"I assumed the investigation was just a formality the sheriff's office had to perform."

"I hope for our client's financial future that you're right. But this could end up in a war. Don't get sucked into Elena Thompson's emotional drama and distracted by her personal issues. You've got to think like a lawyer, not a counselor. A lot of what you're telling me has to do with the client's mental state, not her legal status. You'll best serve her if you focus on the law and let Reverend Grantham handle the counseling duties."

"You're right. Elena may have some kind of personality disorder, which is way out of my league. I feel like a ping-pong ball when I talk to her. But I'm sorry for her, even if she pressures me in an uncomfortable way."

"Don't stay in that place."

"Yes, sir," Liz answered. "Also, Elena wants us to find out what the sheriff's department has discovered so far. Is there anyone on the inside you can contact? I didn't promise anything, but she's been insistent."

"There's someone I can call, but it's too soon to play that card. My insider isn't going to give me multiple updates."

"Okay." Liz took a deep breath and sighed.

Harold eyed her for a moment. "Liz, you can be sympathetic without being distracted from your job. Remember that *you're* the lawyer, not Elena. Handling an unstable client in a professional way is an acquired skill, and this is a good case to practice on. She obviously likes and trusts you."

"I know. Do you think I should attend Matt's funeral? Or is that too much in the personal realm?"

"Your call, but Elena will expect you to be there. In the meantime, start preparing a memo identifying the issues that may come up now that Thompson is deceased and how we're going to respond to them."

"Related to the insurance policies and valuation of the business?"

"Correct. If we assume Thompson didn't change his estate plan, putting a number on the percentage of the company that will pass to Elena will likely be our toughest challenge. Don't send your memo to Elena. Make it for internal use only."

"This is a tough situation," Liz said and sighed once more.

"You're up to the job," Harold replied with a smile. "I don't toss out thousand-dollar gift cards to underachievers."

Connor finalized plans for Matt's funeral service. To his relief, Anne asked only that she and her girls be seated at the front of the sanctuary and that the children's relationship to their father be listed on the program. Neither Elena nor Anne wanted an open casket, and Elena said no to a receiving line at the local funeral home. She didn't want to be stuck in a room with Anne for several hours. The service was set for 2:00 p.m. on Wednesday.

Notice of the funeral was posted on the church website and included in the brief obituary published in the local paper. Connor wrote the obituary based on responses to questions he sent to Elena and Anne. He was standing beside Michelle's desk when the light on her phone lit up signaling an incoming call. His assistant normally wore a headset when on phone duty.

"Good afternoon, Rock Community Church," she said and then put her hand over the tiny microphone. "Do you want to talk to Reg Bullock?"

"Yes, I'll take it."

Connor returned to his office.

"I saw the notice in the paper for Matt Thompson's funeral," Reg said after Connor answered. "Did you have any problems from Elena or Matt's ex-wife in organizing the service?"

"No. It will be a brief ceremony. I'll share a pared-down version of what I said on Sunday."

"You'll do great. The reason I called was to pass along to you the status of the investigation into Matt's death. Andy McNamara says a posse from the Georgia Bureau of Investigation has been crawling all over Burnt Pine Tree for the past two days. I don't think that would happen without a reason. They're looking for something or someone."

"'Someone'?"

"Andy suspects it's some type of physical evidence. The GBI has been running a bunch of dogs during the day and into the night that have spooked every deer on the reserve. Several men from the sheriff's department were there too. Yesterday afternoon they asked Andy to take them to the area where you crossed the property."

"Did they find anything?"

"Not while Andy was with them." Reg paused. "The lead investigator for the GBI asked Andy a bunch of questions about you. Was this the first time you'd been caught on the property without permission? Do you know whether anyone ever complained about you trespassing?"

"I wasn't caught trespassing!"

"That's just the way he put it. Also, the investigator wanted to know if Andy had seen you with Matt or Elena, individually or as a couple."

"What did Andy tell him?"

"That he saw you sitting with Elena in her car a few weeks ago in front of the coffee shop on Dixon Street. Andy knew it was Elena because she drives a baby blue BMW convertible. There's no other car like it in Etowah County."

Connor's heart sank. Elena had wanted to drop off some paperwork at his house prior to a counseling session, and he'd insisted on a public meeting place. He explained the background to Reg.

"Sounds reasonable and innocent to me."

"But it could be interpreted differently by someone who's suspicious. Is this what you were going to tell me on Sunday?"

"No, all I knew then was that the GBI had been brought into the investigation. I've asked Andy to keep me in the loop about what he sees and hears."

"I haven't done anything wrong, but this is still making me nervous."

"I know, and I hate to tell you this. Also, the GBI confiscated all the video footage for the field cams in the area where they found Matt. Andy puts out extra cameras this time of year because the deer are moving around so much during the rut."

"Did Andy check the footage the GBI asked for?"

"Only for the area of the property where Stan found Matt, who didn't show up in any of the frames. That's not surprising. The cameras are set up near the feeding zones, not where hunters park for a shot. Andy independently reviewed the footage from a couple of additional cameras in the area and didn't see anything except hunters he recognized from the company group."

"That's good."

"If it makes you feel any better, he says the investigators asked him and the other employees a ton of questions about the group from Matt's company: whether there were any arguments, people who didn't comply with the lodge rules, anything suspicious, stuff like that."

"'Lodge rules'?"

"No one is supposed to leave the main building once the sun sets unless accompanied by a guide. It's a requirement of our insurance policy."

"Did Andy see or hear anything suspicious?"

"No. Most of his interaction was with me as the host of the event. Both days people not on the guest list showed up. Andy assumed they were part of the group but didn't know for sure."

"What sort of people?"

"Employees of the company who weren't registered as guests at the lodge or on the list to hunt. There was a lot of coming and going."

———————

Liz put the finishing touches on a letter she was going to email to Winston Boone. In the letter, she requested that no corporate action be taken that might impact Elena's rights in the company as Matt's wife and the beneficiary of his residuary estate. She enclosed a copy of the will, which she hoped was still valid. In an attachment to the email, she asked for copies of various financial records and corporate minutes to be delivered within thirty days. An informal request wouldn't have the same power as formal discovery sent in a lawsuit, but Harold assured her that the company's attorneys would be careful in the way they responded because an obvious omission now might come to light later and make the company look bad. It was a strong move so close in time to Matt's death, but Elena was pleased when Liz told her what she was going to do. Thirty minutes after sending the letter to the company, Becky buzzed her.

"A man named Winston Boone is on the phone for you. Says he works with Daughbert Technology."

"Is Harold in his office? I'd like him to be on this call."

"He left ten minutes ago. Should I take a number?"

Liz hesitated. She preferred that Harold be involved in a conversation with Boone but knew her boss would want her to find out what she could.

"I'll take it."

Liz sat up straighter in her chair. "This is Elizabeth Acosta," she said.

"Winston Boone. You're being a bit aggressive, aren't you?"

Liz silently told herself to relax. "I'm not sure what you mean," she said.

"My longtime friend and business partner isn't even buried, and you're firing off demands for thousands of pages of documents and financial records. Is this what Elena asked you to do?"

"We're simply being proactive," Liz replied, trying to sound professional. "And I realize it will take time to provide the information requested."

"Does being proactive include Elena communicating directly with my former administrative assistant?"

Liz froze for a moment. Elena's actions had cost a woman her job.

"Are you still there?" Boone asked.

"Yes."

"I left Elena two voice messages offering my deepest sympathy over Matt's death, which hit all of us hard too. When she didn't call back, I assumed she was grieving and intended on extending my condolences at the funeral on Wednesday. Now I know she had other things on her mind. Will I be able to speak to her at the funeral or is all communication between us going to be via your law firm?"

"I'm sure Elena will want to talk with you."

"If she does, I won't let her know how much her actions have hurt me and the rest of the management team. You can be the one to pass along that piece of information. And when you do, make sure Elena understands that if she wants our cooperation resolving Matt's business affairs, she'd better adopt a different approach. Is that clear?"

"Yes," Liz said in a voice that she hoped didn't tremble.

The phone call ended. The businessman's words had flowed through the phone line like liquid fire. Liz tried to calm down as she typed a memo for Harold about the conversation. She hoped she wouldn't encounter Winston Boone at the funeral.

━━━━━━━━

Connor paced back and forth in his office as he waited for Elena and Anne to arrive. Michelle opened the door.

"Anne Thompson and her daughters are here. I put them in the senior adult classroom. The ushers know to take Elena there when she arrives."

"Okay."

"There are already people in the sanctuary. I peeked and recognized only a few."

"Most likely they're from Matt's company."

Connor made his way down the hallway. Entering the classroom, he saw Matt's daughters and struggled to retain his composure. Abigail, the younger daughter, was a mini version of her father. Mariah, the older child, looked more like her mother. Anne was wearing a black dress. Both girls wore gray skirts with white shirts that reminded Connor of school uniforms.

Anne spoke. "Reverend Grantham, this is Mariah and Abigail."

The girls were serious and sad.

"I'm so sorry," Connor said to them. "I know your father loved you deeply, and I want this service to honor him."

The girls didn't respond.

"Thank you," Anne said.

Everyone sat on brown plastic chairs. Connor briefly went over in his mind what would take place. He avoided looking at Abigail. Mariah was only a year younger than he'd been when his mother died. Being in the classroom at that moment was the most difficult thing Connor had faced in ministry. He wanted to grieve, too, but his job required him to give comfort and conduct a memorial service. The door to the classroom opened, and Elena, wearing a navy-blue dress, entered. With her was a tall woman in a long brown dress. Elena and Anne exchanged a quick look but didn't speak. Connor extended his hand to the woman with Elena and introduced himself.

"I'm Tracy Kilgore," the woman replied. "Elena's sister."

"Could we speak with you in private?" Elena asked.

"Sure," Connor answered, then turned to Anne. "An usher will come in shortly and escort you to your seats."

Connor led Elena and her sister to his office. Elena was twisting a tissue in her hands.

"What did you want to talk about?" he asked.

"Nothing in particular," Elena replied in a subdued voice. "I just didn't want to be in the room with Anne. It's too stressful. Also, people from Matt's company are already here. Should I greet them now?"

"Not until after the service. Everything is set up for a reception in the fellowship hall."

"Are you sure we should do that?"

"We agreed to it, especially without visiting hours at the funeral home."

"Let Reverend Grantham guide you," Tracy said.

"Time for me to go," he said. "Stay here. As I told Anne and the girls, I'll have an usher escort you to your place on a pew."

"Not next to Anne, correct?"

"The front pew is long enough to provide a buffer."

"I'll sit between you and Anne," Tracy volunteered.

Connor took out his phone and sent a text to the lead usher to have someone come to the classroom and his office. He then took a detour down the hall into the choir practice room to be alone for a few moments. He scrolled through his notes on the tablet. This time, he wasn't going to trust himself to speak off the cuff.

———

Liz found Connor's eulogy less personal and more theoretical than his sermon the previous Sunday. But she didn't internally criticize him. He had a difficult task. When he finished and everyone stood, Liz considered skipping the funeral reception because she didn't want to encounter Winston Boone. But then she remembered a phrase from her grandmother that counseled the only way to overcome cowardice is to face fear. She headed toward the fellowship hall. Waiting in line, she found herself next to Bev and Sam.

"That was a beautiful message, wasn't it?" Bev said, clutching a tissue in her hand. "When he said, 'Every life is full of untapped potential,' Connor was looking straight at Matt's precious daughters."

"I liked it when he challenged all of us 'to see beyond the ordinary into the possibilities planned for us by an infinite God,'" Sam said. "I mean, who says stuff like that?"

Bev touched her husband on the arm. "Honey, you remembered that perfectly. I'm going to cross-stitch that saying and put it up in the den."

In the fellowship hall, Elena was standing in one corner of the room. Anne and her daughters were in another corner.

"I'm going to say something to Elena and get out of here," Liz said to Bev.

As she made her way across the room, she recognized Winston Boone from the Daughbert Technology website. He was of medium height and build with dark hair and black glasses. He looked a bit older than Matt. Liz veered to the right to steer clear of him.

"Ms. Acosta?" a male voice close to her asked.

Liz stopped and turned to face a tall, slender man who looked to be around thirty-five years old with sandy-colored hair and a matching goatee that seemed out of place on his face.

"Yes," she replied.

"I'm Neil Peterson. I worked with Matt."

Liz hoped she wasn't going to get chewed out again. The man extended his hand, and she shook it.

"I provide technical support for the marketing team and track sales figures."

"How do you know who I am?" Liz asked.

"I received a copy of the memo you sent to the company. Some of the information you asked for will come from my department."

"There's no rush," Liz said. "And I hope it wasn't—"

"I was in Winston's office when he called you earlier this week."

"Oh."

"I want to apologize for the way he spoke to you. It makes sense that an attorney should look out for Elena's interests. Matt would have felt the same way."

"I appreciate you saying that."

"Feel free to call me directly if you have any questions. I want to make sure we have an open flow of communication. My contact information is on the company website."

"Thanks."

Peterson moved on. Liz made her way closer to Elena, who was surrounded by people. It took several minutes for a space to open. As soon as Elena saw Liz, she stepped forward and gave her a hug.

"Thanks for coming," Elena said. "It means so much having your support."

"You're welcome."

Elena lowered her voice. "I'd like to meet with you tomorrow. Send me a text about the best time."

"At the office?"

"Yes, my sister will still be staying with me, and I don't want her involved in my business affairs."

"Okay."

Glancing over her shoulder, Liz saw Winston Boone. She stepped aside as he approached Elena and positioned herself to see how the two of them interacted. When Boone leaned over and spoke to Elena nothing in his face indicated that he was saying anything negative. Liz moved farther away. A familiar voice caused her to turn around.

"What did you think of the service?" Connor asked.

Liz repeated what she'd heard from Bev and Sam. Connor seemed relieved.

"Everything about this is tragic," he said. "Seeing Matt's

daughters was the toughest part yet. At one point, I had trouble keeping my emotions in check."

"I wouldn't have blamed you if you'd shed a tear or two. You're human."

Connor smiled slightly. "Becoming more human is one of my life goals."

"Keep working on it, and I believe you'll get there."

Connor glanced past Liz's right shoulder. "There's Reg Bullock. He gave me an update on the GBI investigation into Matt's death."

"The GBI?"

"You don't know about that?"

"No. Why were they called in?"

"Not here, not now," said Connor, glancing around.

"Could we meet for coffee in the morning? Elena wants to come to the office later in the day, and it would be helpful to give her an update."

"Where?"

"Seven at the Sunnyside Coffee Shop."

"Okay."

As she left the room, Liz saw Winston Boone talking to Neil Peterson. The younger man was nodding his head in agreement at what was being said.

CHAPTER 16

CONNOR WOKE UP EARLIER THAN NORMAL. STILL groggy, he rolled over in bed to grab another forty-five minutes of sleep before his breakfast meeting with Liz. But when he closed his eyes, he knew additional rest wasn't going to happen. Too much turmoil had invaded his tranquil life in the mountains. When he arrived at the coffee shop, Liz was sitting at a table for two with a tall cup of coffee in front of her. She smiled when she saw him.

"Hope it's okay that I went ahead," she said. "I was in the mood for a café Cubano. I couldn't believe it when the barista knew what I was talking about."

"It's sweet, right?"

"Yes, the first drops of espresso are mixed with brown sugar and then added to the rest of the coffee. Have you ever tried one?"

"No."

"You look like you could use a jolt of something," she said.

"I'll stick with the familiar. Do you want a pastry?"

"Surprise me."

Connor went to the counter and ordered a breakfast-blend coffee, an apple Danish, and a slice of toasted French bread for Liz. He returned to the table with his drink and the food.

"Perfect," Liz said.

Liz carefully and evenly spread butter across the surface of the bread.

"I've never seen someone spread butter like that," he said. "You're reaching every corner."

"That's the way my father does it. I always enjoyed watching him butter bread when I was growing up." Liz took a bite and nodded. "Okay," she said. "Tell me about your conversation with Reg Bullock."

Connor summarized his talk with Reg. The last thing he mentioned was the probe from the GBI investigator about Connor spending time with Elena, including sitting in her blue BMW in front of the coffee shop.

"I set that up to avoid being with her alone in private," Connor said.

"That sounds like a soap opera, not police work. I've seen how careful you are about avoiding anything that looks inappropriate for a minister. You don't have anything to worry about. But when I tell Elena the local sheriff's department has brought in the GBI, she's going to react. It was bad enough for her to consider the possibility of talking to Detective Norman. Now she's going to be interviewed by a more sophisticated investigator from the state."

"You'll be with her, right?"

"Yes," Liz said, then paused. "If we allow anyone to interview her at all. That's something I'll have to talk over with my boss."

"Elena can be stubborn."

"I'm well aware of that."

Arriving back at the office, Liz checked her voice-mail messages. The last one was from the Etowah County Sheriff's Department: "This is Detective Norman. I'd like to schedule a time to interview Elena Thompson either at the sheriff's department or at your law office. Let me know as soon as possible."

166

Liz forwarded the message to Harold, along with a request to discuss the issue as soon as possible. There was a light knock on her door, and it opened. Jessica had a serious expression her face.

"A friend called last night and said the GBI has been brought into the investigation of Matt Thompson's death. Have you heard anything about that?"

"It's true. Connor Grantham told me this morning over coffee at Sunnyside."

Jessica's countenance suddenly brightened. "Forget about the GBI. I'm here if you need me for relationship advice. Not that I have any experience dating a preacher, and it's hard for me to imagine one keeping you interested."

"We're not dating. Both of us are trying to help Elena Thompson."

The phone on Liz's desk buzzed, and she pressed the speaker button on the receiver.

It was Becky: "Neil Peterson is on the phone."

"I'll take it," Liz responded.

Jessica turned to go. "Remember, I'm available if needed," the assistant said, tapping her heart with her right index finger.

For a second, Liz debated whether to record the phone call. It was legal in Georgia for one person to record a conversation without telling the other party, but she'd never asked Harold whether it was an acceptable practice at the law firm. She decided to place the call on speaker and take notes instead.

"This is Liz Acosta," she said.

"Neil Peterson. We met at Matt Thompson's funeral."

"Of course, I remember."

"You're not recording this call, are you?" he asked. "If so, I'm hanging up."

"No."

"Are you on a speaker phone? I'm hearing an echo."

Liz picked up the receiver and held it to her ear. "Is that better?" she asked.

"Much. This conversation is off the record, okay?"

"Agreed."

"Everything I tell you can be independently verified, but I don't want to be identified as the source of any information. Does that make sense?"

"Yes."

"I'm calling because of my friendship and loyalty to Matt. Not only did we work together at Daughbert, but he also recruited and hired me."

Liz wanted to believe Neil Peterson was trustworthy but knew she had to be cautious. "I'm listening," she said.

"The biggest asset in Matt's estate may not be the market value of Daughbert Technology. The company has been struggling and trying to find a buyer before the balance sheet scared off any suitors. We could point to past cyclical ebbs and flows to explain the current downturn as part of doing business in this field. But we all knew the company might not make it another eighteen to twenty-four months. And without Matt, it wouldn't last that long. He kept it afloat."

Liz cleared her throat. "If the company isn't in good shape, what's the biggest asset for Matt's estate?"

"Life insurance proceeds. Hold on."

The phone was silent for over a minute.

"I'm back. I know Matt took out life insurance payable to both Elena and Anne. He explained what he'd set up when I asked for his advice about what I should do for my current wife and my ex-wife and son. Matt even told me the amount he'd bought. But that's not the insurance I'm talking about. The company took out high-value keyman life insurance policies."

"'Keyman life insurance'?"

"For Matt and Winston. Life insurance policies that would pay if one of them died while the company was still in business."

"Do you know the details of the policy?"

"Some, but not all. Winston asked me to be in charge of organizing a lot of the materials you requested. In an effort to save money, we're handling that internally rather than bringing in a lawyer to do it. Scrolling through the file index, I saw a reference to life insurance policies. The file included a policy taken out on Matt's life for ten million dollars. There was an identical policy bought on Winston's life. According to a recent memo from Winston, the policy for Matt may pay out twenty million dollars."

"There's a double indemnity clause."

"That makes sense," Neil replied.

"If Daughbert Technology is the beneficiary of the policy, it would increase the cash in the company by twenty million dollars with Matt's estate entitled to forty-nine percent."

"Is that how much of the company Matt owned?" Neil asked.

Liz wished she'd not revealed the percentage so casually.

"That's my understanding," she replied. "But there would be other factors that would go into a valuation. Was the company the beneficiary of the policy?"

"I'm not sure. It was payable to something called the Daughbert Technology Trust. I don't know what that is and didn't see another reference to it in the index. Yesterday, when I checked the index again, the references to the keyman policy, the trust, and Winston's memo had been deleted from the main server, but I had a backup on my computer and downloaded it to a flash drive. I want Matt's family to be treated fairly."

Liz tucked a strand of hair behind one ear. "Can you get that flash drive to me?"

"Yes."

"Does the index contain the financial information revealing the bad state of the company?"

"It should. I saw references to our quarterly profit and loss statements."

Liz tapped one finger against her desk. "Have there been any discussions at the company about the cause of Matt's death?"

"Just what happened. Accidental gunshot to the abdomen. Why?"

"The police are conducting an investigation."

"I'm not surprised. I think a detective from the local sheriff's department interviewed everyone who was on the company retreat."

"Were you there?"

"No, I had to cancel at the last minute. Sorry, but I have to go. You'll honor my request for confidentiality, correct?"

"Absolutely."

===

Connor walked out to Michelle's desk. "What should the topic for my message be on Sunday?" he asked.

Michelle raised her eyebrows. "Shouldn't you be asking God, not me, about that?"

"I did and didn't get an answer."

"Maybe that's your message: 'What to Do When God Is Silent.'"

"Would you want to hear that kind of sermon?"

DOUBLE INDEMNITY

"No, because I probably wouldn't like the reasons. There's probably some kind of repentance needed to remove any blocks to communication."

"I like that," Connor said. "I'll also give you credit for the inspiration by telling the congregation that God spoke to me through you."

"Please don't do that." Michelle shook her head. "For years, Duke has claimed I order him around the house like God. If he believes I'm doing the same thing here, he'll never let me hear the end of it."

An hour later, Michelle buzzed Connor's phone.

"Elena Thompson is on the line," she said.

Connor took a deep breath. "Okay, I'll take it."

Elena spoke immediately. "Tracy saw you and Liz at the Sunnyside Coffee Shop this morning. Were you talking about me?"

"Both of us want to help you as much as possible."

"Don't get defensive," Elena said, then continued in a lighter tone of voice. "Tracy and I had a good day together. She helped me go through some of Matt's things, which would have been extra tough on my own. We even laughed over some photos Matt tucked away in a chest of drawers in our bedroom. Also, there were trinkets and souvenirs he'd saved from our trips that I didn't know about. Mementos that brought back happy memories."

"I'm glad you had that time."

"Yeah, I know I'm going to have a lot of ups and downs in the days and weeks ahead. I'd like to book a regular appointment on your schedule."

"How often?"

"Weekly unless I need more."

Connor couldn't go back on what he'd just said about being there to help Elena. But he knew frequent interaction with her would be draining.

"We'll set something up, but I think it would be good for you to also meet with a female counselor. Somebody with expertise in working through grief."

"Is there a counselor like that in Bryson?"

"Not that I know of, but I'll try to found out."

"In the meantime, what day and time works best for you on a regular basis?"

Connor's calendar was up on his computer monitor. It was peppered with meetings, appointments, and fewer time slots marked off for no activity than he liked.

"Nothing that I can set for the same time every week. Let's start with next Tuesday morning at eleven if that's good for you."

"Let me check."

The phone was silent for a moment. "Got it," Elena said. "Maybe we can grab lunch after we finish."

"Not next week."

"Then after another meeting."

———

"We have to move quickly," Harold said to Liz as they sat in his office. "When you have insider access like Peterson you have to take full advantage of it before any lawsuits are filed and the ability to talk to people who can be classified as a corporate representative goes away."

"'Goes away'?"

"You can't talk directly to another lawyer's client. And when the client is a corporation, that usually includes almost anyone in management."

"Okay, I've not had any experience with this sort of thing."

"You're about to. Have you talked to Elena about your conversation with Peterson?"

"No, I wanted to discuss it with you first."

"Good, don't. She already got the assistant of what's-his-name fired."

"Winston Boone."

"Right. And I don't want Elena messing this source up by calling him directly and scaring him off or discussing him with someone who informs on him and causes him to lose his job too."

Liz shifted in her chair. "But don't we have an obligation to let Elena know about Peterson? This is her case."

"What do the rules of professional responsibility say? You took the bar exam a lot more recently than I did."

"I'm not sure."

Harold swiveled in his chair and picked up a thin book. He held it up for Liz to see.

"You should keep one of these handy," he said. "If not a paper copy, then an accessible file on your computer."

Harold read excerpts from rule 1.4 regarding the client-lawyer relationship out loud. "Sound familiar?" he asked.

"Yes."

"Now, listen to this," the senior partner said. "'In some circumstances a lawyer may be justified in delaying transmission of information when the client would be likely to react imprudently to an immediate communication.'"

Harold looked up at Liz. "Does that apply here?" he asked. "Based on this, can we ethically delay telling her about Peterson?"

"Yes, because Elena has already shown she can act imprudently." Liz paused. "But she'll be furious when she finds out we withheld information from her."

"Not if we wait until the right moment, and she can see that we've set her up for success. A client is less concerned with the process than the outcome."

Liz returned to her office and immediately marked a copy of the rules for instant access via her computer. While she was on the clock for Elena, she decided to call the sheriff's department about the request to interview the client. Expecting to leave a message for Detective Norman, she was surprised when he was available.

"You'd asked me to contact you about interviewing Mrs. Thompson," Liz said. "I hope we can schedule in a couple of weeks."

"Next week would be fine if she's ready to meet with me," the detective replied. "I suspect she's still grieving. When you talk to her, please reassure her that I'm just doing my job. I don't want to upset her more than she already is over her husband's death."

Liz was startled by the difference in the detective's words and attitude from the way he came across at the Burnt Pine Tree Lodge.

"Thank you," she said. "Is there anything she needs to bring with her? Paperwork? Documents?"

"Not that I can think of at this time. I'll let you know if that changes."

Liz decided to take advantage of the detective's collaborative tone and pose the question she knew Elena would expect her to ask: "What's the status of the investigation and how close are you to wrapping it up?"

"It's impossible to say at this time."

Liz regretted the compound question. The detective had responded to the second part and ignored the first.

"Is there any indication that Mr. Thompson's death wasn't an accident?" she asked and then held her breath.

"Is his wife concerned that's the case?"

"No," Liz replied quickly. "She believes it was an accident."

"What's the basis for her belief?" the detective asked.

"Uh, what she understands happened at the hunt and what the doctor told her about the gunshot wound."

"How does she know what happened at the hunting preserve? Who has she talked to? What information does she have regarding the cause of death other than what the doctor told her?"

Liz regretted bringing up the subject. "I'm not sure," she replied.

"Then I'll ask her when we get together. Anything else today?"

"No," Liz said, relieved to end the call.

Liz put Elena's case to the side and worked on something else.

CHAPTER 17

CONNOR STOPPED AT THE HAMILTON HOUSE ON HIS way home from the church. Rascal, who seemed twice as big as the last time he'd seen him, was in a pen at the rear of the house. The dog yelped and started racing around the enclosure when he saw Connor. Josh opened the front door of the house.

"Hey!" he called out. "I'll get my dad."

Connor waited on the front porch. Lyle wheeled himself to the door. Josh stood behind him.

"Would you like to see what I've taught Rascal since the last time you were here?" Josh asked.

"Sure."

"I'll get him," Josh said, running off.

Lyle rolled his chair outside.

"Should we go down the ramp to the yard?" Connor asked.

"No, this is fine," Lyle said in a subdued voice.

Josh appeared with Rascal pulling hard on a blue leash. The boy had an orange Frisbee in his hand.

"I think I know what's about to happen," Connor said.

"Yeah, they've been working on this every day for the past week," Lyle said.

Josh unleashed the dog and waved the plastic disc back and forth. Rascal tried to jump up and grab it from the boy's hand. Josh threw it, and Rascal took off as fast as he could go. The dog snagged the Frisbee out of the air before it hit the ground. He trotted back to Josh, who ran over to Connor and his dad.

"Great," Connor said to the boy. "And what's most impressive is that he brought it back to you."

"Will you throw it, Dad?" Josh asked.

"I'm not feeling too good," Lyle started. "You—"

"Please?" Josh interrupted. "Mr. Connor hasn't seen you throw a Frisbee."

"And I'd like to," Connor said.

"Okay," Lyle said reluctantly. "But just once."

His eyes glued to the orange disc, Rascal stood attentively in front of the stoop. Leaning forward in his wheelchair, Lyle curled his arm around the Frisbee and then released it with a snap. It shot out and then began to climb in stages, higher and higher in the air. Connor had never seen anything like it. When it reached the end of its flight, it came down softly, as if descending on an elevator, and into the waiting mouth of the dog, who grabbed it in his teeth.

"How did you learn to do that?" Connor asked.

"Disc golf," Lyle replied. "I've played since I was a kid."

"Getting it to drop out of the sky where you want it to is the hard part," Josh said. "That way it lands in the metal basket."

"You could still play disc golf, couldn't you?" Connor asked.

"That's what I've been telling him," Josh said.

"Maybe, unless the ground is too uneven," Lyle replied. "But it wouldn't be the same."

"And I want him to teach me," Josh added.

Lyle didn't respond. Connor took the Frisbee from Rascal and threw it in an arc that caused it to nose-dive and roll across the yard. The dog took off after it.

"Looks like I need a lesson more than Josh," Connor said.

"Yeah," Lyle replied with a slight smile. "We'd have to start at the beginning."

"Here's how I'll pay for my lessons," Connor said.

Connor told Lyle about the skeet shooting facility. Josh's eyes widened.

"There's a section that is completely wheelchair-accessible. I thought we could drive down early one Saturday morning. They have a station that would allow Josh to give it a try. Guns and ammo are included."

"Yes!" Josh replied excitedly.

"Put Rascal in his pen while I talk to Mr. Connor," Lyle said to his son.

"We can go, right?" Josh asked. "You know it would be fun!"

"Get the dog and put him up," Lyle repeated.

Lyle waited until Josh disappeared around the side of the house.

"We got some bad news this morning," he said to Connor. "Sarah has breast cancer."

Connor's shoulders sagged. "How advanced?" he asked.

"Pretty bad. We haven't told Josh yet and aren't sure whether to do it now or wait until she starts treatment. When her hair starts falling out everyone will know."

Connor flashed back to images of his mother. "Where is Sarah now?"

"Inside fixing supper. Would you like to see her?"

"Of course."

"Let me check with her first and figure out how we can occupy Josh while we talk."

Lyle went inside the house. Still reeling from the sad news, Connor waited on the front porch. The Hamilton family had already suffered so much. It took a couple of minutes for Lyle to return.

"Come in," he said. "Josh is getting extra time on his gaming station so he's in his room with his headphones on."

Connor followed Lyle into the small house. The front door led directly into the living room. The kitchen was to the right. Sarah came out of the kitchen.

"Hey," she said to Connor. "Lyle told me what you want to do for him and Josh. I think they'll have a great time."

"I hope so." Connor cleared his throat. "I just wanted to tell you how sorry I am about your diagnosis. I'm sure folks in the church will want to do anything they can to help. That's up to you, of course."

"We'll have a lot of family support for practical things, just like there's been since Lyle's accident."

"I'm here for you too."

"Thanks," Lyle said.

"When he said you wanted to come in and see me, I assumed it was to pray with us?" Sarah asked.

"Yes, I'd like to."

Sarah sat on a cracked leather sofa. They'd cleared a space at one end of the sofa where Lyle could park his wheelchair. Connor sat in a soft beige side chair with slightly worn arms. Lyle reached out and Sarah gave him her hand. Connor leaned forward with his hands clasped in front of him.

"Before I pray, I need to tell you something," he said. "When I was a teenager, my mother was diagnosed with cancer. I prayed, but she died."

"And you're wondering if your prayers now can really make a difference?" Sarah asked.

"Yes."

"There's a mystery to the ways of God that I haven't figured out," Sarah said. "I've seen miracles, not just read about them in the Bible. Lyle and I believe in trusting and asking."

"I want you to have a miracle," Connor replied earnestly.

"That makes three of us," Lyle said.

Connor paused for a moment. "One more thing. Before I pray for you, I'd like you to pray for me. Is that okay?"

Sarah smiled. "God gives grace to the humble."

Connor closed his eyes. They sat in silence for a few moments. His heart started beating a little bit faster. Then, Sarah Hamilton prayed. The woman's words reminded Connor of a freight train slowly pulling out of the station. They carried a weight and power that couldn't be ignored. Something big and powerful was on the move. Sarah spoke as one who knew what she believed and expected God to listen. Connor felt confidence well up inside him as she combined Bible verses that she'd memorized with words from her own heart. Connor now understood why Lyle welcomed his wife's prayers for him every evening. The pace of the prayer increased. Several minutes passed before Sarah finished with a resolute "In the strong name of the Lord Jesus Christ, amen."

When Connor opened his eyes, Sarah was staring at him. The fire in her countenance had never been more apparent. But instead of looking away, Connor met her gaze.

"I know it doesn't make sense," he said to her. "But there toward the end, it seemed like you were listening while you were speaking."

"That makes perfect sense," Sarah said with a nod. "Your turn."

Connor took a deep breath and waited again. But this time there was a hint of expectation in his heart. Then, after a few moments, he experienced something new. A thought whose origin wasn't in his conscious intellect formed in his mind. He suspected this was what he'd sensed in Sarah. But the thought wasn't the sort of thing he'd normally say when faced with a situation as serious as the one confronting the couple sitting across from him. To do so, would, in his opinion, be irresponsible. But after delaying another split second, he decided to forget about his reservations and speak it out loud.

"God, nothing is too hard for you," he said.

The simple declaration released a flood of thoughts and words that cascaded after it. Connor found himself doing what he'd heard Sarah do. Not as well. Not as smoothly. He stumbled over snippets of verses he'd read but not committed to memory. And there were fits and starts to some of his thoughts. But just when he thought he was about to fall flat, something else would come to mind. He'd speak it, and the words would enable him to continue. He prayed for Sarah. He prayed for Lyle. He prayed for Josh. He wasn't sure exactly how long he prayed. But it was far, far longer than he had prayed at any other time in his life for a person in the congregation. When the slate was finally clear, he finished with a simple "Amen."

"Amen," the other two people in the room echoed.

"Thank you," Lyle said. "It's good to know that you're with us in this fight."

"I want to believe," Connor replied. "And being around the two of you makes that seem possible."

"After what happened with your mother, I appreciate your willingness to try again," Sarah said.

"That's what she'd want."

Sarah turned to Lyle. "Listening to Connor, I think we should go ahead and tell Josh about my diagnosis sooner rather than later. He should be part of this from the beginning. Just because he's ten years old doesn't mean his prayers aren't as effective as ours. There's no junior Holy Spirit."

"I agree," Lyle said. "We'll talk to him after supper."

Liz was finishing a salad while watching TV when there was a knock on her door. It was dark outside, and she turned on the outside light. It was Elena. The client was wearing a long dark coat against the evening chill.

Liz opened the door. "How did you know where I live?" she asked.

"My private investigator told me." Elena glanced over her shoulder. "I didn't want to call you because I don't know who might be listening on my phone. Can I come inside?"

Liz moved aside so Elena could enter. They stood in the living room area.

"Why do you think someone is listening to your phone calls?"

Elena took her phone from her purse. "It's turned off now, but all afternoon I would be on a call and there would be a faint beeping in the background."

"Who would want to record your calls?"

"I don't know, but it scares me to death."

"What did you want to talk to me about?"

"The police investigation. All sorts of crazy thoughts are racing through my head. Have you talked with the detective?"

Liz told her about the conversation with Detective Norman. As she talked, Elena became more and more agitated.

"Why couldn't you get any information about the investigation from him?" Elena demanded. "That's what you're trained to do as a lawyer, isn't it? Get people to talk. It's all about asking the right questions. You should have started with something easy that you knew he'd answer and worked deeper from there. Unless you're leaving out a lot of what was said, it sounds like you jumped to the big issue too quickly."

Liz bristled at the criticism. "No matter what I asked, I don't believe Norman would have offered to open his file and let me look at it. The next step for us is to set a day and time for you to talk to him. Is there a day that works better for you?"

"I'll need to check my calendar on my phone."

Elena turned on her phone. She raised her index finger to her lips. "Don't say anything while I look at my schedule."

Liz waited. Elena swiped her finger across the screen. A few seconds later, she called out, "It happened again! The beeping sound."

"Hand me the phone," Liz said.

The welcome screen was covered with apps. Liz scrolled over to at least five screens filled with apps.

"Have you downloaded any new apps recently?" she asked.

"A few. Why?"

"One or more of them could be sending you notifications, and you're hearing the beep in the background."

"Oh," Elena replied, holding out her hand.

Liz returned the phone and waited.

"I think I found it," Elena said. "Yesterday, I downloaded a shopping app that lets me know when items I want to buy become available."

"How many notifications has it sent you?"

"Over fifty. I'm going to delete it."

"Good. Now, please check your calendar."

A few seconds later, Elena spoke. "Next Wednesday morning would be best for me. I'd want to meet at your law office, not the sheriff's department."

Liz quickly noted that her morning was open. "That will work. I'll try to confirm first thing in the morning."

Elena put away her phone and looked around the interior of the unit.

"This is cozy," she said. "It reminds me of the place where I lived in college."

"I've enjoyed it. My landlady is the one who invited me to visit Rock Community Church. Her name is Beverly Devon. She's married to Sam."

"Never met them," Elena replied. "But Connor is the reason I started going to the church. I saw him walk into the Sunnyside Coffee Shop one morning and asked one of the baristas who he was. I was surprised when the girl told me he was a minister at a local church. Connor didn't look like a minister to me."

"Why not?"

"Come on." Elena smiled. "Connor could be a fashion model in a men's clothing magazine. That day I had an intuition he would be an important person in my life. And when that happens, it always comes true."

Liz's skin crawled. Elena's thoughts dishonored her marriage to Matt, and Liz didn't want to hear about the recent widow's intuitions related to Connor Grantham.

"I'll be in touch with you as soon as I confirm with Detective Norman," she said briskly.

"One last thing. Any news from Matt's company?"

"It's going to take awhile for them to respond to my request. I asked for a lot of information. Good night."

Liz almost pushed Elena out of the apartment. After she shut the door, she leaned against it and closed her eyes.

CHAPTER 18

CONNOR DROVE HOME FROM THE HAMILTON RESI-
dence. Instead of fixing supper, he grabbed a bottle of water from
the refrigerator and sat in one of the side chairs in his living room.
He didn't want to eat. He didn't want to read. He just wanted to sit.
And exist in the place where the prayers with Lyle and Sarah took
him. He also knew what he wanted to talk about in his sermon. He
turned on his tablet and began writing.

Sunday morning, Connor took his place behind the pulpit with a
mixture of nervousness and anticipation. His text was Luke 5:16:
"But Jesus often withdrew to lonely places and prayed." The previous day, he'd taken a long hike in the woods to practice what he
intended to preach.

"Today, I want to talk to you about prayer," Connor began. "A
topic I know very little about. That may sound surprising coming
from a minister, but it's true."

Starting with a confession got the attention of the congregation.
But as he read his notes, Connor realized that he wasn't making as

much sense as he'd hoped. He strayed from his prepared remarks, but when he did, he lost his train of thought and quickly returned to what he'd written. When he reached the incident at the Hamilton house, he felt the story came across as vague and indistinct.

After the sermon, the comments he received at the rear of the sanctuary after the message confirmed his fears. Most people simply shook his hand and smiled. Lyle and Sarah paused.

"I hope it was okay to tell that story so long as I left out your names," Connor said in a low voice. "I want to respect your privacy about what you're going through."

"No problem," Lyle responded with a smile. "Sarah nudged me hard when you started down that road."

"Were you fine with it?" Connor asked Sarah.

"Yes, but a seed needs to germinate in the ground before it sees the light of day."

Connor swallowed at the gentle but accurate rebuke. "You're right," he sighed.

"And it's okay," Sarah responded.

Liz approached. Connor hadn't seen her in the congregation during the service.

"Are you having one of your lunches with visitors today?" she asked.

"No."

"Could I offer you a free meal at the Olive Tree?"

Connor hesitated. Part of him wanted to go home as soon as possible, be alone, and maybe take a nap. The friendly expression on Liz's face convinced him otherwise, though.

"Yes."

"I'll meet you there. Don't rush. I'm going to order one of those lemon drinks."

Liz took a sip of her mint limonada and wondered if she should say anything to Connor about Elena. Her phone vibrated. It was Harold calling.

"I'm at the office, and an email for you came in through the firm website regarding Daughbert Technology," the senior partner said. "There's no name listed as sender, but I assume it's from the guy you talked to the other day."

"What's included?"

"A copy of the insurance policy. It has a face value of ten million with a double indemnity clause. Payable to the Daughbert Technology Trust."

"Any trust documents?"

"No, but the policy was purchased two months ago."

"Peterson said it was recent."

"Also, there's a balance statement for the company from around the same time the policy was purchased. I'm not a CPA, but I've read enough financial reports to recognize when a company is cash-strapped and on life support."

"If that's true, Elena Thompson may own forty-nine percent of nothing."

Out the front window of the restaurant Liz saw Connor pull in behind her car.

"I have to go," she said.

"One more thing," Harold said. "The sender included a page with a phone number scribbled on it and a message to call if you have any questions. No name associated with the number. I'll text it to you."

"Thanks."

Connor entered the restaurant and waved. "This is our table," he said with a smile as he came closer.

"Yeah," Liz replied. "I hadn't noticed that."

"Are you okay?"

"My boss called me about some information that just came through about a big case."

"He was at the office?"

"Yes, you're not the only person who works on Sunday."

A waitress arrived and took their orders.

"Good sermon this morning," Liz said when the woman left.

"Do you really think so?"

Suddenly, Liz couldn't recall the topic. "Of course," she said. "You're an excellent speaker."

"But did it make sense?"

Liz tried to remember something from Connor's message. "Totally," she said. "It was about Jesus, right?"

"Yes." Connor chuckled. "I shouldn't be surprised that it's tough for someone to remember what I said thirty or forty-five minutes later."

"You told a story about going to see a couple and praying with them. I assume it was someone in the church who wanted to remain anonymous for some reason."

"Okay." Connor held up his hand.

"And then you took a walk in the woods to pray like Jesus did when he was alive." Liz spoke faster. "He even prayed all night one time, which is mind-blowing when you think about it. The only time I stayed up all night was to study for a chemistry exam when I was in college. I drank energy drinks and barely remember taking the test. I think I made a D in the class. I bet you've never received a D in your life."

Connor laughed. "Enough. It wasn't fair to put you on the spot."

"You clearly work hard on your sermons, and it's not unreasonable to expect people to pay attention."

"I wish everyone shared your perspective."

"Don't dodge my question. Have you ever gotten a D in school? Go back all the way to high school."

"No."

Liz nodded. "I knew it. A lawyer is never supposed to ask a question unless she knows the answer."

"I was wired for school. Put me in a lecture hall followed by a few hours in the library, and I'm happy."

"I have a touch of dyslexia, so school was a challenge for me."

"To overcome that and become a lawyer is impressive." Connor took a sip of his drink. "But what I tried to communicate this morning in the sermon had nothing to do with academics. It came from an experience."

Connor told her about his time with Lyle and Sarah Hamilton. Liz was impressed with the passion in his voice.

"I never thought I'd go to lunch and listen to a man talk about how excited he is about praying," she said. "Why didn't you share this additional information about the couple?"

"I didn't mention Sarah's name because she just received the diagnosis, and they've not told anyone about it."

"That makes sense." Liz took a deep breath. "Did this make you think about your mother?"

Connor stared at her for a second. "Yes. But I couldn't talk about her either. It's still too painful."

The food arrived. The lamb was perfectly cooked and seasoned. Liz especially liked the couscous.

"Maybe you should focus some of your newfound prayer energy toward Elena," Liz said. "She's not doing well."

"I'm meeting with her on Tuesday."

"Be careful."

"What do you mean?"

"At times, I believe she's mentally unstable. Not incompetent. Just irrational and off track in her thoughts."

"One thing I'm strongly encouraging her to do is seek professional help from a psychiatrist or psychologist."

"I hope she takes your advice."

─────

Driving home from the restaurant, Connor thought about Liz. He really liked her honesty. And she was attractive.

Before going inside the house, he checked his backyard garden. In the summer, he raised heirloom tomatoes, squash, okra, and bush beans in raised beds. When the weather turned cooler, he tried to nurse a few asparagus plants from the soil. They wouldn't grow in Georgia clay, but Connor had brought in rich composted dirt, and his asparagus experiment looked promising. It would be fun to invite Liz over for a dinner that included venison and asparagus he'd harvested.

His phone vibrated. It was a text from Reg Bullock:

Available? Need to talk.

Walking across the yard toward his house, Connor made the call.

"Sorry to bother you on Sunday afternoon," Reg said. "But I

thought you should know about a conversation I had with Andy McNamara. The GBI agents were wrapping up yesterday at Burnt Pine Tree and held a meeting with Detective Norman and some other officers from the sheriff's department. Andy took some bottles of water into the conference room and heard one of the GBI agents mention your name as a 'person of interest' in the investigation."

Connor stopped in his tracks. "Why? Because of the video I took?"

"Maybe, but the GBI agent and Norman continued to discuss you as Andy left the room."

"What did they say?"

"I hate to say this, but they suspect there might be an improper relationship between you and Elena Thompson."

"That's ridiculous! I was trying to help save her marriage to her husband!"

"I know."

"Did Andy hear anything specific?"

"Only that they had to follow up with all sources."

"Sources? Who?"

"I'm not sure. Bryson is small enough that any gossip ends up in the open."

"I can't stamp out what didn't happen," Connor said with frustration.

"I hated bringing this up but thought you'd want to know."

"I do," Connor sighed. "Now if the police want to talk to me about Elena, I won't be surprised."

The call from Reg wrecked Connor's good mood. He considered calling Liz to ask her advice about the investigation but didn't want to bother her. If his interaction with her went beyond her attendance at the church, he didn't want it to include anything negative.

Tuesday morning before Elena's appointment, Connor asked Michelle to come into his office and close the door.

"Am I in trouble?" she asked.

"No, and what I'm about to tell you is totally confidential. Agreed?"

"I treat everything around here as confidential unless you tell me otherwise. Duke thinks all I do at work is play games on my phone."

"Keep it that way."

Connor told her what he'd learned from Reg Bullock. Michelle's face reddened.

"That's wrong!" she exclaimed. "The Bible talks about going the extra mile. You've gone ten extra miles with Elena Thompson! I'd like to talk to Detective Norman and whoever else is spewing this nonsense at the GBI. I'll straighten them out!"

Connor had never seen this fiery side of his assistant. "That's not what I'm asking you to do. But there's a possibility the police may contact you. You can tell them Elena and Matt came to see me individually and together."

"And that your door is cracked open when you meet alone with any woman, and I'm always sitting here less than ten feet away."

"Yes."

Michelle continued to fume. "Because you're single, there is always going to be speculation about you. Elena crossed the line, but I've never heard anyone in the congregation accuse you of being improper toward her or anyone else."

"Any gossip in the community?"

"Not that I've heard," Michelle said in a more relaxed voice. "But recently, there's been speculation about you and Liz Acosta. That's not a problem. She's single and fair game."

Connor leaned back in his chair. "What do you think about Liz?"

"I don't have an opinion, but Bev Devon says she's a great tenant." Michelle paused. "What do you think about her? That's the important question."

"I like her," Connor said. "And that's confidential."

———

Elena was late for her appointment. When she arrived, Connor ushered her into his office and left the door cracked open wider than usual.

"Sorry I'm late," Elena said. "Tracy was finally leaving to go home, and I wanted to see her off. She stayed longer than planned."

"I'm sure she's been a big support."

"Not really." Elena shrugged. "She's hoping I'll share some of the inheritance money with her. Tracy's husband has always had trouble finding and keeping a good job. Matt and I loaned them money several times over the past few years."

"Do you think you should help her out?"

"Only with an interest-bearing loan. That's the way we handled it before. I want to keep family and finances separate."

Connor shifted in his chair. "Would you be interested in what the Bible might say about that situation?" he asked.

"Not really. I'm not here to talk about Tracy."

Connor waited. Elena looked past him at the windows offering a view of the mountains.

"Are you still taking hikes?" Elena asked. "You talk about it a lot in your sermons."

"Yes, I like being alone in the woods. It's one of my favorite places to think. And pray."

"I can't stay cooped up in the house all the time with my grief. I think getting outside would be good for me. When are you planning another hike? I'd like to join you."

"Nothing on my calendar right now."

"Let me know."

"My next hike is going to be with Liz Acosta," Connor blurted out.

A cloud seemed to pass over Elena's face. "Have you checked Liz's social media accounts? Someone told me she has a longtime boyfriend who lives in Florida. He comes up to see her all the time."

"No, that hasn't come up."

"Glad I warned you."

Wanting to end that part of the conversation, Connor passed a sheet of paper across the desk to Elena.

"This is for you," he said. "It's a list of resources that may help you deal with grief. I know you like to read as well as listen to podcasts, so there's a mix of information. I also researched professional counselors and suggest you find one with expertise in helping people in your situation. Unfortunately, there isn't anyone in the immediate area, but more and more people are offering remote office visits. You're great about following up on suggestions, and I believe that would work fine for you."

Elena frowned as she took the sheet from him. "What's your role going to be in helping me?" she asked. "I feel like you're trying to dump me."

Connor winced. "I'm your pastor. And part of my job is to help you find the best help available. That's why I'm suggesting professional counseling. I'm still willing to meet with you here at the church on a regular basis to talk about the struggles you face. And pray with you."

"I'm a woman. Not a bundle of problems."

"I don't see you as a bundle of problems. You're going through incredible trauma. I want to be there for you in every way I can."

"That sounds better," Elena sighed. "I miss Matt. He had his flaws, but I believe he really loved me."

"He told me he loved you."

"When did he say that? Was I out of the room?"

"We met a few times one-on-one."

Elena raised her eyebrows. "More than once? I only know about the day Matt stayed after I left."

"It's often part of the marital counseling process," Connor quickly replied. "Remember, I met one-on-one with you as well. I used the opportunity to support your marriage to Matt. He and I ended up having some great conversations about life. That's what I was referring to at the funeral."

"Okay," Elena said. "Matt did bring that up. I wasn't sure about the circumstances. He said he'd listened to a podcast that changed his outlook on what was important but didn't give a lot of details. Matt was always a bottom-line guy."

Connor told her the story of the wrong podcast, and the impact the message had on Matt's thinking.

"That's what I'd been telling Matt for years," Elena jumped in. "His work was always number one, leaving me in a fight for number two with Anne and his kids."

"The message flipped Matt's outlook about a lot of things, including you." Connor could tell Elena was skeptical. "Oh, and Reg Bullock says Matt mentioned some of the same things to the

196

group from his company after dinner on Friday night at Burnt Pine Tree. I think Matt was serious."

"He did?" Elena asked in surprise. "Do you know if they recorded the talk?"

"You'd have to ask Reg."

"Did you record the conversations when you talked with Matt, just the two of you?"

"No, I've never recorded any of our conversations."

"I have. It's helped me remember what was said."

"Are you recording this conversation?" Connor asked in surprise.

"Yes," Elena said and tapped her purse, which she'd placed on Connor's desk. "It helps me to listen multiple times to what you say."

Connor's mouth dropped open. "Will you tell me before you do it again?"

"Sure. Anyway, I'm glad you think Matt's mind was in a good place when he died."

"I believe it was."

The session continued for another hour, mostly focused on Elena's concerns about how she was going to be treated by Matt's company and whether she was going to end up in a legal fight with Anne. It was a conversation more suited to Liz's office than his. As they reached the end, Connor knew he ought to pray with Elena, but at that point he didn't want to prolong the meeting. He ushered her out of his office, then stayed behind at Michelle's desk but said nothing until he heard the bell chime, signaling the exit door had been opened.

"How did it go?" Michelle asked.

"Did you hear anything?"

"No, I don't eavesdrop."

Connor paused. "It's hard to know if I'm doing any good or not. But for now, it's unreasonable to expect Elena to do much except grieve."

"She doesn't look very grief-stricken to me."

Connor returned to his office. He logged on to social media and checked Liz Acosta's relationship status. There were photos of her with a boyfriend taken three months earlier. Connor stared at Raphael's face. He didn't look trustworthy. He returned to Michelle's desk and told her what he'd found.

"Oh, that relationship ended," the assistant immediately responded.

"How do you know?"

"Becky Carrington told me. She works at the same law firm as Liz."

"Why were you talking to Becky about Liz?"

Michelle hesitated. "Maybe what I said earlier—that there wasn't any gossip about your social life—isn't quite true."

CHAPTER 19

LIZ MET WITH HAROLD ABOUT ELENA'S UPCOMING appointment with Detective Norman.

"Should I have her invoke her Fifth Amendment right not to incriminate herself?" she asked.

Harold raised his eyebrows. "Is there any suspicion in your mind that Elena Thompson is responsible for her husband's death?"

"I don't have any reason to believe she had anything to do it."

"Have you asked her?"

"No, and if I did, I can only imagine how she would react. She'd get really upset and fire me."

Harold leaned back in his chair. "You've got to let her know that Norman may ask her insinuating questions. Getting mad at him isn't an answer. A simple 'No' should be her starting and ending point."

"Right."

"Make sure she doesn't answer any compound questions containing facts that may not be true or questions that assume facts adverse to her as part of their foundation."

Liz recalled her own error in asking the detective a compound question.

Harold checked his watch. "Gotta go," he said. "I'm out of town tomorrow, but I'll be here early in the morning on the following day if you think of anything else."

Liz stayed late to research the types of questions Elena shouldn't answer. It was a frustrating exercise. When she read examples of objectionable questions, Liz could see the problem but struggled to come up with similar questions herself. Developing her ability to create them was linked to her ability to spot them. She left the office hoping the local detective was a lot less capable than some of the experts who wrote the articles.

Instead of going home, she drove to the taqueria on Kenilworth Avenue. Manuel was at his usual place on a stool beside the cash register.

"Hola!" he said. "It's late for supper in America."

"And I didn't get to take a siesta this afternoon. I'm hungry."

"What would you like?"

"Antojitos," Liz replied, using the common term for Mexican street food, which meant "little cravings." "You know what's best in the kitchen this evening. Surprise me."

Manuel jumped off his stool and stuck his head into the kitchen. Liz couldn't hear what he said.

"Are you working too hard?" Manuel asked when he returned.

"Are *you* working too hard?"

"Only if you call sitting here and talking to people work," Manuel replied with a smile. "I have a new partner who's bought a piece of the restaurant. He's already taken over the kitchen, leaving me to greet customers and count the money."

"Who is he?"

"Raul Vasquez. He used to work at the fancy hunting property a few miles out of town. He was in charge of smoking all their meats."

"Burnt Pine Tree Lodge?"

"Yes, that's it. What an odd name for a place. Who would want to go there? Pine trees aren't good for much. And a burnt one even less. Anyway, he's been saving his money, and I agreed to sell him an interest in the restaurant. I'm getting too old to be here all the time."

"Congratulations. I hope he's not going to change the tamale recipes."

"Oh, the menu is going to get better. Raul is a real chef."

Liz paused for a moment. "Was he working at Burnt Pine Tree when one of the guests recently died in a hunting accident?"

"I don't know. You can ask him when he brings out your food."

While she waited, Liz talked to Manuel about his family. He had a new granddaughter and showed her a photo on his phone of a tiny infant with a pink bow stuck to the top of her head. A few minutes later, a short, stocky man in his forties with black hair and wearing a white apron came out of the kitchen carrying a plate. Manuel introduced him to Liz.

"I made you elote cut from the cob and carnitas pambazos," Raul said.

Elote was a corn dish and pambazos were small tortas. On a separate plate the chef had laid out some coconut bars colored with three bands of green, white, and red.

"And some cocada for dessert," he said.

"Looks great," Liz said. "Manuel says you used to work at the Burnt Pine Tree Lodge."

"Yes."

"Were you there the day the guest died in a hunting accident?"

"I was," Raul said with a sad shake of his head. "He and some other men came into the kitchen that morning, and I fixed them sausage biscuits. The man who died gave me a big tip. I don't think he was very interested in hunting."

"He didn't want to hunt?"

"No, he told the other men he wasn't feeling good. Later that morning, I found out that he'd been shot. An ambulance took him to the hospital. Then I heard he died. It made me really sad. I mean, if he hadn't gone hunting, he would still be alive."

———

Tuesday afternoon, Connor was working on his sermon when Michelle knocked on the door of his office.

"Sorry," she said. "I know you told me to hold your calls, but the phones have been blowing up for the past half an hour."

"Why?"

"The article in the newspaper this afternoon about Matt Thompson's death."

The *Etowah Gazette* was an afternoon paper that came out three times a week. The church was the last stop on the delivery person's route. The newspaper was so old-fashioned that it didn't offer an online subscription.

"What does it say?"

"A reporter claims there's a full-blown investigation by the sheriff's department and GBI into the cause of Matt's death. Your name was mentioned in the article. According to an anonymous source, you were questioned by a detective at Burnt Pine Tree Lodge about what happened. Is that true?"

"Yes, but not because I knew anything. Everyone from Matt's company was questioned as well."

Connor told her about the video he'd taken and the interview by Detective Norman. "That's all I know," he said.

"People in the congregation want to talk to you about the article."

"Who?"

Michelle glanced down at the notepad in her hand and rattled off seven or eight names. Neither Elena nor Reg Bullock had called. At least not yet.

"I'll see if our paper is here," Michelle said, turning to walk back toward her desk.

A minute later, she returned with the newspaper. She spread it out so both she and Connor could read it. The article was the lead story on the front page.

The headline read "Local and State Law Enforcement Officers Investigate Death at Burnt Pine Tree Hunting Lodge." Connor quickly skimmed the text. It gave basic background information about Matt and his company. The cause of death was described as "a gunshot wound to the abdomen." The sentences that mentioned Connor stated: "Among those interviewed by the sheriff's department was local minister Connor Grantham, who was on the property at the time and the only guest not employed by Daughbert Technology. According to official sources, Reverend Grantham is considered a person of interest to the investigation."

"'Official sources,'" Connor said, standing up. "And 'person of interest'? What's that supposed to mean?"

"Slow down. I'm still reading," Michelle said. "I'm not surprised they didn't get the facts straight. Whenever I read something in the paper that I already know about there's a mistake. 'Person of interest' sounds ominous."

"Yeah," Connor replied grimly. "I wish they hadn't written that. I understand why people are calling the church."

The light on Michelle's phone blinked to signal an incoming call. She leaned over, answered it, and listened for a few seconds.

"Let me see if he's available," she said, placing the caller on hold. "I assume you want to talk to Liz Acosta?"

"Yes."

Connor went into his office.

"Have you seen the newspaper article?" she asked.

"Yes, and I don't like the slant it takes."

"Me either. According to my boss, this is only the first of several articles. More are coming."

"How does he know that?"

"I can't tell you."

"That's not very helpful." Connor shifted in his chair. "This could create a huge problem for me."

"I know, and I wish I could say more, but I can't."

Connor thought for a moment. "Would that change if I hired you to represent me?"

"No."

"You don't want to help?"

"No, no. I'm sorry. There's nothing more I can say, but it's not because I don't care or wouldn't want to help."

"This doesn't make sense."

"Please, that's all I can say. Has Elena called you yet?"

"No, but the phones have been busy here at the church."

"Elena left me a message a few minutes ago. I'm sure you'll hear from her."

The call ended, leaving Connor frustrated and worried. His desk phone lit up again.

"Elena is on the phone," Michelle said. "This is the second time she's called in the past five minutes."

"Put her through."

───────────────

Liz had delayed calling Connor because she was still trying to process what she'd learned from Harold Pollard when he came into her office two hours earlier.

"I have a scoop on an article that's coming out in today's newspaper," Harold had said. "The investigation into the cause of Matt Thompson's death is heating up. And once the insurance companies find out about it, they'll put the brakes on any prompt payout to Elena Thompson."

"What's going to be in the article?"

"It mentions the existence of an investigation involving both the sheriff's department and the GBI. Once the GBI is mentioned, that changes the public and legal perception of everything."

A puzzled look on her face, Liz asked, "Does the reporter think Matt was murdered?"

"So far, the newspaper isn't claiming that anything is going on except a criminal investigation. Our focus has to be on helping Elena Thompson. Technically, a murder doesn't keep her from collecting the life insurance proceeds payable to her."

"But it would nullify the double indemnity provisions."

"What does the policy say?"

"I don't know."

"Let's look at it."

Liz left and returned with her laptop and a paper copy of the insurance policy that she gave to Harold.

The senior partner put on his reading glasses. "Typical language," he said, placing the policy on his desk. "The double indemnity provision excludes death by natural causes, suicide, gross negligence of the decedent, or murder by a beneficiary or in collusion with someone else."

"So Elena could still collect double if Matt was murdered?"

"As long as she didn't kill him or have him killed."

"What about the gross negligence exclusion?"

"Matt was certainly negligent in use of a firearm, but gross negligence—"

"Requires evidence of a conscious action in reckless disregard of safety," Liz finished. "Like playing roulette with a loaded pistol."

"Are they still using that example in law school?"

"Yeah."

Liz thought for a moment. "What about Elena's meeting in the morning? Do you think a GBI agent might show up too?"

"Possibly," Harold said.

"If so, what should I do?"

"Be her lawyer."

Liz felt her face flush.

"How's your preparation going?" Harold asked.

Liz pulled up the file on her computer and read from some of her notes.

Harold cut her off. "That's good," he said. "You also

need to let the client know that she's going to be asked about the preacher who took the cell phone video you showed me. I knew that might possibly be a problem for us, but it may be a problem for him too."

"Why? Reverend Grantham was just out for a walk in the woods. He does that all the time."

"How do you know that?"

"I've visited the church several times. He's mentioned going for hikes in his sermons."

"But do you know that's what the preacher was doing the day Thompson died?"

"Connor Grantham is a suspect?" Liz asked in disbelief.

"He's going to be identified in the article as a 'person of interest,' which is a euphemism for a suspect." Harold shook his head. "In my opinion suggesting that a local minister is a murder suspect is a far-fetched theory by overzealous law enforcement. But for whatever reason, that's the way it's going to be pitched in the newspaper. It could be a strategy to make a more serious suspect relax."

Liz's thoughts scattered in multiple directions. "The impact on Connor will be catastrophic. He could lose his job. Could you talk to Mr. Barnwell at the newspaper?"

"What would I say?"

Liz paused. "I don't know," she said.

"Look, the police are interested in every detail of Grantham's whereabouts on the day Thompson died. Pat Barnwell told me the preacher was on the Burnt Pine Tree property without permission before and after the shooting incident. There's supposedly other evidence that raises suspicions about his activities."

"What other evidence?"

"Pat wouldn't tell me. But the reporter working the story believes it may exist."

Stunned, Liz didn't know what to say.

Harold continued. "Pat also told me they've checked into Grantham's background. He grew up in Atlanta and went to an Ivy League seminary."

"That's true."

"And he comes across as the smartest person in the room."

"Not true. He's humble." Liz bit her lower lip. "I need to talk to Connor."

Harold raised his index finger in the air. "Be careful. Pat is a client and spoke to me confidentially. He knows we're trying to help the widow and is sympathetic to our cause."

"But—"

"I gave my word to Pat. We have to honor that. Let's get back to what's important. Given this new information, how are you going to prepare Elena for questions about the minister?"

Liz thought for a moment. "Tell her not to describe Connor Grantham as a male model."

"She would say that?"

"I've already heard it from her lips."

"You need to script Elena carefully and keep her comments as short as possible. That type of wording should be totally off-limits."

"Easier said than done." Liz hesitated before saying, "And Mr. Barnwell needs to be careful that he doesn't print something about Connor Grantham that opens the door to a libel suit. As our client, you could tell him that."

"Pat knows the rules. Everything will be attributed to sources, no speculation."

"Speculation is all I'm hearing."

CHAPTER 20

CONNOR HELD THE PHONE AWAY FROM HIS EAR AS Elena spewed out words like a fire hydrant. He'd given up trying to carry on a conversation with her about the article in the newspaper until the flow subsided.

"I know it's hard—" he started again when she paused.

"'Hard!' That comes nowhere close to describing what I'm going through! Tomorrow morning, I have to be at Liz's office to be interrogated by the detective who stirred up this whole thing. She says he's the same one who questioned you at the hunting lodge. Tell me again what he asked you."

Connor repeated what he remembered.

"To insinuate that you had something to do with Matt's death is so insulting!" Elena replied. "That's the crime! I'm sure this so-called detective will do the same thing with me. And when he does, I'm going to let him have it!"

"Discuss how to respond to the questions with Liz," Connor said. "She'll guide you."

"I'm not going to let him or anyone else bully me! You have to be polite because you're a minister. Look where it got you. What else did he ask you? Oh, and I hope it's okay that I'm recording this call."

"I thought you were going to let me know in advance."

"I was so upset, I forgot."

Elena said something Connor couldn't make out.

"Are you alone?" he asked.

"Of course I am. I can't be all calm and collected like you. Since we're not meeting in person today, will you be available to talk to me tomorrow when I finish?"

Connor looked at the ceiling and offered up a silent plea for help. "Unless I'm on another call or meeting with someone. If so, leave a message with Michelle, and I'll call you back."

As soon as he finished with Elena, Connor started returning calls to members of the church who wanted to ask about the newspaper article. Most people weren't contacting him for a detailed statement about his activities. They simply wanted reassurance that, as their minister, he was doing what he should, and there was nothing to worry about.

"I'm going to do everything I can to assist the sheriff's department in their investigation," he told one elderly lady. "If they want to talk to me again, I'll be glad to do so."

"Oh, so you're trying to help them."

"Yes, ma'am."

"That makes me feel so much better."

Connor returned ten other phone calls, six positive, four less so. People were understandably troubled by the "person of interest" statement, and Connor's effort to reassure them that he wanted to help the police wasn't going to be universally accepted.

"I believe in giving someone the benefit of the doubt, but you have to keep your nose cleaner than anyone else," one man said.

Connor glanced at the box of tissues he kept in his office in case someone cried during a counseling session.

"You're right," he said. "Thanks for the reminder."

On the way home, Connor didn't dwell on his phone calls. He thought about Liz and the confusing conversation with her. He took a quick turn toward her apartment and soon after rang the bell.

"Come in," Liz said, a look of surprise on her face.

"I should have texted or called."

"No, it's okay. Have you eaten supper?"

"I'm not here to barge in—"

"You did, but I'm glad to see you."

Connor followed Liz into the small kitchen. There was a metal bowl on the counter with the makings of a salad beside it. She motioned for Connor to sit at the table. There was only one chair.

"I'm throwing together a salad. Would you like some grilled chicken on top?"

"Chicken would be great."

Connor glanced around. The apartment was neat and un-cluttered.

"I felt trapped earlier when we talked, and it's been bothering me ever since," Liz said as she cut up a tomato. "Our firm represents the newspaper, so there are aspects of the investigation I can't discuss because they were shared in confidence with my boss by the publisher."

Connor felt a knot in the pit of his stomach. "I've not done anything wrong," he said.

"And I believe you. This is going to blow over and not become a big deal."

Liz's simple statement had more impact on Connor than anything he'd heard from members of the congregation. He leaned back in the chair and watched as she continued preparing the salad.

"Okay, no more discussion about that topic," he said. "Would you like to go on a hike with me? I was thinking about Saturday?"

Liz lowered her knife to the counter and turned around. "Yes, I would."

―――――――――

"Bring a chair from the living room," she said after agreeing to join him for a hike. "The wooden one in the corner will be fine."

"With the cushion on the seat?" Connor asked a moment later. "Is it an antique?"

"Only old. One of my aunts stitched the birds on the cushion."

"I don't want to sit in it. What if I drop a piece of salad?"

"I'll risk it."

Liz placed two bowls on the table and shook the bottle of dressing. "It's homemade," she said. "A mixture of spice and sweet."

Connor generously doused his salad with dressing. Liz never prayed before she ate, but with Connor present, a prayer seemed to be in order. She thought about asking him but that would be cowardly. She folded her hands in front of her and closed her eyes.

"God, thank you for this food. Amen," she said.

"I like that," Connor said. "Direct and to the point."

"Eat." Liz pointed her fork at him. "You're a minister, but you can only critique the salad, not the prayer."

Connor took a bite. "Delicious," he said.

"What do you like to fix for supper?" Liz asked.

Connor told her about his garden.

"More like Wendell Berry every day," Liz replied.

"Maybe." Connor grinned. "Let me tell you about some options for our hike."

While they ate, he described several trails in the surrounding hills and mountains.

"You've been to all these places?" Liz asked.

"Multiple times."

"Always alone?"

"Mostly."

"I like the idea of a waterfall, even if it's not huge."

"That narrows it down."

Connor told her about two destinations. Both sounded good to Liz. He finished one bowl of salad and ate another.

"I don't have any dessert," she said.

"That salad was plenty for me. Thanks again for opening the door and inviting me in."

Liz smiled. "You're welcome."

Cleanup consisted of putting the bowls and utensils in the dishwasher. Connor helped.

"Do you have a busy day tomorrow?" he asked as he dried his hands on a towel.

"Yes."

"Elena told me Detective Norman is going to question her at your office."

"That's the plan."

"I told her to follow your advice."

"I hope she heard you."

After Connor left, Liz sat on the sofa in the living room and propped her feet up on a coffee table. Throughout the meal, she wasn't thinking about trails and waterfalls but what might be printed in the newspaper. Connor's interaction with Elena, even if entirely professional on his part, was a ticking bomb. But Liz didn't know how to bring it up or what exactly to say if she did. So she kept silent.

The following morning, Liz arrived early at the office to continue getting ready for the interview that was scheduled for 10:00 a.m. Elena was supposed to arrive at 9:00 a.m. At 9:15 a.m., Liz buzzed Becky.

"No word from Elena Thompson?" Liz asked. "She was supposed to be here fifteen minutes ago."

"Do you want me to call her?"

"I'll do it."

Liz called Elena's cell number and left a message. There was no answer at the home number either. Getting nervous, Liz left her office, went to Jessica's desk, and told her what was going on.

"Sometimes you have to tell clients to come a lot earlier than you need them because they're likely going to be late."

"I did that, and Elena has always been prompt to her appointments."

"But she wasn't going to be questioned by a detective from the sheriff's department."

"Yeah, I should have thought about that."

Jessica glanced past Liz and spoke in a softer voice. "I'm sure you read the article in the newspaper about Matt Thompson's death. I didn't like the way they made it sound like Connor Grantham may have something to do with it. Calling him a 'person of interest.' I know they're trying to sell a few more copies of that fire-starter of a paper, but it hit me the wrong way."

"Me too," Liz replied. "Even a false insinuation could ruin his career."

Before Jessica responded, Harold appeared. "Elena Thompson is in the reception area. You need to prep her. Take her into the main conference room. I'll delay the detective and then join you."

"You're going to sit in?" Liz asked in surprise.

"I think I should. Are you okay with that?"

"Yes, sir."

Elena was impeccably dressed. Liz took her to the conference room.

"Am I overdressed?" Elena asked.

"No, you're fine," Liz replied. "There are some things we need to go over before the detective arrives."

Liz moved as rapidly as she dared through her notes, omitting most of the places where she'd planned on conducting a role-play with Elena.

"Are you okay if Mr. Pollard sits in on the interview?" she asked.

"Yes, so long as you're here too."

Liz was less than halfway through the prep work when Jessica interrupted them.

"Detective Norman is here," she said.

"Let Harold know. He's going to stall him until I finish with Elena."

"Oh, I'm ready," Elena said confidently. "I want to get this over with as soon as possible."

"But there are still some things we need to—"

Elena turned to Jessica. "Tell Mr. Pollard what I said. I expect him to bring in the detective within the next five minutes. Will you do that?"

"Yes," Jessica said with an eye-rolling glance at Liz before she left.

"I know you're trying to do your job, but there's no need to pretend I'm auditioning for a part in a fifth-grade play," Elena said.

"There will be questions about you and Connor Grantham," Liz responded quickly.

"He's a minister who provided valuable marriage counseling to Matt and me. That's it."

"The detective may come at the topic from different angles."

"And he'll get the same answer. I blew up yesterday when Connor and I talked about the snarky article in the newspaper, but I've had a chance to calm down and process the situation. Don't worry about me."

There was a brisk knock on the door. Harold, Detective Norman, and a young man in his late twenties with light brown hair and wearing a gray suit entered.

Harold handled the introductions. "This is Agent Chris Flannery with the GBI," he said.

Agent Flannery made direct eye contact with Liz when he shook her hand. She caught the hint of a smile that came across as a smirk.

"I'm primarily here to observe," Flannery said.

They all took a seat at the table. Norman took out the same recording device Liz saw when the detective came to Burnt Pine Tree. He faced Elena, who was sitting with her back ramrod-straight in a chair directly across the table from him.

"Mrs. Thompson, are you ready to proceed?"

"Yes," she said in a confident voice.

For the next forty-five minutes, Liz listened in amazement to Elena's performance. The client was poised and concise. She cried briefly when talking about her time at the hospital and the hope that Matt might pull through surgery. She was candid about their need for marital counseling and praised Connor for his assistance, particularly his positive influence on Matt. As promised, Elena kept her answers brief.

"Reverend Grantham always treated me with respect and

constantly reminded both Matt and me that he was there to help our marriage. Everything we did individually with him and as a couple had the same goal."

"Did you ever meet with Reverend Grantham alone?"

"On several occasions at the church, but only with the door to his office open and his administrative assistant close by. I met with him briefly once at the Sunnyside Coffee Shop to give him some homework he'd assigned for an upcoming session with Matt."

At that point, Agent Flannery spoke. "Detective Norman, I'll take over now."

Norman turned toward the GBI agent. "This is my interview," he said.

"And your part is over. Check with the sheriff if you doubt me. I believe he'll inform you that he's received instructions from Atlanta authorizing me to proceed as I choose."

A scowl on his face, Norman left the room. Liz jumped slightly as the detective slammed the door behind him. Unperturbed, Agent Flannery took a tablet from a thin briefcase and placed another recording device on the table.

"Mrs. Thompson, this has been running the whole time so there's no need for me to cover anything already discussed."

"Okay," Elena replied cautiously.

Agent Flannery went immediately into a long list of questions about Matt and Elena's financial situation. To Liz, they seemed overly technical. Flannery either had a degree in accounting or someone had prepped him for the session. Elena began to get flustered. Liz glanced at Harold, wondering if he was going to object, but her boss remained impassive and silent. When the agent went through the life insurance policies, Liz held her breath. Elena told what she knew, and Flannery didn't mention anything about a policy payable to Daughbert Technology. After more than an hour passed, Flannery leaned back in his chair and closed his eyes. Elena glanced at Liz, who shrugged.

Flannery opened his eyes, then launched into a second round of questions about Elena and Connor's relationship. Some of the questions were repetitive, but an emphasis on their interaction at the hospital after the shooting was new.

"There wasn't much talk between us at the hospital," Elena replied. "One of the nurses told me Reverend Grantham spent most of his time in the chapel praying. When I found out Matt passed away, Reverend Grantham was there to comfort me."

"What did that consist of?"

Elena took a tissue from her purse and touched her eyes. "Being with me while I cried."

"Did he embrace you?"

"He held me briefly when he first arrived. I was on the verge of collapsing."

Flannery checked his tablet. "Mrs. Thompson, if someone wanted to harm your husband, who do you think it might be?"

"I don't know anyone who would want to hurt or kill him."

"He never mentioned receiving any threats?"

"No."

"Did he indicate that anyone at Daughbert Technology was upset with him?"

"Only about the sale of the company. There was a difference of opinion between Matt and Winston Boone, one of the other owners."

"When did you become aware of the life insurance policy the company took out on your husband's life less than two months before his death?"

Elena glanced at Liz before answering. Liz felt the blood drain from her face.

"I have no idea what you're talking about," Elena replied.

"Are you sure about that?"

"Yes."

"No more questions."

CHAPTER 21

THE INCREASING ONSLAUGHT OF PHONE CALLS AND emails Connor received about the article in the newspaper was wearing him down. His initial perspective about what people were interested in hearing hadn't panned out. He received an email that the church's board of directors was scheduling an emergency meeting.

"This is out of control," Connor said to Michelle when he gave her the news.

"What are Reg Bullock and Jim Morgan saying? They're cochairmen of the board."

"They were copied on the email setting the meeting, but I've not heard from either one of them."

"They've been your strongest supporters among the leaders. Do you think you should call them?"

"That's probably a good suggestion." Connor sighed. "But I've wondered if Reg and Jim have stayed silent because they're against me too. Neither one of them objected to the special meeting."

The light on Michelle's phone lit up, and she answered. "I'll put you through," she replied after listening for a moment.

"It's Reg," she said. "I assume you want to talk to him."

"Yes."

Connor went into his office and closed the door. Taking a deep breath, he picked up the phone.

"How are you holding up?" Reg asked.

"It's worse than I thought it would be," Connor replied. "The first calls were running fifty-fifty between attacking and defending. But it's been ninety percent negative this morning. I thought that I had a bigger bank of trust built up with the congregation. Did you receive the email I sent out late yesterday? I hoped it would help, but it seems to have stirred up more controversy."

"I thought it was excellent. I've been on the phone all morning trying to settle people down."

"Thanks. What about Jim? I've not heard from him."

"He's having a heart catheterization."

"I didn't know anything about it. I would have checked on him."

"It came up suddenly. Peggy left me a message about an hour ago. I don't think they wanted to bother you."

"They should know I'd want to help."

"Send him a text as soon as we hang up. Depending on what they find, they'll either send him home or keep him overnight. If it's serious, they'll transport him to Atlanta."

"Okay."

Reg coughed and cleared his throat. "I waited to call until I could find out more about the newspaper article. My wife's nephew works in advertising, but he knows what's going on. He says they have a copy of the video you took on your phone."

"They must have gotten it from Detective Norman," Connor replied. "That's wrong."

"And they're reviewing surveillance footage from trail cams near the lodge."

"There aren't any videos with me in them on Saturday unless I triggered a camera in the area I passed through. I thought Andy checked the trail cam footage and didn't see anything."

"He did."

"Whatever they have, I want to see it," Connor said firmly. "Can you make that happen?"

"I'm not sure what the GBI demanded."

Connor thought for a moment. "Do you think the newspaper is going to claim I was illegally in the area around the time of Matt's accident?"

"Based on what Andy's telling me, I think the chances of that are high, even though he told the GBI and the newspaper reporter that we didn't care about it."

Connor felt like he'd been punched in the stomach.

"I'm not sure what to say or suggest," Reg continued. "It will be a couple of days before another edition of the paper is printed. But we have the church board meeting tonight."

"Please don't say anything about what Andy told you," Connor said. "We need time to find out more and don't know what the reporter is going to write. Anything vague is just going to fuel speculation."

"Agreed." Reg paused. "Do you think you should consult with a lawyer?"

"If I do, some people will assume I'm guilty. I've done nothing wrong and haven't been accused of anything, not even trespassing!"

"Just a thought."

"I know you're trying to help. Do you know the DA? What's his name? Nelson?"

"Tom Nelson. I don't have any connection to him, but I believe Jim was on his election committee. I gave money to Nelson's opponent so I'm not the one to communicate with him."

Liz, Elena, and Harold remained in the conference room after Agent Flannery left. Liz apprehensively told Elena about the life insurance policy payable to the Daughbert Technology Trust.

The client furrowed her brow as she listened. "When will you find out the details about this new insurance policy?" she asked.

"I'm following up on it," Liz replied. "Hopefully, we'll receive what we want voluntarily."

"I'm not sure you can trust Neil Peterson," Elena said. "Matt said he was slippery. Why didn't you mention this before?"

Harold spoke before Liz could. "That was my decision," he said. "We want to give you accurate information, not speculate."

"But I like to be kept up-to-date."

"And that's what we'll do," Harold continued. "Let us focus on what needs to be done and how to make it happen. Leave the investigation up to us. If anxiety creeps into your mind, tell yourself that's why you hired our law firm. I often tell clients our job is to worry. Your job is to roll your fears and concerns onto our shoulders."

"I'll try to do that," Elena said slowly.

Harold stood, signaling the end of the meeting.

Elena remained seated. "One other thing. I'm really concerned about Connor Grantham and the nasty things they said about him in the newspaper," she said. "His name is being dragged through the mud for helping Matt and me."

"Connor has been talking to me about it," Liz said.

"Has he hired you to represent him?" Elena asked.

"No."

Elena was silent for a moment. "If he does, I'm okay with it. I don't want him to suffer because of me."

Liz escorted Elena from the conference room, then joined Harold in his office.

"Overall, that went well," Liz said, plopping down in a chair opposite Harold's desk.

"I have two areas of concern," Harold replied.

"What are they?"

"Whether we'll get what we need voluntarily from Matt's company, and the possibility of a conflict of interest between Elena and the minister if he hires us."

"What sort of conflict?"

"We don't know what may happen down the road, but if a problem surfaces, Elena takes precedence. Agreed?"

"Yes, sir."

―――――――――

Connor and Reg lingered at the church after the meeting with the board ended. The process had been painful for Connor, but Reg did a skillful job. Instead of jumping in immediately to defend Connor, the businessman let people vent their negativity about the situation, then gently maneuvered everyone in the room to a place where they were willing to wait and see how things developed. Connor would have preferred an unequivocal vote of confidence in his integrity, but that wasn't possible.

"Thanks, Reg," Connor said. "You handled that much better than I could have."

"I've suffered through plenty of contentious board meetings over the years. A few nuggets of knowledge about how to handle situations have made their way into my brain. The most challenging scenarios are nonprofit organizations like the church, a civic group, or a homeowner's association. It's tough dealing with board members who don't have to worry about repercussions if they revert to third-grade interpersonal skills."

Connor shrugged. "I'll not identify who acted most like a third grader tonight."

"You don't need to. But all we got was a temporary reprieve. What comes out in the newspaper and through the gossip channels is going to dictate the narrative moving forward. That's what's frustrating. We can't control the discussion. We're forced to respond."

"Yeah. I've never been in a situation anything like this," Connor said as he locked the side entrance to the church. They walked across the parking lot. "Is it too late to call Peggy and check on Jim?"

"Go ahead. I'm sure they'd like to hear from you again."

―――――

It was Thursday afternoon. After four attempts over two days Liz finally reached Neil Peterson. She didn't have the Daughbert Technology employee's cell phone number and was reluctant to leave voice mails because she didn't want anyone else at the company to know she'd called.

"Do you have time to talk?" Liz asked.

"Yes, but only for a few minutes."

"I'll be brief. When do you think you'll be able to send the documents we requested, and can you include specific information about the insurance on Matt Thompson's life payable to the Daughbert Technology Trust?"

"It's going to be at least a couple of weeks before you receive any documents. The profit and loss statements are going to be a shock to your client and confirm what I told you the other day.

The company was in dire straits financially with serious cash-flow problems. They're still trying to attract a buyer, but every day makes that tougher."

Peterson sounded like he was telling the truth, but Liz was skeptical. "Please expedite delivery of the information if you can. I'm sure we'll hire a firm to perform a review or conduct an audit. What about my second question?"

"Hold on, I'm going to close the door of my office."

While she waited, Liz tapped her index finger against her desk.

"I've read the trust documents," Peterson said when he was back on the line. "I'm not a lawyer, but I think if either Matt or Winston died, the proceeds of the policy would be paid to the survivor individually."

"None of the money went to the company?" Liz asked in surprise.

"Not the way I read it."

"Or the family members of the person who died?"

"No, it was set up to compensate them for loss suffered if one of them couldn't contribute to the success of the company."

"How soon can you send the trust agreement to me? Do you have to wait on your company lawyers to give you the okay?"

"Yes. I'm taking a big risk talking to you at all. I know the arrangement I've described won't sound fair to Matt's wife."

"Yes, she's going to be very upset. Did Matt sign the documents setting up the trust?"

"Yes. Both he and Winston are listed as trustees."

"Whose idea was it to do this?"

"I don't know for sure, but my guess would be Winston. He's always been the one who ran the internal affairs of the company. Matt made it grow. Without Matt, there wouldn't be a Daughbert Technology."

"He was that important?"

"In my opinion, yes."

"Is there anything else you can tell me?"

"My cell phone number. Use it in the future. Don't call me at the company."

"Of course, thanks."

After she hung up, Liz wanted to update Harold, but the senior partner had left the office to play golf.

She went to Jessica's desk. "Should I call him on the golf course?" Liz asked.

"You can try, but Harold hates being interrupted when he's playing golf."

"I'll wait," Liz decided and returned to her desk.

A couple of minutes later, Becky buzzed her. "Elena Thompson called," the receptionist said. "She wants you to come to her house."

"Why?"

"She hadn't heard from you since yesterday and wants an update. She said she was still in her pajamas and didn't feel like getting dressed and driving to the office."

"I can give her an update over the phone."

"She told me she expects you to show up when she needs you. Text her when you're at the front door."

Liz's calendar was clear for the rest of the day.

"Okay," she said grudgingly.

———

Liz checked her appearance in the sun-visor mirror. Elena might be lounging in her pajamas, but Liz wanted to look professional. She dreaded breaking the news she'd received from Neil Peterson.

It was an unseasonably warm, sunny afternoon. Liz took out her phone and sent Elena a text letting her know she'd arrived. A few seconds later, a message came back:

Hozmile nkleim

Liz stared at her phone and then typed a reply:

It's Liz.

This time, the response from Elena's phone was shorter:

Zimen

Liz didn't want to trigger the burglar alarm, but she was worried. She tried the door. It was unlocked.

Going inside, she quickly looked around. It was quiet in the foyer.

"Elena," she said tentatively.

Liz walked from the foyer into the den and to the kitchen. The refrigerator door was open. Liz closed it. Several glasses and plates were in the sink. The remains of a grapefruit lay on the counter. Three empty wine bottles were in the trash bin.

"Elena!" she called out. "Where are you?"

Walking rapidly, Liz went into every room on the ground floor of the house. There was no sign of Elena. She checked the three-car garage. Elena's blue convertible was there along with a couple of other cars. Liz returned to the foyer. She'd never been upstairs. Ascending the steps, she continued to call out for Elena without receiving a response. The first room to the right at the top of the staircase was a guest bedroom. Beyond that was an upstairs study. There were two other bedrooms filled with expensive furniture on the left. At the end of the hall was a room with the door closed. As she approached it, Liz's heart was beating faster. She knocked on the oversized door. No answer. Turning the knob, she opened the door and peeked inside. It was the master bedroom. The room had a vaulted ceiling and large plate glass windows that offered a view of the mountains. Still no sign of Elena.

"Elena," Liz said in a softer voice.

Moving past the unmade bed, Liz approached a closed door that she suspected was to either the master bath or a large walk-in closet. She had to step over clothes that were strewn about. She opened the door. It was the bathroom. Elena was on the floor in front of the tub. Dressed in light blue pajamas, she was lying on her stomach at an odd angle with her right arm splayed to the side. There was a cell phone on an ivory-colored rug. Next to the phone was a medicine bottle.

Liz gasped. Not trained in CPR, she was afraid to touch the body. She took out her phone and with trembling fingers called 911.

CHAPTER 22

ONCE AGAIN, CONNOR FOUND HIMSELF SITTING IN THE hospital chapel while he waited for an announcement of life or death. Shifting his weight on the short pew in the claustrophobic room, he tried to pray. He checked the time on his phone but knew he wasn't going to leave until he found out if Elena had ingested a lethal dose of some kind of drug. The door to the chapel opened. Liz entered.

"One of the nurses said I'd find you here," she said. "I was finally able to reach Elena's sister. She's on her way and should be here within a few hours. Any word from the doctors?"

"She's alive. They can't really tell me anything specific. I don't know if she's conscious, in a coma, or in between."

Liz sat on the pew.

"I'm sure they're doing everything they can," Connor continued. "Did Elena leave a note? I forgot to ask you earlier."

"I didn't see one in the bathroom or look around the house. Once I found her, I was in a panic. I didn't handle the situation very well."

"You dialed 911, which was the right thing to do. I've spent most of my time since I arrived wondering what I could have done to help her. Did she ever talk to you about suicide?"

"She mentioned taking too many sleeping pills once but quickly told me she wouldn't really consider doing something like that."

They sat in silence for a few moments. Connor ran his fingers through his hair.

"Elena has always come across as a fighter, not a quitter," Liz said. "You've been there for her as much as you could. Don't beat yourself up."

The door opened and a muscular young man wearing hospital scrubs entered. "Reverend Grantham?"

Connor quickly stood. "Yes."

"Mrs. Thompson is awake and would like to see you. She told me you'd probably be here."

Connor glanced at Liz. "Would you like to go with me?" he asked.

Liz shook her head. "I'll wait. If she wants to talk to me after you finish, let me know."

Connor and the orderly took the elevator and entered a hospital corridor through a locked gate.

"Is she in the ICU?" he asked.

"No, she's on the psych floor."

They walked down a cheerily decorated hallway. Elena's room was at the end on the right. The man tapped lightly on the door. Connor recognized the female voice that responded.

"Come in," she said.

Elena was sitting up in bed with a white sheet pulled up to her chin. Without makeup her eyes seemed to disappear into her face.

"I look terrible," she said.

"You're alive," Connor replied. "That's what counts."

Tears appeared and ran down Elena's cheeks. She lowered the sheet enough to reach out and pluck a tissue from a box on the nightstand beside the bed. She was wearing a hospital-issue gown.

"I didn't try to kill myself," she said, sniffling. "You believe me, don't you?"

Connor reached out and squeezed her hand, then released it.

"If I wanted to die, I would have succeeded," Elena said, speaking more rapidly. "The doctor claims I took an overdose of opioids, but I've never filled a prescription for something that strong. I had a few extra bottles of painkillers lying around the house from a year ago when I sprained my ankle in a fall on the ice. I took a couple of them earlier today because they help numb all kinds of pain. The whole situation since Matt died has gotten to be more than I can—" Elena stopped and more tears appeared.

Connor pulled a chair close to the side of the bed and sat down. "You don't have to explain anything to me," he said. "I'm here to let you know there are people who care about you."

"Sometimes, it's hard to believe that's true," Elena managed.

"It is. Liz is outside in the chapel."

"Yes," Elena said, nodding between sniffles. "She's been more than a lawyer to me. They said she's the one who found me. Thank God I asked her to come to the house for our appointment." Elena closed her eyes for a moment.

Connor waited until she opened them before speaking. "Is there anything you want me to do for you?" he asked.

"I don't want to be left alone." Elena blew her nose on a tissue. "That's the hardest part of all this. Matt would take off for Atlanta and be gone for days at a time, but I always knew he'd eventually come back. Now, the house feels more like a prison than a home."

"Your sister is on her way. Liz was able to reach her."

"Did she tell Tracy that I overdosed?" Elena asked sharply.

"I'm not sure what she said."

"Make sure you don't mention the word 'overdose' to

anyone because it's not true," Elena continued in a stronger voice. "Promise?"

"Yes."

Elena seemed to relax a little bit. They sat in silence as the minutes passed. Connor glanced around the room. There was nothing to indicate it wasn't a regular hospital room. The only difference he'd seen was the locked door upon entry to the floor. But the stigma of an admission to the psychiatric unit, even if warranted by a legitimate medical condition, was itself a wound.

Despite Elena's words, Connor believed she'd overdosed. Even her plea that she'd not tried to end her life was a cry for help. Lying motionless in the bed, Elena looked weak and fragile. Connor felt compassion for her well up inside him. Heartache and loss is an inescapable part of life, but the woman in the bed had been hit with a double portion. Connor silently prayed that she'd find peace and receive healing in the invisible places.

"The doctor claims they found a high concentration of opioids in my blood and asked if I'd ever taken anything with fentanyl in it, but that's impossible," Elena suddenly said. "I've never filled a prescription for anything that powerful."

"I know," Connor replied softly. "You told me a few moments ago."

"I did?" Elena gave him a confused look.

"You mentioned having leftover pain pills prescribed after you fell on the ice."

"Yeah, yeah," Elena said. "That's right. Matt and I were skiing at Vail, and I fell outside a restaurant. You can check the bottle. The pharmacy was in Colorado."

Elena closed her eyes again. She seemed to be asleep. Connor considered trying to slip quietly from the room.

"Don't leave," Elena said, opening her eyes. "What are you going to tell people when they ask what happened to me?"

"I don't have to say anything."

"No, that wouldn't work."

"What do you want me to say?"

Elena was quiet for a moment. "Am I on the mental floor? I saw a man strapped to his bed when they brought me here. He was awake and yelling."

"Yes, this is the psych ward," Connor said and braced himself for Elena's reaction.

"That helps," she said calmly. "Tell people I had an emotional breakdown because of Matt's death. That makes sense."

"I'll be more comfortable just mentioning that you'll appreciate prayers for a quick recovery."

"But I'm not sick."

"Would you like to see Liz?" he asked again.

Elena glanced past Connor toward the door. "Only if I can be sure no one is listening to our conversation," she whispered. "Go quietly to the door and jerk it open to see if anyone is there trying to eavesdrop."

"Elena—" Connor began.

"Just do it!" she said in a more intense whisper.

Reluctantly, Connor made his way to the door. He didn't jerk it open, but he pulled it back quickly. He looked over his shoulder at Elena.

"No one is there," he said.

"Okay," she replied in a slightly more normal tone of voice. "Ask Liz to come back."

"You'll need to let one of the nurses or an orderly know that you want to see her."

"Find Robert, the one who brought you, and send him in. He'll do what I want."

The orderly was lounging around at the nurse's station. He accompanied Connor to the chapel. Liz wasn't there. Connor checked his phone. There was a text from her telling him that she'd left the hospital and would try to see Elena the following morning. Connor turned to the orderly.

"Please let Mrs. Thompson know that Liz Acosta will visit her tomorrow morning."

———————

Feeling cramped in the chapel, Liz returned to the office. As she pulled into the parking lot, she received a text from Neil Peterson:

Sent the trust documents to your office email.

She found the email. Attached was a document labeled "Daughbert Technology Trust." Liz read it quickly. The language confirmed everything Peterson had previously told her about the life insurance policies purchased by the trust and payable to either Matt or Winston Boone, not the company or their families.

Liz closed the file. This wasn't something she wanted to discuss with Elena while her client was recovering from a drug overdose. Her cell phone lit up. It was Connor.

"Elena is on the psychiatric floor," he said.

"That makes sense," Liz replied. "Drug overdose, suicide attempt."

"Don't mention either one of those."

"Why?"

Liz listened to Connor's summary of his discussion with Elena.

"Did you tell Tracy that Elena overdosed?" Connor asked.

"No, just that she was unconscious with a pill bottle beside her. She can draw her own conclusion."

"Good. Elena wants to control the narrative about what happened. She's really vulnerable."

"I'm not going to say anything to anybody except my boss. He needs to know as part of our representation."

"Are you going to visit Elena in the morning?"

"Yes."

"Talking with her may be challenging."

"That's nothing new."

The following morning, Liz was awakened at a few minutes after six by her cell phone vibrating on her nightstand. Rolling over, she grabbed it. It was Elena.

"You need to get me out of here!" her client demanded as soon as Liz answered.

Liz sat up in the bed. "I'm sure they have a protocol to follow to make sure you're stable before releasing you," she said. "Have you talked to the doctor?"

"Yes! That's why I'm calling you. She just told me I'm going to have to stay at least three days. That's ridiculous!"

"I'm not sure what the law says about this," Liz replied slowly. "How are you feeling?"

"Fine! That's why it makes no sense to keep me against my will. Did you talk to Connor?"

"Yes, he called last night."

"What did he say?"

"Not a lot. We're both glad you're okay. That was scary."

"Did he say I tried to kill myself by overdosing on fentanyl?"

"No."

"I woke up to a bunch of texts from Tracy. She got into town in the middle of the night and wants to see me. I just want to get out."

"Where is Tracy staying? At your house?"

"No, a hotel." Elena paused. "My house is a wreck, and Tracy always judges me when it's messy."

"It didn't seem that bad to me when I was there yesterday. There were a few dirty dishes in the sink."

"Yes, and the upstairs bedroom where she sleeps is a mess. I haven't washed the sheets since she was here for the funeral."

"I'm sure Tracy will understand that under the circumstances you couldn't—"

"Will you go and straighten up before I invite her to spend the night? Then, do whatever it takes to get me out of here!"

Liz was struggling with Elena's irrational anxiety about the condition of her home. Now her client was asking her to provide maid services in addition to legal representation.

"Don't you have a cleaning company?"

"Yes, but I don't trust them to be in the house unless I'm there too."

Liz shook her head at this new facet of Elena's growing paranoia.

"I'll let you in remotely with my phone once you're there and text you the things to do," Elena continued, speaking rapidly. "How soon will you be there? It needs to be early, because once you finish, I want you to be at the courthouse when it opens so you can get an order from a judge forcing them to let me leave the hospital."

Liz took a deep breath. "I'll work on getting you out, but I'm not going over to your house."

Elena was silent for a moment. Liz braced for an explosion. She had to draw the line somewhere.

"Connor will do it," Elena said. "Just get me out of here."

Later, as her coffee brewed, Liz called Connor. "Did I wake you?" she asked.

"No, I've already been on the phone with Elena."

"Me too. Did she ask you to go over to her house?"

"Yes."

"Did you agree to do it?"

"Yes, just to straighten a few things up before Tracy gets there. I don't blame you for turning her down, and I may regret agreeing to go over there, but Elena has me on edge. If I don't go along with her request, I'm afraid she may turn on me and accuse me of something crazy. You know how your mind can go off on wild tangents in the middle of the night. I spent a couple of hours worrying about what she might say about me."

"You can't let Elena manipulate you like this."

"There's no harm in checking on her house."

Hearing Connor, Liz almost wished she'd agreed to Elena's demand. But there was no point in criticizing him. The minister was under a lot of pressure.

"You're a full-service pastor," Liz said in a lighter tone of voice. "Call me later."

CHAPTER 23

CONNOR ARRIVED AT ELENA'S HOUSE. THE SUN WAS up, and the early rays of diffused light shone across the yard onto the wood-and-stone exterior. Daylight banished some of the dark, ominous thoughts that had tormented him the previous night. The large residence had an empty look to it. Connor grew up in a big house in Atlanta, but two people didn't need so much space. He texted Elena that he'd arrived, and she unlocked the front door remotely.

Once inside, he went into the kitchen. Elena had asked him to put the dirty dishes in the washer and take out the garbage. The kitchen was clean, and there was no trash in the container. He suspected the cleaning service had already come. He went upstairs to the bedroom where Elena wanted Tracy to stay. The bed was unmade and the sheets were partially on the floor. Connor made the bed, then put fresh towels in the connected bath. When he turned to leave the bathroom, Connor saw two small pills on the corner of a rug on the floor. He leaned over and picked them up. One was a bluish gray with an "M" on the front and a "30" on the back. The other was gray without any identifiable markings.

Connor took a photo of the first pill and opened an app that analyzed medications by appearance. It was immediately identified as a 30 mg oxycodone tablet. He took a photo of the second pill and repeated the process. It took the app longer to respond. When he saw the result, Connor shook his head. It was most likely illegally manufactured fentanyl.

Not wanting to leave the pills in the guest bathroom, Connor considered throwing them away. Instead, he walked down the hall to the master bedroom. It was also neat and tidy. To the left was the master bath. The large room featured a massive walk-in shower, whirlpool tub, and as many cabinets as Connor had in his entire house. He carefully placed the two small pills on the counter beside one of the sinks.

———————

It was still early when Liz arrived at the office. No one else was there. Her research revealed that it would take two doctors and a mental health worker to designate a patient like Elena for involuntary commitment. Otherwise, she would have to be discharged within forty-eight hours of admission. Liz didn't see anything in the law about the three-day confinement Elena had mentioned earlier. She called Elena's cell phone, but there was no answer. Liz's cell phone vibrated, and Connor's number appeared.

"I'm leaving Elena's house," he said. "The cleaning service had already been there to straighten up the kitchen and her bedroom."

"She was probably confused about that."

"Yeah. But the bed in the guest bedroom needed to be made. When I put towels in the bath, I saw a couple of pills on the rug. One was an oxycodone 30 milligram, and according to an app, the other was bootleg fentanyl."

Liz sat up straighter in her chair. "What did you do with the pills?"

"Put them on the counter in Elena's bathroom."

"Are you going to say anything to her about it?"

"Probably not. What do you think?"

"I'm not sure. My number one job is getting her out of the hospital."

Shortly after the call ended, there was a knock on the door, and Harold entered.

"I thought I'd be the first one to the office today," he said.

"I was on the phone with a client around six this morning," Liz replied.

She told him about the call from Elena.

"At your hourly rate that would have been the most expensive maid service Elena Thompson has ever paid for."

"When I turned her down, she twisted Connor Grantham's arm, and he went over there. He just called and told me he found an oxycodone and street-manufactured fentanyl on the floor of one of the bathrooms."

"What did he do with the pills?" Harold asked sharply.

"Put them on the counter in Elena's bathroom."

"He shouldn't have gone over there," Harold said, shaking his head. "Or touched anything, especially a scheduled narcotic."

"He went because he didn't want to upset Elena and cause her to say something negative about him while he's being scrutinized by the newspaper."

"Trying to avoid one risk may have opened the door to a greater one. If Elena Thompson wants to get Grantham in trouble, all she needs to do is accuse him of planting drugs at her house."

Liz swallowed. "Hopefully, that won't happen."

Connor took the elevator to the psych ward. Depression and anxiety were common maladies in every town, big or small, but during his years in Bryson, he'd never visited a member of the congregation who was receiving inpatient mental health treatment. He stopped at the nurse's station outside the locked doorway and introduced himself to the woman seated behind the counter.

"Is Robert on duty?" he asked.

"No, he works second shift."

"I'm here to see Elena Thompson. I'm Connor Grantham, her pastor."

The woman hit several buttons on her keyboard while she stared at a computer monitor. "Okay, wait here. Someone will escort you to the patient's room."

It was several minutes before the doors opened, and an older man came out. "Reverend Grantham?" he asked.

"Yes." Connor stepped forward.

"Sorry, but we have to monitor what enters the unit. Do you intend on giving anything to the patient?"

"No."

As he followed the orderly, Connor was glad he'd not stuck the pills in his pocket to give Elena later. They neared Elena's room.

"I know where it is," Connor said to the orderly, who didn't reply but continued to accompany him to the room.

"I'll be waiting here by the door," the man said.

Connor knocked.

"Yeah!" Elena called out curtly.

Connor entered. Still wearing a hospital gown, Elena was sitting up in bed with the TV on and the volume turned up loud. She was watching a reality show.

"Hi, Connor," Elena said in a normal tone of voice as she pressed the button to turn off the TV. "I thought it was one of the hospital staff. They've really made me mad this morning. I'm ready to get out, but they want me to see another doctor first. I had no idea it was this easy to keep someone in the hospital against her will."

"Hopefully they'll get it straightened out soon."

"They'd better." Elena pulled the sheet up higher on her chest. "Liz is working on it for me from the legal end. Was anyone screaming when you entered the unit?"

"No."

"It was terrible last night. I had trouble sleeping through the racket. It sounded like they were torturing one of the patients, which wouldn't surprise me after what I've been through."

Connor pulled up a chair and sat beside the bed.

"Did you go by my house?" Elena asked.

"Yes. Are you sure the maid service didn't come?" he asked.

"No. They come on Thursday."

"Yesterday was Thursday."

Elena looked puzzled, "They're supposed to call first."

"Do they have a key?"

"Yeah, but they don't know how to deactivate the alarm system."

"The alarm wasn't on when I arrived."

"How did you get in?"

"You unlocked the door using your phone."

"That's right." Elena shook her head. "The meds they're inject-ing into my IV make me feel loopy. Thanks for straightening up the guest bedroom. I've been staying there some since Matt died."

"I made the bed but didn't change the sheets."

"Tracy won't know the difference."

Connor cleared his throat. "There were a couple of pills on the rug in the guest bathroom. I didn't think you'd want them there when Tracy arrives. I put them on the counter in the master bath."

"What kind of pills? What did they look like?"

"Small and round," Connor answered cryptically.

"Don't be evasive. Be specific."

"I scanned them on my phone. One was oxycodone, the other fentanyl."

Elena was silent for a moment. "I had a few oxycodone in the house, but you're wrong about the fentanyl. I wish you'd brought the pills to me. It's not a good idea to leave medication lying around the house."

"The hospital won't allow a visitor to bring anything to a patient's room."

"The people who run this hospital are crazier than some of the people locked up in here."

The door opened, and a female nurse entered. "Good morning, Mrs. Thompson," she said.

"It won't be good until I'm released from this place."

The nurse ignored Elena's comment and took her vital signs. "Did you eat your breakfast?" she asked.

"I sent it back. No one should have to eat that garbage."

The nurse finished and left.

"That might not be the best way to interact with the staff if you're trying to convince them to let you go home," Connor said.

"It's the truth," Elena said and sniffed. "And doesn't the Bible say that the truth will set you free?"

Liz grabbed her phone as soon as Connor's name popped up.

"Where are you?" she asked.

"Just leaving the hospital."

"How's Elena?"

"Cranky and upset. I ended up telling her about the pills I found. She wished I'd brought them to her at the hospital."

"What?"

"Yeah."

"I wish you'd left them on the rug where you found them, but I'm not going to bring it up again. Elena's main goal is to get out of the hospital. There are technical hoops the doctors have to jump through to keep her as a patient. I suspect what the doctor told her early this morning was just a recommendation rather than a requirement, and Elena took it the wrong way."

Connor stopped at a red light. "Does your boss know whether the newspaper is going to print anything else about Matt's death in today's edition?" he asked. "I've included something about him in my sermon on Sunday, but if new allegations or innuendos surface, that will have to change."

"He's not said anything. Are you still getting calls and emails from people at the church about it?"

"Not as much. Some of my supporters have been urging people not to jump to conclusions."

"Would Bev and Sam Devon be supporters?"

"I hope so. I've not talked to either one of them."

Liz was silent for a moment. "With all that's going on, do you want to call off our hike to the waterfall tomorrow?" she asked. "I'll completely understand."

"No, spending time in the woods is exactly what I need to do. I'd sneak away by myself this afternoon if I didn't have to wait around for the newspaper to come out."

After the call ended, Jessica stuck her head into Liz's office. "Good morning. May I come in to see you?"

"Not if it's bad news."

"Is there any other kind? Elena Thompson is in the hospital on the mental ward after a possible suicide attempt."

"Yes, I'm the one who found her and called the ambulance."

"You did?" Jessica's eyes widened.

Liz told her what happened. "How did you hear about it?" she asked Jessica.

"From a friend who works at the hospital. I'm not going to tell you my friend's name. Anyway, I thought you should be aware that Elena hasn't been certified for involuntary commitment. I remember that being a big deal in a case Harold worked on a few years ago."

Liz leaned forward. "That means she can walk out of the hospital even if it's AMA," she said.

"What's AMA?" Jessica asked.

"Against medical advice. That's a term I learned earlier this morning in my research. Elena needs to know her rights. I'm going to the hospital."

━━━━━━━━

Connor drove to the Hamilton home. Sarah opened the door.

"Sorry to keep dropping by without calling," he said. "But—"

"Come in," Sarah said, stepping to the side. "I'll get Lyle. He's in his shop."

"What's he doing?"

"Woodworking. His latest project is carving custom hiking sticks. There's an outdoor store in Blue Ridge that wants to sell as many as he can make."

"I'd like to see his work."

"Go."

Lyle's shop was in a small building at the rear of their property. The door was propped open. Rascal appeared and barked sharply as Connor approached. The brown dog's bark was deeper than the last time Connor came by the house.

"Quiet!" Lyle commanded. "Down."

Rascal immediately lay at Lyle's feet. His tail wagged against the concrete floor of the compact building.

"He's getting to be a big boy," Connor said as he held his hand down for the dog to sniff.

"Yeah. One thing about being home is that I have time to train him. He's really smart and wants to please. He has some bird dog in him. That behavior has been coming out."

"Sarah says you have a new project."

Lyle reached over to a pile of wooden sticks, picked one up, and handed it to Connor. It was about five feet long with the bark stripped off, exposing the light-colored wood beneath. What caught Connor's attention was the carving on the top of the stick. It was the silhouette of a face that looked familiar.

"Is this Reg Bullock?" Connor asked, turning the stick from side to side.

"Success." Lyle grinned. "I didn't get Reg to pose but used the photo in the church directory."

"Does he know about this?"

"He knows I've been carving faces in some of the sticks, but not that I'm doing one for him."

"Why Reg?"

"He's quiet about everything, but he's really helped us out since my injury. I want to do something for him."

"He's going to love it. There's only one problem."

"What's that?"

"It's a work of art, not something he can use when he goes for a walk in the woods. Reg is going to display it on the wall of his trophy room."

"That's up to him."

Connor leaned against one of the supporting beams for the shed. "I've got the information for our trip to shoot clays with Josh," he said. "Two dates are possibilities."

Lyle checked the calendar on his phone. "Either one of those works for me," he said. "Josh will be excited."

"How's Sarah doing?"

"She had a follow-up visit with the oncologist after they completed all the tests. They're mapping out a program of chemotherapy and radiation followed by surgery. It's depressing to me, but her faith is strong. She's praying that she'll be around for Josh's wedding."

"Could you take a break so the three of us could pray together?"

They returned to the house. Lyle rolled his wheelchair across the yard as fast as Connor walked. He barely slowed down as he ascended the ramp to the back deck. They entered the kitchen.

"Fresh coffee," Sarah said. "How do you want it?"

"Black," Connor replied.

"With two sugars for me," Lyle said.

"I already know that," Sarah answered with a slight smile.

They sat at a small round table at one end of the kitchen.

"Lyle told me about your visit to the doctor, and the recommended treatment," Connor said. "And your prayer that you'll be alive to see Josh get married."

"Lyle—" Sarah started.

"I'm glad he told me," Connor cut in. "And I want to pray the same thing."

Connor took a sip of coffee. "But I'm also here for a selfish reason," he said. "I guess you read the article about Matt Thompson's death in the newspaper. The reporter described me as a 'person of interest' in the investigation. It's stirred up trouble for me."

Lyle and Sarah exchanged a look.

"We've been asking the Lord to sort it out," Sarah said.

Connor was about to speak, but Sarah's simple statement stopped him.

"Could you explain what that means to you?" he asked.

Sarah clasped her hands together in front of her on the table. "God knows the end from the beginning, whether the path in between is long or short, complicated or simple, and how everything fits into the destiny and destination he has for each person's life. I learned that prayer from my grandmother. She also taught me not to stop there. It's important to seek the Lord for any specific details that he's willing to provide."

"Has he shown you any details for me?" Connor asked.

"I'm still working on it," Sarah replied.

Connor turned to Lyle. "Can you help me out here?" he asked.

"Maybe she wants to be around for your wedding too."

All three of them burst out laughing. In the midst of deadly serious issues there was still room for humor.

"That will take great faith," Connor said.

Lyle bowed his head. "Father, thank you for Connor. Because he loves you, I pray that you will cause all things to work together for his good according to your purpose for his life. And may he know that no matter what, Sarah and I have his back."

Lyle and Sarah went back and forth for several minutes. Connor kept quiet. It was nice to be free from the expectation to lead the way. The heaviness he'd brought onto the Hamiltons' property lifted. And when there was an opening, he poured his heart out for Sarah and Lyle. They opened their eyes.

"Thank you," Sarah said. "Do you want me to warm up your coffee?"

"No, thanks," Connor said, then paused. "I know it sounds odd, but when you were praying the whole room got hot."

"Lyle, is the heat set too high?" Sarah asked.

"Still on 68 where we always keep it," Lyle replied, turning to Connor. "Saves on the propane bill."

———————

Liz walked through the main entrance to the hospital and stopped at the information desk.

"Which floor is the psych ward?" she asked the older man on duty. "I need to see a patient. It's urgent."

"Four east," the man replied. "Name, please, and I'll need to see your driver's license."

"Elizabeth Acosta. I'm an attorney here to see a client." Liz took out her license and handed it to him.

The man scanned it on a small machine beside his chair. "You'll need this," he said, reaching beneath the counter for an orange peel-off sticker.

"Will this give me access to see one of the patients?" she asked.

"No, but it will keep them from sending you back down here so I can record your name and scan your ID."

Orange sticker prominently displayed above her heart, Liz took the elevator to the fourth floor and approached the station set up outside a set of double doors. A sign announced "Visitor Check-In." There were two people on duty, a younger man and a middle-aged woman.

Liz introduced herself. "I'm the attorney for a patient named Elena Thompson. I'd like to see her immediately."

The woman tapped the keyboard in front of her. "What's the name again?" she asked.

"Elena Thompson."

"Let me check to see if she was transferred to another facility," the woman said.

"Another facility?" Liz asked.

The woman continued to type. "Mrs. Thompson is no longer a patient," she said. "She was discharged a few minutes ago. That's why her status wasn't clear in the system."

"Did she leave AMA?"

"No, her treating physician cleared her. Anything else?"

"Uh, no. Thanks."

As soon as she was in the hallway in front of the elevators, Liz sent Elena a text:

> Came by the hospital to see you. They say you've been discharged. Where are you??

Seconds later a reply appeared:

> In the lobby waiting on Tracy to pick me up and take me home.

Liz pressed the button for the elevator and rapidly tapped her foot against the floor while she waited for it to arrive.

CHAPTER 24

LOOKING SLIGHTLY DISHEVELED AND SITTING IN A wheelchair, Elena was wearing a white blouse and dark slacks. A muscular young man stood behind her. Liz walked over to her.

"How are you?" she asked.

Elena glanced up at the orderly. "Perfect," she said. "Robert is taking great care of me, but he can go now that my sister is here."

"This is your sister?" the orderly asked, eyeing Liz suspiciously.

"Yes," Elena responded before Liz could speak. "I'm adopted, and we don't look anything alike."

With a shrug, Robert handed some papers to Liz. "This includes the date and time for her follow-up appointment with the doctor along with her medication list."

When Robert left, Elena leaned close to Liz. "I have to be careful what I say in front of the prison guards," she whispered.

Elena stood and abandoned the wheelchair. Outside, she took a deep breath of air.

"Freedom," she said with a glance skyward. "Thanks for going along with the sister story. I couldn't stand another second being locked up. Tracy is on her way. I'll let her know we're outside."

They sat on a bench in front of some shrubs.

"What happened this morning?" Liz asked.

"The two doctors responsible for my care disagreed about whether to keep me. I guess it takes more than one doctor to sign off on an involuntary commitment."

"I discovered that when researching whether they could keep you."

"Let's practice."

"Practice what?"

"Your story for Tracy. Tell me what happened when you arrived at my house. Where did you find me?"

"In the bathroom. Do you recall going in there?"

Elena shook her head. "No, the last thing I remember is eating a grapefruit in the kitchen. Next thing, I'm waking up in the ER and hearing them talking about putting me in the psych ward."

Elena pushed her hair back from her face. "I look like a mess, but whatever they pumped into my IV makes me feel good. I may get the prescriptions filled. How do I seem to you?"

"Better."

Elena stared in front of her. "Each day is a struggle."

"Maybe next week we can get together and go over your legal issues," Liz said. "I think you should take it easy for a few days."

"You're probably right." Elena looked away. "Connor claims he found some pills on the floor of the guest bathroom at my house and that one of them was a fentanyl. He's wrong, of course. Why would he do that? I thought I could trust him."

"You can," Liz quickly replied. "Maybe you could get the pill analyzed."

"There's no point in that. I've never filled a prescription for fentanyl and never bought any drugs except at a pharmacy. I don't know what they claim they found in my body at the hospital. I believe I passed out from all the stress I've been under."

Tracy pulled up to the entrance. Getting out of the car, she rushed over to Elena and hugged her.

"I'm so glad to see you," Tracy said between sniffles. "I've been worried to death."

"I'm fine now that I'm out of that hospital," Elena replied as she pulled away. "Let's go home."

———

Liz phoned Connor on her way back to the office. "Elena was discharged from the hospital," she said. "Tracy met us there and took her home. Elena believes she passed out from all the stress she's been under. I'm curious what the lab report on her blood revealed but didn't ask her."

"I'm glad she's with Tracy."

"And we're still on for tomorrow?" Liz asked.

"Yes. Pick you up around eight o'clock? Is that too early?"

"Perfect. That's over two hours later than Elena's phone call this morning."

———

Connor skipped lunch and put the finishing touches on his sermon for Sunday morning. Normally, he didn't ask Michelle to preview what he intended to say, but this week would be different. He'd never had to publicly refute an insinuation of criminal charges against him. He read to her what he'd written about the situation while she sat across from him in his office.

"How does that sound? I know it's short," he said when he'd finished.

"Short is good. The more you say, the more people will start to think there's something to this. I have only one suggestion."

"What's that?"

"Cut the line about being available to talk to anyone if they have additional questions. That encourages people to harass you. Even more than you've already experienced. Of course, I have a selfish motivation. I don't want to answer a bunch of phone calls and listen to people vent to me before they talk to you."

"But I want to communicate that I don't have anything to hide."

"You say that very eloquently when you talk about your duty to the congregation as their pastor and to God. And it's good to remind people you work for the Almighty, not them. You should do that at least twice a year."

A bell chimed signaling someone had entered the door for the church office suite.

"I don't have any appointments on my calendar," Connor said, glancing at his computer monitor.

"It's probably a friend who delivers the newspaper. I asked her to bring one by before she runs her regular route."

Michelle left. Connor looked out the window at the mountains in the distance. The prayer meeting with the Hamiltons had really helped. But he longed for the day when he could enjoy the beauty in the distance without anxiety about the future. It took Michelle longer to return than it should have. Connor suspected she was reading the newspaper to discover what it said about him. He went to her desk. The assistant had the paper opened.

"So far so good," she said without looking up.

Michelle turned to an interior page. "Nothing about you," she said. "It's mostly about Matt Thompson's business."

"Matt's business?"

"Yeah. The reporter talked to an 'anonymous source' who claims Matt's company was in big financial trouble with a lot of disagreement among the owners about what to do in the future. That's why they were meeting at Burnt Pine Tree."

"What would that have to do with Matt's death?"

Michelle closed the newspaper and handed it to Connor. "I don't know. The article asks questions but doesn't give any answers. It's like the reporter leaves everyone hanging until the next installment."

Connor quickly read the article. If Daughbert Technology was in serious financial trouble, that would have been relevant to Matt and Elena's marriage. Connor folded up the newspaper and returned it to Michelle.

"This was good for me but not for Elena," Connor said. "If Matt's business was in bad shape, she won't have the financial stability she expected."

"Unless there's a bunch of life insurance," Michelle replied.

"Yeah. I have no idea."

"I bet you'll hear from Elena about something before you close your eyes tonight."

———————

Contrary to Michelle's prediction, Connor didn't receive a call or text from Elena. The following morning, he prepared for his hike with Liz. There was a chance of rain, but absent the threat of a severe thunderstorm, Connor rarely called off a hike. He had the gear to keep dry and warm in the rain and enjoyed every face the forest showed him. Liz might have a different opinion. He packed waterproof items. Dark clouds were rushing across the sky when he arrived at Liz's apartment. She had a cup of coffee in her hand.

"Good morning," he said.

"Is it?" she replied.

Liz was wearing jeans, a long-sleeved shirt, and socks but no shoes. There was a black ball cap on her head with her dark hair in a ponytail through the back.

"Yeah, the weather is iffy," he replied. "Are you still up for this?"

"I'm not sure."

"I'll get my pack from the car and show you how I prepare for a day like this."

Connor laid everything out on Liz's kitchen table. She picked up the blue rain jacket he'd brought for her. Beside it was a pair of camouflage rain pants.

"The jacket and the pants aren't color coordinated," she said.

"Function over fashion," he replied. "Try them on."

Liz slipped on the jacket, which was big but serviceable. Connor unzipped a pocket behind her neck and put the hood over her head. The hood extended beyond her face and could be secured with a drawstring.

"No rain can get past that," he said. "And you'll put your hands in your pockets."

"Okay, but the pants," Liz said.

"Never worn. I ordered the wrong size and decided not to send them back in case I needed to let someone borrow a pair."

"You like the camo look?"

"Better on you than me."

Liz slipped on the pants that were way too long.

"You could walk through water up to your neck and not get wet," Connor said, stepping back. "Except for one issue."

"My shoes," Liz said.

"Yes."

Liz left him and went into her bedroom. She returned with a pair of brown lace-up boots. She handed them to Connor.

"Will these work?" she asked. "They're water-resistant."

"These are very nice. Have you been holding out on me about your experience as a hiker?"

"Remember, I'm from Florida. It rains a lot there, and I needed something to keep my feet dry in sloppy weather. Those boots have taken me through a couple of hurricanes and several tropical storms."

"So it's a yes for today?" he asked.

"Can you guarantee no lightning?"

"No, but it's not in the forecast."

"Fair enough." Liz nodded. "One more thing. Even though I'm sure the snacks you've brought taste great, I'd like to bring something more for lunch."

Liz opened an insulated sandwich bag on the counter and took out the contents. "I made wraps with dried prosciutto, bacon, and Swiss cheese. There's coleslaw mix in this baggie, and I thought we could use mustard and mayo packets."

Connor smiled in appreciation. "I'd eat that if all we did was drive to the trailhead and stay in the Jeep."

They loaded everything into Connor's vehicle. Liz hoisted herself up into the passenger seat. "Oh, there's Bev and Sam Devon," she said. "We should say hi to them."

Connor drove over to the couple and lowered his window.

"Where are you going?" Bev asked with a smile.

"Holly Creek Falls," Connor replied.

"It's a beautiful morning," Bev said.

Sam eyed his wife. "You just told me I couldn't go with Fred to look over that piece of property he's thinking about buying because I might get struck by lightning."

"Oh, Connor and Liz will be fine," Bev said with a nervous laugh.

"It's supposed to clear up later," Connor said.

"Bev and I don't want to hold you for a marriage counseling session," Sam said. "After forty-eight years, we'll work it out."

"Have fun!" Bev said.

Liz and Connor drove away.

"Do you think Sam will go with Fred?" Liz asked.

"Yeah, he can use us as exhibit A when he argues his case."

The tires on the Jeep created a loud noise when Connor reached highway speed and made it difficult to carry on a conversation. Liz leaned back in the seat and kept her eyes on the clouds that were now thicker and darker. After thirty minutes, they left the paved road for a gravel road. Connor slowed down, but the ride was now both bumpy and noisy.

"This road is maintained by the state's Department of Natural Resources," Connor said over the racket.

"Is that going to be a question on a test?" Liz replied, trying to keep her teeth from chattering.

"No, it's completely useless information," Connor said with a glance in her direction. "And a terrible way to start the tour."

They made a couple of turns. Connor obviously knew where he was going.

"Did you bring a compass?" Liz asked as they reached a narrow dirt road.

The limbs of the trees alongside the road almost created a wooden tunnel.

"Yes, and a trail app on my phone along with a backup paper map," Connor answered, holding tightly to the steering wheel that jerked back and forth in his hands.

"I thought you knew where we were going."

"I do. I've been there many times. But it's good to be prepared."

"Were you a Boy Scout?"

"Yes, Eagle rank."

"That makes sense."

"Why?" he asked.

"Just who you are. You know, be prepared. Keep your wood dry."

"'Keep your wood dry'?"

"Isn't that a good idea?"

"Yes, but it's not a main theme in the *Boy Scout Handbook*."

Connor navigated through a deep rut in the road that tossed Liz back and forth.

"Not far now," he said. "The trailhead is around the next bend."

Connor pulled off the dirt road and stopped in front of a ditch. He turned off the motor. Suddenly, everything was quiet.

"I don't see any signs," Liz said.

"There aren't any. We go north by northwest through the woods for about half a mile and intersect the waterfall trail. This cuts out the boring part of the hike."

"Did you figure this out on your own?"

"Yes."

Liz sensed Connor's energy while they loaded up the gear. "You love this, don't you?" she asked.

"I do," he said, smiling. "Stay directly behind me."

"Will you scare off the snakes?"

"Absolutely. They want to avoid us more than we want to avoid them."

Connor plunged into the woods. Liz followed. After about thirty feet, he turned right at a large tree. A few feet farther, he turned left. This happened several times in rapid succession.

"I'm lost," Liz said. "I have no idea of the direction to your Jeep."

Connor stopped and pointed at the ground. "I do. Look down and tell me what you see."

Liz examined the forest floor but couldn't discern anything remarkable about it. "Pine needles, leaves, and twigs," she said.

Connor pointed to the left. "And in that direction?"

Liz started to say "trees" but paused to consider the question more carefully. "Maybe there's some kind of a path, but I'm not one hundred percent sure," she said. "Is this the trail to the waterfall?"

"No, we've only walked a couple hundred yards. This is a game trail made by the animals who live here."

Liz looked behind her. She could now see the narrow way more clearly. "I had no idea they did that. I thought animals just made their way randomly through the woods."

"No, they're very efficient. They figure out the best way to access food and water so they don't waste calories."

As Liz followed Connor, she could occasionally make out the trail, but at other times, it seemed to disappear. Connor certainly didn't have that problem.

"You're really good at this," she said after several minutes passed.

"The Cherokees who lived here for a thousand years or so before the white settlers showed up often utilized game trails in setting up their highways through the forest."

Liz was intrigued by the possibility that she might be walking in the footsteps of people from so long ago.

Connor stopped. "Here's where the game trail intersects the trail to the waterfall."

At her feet was a typical hiking path about a yard wide. "I'm sorry to leave the game trail," she said. "That was interesting."

"I'm glad you liked it. From here it will take us about two hours to reach the waterfall."

Connor turned away before he could see the surprised expression on Liz's face.

"Do we have to climb any mountains?" she asked, hoping her voice didn't betray her apprehension.

"No," Connor replied without looking back. "Only a few hills."

Soon, a few raindrops started to fall. They both put on rain gear. A steady rain began. It was different from dashing under an umbrella across a parking lot. The rain wrapped itself around them. There wasn't any lightning or thunder. Thirty minutes later, the sun came out. Liz had remained dry.

"I liked the rain," she said.

"I'm glad you did."

Connor offered occasional comments about the plants and rocks. His knowledge was impressive. Liz tried to ask intelligent questions. Connor set a reasonable pace, and Liz settled into a rhythm. She especially liked to smell the air. It was a basket of aromas.

Connor's definition of a hill proved, for the most part, to be accurate until the final ascent to the waterfall. Liz could hear the sound of the water before they rounded a corner, and a glint of white came into view through the clustered tree trunks. She hoped the increasing noise of the water hid the sound of her breathing. Connor suddenly took a side path to the left. A few seconds later they were standing at the bottom of a rocky cliff and looking up at a narrow stream of water that burst over the edge of the earth at least a hundred feet above them. It crashed down several ledges before accumulating in a shallow pool not far from where they stood. There the stream reformed and disappeared into the forest.

"What do you think?" Connor asked. "Was it worth the walk?"

"It's spectacular," Liz said as she caught her breath.

Connor pointed across the stream. "There's a path that goes to the top, but it's pretty rugged and can be treacherous when there's been a rain shower. We won't try that."

"Good idea," Liz quickly replied. "I don't want to hurt myself and make you carry me out."

CHAPTER 25

CONNOR SLIPPED OFF HIS BACKPACK. HE'D BEEN impressed with Liz's stamina and pace on the hike. "Ready for lunch?" he asked.

"I'm starving."

Connor handed Liz her water bottle. "Finish it off," he said.

"Shouldn't I save some?"

Connor pointed to the stream. "There's plenty of water in front of us."

"Is it safe to drink? I thought you could get sick."

"We won't." Connor took out a small device from his pack. "I'm going to purify some water."

Placing the exit tube inside Liz's water bottle and the intake end into the stream, he quickly filled the bottle. Liz took a drink.

"It's cold and good," she said.

There was a large, flat rock at the edge of the pool where they laid out the food. Liz finished preparing Connor's sandwich. He appreciated her simple act of service in squeezing mustard and mayo from the packets. Before they ate, Connor closed his eyes to pray. Instead of a short sentence or two, he found himself thanking God for not only the food but also the hike, the forest, the waterfall, their conversation, and that Liz agreed to join him in the first place.

"Sorry," he said when he finished.

"That's okay, but if you'd gone on much longer, I was going to start eating and let the prayer take effect in real time."

Connor sat with one leg propped up on the rock. "This is a great wrap," he said after his first bite. "Everything tastes better in the woods."

"I was surprised we didn't see anyone else on the trail."

"Maybe it was the threat of rain. There were fresh footprints from a group of three hikers who came before us."

"You could tell that?" Liz asked, raising her eyebrows.

"It wasn't hard. I counted the boot prints in the muddy spots on the trail."

"I didn't notice."

"I'll show you on the way out."

After they ate, Liz took off her boots and socks and dipped her red-painted toenails into the pool. "It's brisk," she said, "but refreshing."

Connor watched as Liz leaned over and picked up a smooth white stone from the pool.

"What is this?" she asked, holding it up.

"Either calcite or quartz. Let me see."

Liz handed him the rock. Connor scraped it against another darker stone.

"Quartz," he said, returning the rock to Liz. "It's much harder than calcite."

"Is that also going to be on the test you give me during the drive home?"

"Yes."

Liz glanced over at Connor. "I like the nature and scientific side of you," she said.

Connor leaned back and braced himself with his hands on the rock beneath him.

"And I've really enjoyed spending time with you," he said. "Not just today. I guess that's obvious to you, not just Bev Devon."

"Bev's a romantic." Liz smiled.

They stayed long enough beneath the waterfall for Connor to refill their water bottles from the stream.

"I really like this," Liz said, taking a long drink. "It's much better than the spring water they sell at the store."

"That stuff loses something in the industrial process."

Liz put back on her shoes and socks. She stood and stretched. "If we don't head back, I'm going to get stiff."

"Do you want to lead the way?" Connor asked.

"Why?"

"You can see more than my back."

"Okay, but I'll never recognize the intersection with the game trail."

"I'll handle that part."

During the return hike, Connor was able to point out things in front of Liz as she approached them. He showed her the boot patterns in the mud.

She eyed them skeptically. "I can't see three different sizes. They run together."

Connor broke off a twig and used it to illustrate the different lengths. "And this hiker needs a new pair of boots. Some of the treads are almost totally worn down."

The sun came out from behind the clouds. The return hike seemed quicker than the walk to the waterfall. Letting Liz set the pace, Connor checked the fitness tracker on his wrist. They were moving faster.

"Here's the game trail," he said.

"If we kept going on the main trail, how far would we end up from your vehicle?"

"About three quarters of a mile. We'd have to walk along the dirt road to return to my Jeep."

"I'd like to do it," Liz said.

"Okay."

There were two trucks and a single car parked at the trailhead. They started down the dirt road. Now they walked side by side.

"When you recorded the video on the Burnt Pine Tree property, were you on a game trail?" Liz asked.

"No, that was strictly cross-country, although I usually follow the same general route."

"Could we do that hike?"

"The destination is the top of a steep hill with a fantastic view. I rarely see anyone up there because it's only accessible by a scramble over boulders for a hundred yards or so."

"Do you think I could do it?"

"If we take our time."

They reached Connor's vehicle an hour later. Once they left the bumpy gravel road, Liz leaned her head to the side and closed her eyes. She opened them as they neared town.

"That was rude," she said, shaking her head. "I passed out."

"A nap after a hike is almost as good as a sip of water from a mountain stream."

Liz opened her water bottle and took a refreshing drink. When they reached her apartment Connor pulled her backpack from the rear of the Jeep.

"I had a wonderful day," Liz said.

"Me too."

Liz stepped forward and gave Connor a hug. He pulled her closer for a few seconds before they parted.

"Will I see you in the morning at church?" he asked.

"Yes, but there's a chance I won't pay attention to the sermon."

"Why not?"

"I may be thinking about game trails and waterfalls."

———

Liz went to bed early. Normally, she didn't remember her dreams, which often fell in the category of unconsciously working out the stress of her day. Tonight, she woke less than an hour after falling asleep from a dream in which she was sitting beside a stream slightly bigger than the one she and Connor visited on the hike. He wasn't there. She was alone. The flowing water shimmered with reflected sunlight. In the dream Liz leaned over, cupped her hand, and brought some of the water to her lips. Just before she drank, the thought flashed through her mind that she'd not purified the water. She brought her hand to her lips anyway. The clear liquid was cool when entering her mouth but instantly became warm as it flowed through her body. Both sensations were pleasant, but in different ways.

Liz woke up thirsty. Going into the kitchen, she turned on the faucet and filled a glass half full. Taking a drink, she frowned. The water for the apartment came from a deep well on the property and was better than any municipal water she'd ever had. Liz took another drink that was barely better than the first. The water from the tap wasn't as good as the water Connor gave her and much inferior to the water in her dream. Returning to bed, she quickly fell asleep and didn't awaken until after her usual time.

Rolling over, she groaned as multiple muscles voiced their complaints about the exertion of the previous day. Sitting on the side of the bed, she remembered the dream. It remained as vivid as when she'd awakened earlier.

Gentle stretching helped loosen her muscles, but she walked slower than normal across the church parking lot. Inside, the congregation was smaller than at any other time she'd visited the church. There was a wide-open space on the pew beside Bev and Sam. Liz joined them.

Bev smiled when she saw her. "How was the hike?" she asked.

"Great. Did Sam go with Fred?"

"Yes."

"I'm glad he didn't get struck by lightning."

Bev chuckled. The service was scheduled to start in about five minutes. Liz shifted in her seat and moved her legs to keep them from stiffening up. Out the corner of her eye, she saw Elena and Tracy walking down the center aisle toward the front of the sanctuary. People turned to watch the sisters. Liz could see people lean over and whisper. Compassion for Elena rose within Liz. Her client had been through so much.

The choir entered with Connor behind them. Liz settled into the familiar routine of the service. When Connor stepped forward to begin the sermon, she hoped they would make eye contact. Instead, he started speaking by quoting a Bible passage:

On the last and greatest day of the festival, Jesus stood and said in a loud voice, "Let anyone who is thirsty come to me and drink. Whoever believes in me, as Scripture has said, rivers of living water will flow from within them." By this he meant the Spirit, whom those who believed in him were later to receive. Up to that time the Spirit had not been given, since Jesus had not yet been glorified.

Connor explained the context of Jesus's words related to the celebrations of the Jewish calendar. Liz didn't pay attention to what he was saying. Her threat of mentally zoning out during the sermon came true—but for an entirely different reason. Instead of a day-dream, she revisited her dream in the night and wondered if what she'd encountered in the experience was living water. It was a crazy thought. She knew Jesus was speaking metaphorically. But it was impossible to deny the vividness of what she'd seen and felt. The refreshing coolness, followed by pervasive warmth. Only something alive could create such a unique impact.

Grabbing a Bible from the pew rack, she turned to the gospel of John and began reading from the beginning of chapter 7. The account was all about the identity of Jesus and whether he was the Christ. A note at the bottom of the page explained how in the con-text of the passage he was the promised Son of God and Savior of the world. Jesus spoke directly to the issue, culminating in the verses Connor quoted. Liz felt herself dropped into the middle of the story. The choice was clear: believe or reject who Jesus was. Both types of responses were clearly described. No middle ground was possible. Staring at the words on the page, Liz knew she had to decide. Taking a deep breath, she chose to believe.

The rest of the sermon was a blur. Toward the end of the service, she heard Connor make a reference to the newspaper article. When that happened, Liz shifted in her seat to gauge Elena's reaction but couldn't see her clearly. Bev nudged Sam. Liz glanced down at the open Bible in her lap. She wanted to read the verses about water again. She finished as Connor gave the closing prayer. The congregation stood for the benediction.

Bev leaned over to Liz and whispered, "I told Sam there wasn't anything to that article in the newspaper."

Liz could see Sam move away from them toward the aisle.

"What did he think?" she asked.

"That the newspaper is only good for finding out what's on sale at the grocery store."

"Will he be satisfied by what Connor said today?"

"He'd better be. Otherwise, he's going to be eating cereal for supper."

Liz looked toward the front of the sanctuary. Instead of making his way down the aisle to shake hands with people as they left, Connor was talking to Elena and Tracy. But he was obviously looking past them.

Liz quickly made her way forward and interrupted the conversation. "I know you need to get to the rear of the sanctuary," she said to Connor. "I'd like to speak with Elena and Tracy."

With a grateful look, Connor left. Elena had put on makeup and was wearing a cream-colored dress.

"How are you feeling?" Liz asked her.

"Upset," Elena replied. "And Connor won't listen to me about being proactive. If his name gets dragged through the mud, then mine won't be far behind. Now the whole county knows Daughbert Technology was in financial trouble. Writing something slanderous about me and Connor is next."

"Why would the paper do that?" Tracy asked, looking at her sister in surprise.

Elena motioned to Liz. "Ask Liz. She knows."

"Anything is a possibility," Liz replied. "But that doesn't mean it's going to happen. I hope the reporter writing the articles has enough journalistic integrity not to print something without any factual support."

"If he does, I want you to sue," Elena said emphatically. "I may not have as much money as I thought I would, but I'll pay whatever it takes."

Liz didn't respond. It wasn't the time to inform Elena that she couldn't sue another one of the law firm's clients.

"And I'm ready to schedule a time to come to the office," Elena said. "Tracy is going home tomorrow morning."

"Are you sure it's a good idea for Tracy to leave so soon?"

"We've talked it over," Elena replied before her sister could speak.

From the look on Tracy's face, Liz guessed they'd not been in agreement.

"Elena knows I'll come back if she needs me," Tracy said.

Liz stepped aside as Elena moved past her with Tracy trailing behind. When the sanctuary was mostly empty, she made her way to the foyer. Connor was still shaking hands with people as they exited. She waited until he was alone.

"Good morning, Ms. Acosta," he said, bowing his head slightly. "I hope you enjoyed the service."

"More than you can imagine." Liz smiled.

"Why? Tell me."

"Aren't you tired of spending time with me?"

"Don't you remember what I said at the waterfall? Let's do lunch at the Olive Tree."

CHAPTER 26

CONNOR THOUGHT ABOUT THE MORNING'S SERVICE as he drove to the restaurant. It wasn't break time for the local schools or a holiday on the calendar, but the number of people in the pews that day had been lower than normal. There was no logical explanation other than the controversy caused by the newspaper article. Connor had done his best to take the sting out of the issue, but there had been a negative impact.

During the early part of the service, he checked off who wasn't there by vacant spaces in the pews where people usually sat. Some weren't a surprise. They were individuals and couples who were resistant to what he'd said to them in a phone call or written in an email. Others were more surprising.

He reached the restaurant and parked behind Liz's car. They walked side by side along the sidewalk.

"This is as far as I want to hike today," she said when they reached the entrance.

"Sore muscles?" he asked, holding the door open for her.

"Are you telling me that you're not stiff or sore?" she asked.

"Not really."

"Which means not at all?"

Connor shrugged his shoulders. "Maybe a tiny bit in my left deltoid. I didn't have the strap on my pack adjusted exactly right."

"Every deltoid, quadricep, calf, and gluteus is letting me hear from them," Liz said.

"But not your bicep?"

Liz flexed her right arm. "No, it handled my morning cup of coffee without a whimper."

The waitress brought two glasses of water.

"Elena and Tracy made it to church," Liz prompted.

"Yeah, I'm glad Elena felt well enough to show up. And thanks for rescuing me. I needed to get to the rear of the sanctuary. Usually, people realize that's the case and don't try to slow me down."

"But not Elena."

"She gets a pass on church etiquette after what she's been through."

The waitress arrived, and they ordered their food.

"Why did you enjoy the service?" Connor asked.

Liz paused for a few seconds before she answered. "I'm not sure where to begin, but it started with the hike, followed by a dream, which was connected to the verses you read from the Bible."

Connor's eyes brightened. "I'm eager to hear whatever you're willing to tell me."

Connor had never heard anything like the story that came from Liz's lips. If he'd not seen her analytical side as an attorney, he would have been skeptical and assigned her a place alongside some of the mystics he'd read about in church history. While she talked their food arrived.

He barely touched his plate. "I can understand you having a dream about a stream after going on our hike to the waterfall," he said.

"But what about the physical sensations that I experienced in my body?" Liz asked, picking up a fork. "It felt as real as this fork in my hand."

"That's out there," Connor replied, shaking his head.

"And then you began your speech at the church reading from the Bible about living water, which would have sounded totally metaphorical to me yesterday but completely practical today."

"Sermon," Connor corrected.

"Sorry, I whiffed on the lingo. I spent part of the rest of the sermon reading the entire chapter. That helped me put what Jesus said into context."

Connor ate then as Liz talked.

"So do you think I'm way out of bounds?" she asked when she'd reached the end of her retelling.

"No. What you describe is so beautiful that it makes me—" He stopped.

"What?" Liz asked.

"Jealous. But in a good way."

That night Liz slept soundly without being interrupted by vivid dreams. Less sore in the morning, she spent extra time stretching until she was able to move freely. While drinking her coffee, she downloaded a Bible app on her phone and opened it to the gospel of John. Instead of going directly to chapter 7, she began with chapter 1. Liz had never had an interest in reading the Bible, but after what had happened the previous night and day, she was curious. She quickly realized that the same questions about the identity and nature of Jesus reported in chapter 7 came up as early as chapter 1. It took a large cup of coffee to make her way through chapter 3. After finishing, she sent Connor a text:

Read John chapters 1, 2, and 3 this morning.

He quickly replied:

Any more dreams?

She sent him a thumbs-down emoji followed by a frowny face.

At the office, Liz stopped by Jessica's desk. The assistant had been away with her husband to celebrate their tenth wedding anniversary.

"How was the getaway?" Liz asked.

"Beyond wonderful," Jessica replied, then lowered her voice. "When we were dating, Max was super romantic, but once he convinced me to marry him, the romantic rush became a tiny trickle."

Jessica held up her index finger on her right hand. "See this amethyst? He picked it out and designed the setting himself for a jeweler to make. There's no other ring like it on the planet. He gave it to me at a special dinner prepared by a private chef and served at the cabin where we were staying." She paused. "What did you do this weekend?"

Jessica's eyes widened as Liz told her about the day spent hiking to the waterfall with Connor.

"Sounds like he's inviting you into his private little world."

"Yes," Liz agreed. "I hadn't thought of it that way, but you're right."

"You and a preacher?" Jessica shook her head. "As romantic as I feel after the weekend with Max, I'm not sure I have the faith for you to find happiness in that sort of relationship."

Becky came in from the reception area. "Elena Thompson is on the phone and wants an appointment this morning. I checked your calendar, and it's clear until noon. Should I tell her to come in around ten thirty?"

"That will be fine. Thanks."

Knowing that the meeting with Elena would likely take up a considerable amount of time, Liz left Jessica's desk and worked on several other projects. Shortly before ten thirty, Harold knocked on her door.

"Is Elena Thompson still in the hospital?" he asked.

"No." Liz brought the senior partner up-to-date. "She's scheduled to come in to see me in a few minutes."

"Did you read the article in the newspaper claiming that her husband's business was failing?"

"Yes, and that's consistent with what Neil Peterson told me."

"Have you filed the claim for payment of the life insurance?"

"No, but I'll bring it up with her today."

"Do that. Keep the ball rolling." Harold ran his fingers through his thinning hair. "At least neither Elena nor the minister was mentioned in the newspaper article on Friday."

"Yes, but both of them are worried it could still happen. Do you have any inside scoop?"

"Not yet."

Elena was late for her appointment. Liz continued working until Becky buzzed her.

"I'll meet with her in the main conference room," Liz said.

"She's not alone. There's a man with her."

"Who is he?"

"She didn't tell me."

———

Connor was at the church waiting for Reg Bullock to arrive.

"Did he say what he wanted to talk about?" Michelle asked.

"No, he sent me a text last night. You and Duke were at the service yesterday. How do you think it went?"

"Fine, but I'm biased, and Duke knows that it's easier to agree with me than try to convince me differently. I'm always right."

"Always?" Connor smiled.

"Ninety-one percent of the time. I'd like to get to one hundred percent, but that's going to be tough."

Connor looked at his computer monitor. He'd pulled up the statistics from Sunday. "Both attendance and giving were down," he said.

"There are people who've left and say they won't be coming back," Michelle replied.

"Who?"

Michelle recited ten or eleven names. "Most of them were shaky anyway," she concluded.

A few seconds later, Reg came through the door. "Good morning," he said to both Connor and Michelle.

"Come on in," Connor said as he led the way to his office.

"Would you like coffee, Mr. Bullock?" Michelle asked.

"No, thank you. I've already had my limit."

The assistant closed the door. Reg sat down across from Connor and looked past him at the panoramic view.

"You have the best view in Bryson. I'm so glad the architect who designed the church positioned the pastor's office so he could see the mountains. We talked about making this the view from the front of the sanctuary but decided it would be hard to concentrate on the service."

"Not hard, impossible. What's on your mind?"

Reg took a deep breath. "The GBI spent all day Saturday at Burnt Pine Tree. Detective Norman from the sheriff's department was with them."

Connor felt his throat tighten. "Did it have anything to do with the field camera footage?"

"No. They already have that, but they wanted to know if there was any additional surveillance from the cameras set up in the lodge. Andy had given them everything from inside, but they wanted the cards for the outside of the building."

"I wasn't anywhere near the lodge, inside or out, on the day Matt died."

"I know, but the agents specifically asked Andy if he remembered seeing you by the side of the house shortly after breakfast and before the hunt."

"Is somebody claiming I was there for breakfast?"

"I'm not sure, but Andy said he didn't remember seeing you. Of course, it was dark when the group left to set up for the hunt, and the guides were milling around outside."

"They need to talk to Stan Maxwell. He'll confirm I wasn't there."

"The GBI told Andy they spoke with Stan and the other three guides but didn't say what they'd said."

"I want to talk to the guides myself."

"You don't have to," Reg replied. "I did it for you. I caught up with Stan and the others yesterday afternoon. None of them remember seeing you on the morning of the hunt."

"That should be the end of it," Connor replied in frustration. "Instead of trying to make me look like I've done something wrong, the GBI and Detective Norman should be trying to identify the man in the video I took. What was he doing that morning running away from the property with a rifle in hand? Does he show up in any of the trail cam footage or the surveillance cameras at the lodge?"

"I totally agree," Reg replied. "Also, a group of us are doing everything we can to stamp out any gossip swirling around the church."

"I appreciate that," Connor sighed. "There were quite a few people who didn't show up yesterday."

"And some who did weren't satisfied with what you said about the situation in your sermon."

"What more should I have said?"

"I don't know, but there are new rumors, not about Matt's death but about your interaction with Elena Thompson. People saw you going into the hospital to see her."

"I'm her pastor!" Connor exploded. "That's part of my job!"

"No argument from me about that, but for the time being I suggest you not meet with her alone. Anywhere at any time."

"It's always been my policy not to meet behind closed doors with women in the congregation. How did word get out that she was hospitalized?"

"I'm not sure. Rumor is, she had a drug overdose."

"I can't comment on that."

"Understood. I'm not looking for information, just trying to keep you informed."

CHAPTER 27

SITTING BESIDE ELENA IN THE LAW FIRM RECEP-
tion area was a large, muscular man in his thirties wearing a
cream-colored golf shirt, lightweight jacket, and black pants. He had
long brown hair that he'd pulled back into a bun. He stood when Liz
entered, then slipped off his jacket to reveal a short-sleeved shirt.

"This is Tyson," Elena said.

Liz introduced herself. Tyson extended his hand. When he did,
Liz could see a portion of a lion's head tattoo higher up on his broad
bicep.

"Nice to meet you," he said in a clipped accent that Liz suspected
was British.

Liz escorted them to the conference room.

Elena waited until the door closed to speak. "Tyson has been
working for me about a year," she said. "He's the private investigator I told you about. I hired him to let me know what was going on
with Matt and Anne in Atlanta. After Matt's death, I asked Tyson
to continue to help me."

"Where's your firm located?" Liz asked.

"We're international with multiple offices," Tyson responded.
"There's a branch office in South Africa. That's where I'm from."

"What's the name of the company?"

"The Fletchall Group Limited."

"That's not important," Elena said. "I wouldn't have asked Tyson to join us today except he's been looking into the circumstances of Matt's death, and there's a possibility I hadn't considered."

"What is it?"

"Suicide." Elena took a tissue from her purse. "Tell her," she said to the investigator. "It's too hard for me to talk about."

The investigator leaned forward and rested his arms on the table. "I recorded multiple conversations between Mr. Thompson and his ex-wife. Matt was depressed over the financial condition of his business and the problems in his relationship with Elena. A couple of times, he mentioned that it was hard for him to see a way out of the situation and believed the people he cared about would be better off if he was dead."

"Did he use those exact words?" Liz asked.

"Yes."

"How close to the time of Matt's death did these conversations take place?"

"Starting about six months ago with the last one three weeks before he died. At that time, his ex-wife asked him to provide her with information about his life insurance policies in case that was the choice he made."

"She didn't encourage him to get some help?" Liz asked in surprise.

"She mentioned a medication that a friend found helpful for depression, but the last thing she did was ask for copies of his current life insurance policies."

Liz turned to Elena. "Did Matt ever talk about his depression with you?"

"I knew he was under a lot of stress, but he never said anything about being better off dead. It hurt my feelings that he'd say something like that to Anne but not me."

"Did you record these conversations?" Liz asked the investigator.

"Only the ones that took place in public. He didn't talk about ending his life when the two of them were alone."

Before Tyson's last statement, Liz had suspected the investigator's surveillance was likely illegal. Even if it was within the boundaries of the law, the activity was dirty.

Elena spoke. "Tyson, wait in the lobby while I talk some more with Liz."

The private investigator left.

"Is Tyson checking into anything else?" Liz asked.

"Whatever I ask him to do, he does," Elena replied. "He also provides personal security if I need it."

"Why would you need personal security?"

"Anyone who has a lot of money or is about to come into money has to be careful."

Liz accepted that she was talking to the more paranoid version of Elena. "What else did you want to talk to me about?" she asked.

Elena placed her phone on the table. Liz glanced down to make sure the conversation wasn't being recorded.

"I've turned off my phone," Elena said. "Do you have your phone with you?"

"No, it's in my office."

Elena spoke softly. "If Matt committed suicide, would that change whether I can collect the life insurance or the amount I'd receive?"

"Death by suicide would nullify the double indemnity provisions. A suicide isn't an accidental death. It's intentional. But I believe the policies payable to you and Anne have been in effect long enough that suicide isn't a defense to payment of the basic benefit." Liz paused. "But the policy payable to the members of the Daughbert Technology Trust was much more recent. I'd have to check the language."

"Can you do that?"

"Yes."

"I'd like an answer," Elena said. "Now."

Liz stood.

Elena continued. "If I was asked in a deposition whether I suspected Matt committed suicide, what would I say? I'd want to tell the truth."

"Based on what Tyson said, that would be a tougher question for Anne to answer than you. Let me think about how you could word a response."

Leaving the conference room, Liz first checked the individual policies. Both the policy payable to Elena and the one naming Anne as beneficiary had the same standard language. After being in effect for two years, benefits could not be contested due to suicide but the double indemnity provision wouldn't trigger. The Daughbert Technology Trust policy contained a one-year period of contestability in case of a suicide.

Returning to the conference room, Liz gave Elena the news. "You and Anne are in the clear on the basic coverage, but not the trust. If Matt committed suicide, Winston and the others wouldn't receive anything."

"That's what I thought," Elena said, then continued, "Would it make sense to let someone at the company know what Tyson overheard?"

Perplexed, Liz asked, "Which company? The insurance company or Daughbert Technology?"

"Daughbert. If Winston Boone was made aware we had information indicating that Matt's death was a suicide, he might be willing to share some of the proceeds of the big policy to keep us quiet."

Liz frowned. "Elena, that's too close to blackmail for me to go along with it."

Elena met her eyes with a steely gaze. "I don't want to do anything dishonest, but I don't like what Winston and the other owners did. They bet big on Matt's death and used company money to pay for the policy. I don't like the idea of them profiting from it."

"I understand. But if you raise this issue, it could backfire on your own claim under the double indemnity provision."

"Not if it's only discussed between the lawyers. Wouldn't any conversations you have with the attorney for Daughbert be subject to the confidentiality rules?"

"Yes, but I'm not going to offer to hide evidence in return for the payment of money."

"There's nothing to stop me from talking to Winston, though, is there?"

"It depends on what you say and how you say it," Liz replied slowly. "My advice is for you to let Harold and me represent you the best we know how."

Elena sniffed in frustration. "One other thing," she said. "What if Matt was murdered? Would I still be able to collect double the life insurance?"

Liz felt suddenly queasy. "The double indemnity provision would still apply so long as neither you nor someone acting on your behalf murdered Matt."

"Okay, that makes sense," Elena replied. "Also, I contacted the cleaning service for my house. One of their employees came in and straightened up after the EMTs left. I demanded they fire her because the company is supposed to let me know every time before they come into the house. Their employee would be the only source for any illegal drugs Connor found in the guest bath. Turns out the woman already quit."

_____

The more Connor thought about the conversation with Reg, the more agitated he became. He went outside and walked around the church grounds. That didn't help. Returning to his office, he tried to call Liz, but she was in meetings and unavailable. Connor left a message and told Michelle to hold his calls except for Liz.

Closing his office door, he tried to refocus and come up with a topic for his sermon. But the living water he'd read about the previous Sunday had run dry. Connor considered and discarded five ideas before Michelle buzzed him.

"Liz Acosta is on the phone," the assistant said.

"Sorry it took so long to get back to you," Liz said. "It's been a busy day."

"Mine too." Connor told her about his conversation with Reg.

"None of this makes sense," Liz said when he finished.

"Which is why I'd like to talk directly with Detective Norman. Do you think that's a good idea?"

"Based on my previous interaction with him, Norman is a one-way street. He takes in information but doesn't give it out. There needs to be some reason why he'd want to talk to you. Telling him that he's wasting taxpayer money isn't going to be enough. And I doubt he cares about the negative impact unsupported insinuations could have on your position at the church."

"I wouldn't begin with anything about me. I was going to lead with my responsibility to Elena as one of the people in the church who are under my care. The stress and uncertainty surrounding the circumstances of Matt's death is putting her life at risk."

"Would you tell him about her hospitalization?"

"No, but he probably knows. Reg mentioned it. Secrets are hard to keep in a town this size. Then I could ask why my name continues to be mentioned in connection to an investigation, especially when everything indicates Matt's death was an accident."

"I think talking to Norman is going to be a waste of time," Liz said. "You have plenty of reason to be upset, but I believe you're going to have to let this play out. You can't control it."

"I don't want to control anything," Connor said, his voice rising. "But the police making it sound like I'm a criminal suspect linked to Matt's death isn't right!"

Liz was silent for a moment. "Would you want me to be there if you meet with Detective Norman?"

"Yes, if you're willing."

"Don't call him to set it up. I'll do it," she said.

"You will?"

"I think coming from me will make it more professional. How open is your schedule for the next few days?"

"Completely for this."

"Okay, I'll send over a contract for the law firm to represent you to make it official. Sign it and return."

"Thanks," Connor replied. "I'm sorry for the hassle."

The call ended. Connor went to Michelle's desk.

"Good call?" she asked cheerily.

"I guess so."

"Your face says otherwise."

"I'm taking the rest of the afternoon off," he said.

Connor didn't want to go home or be alone. He thought about showing up unannounced again at the Hamilton home but that didn't feel right. Instead, he called. Lyle answered.

"I know this is short notice, but I'm going for a short hike and wondered if Josh would like to tag along. We'd be back by suppertime."

"Just a second."

Connor heard Lyle yell: "Josh, have you finished your homework?"

After a brief pause, Lyle came back on the line. "Where are you heading?"

"Along the edge of the Burnt Pine Tree property."

"Can he bring Rascal?"

"Sure."

Thirty minutes later, Connor and Josh reached the road that led to Burnt Pine Tree. Connor parked in his usual spot. Getting out, he smelled the cool air. Rascal yelped from the rear seat.

"Make sure you keep a tight grip on Rascal's leash," Connor said. "If not, he'll catch the scent of something interesting and take off for the next county."

The trees were totally bare of leaves.

"Is that a path?" Josh asked, pointing to an opening in the trees.

"No, that's a firebreak, but it's a good spot to enter the woods. We'll go cross-country."

Josh kept close to Connor while Rascal constantly pulled hard at the end of the leash. Several times, the dog wrapped himself around a tree trunk and had to be untangled.

"Would you like me to hold him for a while?" Connor asked.

"Yes, sir."

Connor shortened the leash and began trying to teach the dog to heel. It was an impossible task in the incredibly sensory experience of the forest. Connor gave up. His thoughts went to Matt Thompson and the businessman's last walk in the woods.

"What kind of tree is this?" Josh asked, touching the dark bark of a thick trunk.

"It's a black birch," Connor answered. "They're not very common around here."

A few yards deeper into the woods they reached the shallow gully near the spot where Connor stopped to watch the large buck pass by in pursuit of the does. He told Josh about the buck.

"I'd love to see a deer like that," Josh replied. "The ones who come into our yard in the evening aren't very big."

Connor walked into the gully that was filled with leaves. When he did, his leg dropped into an unseen hole, causing him to lose his balance. He lost his grip on the leash, and in a split second the dog was thrashing through the leaves. Josh saw what had happened and began running. He dove after the leash, almost disappearing in the leaves. Sputtering, he stood up with the leash in his hand.

"Got 'im!" he called out.

"Good job," Connor answered.

Josh leaned over and stuck his arm in the leaves again. "That's not all," he said, holding up a cell phone in his right hand. "I found this."

Connor joined the boy and the dog. Josh handed him the phone that was splattered with mud on the bottom where the charging port was located.

"Does it work?" Josh asked.

Connor tapped the screen, but the battery was dead. "No."

"I wonder who lost it."

Glancing around, Connor realized the phone might have been dropped by the man in the video. It had rained multiple times since that day in late September, but there was always the chance a dead phone could be revived.

"When I get home, I'll charge it and see if it still works," he said.

CHAPTER 28

"Just remember what I told you the other day," Harold said to Liz when she brought up accompanying Connor to a meeting with Detective Norman. "You can sign Grantham up as a client, but Elena Thompson takes priority."

"Yes, sir. Should I tell Connor that?"

"Not unless it becomes necessary to make a choice."

Liz left the meeting with Harold and called Detective Norman, who was surprisingly cooperative. "I can meet with you and Reverend Grantham at ten thirty tomorrow morning," the detective said.

Liz checked the calendar on her monitor. Harold had entered an appointment with a new client on her schedule for that time slot.

"I need to move something but will make that work."

"You don't need to check with your client?"

"He's flexible."

"Yeah, I guess he only works one day a week," Norman said with a quick laugh.

Liz wasn't in the mood for humor. "We'll meet at my office," she said. "We can use the same conference room where we met the other day."

"No, it has to be here at the sheriff's office."

"Why?"

"That's where I have the entire investigative file."

Liz would feel more comfortable on her own turf. She started to protest but knew Connor wanted to meet with the detective, regardless of the place. "All right. See you then."

"Will you want to record the conversation?" Norman asked.

"Yes."

"Then I will too."

Later, as Liz was getting ready to leave for the day, Harold buzzed her. "When's your meeting with Detective Norman and the preacher?" he asked.

"In the morning at the sheriff's office."

"Would you like me to join you?"

"Yes," Liz replied quickly. "But I'd better check with Connor to make sure it's okay with him."

"Let him know my presence will be pro bono."

"That's generous."

Driving home, Liz called Connor.

"Why does your boss think he should be there?" he asked with concern in his voice. "Does he know something about what's going on that I don't?"

"He realizes this is new to me and wants to back me up."

"Are you sure he'd let you know if he had inside information?"

"Connor, you're sounding like another one of my clients."

"Okay, okay. But there is something else I need to tell you, even though I'm not sure if it's important."

Liz listened as Connor told her about Josh finding the cell phone in the woods.

"I was able to charge the battery and turn it on, but the phone is password-protected. All I could see was the screen saver photo. It looked like the kind of image that comes with the phone."

"Did you try to bypass the password?"

"No. I researched ways to do that but wasn't sure if it was legal. Also, I didn't want to do something that would erase any information. What do you suggest?"

Liz thought for a moment. "We could take the phone to the meeting with Detective Norman. The sheriff's department may not have the expertise to hack into a phone, but the GBI likely does."

"Yeah, I thought about that. But if I give them the phone, there's no way to know what they find unless they tell us. And don't accuse me again of being paranoid. I have reason to be cautious."

"You do." Liz paused. "Bring the phone to our office in the morning, and we'll ask Harold what he thinks about it."

"What time should I get there?"

"Nine fifty. It's a five-minute drive to the sheriff's department."

———

Connor spent a restless night thinking about the meeting in the morning with Detective Norman. The intellectual part of his brain argued that he'd done nothing wrong. But his analytical side retreated when confronted with negative emotions fueled by fear. He even imagined himself being put in handcuffs and placed in a jail cell. Connor threw off the covers and got out of bed. Going into the bathroom, he splashed cold water on his face and stared at himself in the mirror. Returning to bed, he was finally able to drift off around 5:00 a.m. He awoke again at 7:00 a.m. as sunlight peeked through the curtains in his bedroom.

Stumbling into the kitchen, he brewed a pot of coffee. Normally, he enjoyed waking up to solitude. But today, he simply felt lonely. Not wanting to sit idly around the house until it was time to meet with Liz, he drove to the church. He was sitting in his office staring out the window at the mountains when Michelle arrived and poked her head through the open door.

"Good morning," she said cheerily. "I saw you have an open morning. Why don't you take off and go for a hike?"

Connor turned in his chair. "I did that yesterday," he said. "This morning I'm meeting with Detective Norman. Liz Acosta and Harold Pollard are going to be with me."

Michelle's expression turned serious. "Why did the detective want to meet with you?"

"I requested it to find out what they think I did wrong. I can't stand the uncertainty."

"I'm glad you're going. I had trouble going to sleep last night worrying about the Thompson situation."

"That makes two of us. But I don't want you to worry."

"How can I avoid it?" Michelle asked as tears appeared in the corners of her eyes. "I was determined to come in this morning with a positive attitude, and here I am getting weepy."

"I hate that you're upset," Connor said. "But realizing that some-one cares is exactly what I need this morning. Thank you."

Michelle wiped the tears away with her fingers. "It is?"

"Yes. My emotions have been running roughshod over my mind, and it has to stop. I need to remind myself that decent people like you believe in me and support me."

"We do!" Michelle responded. "And there are sincere, good-hearted people in the congregation praying for you."

Michelle told him about two phone calls she'd received over the past twenty-four hours from church members who were praying for him.

"And I forgot to mention Sarah Hamilton. I don't know her very well, but she says the Lord prompted her to pray for you yesterday afternoon. Sarah already has a lot on her plate with the cancer diagnosis and her husband being paralyzed and all."

"She and Lyle have inspired and helped me over the past few weeks."

"Sarah has always kind of intimidated me," Michelle said.

"Yeah, until recently I've felt the same way." Connor stood. "At least I know what I'm going to preach about on Sunday. I'm going to talk about how important it is for Christians to pray for one another. We know that's true but don't appreciate the power it releases. The apostle Paul talked about it all the time when he was facing persecution or locked up in prison." Connor stopped. "But I'm not going to emphasize that he was in jail."

Connor arrived early at Liz's office. Becky greeted him with a nervous expression on her face.

"I saw you were at church on Sunday," Connor said.

"Yes, and I want you to know that I support you one hundred percent no matter what anyone else says," she said, then put her hand over her mouth.

"Thank you," Connor replied with a smile.

Liz appeared. "We'll talk in the conference room," she said. "Harold is waiting for us."

"I'll be praying for you," Becky said.

"Thanks. That means a lot."

Harold Pollard greeted Connor. They sat at the conference table.

Liz spoke. "I told Harold about the cell phone you and the boy found yesterday in the woods at the edge of the Burnt Pine Tree property. Do you have it with you?"

Connor placed the phone on the table. "Should I turn this over to the police?" he asked.

Harold responded. "Not yet. You didn't steal it. You found it. And in my opinion, where you were on the property doesn't fall within the definition of a crime scene."

"What about trying to find out what it contains?" Connor asked.

"If we decide to do that, let's leave it to experts." Harold leaned back in his chair. "I did a little preliminary work before our appointment."

"I would have been glad to handle any research," Liz said.

"Not that kind of work," Harold replied. "I talked to Sheriff Holland yesterday evening. The sheriff is a churchgoing man, and I thought he might have sympathy for your situation. He claims at this point the investigation is being driven by the GBI, not the local authorities. That goes along with our experience when Elena Thompson was questioned."

"Are we wasting our time talking to Detective Norman?" Connor asked.

"I hope not," Harold replied. "He might be more willing to talk if the GBI has marginalized the sheriff's department. The sheriff promised to speak to Norman before our meeting. That should help."

They rode in Harold's Mercedes. Liz offered to sit in the rear seat because Connor was so much taller, but Harold cut her off.

"If this car doesn't have enough leg room for Connor, I need to trade it in for something bigger," he said.

During the short drive, they passed the courthouse. Liz glanced out the window as a line of people streamed up the steps.

"Judge Bradshaw is on the bench this week," Harold observed. "And all the defense lawyers are scurrying in to plead out their cases. She's much more lenient than Judge Conklin. Probation should be her middle name."

"Do you handle many criminal cases?" Connor asked.

"I'm very selective," Harold replied. "A criminal case that looks straightforward can quickly become complicated and suck a tremendous amount of time from a lawyer's day."

"Thanks again for coming with us," Connor said.

"Save your thanks for the return trip, when we'll know whether it's warranted."

Harold parked in a space reserved for sheriff's department employees.

"Is that allowed?" Liz asked.

"Do you remember the big barbecue the law firm hosted last spring for county employees?"

"Yes."

"That gets me preferred parking."

They entered a squat redbrick building that was an annex to the nearby jail. The reception area featured white plastic chairs.

Harold greeted the woman on duty by name. "Maddy, we're here to see Detective Norman."

"I'll let him know, Mr. Pollard."

A few moments later the detective appeared. He shook Harold's hand.

"The sheriff told me you'd be joining us," Norman said.

With a slight nod to Liz and Connor, the detective led the way down a short hallway and into a rectangular room that contained a fake-wood-veneer table and seating for six. The same recording device Liz had seen at the Burnt Pine Tree Lodge sat in the middle of the table. Norman sat at the head of the table and opened a thick file that Liz wished she could copy.

"I'll speak up if need be," Harold said. "Reverend Grantham has a few questions for you."

"Before he asks any questions, I need to serve Reverend Grantham with this." Norman slid a piece of paper across the table to Harold.

The senior partner's eyes widened. "This is dated this morning," he said.

"Yes, it was just sent over from the GBI office in Atlanta. You saved me a trip."

"What is it?" Connor asked.

Harold handed the paper to Connor before replying, "It's a notice prohibiting you from leaving the state pending presentation of evidence to a grand jury."

Liz watched in shock as Connor stared at the piece of paper.

"Can they do that?" she asked Harold.

The senior partner scratched the side of his head. "Normally, I would have expected the GBI to issue an arrest warrant if an agent thought Reverend Grantham was guilty of a crime."

"Me too," Detective Norman said. "I showed this to the sheriff. He's never seen anything like it. The GBI has been constantly interfering during this investigation."

Connor still hadn't spoken. Liz grabbed the sheet. The notice was signed by a woman named Vonda Ramsey, assistant director of investigations for the north Georgia region of the GBI. One person receiving a copy was Christopher Flannery, the agent who'd been present when Detective Norman questioned Elena.

"What are you going to do with this?" Liz asked the detective.

"Deliver it to Reverend Grantham, which is what I just did," Norman said nonchalantly.

"Are you going to give a copy to the newspaper?" Harold asked.

"Hmm. I hadn't thought about that. I'll leave the decision whether to release it to the media up to Sheriff Holland."

"I'd like to talk to the sheriff—" Connor began in a subdued tone of voice.

"Let me do it," Harold cut in, then turned to the detective. "Are you willing to tell us anything about the investigation?"

Norman glanced at Connor before he answered. "The GBI claims they possess hard evidence that Reverend Grantham hasn't been truthful regarding his whereabouts on the morning Matthew Thompson was shot."

"What sort of evidence?" Harold asked.

"Video and eyewitness accounts. They've provided a summary but not access to their entire file."

"Does the summary name the supposed eyewitnesses?" Connor demanded. "I have a right to know!"

"I'm not going to reveal that information at this time," the detective replied. "Your lawyers can explain your rights to information in a criminal proceeding."

"Which doesn't currently exist," Harold replied testily. "Do I have a commitment from you not to notify any media outlet about the notice instructing Reverend Grantham not to leave the state?"

"I already told you. I'm leaving that up to the sheriff."

"Is he in his office?"

"Wait here. I'll check." The detective left.

"Sheriff Holland is a decent man," Harold said. "Given the circumstances, I believe he'll keep a lid on this."

"Until when?" Connor asked, shaking his head. "This is a much more serious threat to my reputation. The GBI wants to charge me with murder."

"Maybe, but they haven't done it yet," Harold said.

"Do you think they knew I was planning a trip to Boston toward the end of the month?" Connor asked.

"I didn't know about that," Liz said.

"There wasn't a reason to mention it to you. It's a theological conference about the Greek and Aramaic versions of the New Testament." Connor stopped. "But who in this building cares about that?"

Harold pointed to the notice that still lay in the middle of the table. "It's good that this wasn't an arrest warrant or an indictment waiting for us this morning. Norman may not have opened his file, but he told me something anyway. The GBI doesn't have any really strong evidence linking you to Matt Thompson's death."

"Because there isn't any!" Liz said.

Detective Norman returned. "The sheriff will see you," he said to Harold, then pointed at Connor and Liz. "The two of you can wait in the reception area."

Before he left the room, Harold gave his key fob to Liz. "Go to the car," he said.

CHAPTER 29

CONNOR LOOKED DOWN AT THE SIDEWALK AS HE and Liz walked to Harold Pollard's car. Weeds had sprouted in the cracks. He and Liz both sat in the rear seat.

"I'm sorry," she said.

Connor didn't respond. He was still in shock.

"And I'm glad you have Harold on your side," she continued. "There's no better lawyer in Bryson to communicate with powerful people on behalf of a client."

"Especially a powerless client like me."

"Remember what Harold said. The fact that the GBI didn't issue a warrant for your arrest is good."

Connor eyed her. "Would you feel that way if you were in my position?"

Liz pressed her lips together tightly. "It does sound kind of shallow," she said.

"I guess I should be thankful Detective Norman didn't put me in handcuffs and haul me over to the jail."

They sat in silence. Connor stared at the entrance to the jail.

"I wonder why it's taking so long?" he asked. "It should be a short conversation."

"He's probably trying to convince Sheriff Holland to tell him more than Detective Norman was willing to share. Harold can be persistent to the point that people will often give him the information he wants just to get rid of him."

"Okay," Connor said, then paused for a moment. "I shouldn't have snapped at you. You're trying to help."

"You don't have to apologize. I can't imagine what you're feeling."

Harold emerged from the sheriff's department. "Stay in the back seat," he said when he opened the door. "We'll talk here for a few minutes, then I'll be your chauffeur to the office."

"What did the sheriff say?" Connor asked anxiously.

"That he'll do everything he can to keep a lid on public disclosure of the notice from the GBI but can't guarantee anything. He doesn't control what the state authorities release to the media. According to Holland, the main source of information to the local newspaper is someone in Atlanta. He doesn't know who that is."

"Anything else come out about the investigation?" Liz asked.

Harold turned more sideways in the seat. "They found a high concentration of opioids in Matt Thompson's blood."

Connor's mouth dropped open. "Fentanyl?" he managed.

"The typical blood test doesn't distinguish the type of opioid, just its presence." Harold looked at Liz. "Do you know if Elena has a copy of the lab results for Matt's blood?"

"No, I never asked if she requested them," Liz said. "Would the Health Care Power of Attorney that Matt signed a few years ago allow her to obtain the information from the hospital?"

"No." Harold shook his head. "The HCPOA is ineffective upon the death of the patient. After that, the personal representative of the estate has the power to access confidential health information."

"Which is Elena," Liz said to Connor. "She's the executrix of Matt's will. But we've not filed the will for probate. It may take weeks for that to be finalized, assuming Matt's ex-wife doesn't show up with a competing will."

"There is no question Matt died from a gunshot wound," Connor said.

"But was he conscious or not?" Liz asked. "And why did Matt take opioids prior to going out to hunt? Or did someone give them to him without his knowledge? The cook who used to work at Burnt Pine Tree told me Matt said he didn't feel well that morning."

"And what is the connection, if any, between the fentanyl in Matt Thompson's blood and the pill you found on the bathroom floor at Elena's house?" Harold asked. "There are a lot of questions that need answers."

Connor didn't speak during the short ride back to the law office. Liz and her boss continued to bounce ideas back and forth. He knew it made sense for them as lawyers to do so, but to him it sounded so impersonal. He stared out the window and wondered how he could restore a sense of normality in his life.

"What should I do now?" he asked as Harold pulled into the law firm parking lot.

"Give me the cell phone you found in the woods," Harold said. "I'd rather it be in my office than in your possession in case they decide to search your house."

"Do you believe that's going to happen?" Connor asked.

"Just in case," Harold replied matter-of-factly. "And don't talk to anyone except Liz or me about any aspect of the investigation."

"Including Elena," Liz added. "Keep your conversations with her about dealing with grief or things like that. I know she tries to draw you into everything that's going on."

They exited the car. Connor gave Harold the cell phone. The lawyer shook Connor's hand firmly. "Talk to Liz first, but I'm here for you too."

Harold walked toward the office building. Liz hung back.

"During the drive back from the sheriff's department I started thinking about the church," Connor said. "Maybe I need to take a sabbatical until this can be resolved. It's impossible for me to function day-to-day."

"Stay put," Liz said. "Otherwise, how can you honestly tell people that God will be with them at difficult times in their lives?"

Connor gave her a wry smile. "If I don't feel like preaching Sunday morning, will you fill in for me?"

"No, but call or text me. Anytime. Day or night."

———————

Liz didn't look back as she walked toward the front door of the law office. She'd remained professional and emotionally strong in front of Connor, but inside, she was falling apart. She marched directly to Harold's office. The senior partner was opening the morning mail that was piled high.

"How worried should I be for Connor?" she asked.

Harold returned the silver letter opener to his desk. "The GBI is coming after him. Somebody at headquarters in Atlanta believes Matt Thompson was murdered and that Connor Grantham was either involved or has relevant information. The notice not to leave the state is intended to put pressure on him. I suspect the GBI is watching him, maybe even listening to his phone calls and tracking his emails."

"Why didn't you tell him that?" Liz asked.

"I have no proof," Harold explained. "And in this case, I don't believe it's good to start throwing out unproven suspicions. I told Connor not to talk to anyone about the circumstances of Matt Thompson's death except you and me. Do you think he'll do what I said?"

"Yes. Would the GBI be able to listen to my phone calls and read my texts and emails to Connor? Aren't those protected by the attorney-client privilege?"

"They should be privileged so long as none of the exceptions such as joint engagement in illegal activity or criminal conspiracy exist."

"What about the cell phone that Connor and the boy found in the woods?"

Harold retrieved it from his credenza and handed it to her. "Find out how to access the phone without damaging anything stored on it."

"Do I have a budget?"

"No. On this case, I'm treating you like a partner, not an associate."

"Thanks."

"One other thing. Did you consider what effect the implication of opioids in Matt's blood stream at the time of his death might have on the insurance policies?"

Liz paused. "If he took drugs before going on a hunt, that might be considered gross negligence and nullify the double indemnity provision," she said.

"Right. You're thinking like a partner too."

Liz placed the cell phone in a FedEx packet for next-day delivery to a company in San Diego that claimed it could access any mobile device without disturbing data.

"No need to tell us what you're looking for," said the female technician who spoke with Liz. "We'll organize everything we retrieve for your review."

"How long do you think it will take?" Liz asked.

"Do you have a deadline?" the woman asked. "Expedited service is an additional charge."

"How much?"

It was twice the normal amount for unlocking the specific type of phone. Liz hesitated, not sure if a week to ten days would make a difference.

"Expedite it," she replied.

"You got it."

CHAPTER 30

WHEN CONNOR TOLD MICHELLE HE COULDN'T PRO-
vide any details about the meeting at the sheriff's department, her
face fell.

"Oh no," she said, putting her hand over her mouth.

"But that's because of what the lawyers told me."

"So it wasn't all bad?" Michelle asked hopefully.

"Nothing is all bad," Connor replied, although he couldn't think
of anything good, except that he'd not been arrested on the spot and
hauled off to jail.

"Okay," Michelle began as she repositioned herself in her chair,
"then I'm going to try to have a positive attitude."

Connor remained isolated in his office, not even going out for
lunch. He fielded routine phone calls and responded to emails. But
when Elena called, he told Michelle to take a message. Midafternoon,
he emerged to the reception area.

"Go home early today," he said to Michelle.

"Are you sure? I have plenty of work to do."

"It can wait."

After Michelle left, Connor went into the sanctuary. He sat in
the front pew and looked up at the large wooden cross surrounded

by river stone. The ancient name for the room—"Sanctuary"—described a place Connor desperately needed. All day his swirling emotions had been draining energy from him like a gaping hole in the bottom of a swimming pool.

He lay down on the cushioned pew and looked up at the ceiling. One of the recessed lights needed to be changed. The only way to do so was with an extra-long extension pole with a suction cup on the end. Connor started to rise to retrieve the pole from the utility closet. But a gentle heaviness that spread over his whole body kept him on the pew. For a split second he thought it might be a problem with his heart. Connor took a deep breath and exhaled. He didn't feel pain. On the contrary, he was relaxed. Folding his hands across his chest, he closed his eyes and sensed a glimmer of energy, a spark of rejuvenation returning to his soul. A feeling of peace that extended from one end of his body to the other followed. Still lying down, he brought his hands together beneath his chin in the classic posture of prayer. Whatever or whoever had been assaulting him was gone. Connor had read about ancient mystics who'd had tangible experiences with God's presence. Now, he'd joined their company.

"Thank you," Connor said. "I really needed this."

He remained on the pew until the afternoon shadows lengthened. Before going to bed at home later, he spent time in his living room thinking about what had happened in the sanctuary. The best way he could describe the experience was as a protective covering of God's presence. He looked up the Hebrew and Greek words and quickly found the one that best fit. It was the Hebrew word *kavod*. The three-letter root for the term was connected to other concepts, including weight and heaviness, but one touched Connor at the deepest level—glory. He'd been covered by the glory of God.

When he woke in the morning, Connor rolled over as a text from Liz popped up on his phone:

Awake?

He immediately answered that he was and a few seconds later, she called.

"Good morning," Liz said. "Have you talked to Elena since our meeting yesterday?"

"No, she called yesterday afternoon, but I haven't gotten back to her."

"I had a short phone call with her," Liz said. "At least short by her standards. We're meeting in person today. Most of our conversation was about legal matters, but your name came up. I asked her a few questions but mostly listened. I hope it's going to be easier for you to interact with her in the future."

"Please explain."

"Elena realizes she's been too demanding on your time. You're responsible for a lot of people, not just her. I used the analogy of the law office. We represent a lot of clients. When we're talking to a specific client, that person has our undivided attention. But we can't devote all our efforts to one client."

"That makes sense," Connor replied slowly. "But Elena has been through two of the greatest traumas in life. Serious marital difficulty and the death of a spouse. She deserves a bit of extra pastoral care."

"Right, right. But you have the chance to reset where you are with her."

"I'll keep that in mind when I talk to her later today."

"Good. At the top of my list of things to do is finding a company that can access the information on the phone you found in the woods. I did some research and found one in San Diego. I'm sending them the phone today with next-day delivery."

"Is this going to be expensive?"

"Don't worry about the cost. Harold gave me the go-ahead to do what's necessary to help you. We'll figure out how to handle the attorney fees and expenses later. No pressure."

Connor, who was about to take a sip of coffee, lowered the cup. "That's generous."

"I thanked him."

"One other thing," Connor said. "Did you say anything to Elena about the police claiming there were opioids in Matt's blood at the time of his death?"

"Yes, but of course I didn't mention our meeting with Detective Norman or the notice you received from the GBI. Elena already knew about the blood test. She said Matt had a long-standing prescription for painkillers that he took whenever one of his knees flared up from an old sports injury. She said he probably took a pill before the hunt because he would be walking on uneven ground. But the fentanyl pill you found came from somewhere. We just don't know the answer."

After the call ended, Connor finished his coffee. He had three counseling sessions on his calendar. After his experience in the sanctuary, he hoped he could do what Liz suggested and devote his attention to the people who needed him. Driving to the church, his cell phone vibrated. It was Reg Bullock. Connor answered.

"Are you free for lunch?" Reg asked.

"Maybe. It depends on how long I'm in a meeting with a man who's coming in with his teenage daughter."

"I bet I know who it is," Reg said. "I told him to call you months ago. Take all the time you need. I'll work with your schedule."

———————

Liz's next item of business was to file Matt's will for probate in Etowah County. The forms weren't complicated. It was much like the coin flip at the beginning of a football game. The real competition would come later. Liz took the documents over to the courthouse and delivered them to the clerk of the probate court. While Liz stood at the counter, the woman glanced over the paperwork and nodded.

"Everything looks in order," she said. "Is service going out to the heirs?"

"Yes."

Liz was required to notify Anne individually and on behalf of Matt's daughters that the will had been presented for probate. Liz suddenly had a question: "Has a competing will already been filed by anyone else?"

"Let me check."

Liz waited while the woman faced her computer monitor and typed on a keyboard.

"No," she said after a minute passed. "But our office has received inquiries about the estate. I knew about Mr. Thompson's death from the obituary in the newspaper and opened a file to store information."

"Can you tell me who contacted you?" Liz asked.

"Yes. Let's see, a law firm in Atlanta representing Daughbert Technology, another firm representing Ms. Anne Thompson, Detective Robert Norman with the local sheriff's department, a man named Mr. Neil Peterson, and a reporter from the newspaper."

"What's the name of the law firm that represents Daughbert Technology?"

There were five named partners. Still standing at the counter, Liz quickly looked up the firm on her phone. There were eighty lawyers in the Atlanta office with twenty attorneys in the trust and estate department. That was a lot of firepower.

"Anything else?" the woman asked.

"What about the firm who contacted you on behalf of Anne Thompson?"

It, too, was an Atlanta law firm. Liz entered the information in her phone without looking it up.

"Thanks for your help," she said.

Two hours later, Liz was meeting with Elena in the big conference room. The client bristled when Liz told her that Anne had hired an attorney.

"Why would she do that unless she intended to attack the will that Matt made out for me?"

"That may be the case, or she could just be looking out for her interests. She didn't hire a big firm. It's a small outfit in Marietta with three lawyers."

"I don't trust her."

"And I'm going to do everything I can to protect you from Anne and anyone else."

"Speaking of that, I've thought a lot about what you should do with Winston Boone and the Daughbert Technology Trust."

Elena took out her phone and read from a list of demands, which again included Liz raising the possibility that Matt committed suicide. At that point, Liz interrupted her. "I already told you I can't do that," she said.

"Not to pressure Winston to give me any money, but when he

hears that Matt possibly committed suicide, he'll get the message. He's a smart man. Personally, I believe it was a horrible accident, but there's no use pretending that's not what everyone thinks."

"The answer is still no."

Elena stared directly into Liz's eyes. "As your client, I'm telling you what to do. Matt died from an accident, suicide, or someone killed him."

Liz wasn't backing down. "And we're going to do everything we can to prove it was an accident so you can collect under the double indemnity provision of the life insurance policy. Please let me do my job the best way for you."

Elena sighed. "Will you at least talk to Mr. Pollard to see if there's a way to communicate with Winston about the possibility of suicide?"

"Yes, but I believe the answer will still be no."

After Elena left, Liz stopped by the senior partner's office to see if he was available. Harold was on the phone but motioned for her to come in.

"I don't care how Judge Conklin ruled in the case you brought last year," Harold said. "Every case has to stand on its own merits."

The senior partner looked at Liz and rolled his eyes. Placing his hand over the receiver he whispered, "Marvin Stancill. This won't take long."

Harold continued to listen for a few seconds. "You know what they say, Marvin," he replied. "Bad facts make bad law. Only in this case your bad facts are going to make good law for me and my client."

Harold smiled. Even though the call wasn't on speaker, Liz could hear Stancill's voice through the receiver.

"That's right. I'll see you in court too," Harold said. "Unless your client decides it's not worth paying your fee to come over the mountain to Etowah County. We're only three thousand dollars apart on settlement."

The call ended.

Harold grinned. "I can't resist baiting him. He's easier to convince to take the hook than a starving trout in a one-acre fish-pond. I've made him a fair offer to settle, but he still tries to bully me for more. Do you think Reverend Grantham would consider how I treat Marvin a sin?"

"You should ask Connor, not me."

"Maybe I will. Marvin has sown enough bad will with other attorneys over the years that he deserves to reap the whirlwind. That's somewhere in the Bible. But you're not here to discuss theology."

"No, I met with Elena and wanted to give you an update."

"Go ahead."

Liz summarized the conversation. "She brought up suicide as the cause of Matt's death. The possibility is stronger now that we know about the presence of opioids in his blood system. Should that turn out to be fentanyl, everyone knows how deadly it can be."

"Yes," Harold said simply. "But based on your research into the policies, death by suicide won't impact Elena's basic claim, only the one by the Daughbert Technology Trust."

"Elena insisted I ask you again about mentioning suicide to Winston Boone as a bargaining tactic. She's thinking that somehow he's going to get the message and offer her money to keep quiet."

Harold snorted. "That's ridiculous and unethical! The lawyer I just talked to on the phone might attempt a stunt like that, but not us. What did you tell Elena?"

"That we wouldn't do it."

"Good. Have you filed the will with the probate court?"

Liz told Harold what the clerk told her. At the mention of the big Atlanta firm Daughbert Technology had hired, Harold raised his eyebrows.

"That's a good group. I went to school with one of the partners. He makes big bucks working in the arbitrage field." Harold rubbed his hand across his forehead. "More reason for us not to act sophomoric. As to Neil Peterson, he's given you two pieces of valuable information. It wouldn't hurt to see if there's anything else in his back pocket that he's willing to share. Let me know what you find out."

"Yes, sir."

CHAPTER 31

REG WAS WAITING FOR CONNOR AT PARKER'S RESTA-
urant. The tables in the bustling diner were crammed close together
to squeeze in a few more lunchtime customers. Reg was sitting in a
booth in the back that provided the best chance for privacy. Connor
made his way to him.

"How were you able to grab this?" he asked as he sat down
across from Reg.

"Vince Parker personally controls who sits here," Reg replied.
"I sent him a text."

"I didn't know about that. I guess it's a secret."

A waitress took their drink orders and left.

"Speaking of secrets," Reg said. "I heard rumor of a letter the
GBI sent to the sheriff's department ordering you not to leave
Etowah County while they continue to investigate the cause of Matt
Thompson's death."

Connor had walked into the restaurant hungry. His appetite
evaporated.

"Who told you?" he asked.

"One of my nieces who works at the courthouse overheard the
sheriff talking to one of the judges. She knows how much I like you
and let me know."

Connor sighed. "Does that mean it's going to be in the newspaper this week?"

"Maybe not. My niece knows how to keep her mouth shut."

"She didn't keep it shut to you."

"But I don't think she'll tell anyone else."

The waitress returned.

"A bowl of chicken noodle soup for me," Connor said.

"Honey, is that all?" the waitress replied. "Can I bring you a slice of corn bread?"

"No, thanks."

"The usual for me, Bessie," Reg said without looking at the menu.

"Fried pork chop, lima beans, and okra with onions and tomatoes," the woman said as she scribbled on a pad.

"And a roll, please; no corn bread. Plus, a sweet tea with extra lemon."

After the waitress left, Connor spoke. "I'm not prohibited from leaving Etowah County, just the state of Georgia. Anyway, I had to cancel my trip to Boston at the end of the month. The organization will refund the cost of the conference to the church, and I'll request a voucher for the flight."

"That's good," Reg said. "You'll need to be proactive about your relationship with the church."

"What do you mean?"

Reg cleared his throat. "If this situation escalates further, it might be best for you to take some time off until it blows over. Performing your duties at the church may become impossible. By calling it a mutual leave of absence, we can justify continuation of your salary for a considerable period of time, maybe up to six months. And once you're cleared, I think a majority of the members of the congregation would want you to resume your role. The board will likely follow. You can count on Jim and me."

As Reg talked, Connor decided hearing this news from a loyal supporter was better than hearing it from one of the board members who'd been a strong critic.

"Thanks for volunteering to talk to me," Connor replied. "I've actually wondered lately myself about taking a sabbatical until this is resolved but had decided to see it through. You and Jim make the call about the timing of any leave of absence. I'll agree with whatever you think best. Rock Community Church doesn't belong to me."

"No changes yet."

The waitress brought their food.

"I'll pray a quick blessing so you can eat," Connor said.

He bowed his head and asked the Lord to bless Reg, Jim, the church, and the food. Before he took a bite, Reg spoke. "Connor, you're mature far beyond your years. I've always been impressed with you. Your reaction to this news only increases my respect."

———————

Liz hung up the phone following a brief and unproductive conversation with Neil Peterson. When she asked why he'd contacted the Etowah County Probate Court about the filing of a will, Peterson brushed it off as an order from Winston Boone.

"Why was that necessary if the company already hired a law firm to represent it?" Liz asked.

"Redundancy, I guess," Peterson responded curtly. "Mr. Boone definitely has OCD tendencies."

"Has there been any internal discussion about the life insurance policy payable to the Daughbert Technology Trust?"

"If so, I've not been part of it. Listen, I have to go. You should have the rest of the documents you requested within the next ten days to two weeks. If you're not satisfied, take it up with the law firm that's representing the company. I'm just a conduit at this point."

"Thanks for your help."

Later, Liz summarized the call for Harold.

The senior partner shrugged. "Peterson's loyalty to Matt Thompson is weakening as time passes. Also, he may be thinking about his future employment in case the company goes under and doesn't want to jeopardize his connection with Winston Boone."

"He'd want to continue to work for Boone?"

"Possibly. Big law firms are the same way. When a large one blows up, there are a limited number of parachutes to go around and multiple attorneys try to hang on to a partner who has one."

"I've never thought about that."

"You don't have to working for a firm like this one. All you have to do is keep me satisfied with your work."

"How am I doing?"

Harold smiled. "You're here, aren't you?"

The senior partner swiveled in his chair and picked up a folder that he handed to Liz. "Do you remember the Neville case?" he asked.

"The lawsuit about racial discrimination at the textile plant?"

"Yes. There are five Spanish-speaking witnesses I want you to interview. Some of them may be reluctant to talk because they're job-scared, but eventually they're going to be subpoenaed by one side of the case or the other, so staying silent isn't an option. I want to know what they're going to say before they're put under oath."

Liz knew the best place to start. She went to the taqueria and showed the names to the owner. Manuel pointed to the first person on the list.

"I know three people with that name."

"I think this Jose Lopez is in his thirties. Does that help?"

"Yes, but it doesn't help you find him," Manuel replied. "If that's the Jose you're looking for, he left town last week to return to Guatemala so he could take care of his sick mother. Let me ask Raul to come out and check the names."

Manuel called back to the kitchen. The former Burnt Pine Tree chef smiled and nodded when he saw Liz. Manuel showed him the list and explained what Liz wanted. Raul pointed to the fourth name on the list, a woman named Esperanza Castillo.

"She goes to my church," Raul said.

"Do you know where she lives?" Liz asked.

Liz jotted down the address. The woman wasn't married and lived with two nieces.

"Would you be willing to call and ask if she'll talk to me?"

"What about?"

Liz explained the situation.

Raul nodded. "Yes, but it will have to be in the evening after we close."

"That would be great."

The chef wiped his face with a rag he pulled from his pocket. "A few days ago, the police came by to talk to me about the man who died at the Burnt Pine Tree," Raul said. "Matthew Thompson. They showed me a picture of him."

"What did they want to know?"

"Same as you. What I remembered from that day. I told them he'd come by the kitchen to get a sausage biscuit."

Liz thought for a moment. "He told you he didn't feel well, but was there anything about the way he acted that made you suspect he might be using drugs or alcohol?"

"No." Raul shook his head. "The police asked the same thing. It was early in the morning."

Taking out her phone, Liz pulled up a photo of Connor from the church website. She showed the picture to Raul.

"Do you recognize this man?"

Raul touched the photo with his finger. "Yes, that's the preacher. The police asked about him too. They wanted to know if he was at the lodge on the day the man died."

"What did you tell them?"

"I wasn't sure. Then they showed me a surveillance video from one of the cameras outside the building. It showed the area behind the building where we had the meat smoker. The preacher was standing nearby in the woods."

"Was it dated?"

"Yes." Raul nodded. "All the videos have the date on them. It was from the morning of the day the man died."

Liz hated to hear that. "Are you sure?"

"Yes, but I can't remember if the preacher came inside or not. Mr. Bullock liked to stop by the kitchen for a country ham and egg biscuit. A few times the preacher was with him."

"Did you see Mr. Bullock the day the man died?"

"I can't say for sure. He was there a lot, so it all runs together."

———————

After lunch, Connor sat in the restaurant parking lot trying to decide what to do. Remembering Reg's statement that nothing had changed yet, he returned to the church.

"How was your lunch with Reg?" Michelle asked brightly. "He always has a positive outlook."

"Less positive than normal. But it didn't affect me as much as it would have a few days ago."

"Huh," Michelle said.

Connor told her what had happened to him the previous afternoon in the sanctuary.

"Wow," she said when he finished. "It's not time for my break, but listening to you makes me want to go into the sanctuary right now."

"Fine with me," Connor replied. "Put the phone on voice mail and I'll work on my sermon."

Michelle stood. "If nothing wonderful happens, maybe I'll take a nap."

"Either way, I won't disturb you," Connor promised.

Going into his office and closing the door, Connor was pleased with how well he was able to concentrate. The main distraction was the possibility that he might have a limited number of opportunities left to speak to the congregation. If so, he had to make every Sunday count.

As he considered how to best illustrate the personal aspect of praying for one another, he called Lyle Hamilton to get permission to mention him and Sarah in the message.

"I guess so, but it's going to be kind of embarrassing," Lyle said.

Connor had a quick inspiration. "And I'd like you to share too," he said.

"Share what?"

"About praying for other people and what it means to you."

"There's no way I'd speak to the congregation," Lyle replied. "That would be scarier than when I used to work with 25,000-volt lines at the top of a 55-foot power pole."

"What about Sarah?" Connor asked. "Actually, I'd rather have her than you."

Lyle laughed. "That makes two of us. Sarah is pretty shy, but let me ask her. I predict she'll turn you down."

The phone was silent for a few moments.

"I would have lost that bet," Lyle said when he came back on the line. "She's a yes. Do you want her to write out what she's going to say so you can give it the okay?"

"At least a few notes, so I can make it fit with my message. I'd like to have her ideas by Friday morning."

"Okay, but it will be short," Lyle said. "Sarah doesn't talk much, but when she speaks, she wants to make it count."

"The world needs more people like Sarah."

CHAPTER 32

AN HOUR PASSED AS CONNOR WORKED STEADILY ON the sermon. The process proved therapeutic. There was a light knock on his door.

Expecting Michelle, Connor said, "Come in!"

The door opened. It was Elena Thompson. She was wearing a casual green top, designer jeans, and high brown boots.

"Where's your assistant?" Elena asked. "I didn't see her car in the parking lot, and I've been waiting for at least five minutes. I didn't want to barge in if you were meeting with someone."

"She should be back shortly," Connor said. "Did you want to schedule an appointment?"

"No." Elena frowned. "I want to talk to you now."

Without waiting for an answer, Elena marched in, closed the door behind her, and sat in what had been her usual chair during their counseling sessions with Matt. Connor walked over and opened the door.

"This needs to be private," Elena said.

"It is. When Michelle returns from her break, I'll close the door most of the way."

"You don't have anything to worry about from me," Elena said in a huff. "It's other people in this town who want to get you into trouble."

Connor didn't respond. "How can I help you today?" he asked.

"Betrayed, again," Elena answered, shaking her head. "And by someone you trust too. Do you want to know who it is?"

"Who?"

"Liz Acosta."

"Anything between you and Liz as client and attorney should remain confidential," Connor quickly replied. "It wouldn't be proper for me to comment."

"Are you defending her?"

"No, but it's outside my role as your minister."

"How can you say that? You don't even know what she's done!"

"You're right, but as a matter of procedure—"

"Don't pretend to go lawyer on me," Elena cut in, followed by a torrent of words. "Being a zealous advocate is what Liz is supposed to do. Recently, she's lost her nerve and won't do what she should to protect my future or fight for my rights. Matt and I were building our financial future together, but now he's gone. People think I have a big house, but it has two mortgages that I can't afford to pay. Matt's business is close to going under. And he gambled a bunch of his retirement savings in cryptocurrency that's worth a fraction of what he paid for it. All I have left are the proceeds of some life insurance policies that Liz isn't willing to collect for me. Because his death was accidental, the amount payable under the policies is doubled. But I've not seen a penny and don't know when I will."

"Slow down and make sure this is important for me to know."

"You need to hear all of this. Matt's ex-wife has both hands out, claiming she's just taking care of her daughters, but she's looking out for herself. There's no telling how much Matt paid Anne directly without telling me about it while he was alive. Oh, and the biggest insurance policy was taken out by Matt's company. Winston Boone, the man who controls some kind of trust that owns the policy, doesn't want to share any of it with me. Liz is afraid to confront him or Matt's ex." Elena finally stopped.

"I'm sorry," Connor said.

"I don't want sympathy. I want you to talk to Liz and tell her to do what's right. She thinks I'm irrational, but she'll listen to you. She knows how smart you are and believes everything you say."

Connor measured his words carefully. "Elena, if you're not willing to trust Liz, maybe you should consider hiring another law firm."

"I don't want to start over!" Elena hit the arms of the chair with her hands. "Liz knows everything about me! Even stuff you don't. I could tell when I met with her that she knew I was right, but she needs the courage to act."

"When did you meet with her?"

"Just now. I came straight from her office to see you."

Connor could imagine how uncomfortable the meeting must have been for Liz.

"If you feel strongly that Liz isn't going to fight for you, then I still believe you should consider changing attorneys. People do it all the time."

"Why won't you talk to her? You didn't have a problem telling Matt and me what you thought we should do."

"You came to me asking for help."

"What if Liz asks you for advice? I like Liz. She listens. And I know she cares about me and my situation. But we've had a breakdown in communication and need to get it fixed."

The way Elena talked and the look in her eyes made Connor

wonder if she was under the influence of drugs or some type of medication.

"Why don't you take a breather, and we'll talk in the morning," he said.

"Only if you promise you'll contact Liz. You have permission to tell her anything I said. You know how to do that summarize thing without bouncing all over the place and being emotional. What do you call it? Reflective listening?"

"Yes."

"Good." Elena stood up.

"I won't talk to Liz unless she calls and wants my advice," he said.

"Okay. I'll send her a text."

Connor followed Elena out to the waiting area and into the hallway. When he did, Michelle was walking toward them.

"Good afternoon, Elena," Michelle said as they approached each other.

Elena continued without responding.

Michelle joined Connor in the office suite. "That was odd," she said.

"Rude would be a more appropriate description," Connor replied.

"I've never exchanged more than a few words with her since she started attending the church." Michelle shrugged. "And I'm sorry I wasn't here when you met with her. I hope that wasn't a problem."

"I don't think so, but with Elena it's impossible to be certain how she views a conversation. I'm not going into any details, but she's very upset with Liz Acosta."

"Just guessing, Liz is more in the right than Elena."

"Probably," Connor agreed. "Have you been in the sanctuary this whole time?"

"No," Michelle replied sheepishly. "I started out there and spent time praying but then started thinking about a caramel latte and drove over to the coffee shop on Baxter Street. The coffee didn't equal your spiritual experience, but it was one of the best lattes I've ever had. I was very thankful as I drank every drop."

Connor grinned. "Then it was worth the trip."

He turned toward his office.

"One other thing about Elena," Michelle said.

"What?"

"I've thought about her reaction to her husband's death. Does she strike you as a grieving widow? I know she and Matt were having marital trouble and came to see you. But I get the feeling she's moved on very quickly. It's sad, but sometimes one spouse is relieved when the other spouse dies. That makes me feel sick in the pit of my stomach. I don't expect you to answer, but it's been bothering me. I've heard she's more interested in collecting a bunch of insurance money than anything else."

"Who told you that?"

Michelle ran her fingers across her lips. "I can't tell you. But it wasn't anyone who works with Liz Acosta."

───────────

Liz was about to leave the office for the evening when she received an email from the company in California that she'd hired to unlock the cell phone. The technician wanted to know how to transmit the information. Liz immediately called and asked to speak to the woman who sent the email. Ms. Hua answered, and Liz identified herself.

"Was it hard to access the phone?" she asked.

"No. Whoever owned it wasn't trying hard to block anyone from getting in. There was a four-number passcode that we cracked in about thirty minutes."

"How much data did you find?" Liz asked.

"Not much. There were no texts or voice-mail messages. The owner wasn't identified by name, but we were able to pull off twenty calls he or she received. Of that twenty, there were only six numbers. I'll send you those along with the dates and times of the calls. Everything took place over a three-day period."

"Three days?"

"Yes, the phone was over a year old, but I suspect the owner frequently changed out the SIM card to prevent a long-term record of activity. I saw from your transmittal information that the phone was found in the woods. Perhaps the phone was lost shortly after a SIM switch."

Liz mentioned the date of Matt's death.

"The last call came through at 7:32 a.m. on that day," the technician replied.

"No videos, no photos?" Liz asked.

"There wasn't anything in the photo or video album." Ms. Hua paused. "But an unusual game I'd never seen before showed up as a download. Something called snooker. It's like billiards. The player's name was Colours 6, which is the number of balls other than multiple red balls and a white cue ball used in the game. It was developed many years ago by British soldiers stationed in India."

Liz knew nothing about snooker. "Okay," she said. "Send over the phone log as an email attachment."

"Even though I couldn't ID the owner, do you want me to see if I can locate the names of the individuals who called the phone? That wasn't included in my work order, but I can try to do it, especially if they weren't trying to remain anonymous."

"Absolutely. I didn't know that was an option."

"I'll work on it before I leave for the day."

Later that evening, Liz kept checking her office email to see if she'd received the identity of the callers to the cell phone. She was in bed and about to turn out the lights when she looked one more time. There was an email from Ms. Hua sent two minutes earlier. Scanning the numbers, she immediately got out of bed and called Connor.

"I hope I didn't wake you up?" she asked when he answered.

"No, are you okay?"

"The company we hired in California successfully accessed the cell phone you found in the woods. Whoever had it received several calls around the time of the hunt. Two of them were from Elena Thompson."

"Elena?"

"Along with a call from Matt's ex-wife, Anne, and a man named Neil Peterson who works at Daughbert Technology. I'll send you the email as soon as we hang up."

Connor didn't respond.

"Are you still there?" Liz asked.

"Yes, just thinking. It makes sense that someone from Daughbert Technology would contact a person who was on the property the day of the hunt. The company had the whole place reserved. But what would be the connection between Elena and Anne Thompson and a guy walking around in the woods?"

"I don't know, but I'm going to ask Elena. There was a string of activity early in the morning on the day of Matt's death. Elena's second call was one of them. Some of the other calls took place the day before."

"Who owned the phone?"

"Unidentified. The owner may have recently replaced the SIM card to scrub it clean."

"Is that what the company in California figured out?"

"By deduction. The phone was a year old. It contained no photos, videos, or text messages."

"No texts? That's odd. And why would an employee of Daughbert Technology have a phone like that in the first place?"

"I don't know."

Liz glanced at the clock on her nightstand. It was close to midnight. She decided not to mention her conversation earlier in the day with Raul.

"Okay," she said. "I wouldn't have been able to sleep until I told you about this. Good night."

Connor spoke before she could hang up. "When are you going to talk to Elena?" he asked.

"Tomorrow. We had a rough meeting this afternoon, and I hope she'll calm down overnight. My boss and I are trying to help her navigate all that's going on."

"Elena left your office and came to see me. She was very upset and talked about a lot of things, including an insurance trust that Winston Boone controls; at least that's the way it sounded to me. I didn't ask for details. She was venting and wanted me to convince you to do what she says. I told her no but suggested that if she's not willing to trust you, she should hire someone else. I hope that's okay. Representing someone who won't take your advice seems untenable to me."

Liz felt the blood rush to her face. All the stressors of the last few days seemed to be piling on top of her at once. She didn't know whether to laugh or cry.

"You told Elena to fire me?" she exclaimed. "She's the biggest client I've brought to the firm since I got here! Granted, she's unpredictable and difficult at times, but working through issues is part of the process. I'm perfectly capable of handling any personality conflicts with my clients, just as you are required to do with your parishioners at times."

"You're right. I'm sorry. I was caught off guard and didn't think about that angle. At the end of the conversation, Elena talked about how well the two of you communicate. I don't think she's going to fire you."

"If she does, I'll know why."

"Liz, I'm really sorry."

"Me, too, Connor. And it's really late."

Still a little confused by Connor's advice to Elena and more than a little irritated, Liz ended the call. But falling asleep quickly was out of the question.

CHAPTER 33

AFTER A RESTLESS NIGHT, CONNOR GOT OUT OF BED while it was still dark. He threw his daypack into the Jeep and left town. He drove to the dirt road adjacent to the Burnt Pine Tree property. Strapping a lamp to his forehead, he plunged into the woods and didn't slow down till he was partway up the hill to the overlook, where he intended to watch the dawn. He'd brought along a couple of bottles of water, an energy bar, and a locally grown apple. Leaning against a tree in the gray light of the approaching day, he took a long drink of water and continued his rapid ascent. He arrived at the top with five minutes to spare. He sat down on the familiar rock and took a bite of apple. He watched as the orange crescent of the sun appeared in the distance above the horizon.

No weight of glory descended upon him, but he felt calmer than when he'd left the house. The sun became huge, the day new. He rubbed his hands together against the morning chill, then put them in the pockets of his jacket. It was always amazing how the sun would slowly appear, then suddenly shoot up into the sky.

It was going to be a clear day. The sun banished the morning chill. He slipped off his jacket and finished eating his energy bar. His phone in the front pocket of his shirt buzzed. He had cell service even in the woods. It was Liz.

"Good morning," she said when he answered. "How are you?"

"Sitting on top of a hill enjoying the new day."

"You went for a hike?"

"Yeah. I left the house before five. I barely slept last night. I'm sorry for what I said to Elena."

"And I shouldn't have been so hard on you last night. I understand why you said what you did."

"That doesn't change my need to apologize. Should I call and tell her I was wrong?"

"Don't do anything. Leave it to me."

"Are you at the office?"

"No, I'm about to get in the car but wanted to clear things up with you before starting my day."

Connor nudged a piece of moss with the toe of his boot.

"Switch to Facetime," Liz said.

Connor waited until the request came through and accepted it. Liz was sitting in her car.

"That's a big tree," she said.

"Not really. Let me show you another one that is actually two huge poplar trees growing out of the same trunk."

Connor moved fifty feet toward the tree made famous in his sermon.

"Are you scrambling over boulders?" Liz asked. "The picture is jumping all over the place."

"Yeah, there's not a trail."

He reached the dual trees and held the phone so that they came into view.

"It's impossible to fully appreciate on a small screen," he said. "But hopefully you get the idea."

He moved the phone so it panned up the trunks.

"Wow," she said. "Could we put that hike on the list for the future?"

"Absolutely. I do this one all the time. It's my favorite. The rock where I was sitting when you called is one of the best overlooks in Etowah County. I took this hike the day Matt died."

"Will you cross the Burnt Pine Tree property on your way down the mountain?"

"Yes."

"Let me know if you find anything else in the leaves."

"I don't know if I want to."

"Did you have any more thoughts about the numbers pulled from the cell phone?" Liz asked.

"Yes, but I'm not sure what to do."

"I wish we could talk to everyone who called and find out what they're willing to tell us, but we're limited."

"Why?"

"Both Winston Boone at Daughbert Technology and Anne Thompson are represented by lawyers. Neil Peterson isn't an official at the company, so I guess I could call him, but the last time we talked he told me he didn't want me to contact him again."

"You can talk to Elena."

"Of course, and I will. It'll give us something else to focus on."

━━━━━━━━

Just as Liz finished the phone call with Connor, the back door of the Devon house opened. Carrying a small package wrapped in aluminum foil in her hands, Bev made her way toward Liz, who lowered the window of the car.

"I saw you talking on the phone through the kitchen window and wanted to catch you before you left," Bev said. "I was up early baking this morning. This is a loaf of homemade honey-wheat bread."

She handed the bread to Liz. It was still warm.

"Why is it wrapped in foil?" Liz asked.

"To keep it from drying out. Wait about ten minutes before you unwrap it." Bev paused. "But you're on your way to work. Maybe I should keep it here and do it for you."

"I'd like to share it with the people at the office. Once they smell fresh bread, I'm sure they'll want a slice."

"That's fine." Bev glanced down at the ground for a moment before looking up with a sadness in her eyes. "Have you heard the news about Connor?"

Bracing herself, Liz asked, "What news?"

"Matt Thompson's death may not have been an accident, and the police believe Connor knows something about it. I'm worried sick."

"Who told you that?" Liz asked.

"A woman whose nephew works at the sheriff's department. Do you know what's going on?"

Liz hesitated. If she told Bev that Connor had hired the law firm, it would send a message that the rumors were true.

"From what I've heard, Connor hasn't done anything wrong. In fact, I was talking to him this morning when you looked out your kitchen window. He went for a hike before dawn so he could sit on a hill and watch the sun come up. He showed me a video of a huge tree with two trunks growing out of the base."

"Oh, he preached a sermon about that." Bev brightened up. "It was really good. You can listen to it on the church website."

"I should do that."

"I'm glad you and Connor have become friends. That makes my heart happy."

The older woman stepped away from the car.

"Thanks again for the bread," Liz said.

Becky saw the bread when Liz walked through the door. Moments later there was a swarm of activity in the kitchen.

"You'd think we were starving without any food in the pantry at home," Jessica said as she waited to cut off a slice.

Once Jessica had a slice of buttered bread on a plate, Liz followed the assistant to her workstation.

"I could tell you wanted me to get back to work," Jessica said, sitting down. "Do you have something urgent that needs to get done? I finished Harold's dictation before I left the office yesterday, so I have a gap in my schedule."

"No, I want to talk with you about Connor Grantham. Confidentially."

"Everything that goes on around here is confidential."

"But it seems everyone in this town eventually learns everyone else's business."

"You have a point, but we know the rules."

Liz told her about the meeting with Detective Norman, her conversation with Raul at the taqueria restaurant, and what she'd just learned from Bev Devon.

"Connor doesn't know what Raul or my landlady told me this morning," Liz said. "I was going to bring it up when he and I are face-to-face."

"Because you want to see his reaction?"

"I hadn't thought about it that way. It just"—Liz paused to take a breath—"Seems like the kind of thing that should be shared in person, not over the phone or a text."

"Here's my take. I know you like Connor, but he's in for a rough time no matter what. He's probably going to lose his job and his reputation."

"Yeah, that's what I think too."

"Maybe you should focus on being his lawyer and put the rest of it on hold."

Going into her office, Liz stared at her computer screen. Concepts like innocent until proven guilty and evidence of guilt beyond a reasonable doubt made sense in law school. But the real world operated according to different standards.

Placing the email from Ms. Hua on her desk, Liz called Elena.

———

Connor made his way down the mountain. He reached the boundary line for Burnt Pine Tree and saw the familiar "No Trespassing" sign nailed to a nearby tree. His feet crunched against the leaves and dead twigs that covered the ground. After zigzagging a few hundred yards, he realized that he'd veered south from his usual route and cut sharply to the left. In a hundred feet he encountered the shallow gully where he'd found the cell phone. He followed the ditch, kicking aside the leaves and dead organic material. All he uncovered was rotting leaves. He was about to move away when he saw something metal on the ground. It was painted white. Leaning over, he picked up an additional "No Trespassing" sign that had fallen from a tree or been pulled off by a trespasser. He carried the sign to his vehicle.

Driving onto the Burnt Pine Tree property, Connor reached the lodge and parked beside Andy McNamara's truck. Andy's office was down a hallway to the left. The door was closed. Connor knocked.

"Come in!" a voice replied.

Andy was sitting behind a simple wooden desk with a laptop in front of him. "Connor!" he said with a surprised look on his face. "Where did you come from?"

Connor held up the sign he'd found. "I was cutting across your property this morning after hiking up to Caldwell's Knob and found this."

"Yeah, we lose those signs all the time. I think people steal them for souvenirs," Andy said. "Hey, I just got off the phone with Reg. We're really puzzled about you showing up on the surveillance video feed from the lodge on the day Matt Thompson died."

"From the lodge?" Connor asked. "I thought someone claimed I was in the woods near Matt, which is completely false. I wasn't anywhere near that part of the property, and I never came into the lodge."

"The video I'm talking about wasn't from inside. The camera is set up at the southeast corner of the building near the smokers where we cook a lot of our meats."

"Show me."

Andy tapped the keyboard of his laptop with his fingers. "I'm not sure I should do this because this was sent to us by the police to verify."

"Call Reg and ask him."

Andy picked up his cell phone, then placed it on the desk in front of him. The familiar voice answered via speaker.

"Connor Grantham is here," Andy said. "Should I let him see the video we discussed?"

"He's there now?"

"Yes, it's me," Connor said. "I stopped by after hiking to Caldwell's Knob."

"Go ahead and play the video," Reg replied. "Connor, call me later."

There was an extra chair in the corner of the room. Andy positioned it so Connor could see the computer screen. His hands slightly sweaty, Connor sat down.

"They didn't seize them all at once, but eventually the GBI confiscated all the video recordings from the day of the accident," Andy said.

"You didn't watch them before they took them?"

"Only the ones from the trail cams in the area where Matt Thompson was supposed to be hunting."

Andy pressed a button on his keyboard.

"What did those cams show?" Connor asked.

"Nothing. They're not panoramic. We focus on game trails. Thompson was supposed to set up near a spot where we put out a lot of deer corn. After the ambulance came, I checked the footage but never saw him come into frame."

"Reg told me Stan Maxwell was guiding him."

"That's right. Stan was working because we had such a large group. He took them out in a four-wheeler and dropped Thompson off, then continued on with the other hunters."

"The sheriff's department claims I showed up on some of the trail cam footage."

"I can't confirm that, but like I said, there was a lot I didn't look at before the police took everything away."

Connor leaned forward in the chair. Andy clicked on a file. The opening image was just as Andy described. It showed the corner of the building with a pair of large black smokers in the foreground, one emitting a visible stream of smoke. No one was in the frame. The date stamp on the video was 8:14 a.m. on the day Matt died. A figure dressed in a dark T-shirt and dark pants appeared and went up to one of the smokers.

"That's Raul Vasquez," Andy said. "He used to work for us as a cook. He was in charge of the smokers."

"I remember him," Connor said.

Raul loaded some wood into the firebox and left. Over a minute passed.

"Wait for it," Andy said. "There!"

Andy pointed his finger at the screen. In the left portion of the image, close to the edge, Connor appeared. He was wearing jeans, a red-checked flannel shirt, and a gray ball cap. He looked directly at the camera, then took a step to the left and disappeared.

"Is that you?" Andy asked.

"Yes," Connor admitted. "And I've seen the smokers in operation a couple of times. But I wasn't wearing that shirt, pants, and hat on the day Matt Thompson died. Someone has tampered with the date."

Andy gave him a skeptical look. "That's not possible. It's part of the image when created."

CHAPTER 34

"Hello," Elena said in a sleepy voice. "I hope this is important because you woke me up. I had a terrible time trying to fall asleep last night."

"Join the club," Liz replied. "I was awake too."

"Why?"

"Do you remember the video Connor took on his phone when he was hiking on the day Matt died? The one with the big male deer and a brief image of a man wearing an orange vest."

"Yeah, what about it?"

"The other day Connor and a young boy were hiking in the same area and found a cell phone that may have belonged to the man Connor saw. I sent it to a forensics lab in California, and they were able to identify your number as a recent caller."

"Whose phone was it?" Elena asked in a more alert tone of voice.

"I was hoping you might be able to help me figure that out."

Liz gave Elena the number. "Is that number listed as one of your contacts?"

"Just a sec."

Liz tapped her index finger on her desk while she waited.

"No, it's not in my list."

Liz steadied herself before asking the next question. "Can you explain why the log for the cell phone Connor found lists calls coming from your cell number on two occasions? One, the day before Matt died, and then again the morning of the accident."

Elena was silent for a moment. "No," she said in a calm voice. "I'm trying to remember who I called, especially the morning Matt went hunting. It could have been a lot of different people. With him out of the house, I spent a bunch of time on my phone."

"Is it possible you talked to someone who worked for Daughbert Technology? My first guess is the phone belonged to an employee of the company."

"Not that I remember, but it's been weeks and weeks with so much happening in the meantime."

"Could you double-check and let me know?" Liz persisted. "No one else except for the people hunting was supposed to be on the property."

"Except Connor."

"Right."

"Can't the cell phone provider tell you the name of the person who owns the phone?" Elena asked.

"Not without a subpoena."

"Okay, I gotta go."

Elena abruptly ended the call before Liz could mention that Anne Thompson and Neil Peterson called the same number. That information would have to wait. Liz walked down the hall to see Harold. The senior partner listened closely.

"I believe whoever dropped the phone worked for Daughbert Technology," he said.

"Yeah, that makes sense to me too."

"Do you still have access to the video Connor took?"

"Yes."

Liz pulled up the video and handed her phone to Harold, who watched it. "There's not much to work with, but maybe the company you contacted in California can do facial recognition enhancements," he said. "If so, get them to blow up a partial image so we can determine if it matches anyone who works for Daughbert."

"I'll ask. What do you make of Elena's reaction to my questions? She brushed me off as if it wasn't important and practically hung up on me."

"It's either very suspicious or another example of Elena not being able to focus on a topic other than what's on her mind at the moment."

———————

Connor explained to Reg why the surveillance video was incorrect.

"I remember a day a couple of months ago when I took you back there to see the smokers," Reg replied. "But I don't recall what you were wearing."

"I don't remember your shirt that day either. But I'm pretty sure I was wearing the red-checked shirt and gray hat in the video."

Reg was silent for a moment.

"Do you believe I'm telling the truth?" Connor asked.

"Connor, with all my heart I want to believe you."

Deflated, Connor didn't know what else he could say.

Reg continued. "The old footage from all the field cams and surveillance cameras is kept on a computer at the lodge for a year or so. That way the guides can track how the deer move across the property. I'm not sure how often they delete the old stuff."

Connor sat up straighter. "If it's still there, we could figure out the day you showed me the smokers."

"And see if you show up in the video," Reg said to finish the thought.

"Yes."

"I'll drive out to the lodge as soon as we hang up," Reg said, speaking rapidly. "When do you think we were out there?"

Connor thought for a moment and narrowed it down to two possible dates.

"It had to be a Friday or Saturday of one of those weekends," he said.

"That's where I'll look first."

Connor drove directly from the lodge to Liz's office and marched into the reception area. "Good morning, Becky. I'd like to see Liz."

"Do you have an appointment?"

"No. Tell her it's urgent."

Becky picked up the phone. Connor shifted his weight back and forth on his feet. A few seconds later, Liz appeared.

"Sorry for not calling ahead," he said.

"Follow me."

They entered a large conference room. To Connor's surprise, Harold Pollard was sitting at the head of the table. There was a speaker phone in front of the older lawyer. Harold pointed at the phone.

"We've been on the phone with Detective Norman for the past ten minutes."

"What's going on?" Connor asked as Liz closed the door behind him.

"Norman has been meeting with the local DA and the GBI about charging you with Matt Thompson's murder," Harold said. "The GBI wants to arrest you, but the district attorney, Tom Nelson, isn't on board."

Speechless, Connor sank down into a chair.

"Detective Norman contacted us as a favor," Liz added.

"I don't understand," Connor managed.

"Maybe it's a jurisdictional turf war between law enforcement agencies," Harold responded. "The local boys don't like people in Atlanta telling them what to do and vice versa. We saw the same thing when they interviewed Elena Thompson."

"This is insane," Connor muttered.

"The disagreement between the local and state authorities could work to our advantage," Harold said.

Connor looked at Liz; he could tell she was on the verge of tears. When their eyes met, she grabbed a tissue from a box on a side table.

Connor returned his attention to Harold. "How?" he asked.

"Buying time. Every minute you've not been charged gives us an opportunity to rebut anything the GBI claims incriminates you."

"I know part of the reason they've become more aggressive," Connor said. "That's why I'm here."

Taking out his phone, he showed Harold and Liz the video forwarded by Andy McNamara. He watched Liz's face closely while she watched it. She bit her lower lip a couple of times without looking at him.

"Something's not right," Connor said when the video ended. "I wasn't on that portion of the property the day of Matt's death, and I wasn't wearing that shirt and hat."

He explained what Reg Bullock was going to do.

"That's a good idea," Harold said.

"I wish I could call Anne Thompson and ask her about the number for the cell phone Josh and I found in the woods," Connor said.

"I can't stop you," Harold said. "But you can't do it at our request."

The legal niceties of the attorney's ethical rules were, at the moment, not important to Connor. Harold left the conference room.

Connor turned to Liz. "Thanks," he said. "It means so much that you and Harold are on my side."

———

Liz walked with Connor back to the reception area. After he left, she returned to her office, shut the door, and closed her eyes. A sick feeling had hit her in the pit of her stomach during the call from Detective Norman. She didn't know if she needed to throw up or burst into tears. Perhaps this was what a panic attack felt like. She'd heard the best response was to take slow, deep breaths. The phone on her desk buzzed. She reluctantly pressed the receive button.

"Yes," she said.

"Elena Thompson is on the phone and wants to speak to you," Becky said.

Anyone else, Liz would have sent to voice mail. She tried to steady herself.

"Hello, Elena," she said.

"Why so formal?" the client responded in a light tone of voice. "I was getting back to you about the cell phone Connor found in the woods. I think I may know who it belongs to. Tyson Nash."

"Who?" Liz asked.

"The private investigator I brought to your office."

"I didn't know his last name."

"Tyson used multiple numbers to communicate with me. I should have recognized that as one of his phones as soon as you asked me about it."

"Why did he have multiple numbers?"

"Probably something to do with his business and the need to conceal his identity if he was conducting an investigation."

"Do you remember calling him the day Matt died?"

"It's possible. We were talking a lot. I'd asked him to check on a couple of things with Matt and Anne."

"What sort of things?"

"The usual stuff. Uncovering if there was more going on between them than sharing parenting duties for the girls. Matt had been so agreeable at our last session with Connor that I suspected he was up to something but didn't know what it might be. My first thought was that it had to do with Anne."

"Anne's number also showed up on the phone Connor found."

Elena was silent for a moment. "That makes sense. Tyson would use certain phones to contact someone and find out information without revealing who he was. You know, he'd create a fake identity and then ask questions."

"The phone also registered a call from Neil Peterson at Daughbert Technology."

"What?" Elena exploded. "Why would someone from Daughbert be talking to my investigator?"

"The person that unlocked the phone identified everyone who called the number. The record only went back a couple of days. They identified you, Anne, and Peterson."

"Wait a minute," Elena said more calmly. "I remember asking Tyson to check into something for me at Matt's company. I forgot that. Tyson knew most of the higher-ups from the corporate office were going to be in Bryson for the retreat. He probably wanted to determine who might be left at the office. Peterson was part of the admin staff in sales for the company."

"Why would the investigator care who was at the Atlanta office?" Liz asked. "All the important people were here in Bryson."

"Uh, I guess I can tell you because you're my attorney. I gave Tyson a key to the company office in Atlanta so he could go in on Saturday and locate some financial documents I wanted to see. I'd overheard Matt having a conversation with Winston's assistant, who mentioned a pro forma financial statement about foreign business activity. It really upset him."

"What's a pro forma financial statement?" Liz asked.

"An estimate of how good or bad a company may do in the future. Matt wanted to see the figures, and she said the information was in Winston's office but that he would go over it with Matt during the retreat. It was the sort of data you and I would need, and I asked Tyson to get a copy before Matt or anyone else changed the figures. I figured if I gave Tyson a key to the office, he wouldn't be breaking in illegally."

"I'm not sure that's true." Liz paused. "But why would Tyson Nash be at the Burnt Pine Tree Hunting Lodge and not in Atlanta?"

"I don't know," Elena replied. "Unless he wanted to actually see who was here before going to Atlanta. Would you like me to call and ask him?"

"Yes." Liz thought for a moment. "Is it okay if I tell Connor that the phone belonged to your private investigator?"

"Why is that important?"

"He wants to know."

"No."

Liz winced. This was going to be tough to navigate with Connor.

"One other thing," Liz said. "Did Tyson obtain a copy of the pro forma financial statement for you?"

"No, even with all the executives and support staff at the

retreat, he said there were a couple of people at the office when he showed up."

"So, he drove from Bryson to Atlanta for nothing?"

"Yes, but based on what you've been told by Neil, it's no longer a secret that the company is in big trouble."

CHAPTER 35

ON HIS WAY OUT, CONNOR STAYED IN THE RECEP-
tion area for a few minutes to talk to Becky. When he asked about
her little brother, the receptionist told him the young man, who was
a freshman in college, was having a lot of trouble adjusting to being
away from home.

"We all know that Bo is my mama's favorite," Becky said. "After
all, he's the baby, and the rest of us girls all had a hand in raising him."

The phone on Becky's desk buzzed and she picked up the
receiver.

"Yes, he's still here." Becky lowered the phone. "Liz wants to
see you."

"What's going on?" Connor asked when Liz appeared.

"Let's go to my office," she said.

Liz's work space had a single chair in front of her desk. She
positioned herself in front of her computer monitor. A small framed
photograph of Liz with a middle-aged couple rested on the corner
of her desk.

"Is that your parents?" he asked.

"Yes."

Connor picked up the photo. Liz had her father's dark eyes and hair but shared her mother's nose and mouth. He returned the picture to the desk. Liz was typing on her keyboard.

"Here it is," she said. "The Fletchall Group Limited. I'll go to their website."

"What's the Fletchall Group?"

"A private investigation firm."

"Is that who Elena hired to spy on Matt?" Connor asked.

"She told you about that?"

"No, Matt mentioned it a few days before he died. I never asked Elena."

Liz spoke. "Listen to this: 'Due to the sensitive nature of our services, we do not list the names of our professional investigators or post photographs. Information is available upon signing a confidentiality agreement.'"

"Why do you want to show me a photo of the investigator?" Connor asked.

"To see if you recognize him."

Connor thought for a moment. "Do you think the investigator might be the man in the video? He had a British accent. Call Elena and ask her if the person she hired fits that description."

"I can't do that."

"Why not?" Connor asked with a puzzled look on his face. "It's a simple question."

Liz simply shook her head. Taking out his phone, Connor searched for the Fletchall Group.

"They have an office in South Africa," he said, glancing up at Liz. "That would connect with the accent of the man I encountered in the woods."

"Please don't say anything to Elena about this."

"Don't worry. I won't. But it bothers me that she didn't want you to tell me."

"I shouldn't have stopped you before you left. It was just—" Liz looked down.

"You meant it when you said you wanted to help me in any way you can."

"Yes," Liz sighed.

Driving home from the law office, Connor received a call from Reg Bullock.

"What can you tell me?" Connor quickly asked.

"The hard drive for the computer that contained the original videos taken on the Burnt Pine Tree property crashed a few weeks ago. There's nothing to document a date different from the one that appears on the smoker video Andy showed you earlier."

"The computer crashed?"

"Or was damaged in a lightning storm. That computer and another one in a spare room weren't plugged into protective strips. I know this is disappointing, Connor, but I still feel your gut instinct is right and the video has been tampered with. I'll keep checking what I can."

Connor took a moment to absorb the bad news. "Thanks, Reg. I appreciate that. Could you ask Andy another question? Was there a private detective on the property the day Matt died? He would have spoken with a British or South African accent. I think he may be the person who shows up in the video I took of the big buck."

"Why don't you call Andy? He knows I want him to cooperate with you. I'll text his number."

At home, Connor phoned Andy, who didn't remember a private investigator being on the property.

"What about a man with a British accent?"

"Yes, there was a guy who worked for Daughbert Technology. I think his name was Jerry or something like that."

"Jerome Rossi," Connor said. "But I know he wasn't in the video I took."

The call ended. Frustrated, and wanting to do something physical, Connor went into his backyard and spent time pulling weeds and repairing the boards for his raised garden beds. He stayed outside until noon. Hungry, he was in the kitchen fixing a sandwich when there was a knock on his front door.

Detective Norman was standing on the stoop. He handed Connor a sheet of paper. "Connor Grantham, this is a warrant for your arrest charging you with the murder of Matthew Thompson."

Norman read Connor his Miranda rights. Connor heard what the detective was saying but struggled to believe it applied to him.

"May I call my lawyer now?" he managed.

"After we book you at the jail. Do you have any weapons on your person?"

"No."

"Get in the patrol car."

━━━━━━━━

Liz told Harold about her conversation with Elena.

"You know what this means, don't you?" the senior partner asked when she finished.

Liz nodded. "That the GBI and sheriff's department need to interview the private investigator who works for Elena and find out why he was on the Burnt Pine Tree property the day of Matt Thompson's death."

"You're right, but we don't work for a governmental agency. We work for Elena Thompson. And if Elena didn't want you to mention anything about her private investigator to Connor Grantham, you should have followed her instructions."

"But Connor has more reason than anyone to find out what he can about Tyson Nash," Liz protested.

"True, but he can't use this law firm as a source of information when it conflicts with our duty to another client. The deeper Connor is sucked into the investigation of Matt Thompson's death, the more certain I am that we can't represent him, even in a limited way."

Liz's face fell. Harold continued. "You've known from the beginning that if a conflict of interest arose between Elena and Connor, she had priority. We agreed to that, and it's time to inform Connor that he needs to find another lawyer."

"Is that what you really want to do? I'd much rather represent Connor than Elena."

"No, that's not possible."

"Is this because of how much money the firm can bill Elena?"

Harold gave her a steely-eyed look. "I'm not going to react to your question as strongly as I might like to. Our decision isn't about money, it's about our ethical obligation to Elena. She specifically told you not to inform Connor about the investigator, and you tried to get around those instructions. There's too much potential overlap to avoid a problem. Tell Elena what you did, and cut Connor loose."

"What if he hires someone like Marvin Stancill?"

"This matter is settled. No further discussion."

Liz bit her lower lip. There was nothing else she could think of to say except "Yes, sir."

Detective Norman's car didn't have wire mesh between the rear seat and the front seat. As soon as Norman was behind the wheel, the detective spoke into a radio receiver. "Grantham is in custody. I'm transporting him to the jail."

"Ten-four," a female voice responded.

Dazed and in shock, Connor sat with his hands in his lap during the short ride to the sheriff's department.

"I left my phone at my house," he said when they pulled up to the rear of the building.

"You won't need it. There's a phone near the booking area you can use to call your lawyer."

When the car stopped, Connor instinctively tried to open the rear door but couldn't. Norman escorted him through a solid metal door that buzzed as they approached. They entered a hallway.

"Sit here," the detective said, motioning to a row of five plastic chairs lined up against a yellow wall.

Across from the chairs was the booking area. Two women sat at desks with computer monitors in front of them. The older of the women came over to Connor and asked if he had identification. He took out his wallet and handed her his driver's license.

"Empty your pockets so I can inventory your personal possessions," she said.

All Connor had was his wallet. He'd not even locked the house. The woman put his wallet in a ziplock plastic bag and returned to her desk. A couple of minutes later she led him into the booking area. Connor sat beside her desk while she asked a series of background questions. She then took his fingerprints and told him to stand against the wall for his mug shot. The first photo was rejected because Connor's eyes were closed.

"Open your eyes," the woman said.

The second photo was acceptable. Connor's heart ached at the thought that the picture would appear in the local newspaper.

"May I call my lawyer?" he asked.

"Yes, we have phones in the interview rooms. Press 9 for an outside line."

The woman took him to a small enclosed space that contained a table and three chairs. A phone sat on one corner of the table. Connor picked up the phone and pressed 9 before realizing he didn't have either Liz's work or cell numbers memorized. He returned to the booking area.

"I need the number for the Pollard law firm," he said.

The woman rattled off the phone number without having to look it up.

"Could you repeat it, please?"

She did so more slowly. Connor returned to the interview room and dialed the number. He recognized Becky Carrington's voice.

"Becky, I need to speak to Liz. It's urgent."

"She's at lunch. Would you like me to have her call you back as soon as she returns?"

"I need to reach her now. What's her cell number? I don't have my phone with me."

There was a brief pause. Connor hoped Becky wouldn't ask him why he didn't have his cell phone. Delay was futile. Within twenty-four hours everyone in Bryson would know he was in jail. Becky came back on the line and gave him the number.

"Thanks so much," Connor said and hung up.

There was a knock on the door of the interview room. Detective Norman entered.

"I need to take you to lock up," the detective said.

"I've not yet reached my lawyer."

Norman glanced down at his watch. "Five minutes," he said. "No stalling."

The petty comment infuriated Connor. In a split second he went from being numb to enraged. The detective closed the door before Connor could respond. He took a deep breath and called Liz.

Wanting to put off her conversations with Elena and Connor, Liz left the office. To distract herself, she went to her favorite salad restaurant for lunch. She was eating and scrolling through her phone when an unknown number appeared. She ignored the call and let it go to voice mail. Seconds later the same number popped up.

"Hello," she said as she lowered her water glass.

"Liz, it's Connor. I've been arrested and charged with Matt's murder. I'm calling you from the jail."

Liz sat back in the chair, her eyes wide. "Who arrested you? The GBI?"

"Detective Norman. I've not seen or heard from anyone at the GBI."

Liz didn't know where to start. She remembered her time serving at the public defender's office.

"Don't say anything or talk to anyone," she said quickly. "Has anyone tried to interrogate you?"

"No. Norman read me my rights while we were standing on the front stoop of my house. I left without my phone, keys, everything except my wallet. I have one phone call to my lawyer. Will you talk to Harold and see what he can find out? I figure he could talk directly to the sheriff and find out why they've done this now."

Liz was frantic. She had to force the words from her mouth.

"We're not going to be able to represent you," she said. "There was already a conflict of interest between you and Elena over the private investigator matter. And now, with you being charged with her husband's murder, it's impossible—"

"You're telling me this while I'm sitting in an interview room at the jail?"

"This isn't my choice!" Liz said so loudly that people sitting at the tables nearby turned and stared in her direction. "I want to help you!"

"I need a lawyer, not sympathy."

Liz steadied herself. "I know, I know. Let me tell Harold what's happened and find out what he says."

"If you're not my attorney, how will we communicate?"

"I'm sure there's a way for people to talk to you at the jail. I'll come see you no matter what. I promise."

"I'm not going anywhere soon," Connor said and hung up.

CHAPTER 36

ABANDONING HER FOOD, LIZ LEFT THE RESTAU-rant. She ignored Becky's greeting and walked rapidly to Harold's office. The senior partner was on the phone, and he lifted an index finger to his lips when she entered.

"I can't budge off that number," he said to the other person on the line. "And if the offer isn't accepted within the next twenty-four hours, I'm going to pull it off the table."

Harold listened for a few moments and nodded his head. "I'm glad we could work this out. I'll send over the settlement documents by the end of the week."

He lowered the receiver.

"Connor is in jail charged with Matt Thompson's murder," Liz said.

"Sheriff Holland sent me a courtesy text ten minutes ago. I responded that we're no longer representing Reverend Grantham. Do you want me to break the news to Connor? I know that would be tough for you to do."

"I just told him we had to withdraw when he called me from the jail. He asked if you could still talk to the sheriff and find out what caused them to arrest him at this time."

"No, you and I have to back away."

"This isn't right!"

"And your personal feelings can't determine what you can do as a lawyer. We've already been over this. It's even clearer now that we can't be involved."

"Yes, yes." Liz pressed her lips together tightly. "May I visit him at the jail?"

"As a friend. Unlike a lawyer, you won't have unlimited access. It will be on visiting days. He'll have to put you on the list of people he wants to see."

"That may not happen after what I've done."

Harold didn't respond.

Liz sat silently for several moments before standing. "I'm going to call Elena and let her know that we're no longer representing Connor and why," she said.

"Good."

_____

The woman in the booking area took Connor to a cell that contained four cots. No one else was there.

"Detective Norman gave orders for you to stay here instead of placing you with the general population. A magistrate will set your bond. That could happen by tomorrow or not at all. Sometimes they don't set bond for a murder charge."

"When can I make another phone call?"

"There's no set time. But you can't abuse the privilege. I'll check back in a couple of hours."

The woman closed the solid metal door with a *clang*. The twelve-by-twelve-foot room had no windows. Connor immediately felt claustrophobic. There was a small metal sink against one wall with an open toilet beside it. Connor sat on the edge of one of the bunks. His next call would be to Reg Bullock.

He couldn't sit still and began pacing back and forth. He was angry. The injustice of the murder charge. The abrupt way in which he'd been jerked away from his home and locked up. The abandonment by Liz and her boss. He stopped and rested his hands against the cool metal of the door, then banged the door with the right side of his fist several times. If anyone heard, no one came.

Connor wasn't wearing a watch and without his phone he had no idea about the passage of time. He was sitting on the cot when the lock mechanism on the door clicked, and the woman from the booking area entered. She handed him a plastic drinking cup.

"I should have given you one of these," she said. "City water comes from the sink. It's safe."

"May I make another phone call?" he asked.

"Not yet. I'll be back later."

The door closed. Connor wished he'd asked how long he'd be in the cell. He'd always liked solitude, but aloneness coupled with confinement changed it from a welcome retreat to cruel torture. He returned to the cot and tried to pray, but the words that formed in his mind weren't escaping his head or penetrating the walls of the jail. He lay down on the cot and stared at the upper bunk. He closed his eyes and then quickly opened them. The idea of falling asleep and waking in this place was a nightmare he wanted to avoid. Without realizing it, he nodded off. He jerked awake at the sound of the door opening. He quickly swung his feet onto the concrete floor.

"You can make your phone call now," the woman said.

Connor followed her to the booking area. There was a clock on the wall. It had been less than three hours since he'd arrived at the jail. The thought of spending hour after hour, day after day confined in a jail cell was overwhelming. Connor was allowed to use the same interview room. Fortunately, he'd memorized Reg's phone number.

"Hello," the businessman said in a tentative voice.

"It's Connor. Have you heard what happened?"

"Yes, the news is all over town."

Connor knew that had to be true, but hearing it was devastating. "Liz Acosta and Harold Pollard aren't going to represent me, so I'm going to need to hire another lawyer. There's a chance a judge will set bail. If that happens—"

"We'll get you out," Reg answered before Connor could continue. "If I can't do it alone, I'll put together a group of supporters who will."

"You believe I have supporters?"

"Absolutely. Anyone who knows you realizes this is a huge mistake. I've been in touch with the sheriff and expressed my concern about how this is being handled. He claims the GBI is behind the arrest warrant. Has anyone tried to question you?"

"Not after I told Detective Norman that I wanted to speak to a lawyer."

"Whether we can get you out or not, we're going to help you find the best lawyer available."

"Who else is on my side?"

Reg mentioned Jim Morgan and three other men, one of whom didn't attend the church.

"Why is Nate Atwood willing to help?"

"Because he's my friend and knows how much I respect you."

Listening to Reg and realizing he wasn't totally abandoned caused a well of emotion to rise in Connor. He cleared his throat.

"I can't tell you how much I appreciate this," he managed. "Please let the others know too."

"I will."

"Could you come see me? I'm not sure when visitors are allowed."

"Yes."

Connor slowly lowered the receiver.

———————

Restless, Liz had to get away from the office. Instead of calling Elena, she decided to talk to her in person. She called the client from the car and asked if she could come by and see her.

"Now?" Elena asked.

"Yes. It's important."

"Just tell me what's on your mind."

"In person is my preference," Liz replied.

"If you insist. Make it thirty minutes. I'm wrapping something up."

It only took ten minutes to drive from the law office to Elena's house. Instead of taking a detour or stopping someplace to wait, Liz parked near the driveway entrance at the base of the hill and rehearsed what she wanted to say to Elena. The clock on Liz's phone had never been more resistant to the passage of time.

A large car with heavily tinted windows exited the driveway and turned quickly in the opposite direction from where Liz waited. The vehicle had a Georgia license plate with a sticker for Fulton County, which contained the downtown area of the city of Atlanta. A few moments later, Liz drove up to the house and got out. Elena opened the door before Liz reached it.

"I already know," Elena said. "The police have arrested Connor and charged him with murder. Come in. We can talk in the office."

Liz followed Elena. Stacks of papers covered the desk in Matt's former home office. Liz sat in a leather side chair. Elena was surprisingly composed.

"What else did you hear?" Liz asked.

"Nothing, but I don't think a jury will convict him."

"I hope not," Liz replied. "But I've not thought that far ahead. I came over to apologize to you. After we talked yesterday about Tyson Nash, I let it slip to Connor that Nash may have been the person in the video Connor took on the day of Matt's death. As your attorney, I should have honored your request to keep that confidential. And now that Connor's been charged with Matt's murder, our law firm isn't going to represent him."

"That makes sense," Elena said calmly. "Don't worry about what you said to Connor about Tyson. I'm sure it will come out that he was on the property too. Have you talked to Connor since he was arrested?"

"Yes, he called me from the jail, and I told him we couldn't help him."

"I want to see him," Elena replied. "Can you arrange a visit? The sooner the better. I don't want to waste a trip."

Liz stared incredulously at Elena. "Why do you want to see him?"

"To reassure him that I don't believe he killed Matt. I'm sure he's wondering what I think. Matt died in a hunting accident or by suicide. All this stuff with the police is nonsense."

"I'll inquire," Liz replied slowly. "But I doubt Connor is going to want to see or communicate with me."

"Do your best." Elena held up one hand, seeming to inspect

her latest manicure. "And I'm glad your firm is choosing me over Connor. No offense, but he needs a real criminal defense lawyer. This is way over your head."

Elena stood, signaling the end of the meeting. They walked to the door, stopping in the foyer.

"Do you think this is going to slow payment of the life insurance money?" Elena asked.

"Harold has said all along that insurance companies will use any excuse to delay payment."

Elena frowned. "I'm expecting you to force them to act. Sometimes you come across as too nice. Use any of your legal tricks to make them pay up."

Almost every encounter with Elena left Liz feeling like she'd met with a different person. She tried to process the conversation during her return trip to the office. When she entered the reception area, she could tell that Becky had been crying.

"Are you upset about Connor?" Liz asked as Becky wiped one of her eyes with a tissue.

"Yes," Becky said between sniffles. "It's so horrible."

Liz continued to Harold's office and told him about her meeting with Elena. The senior partner listened without comment until she mentioned Elena's request to visit Connor at the jail.

"I didn't see that coming," he said.

"Neither did I, but I guess it makes sense. If she genuinely cares about him, she'd want Connor to know her opinion about the charges against him."

"I'll see what I can do."

"And Elena says Connor needs a better criminal defense lawyer than this firm can provide."

Harold grunted, then scowled.

Connor returned to solitary confinement in the four-person cell. He passed the time by pacing, sitting on the edge of a bunk, and lying down. And worrying. Uncertainty about what might happen had ended. The worst possible scenario had come true. He was in jail. His reputation in the community was destroyed. Regardless of the outcome, his life would now be divided between the time before his arrest and the time after. Despair closed in tighter than the walls surrounding him.

A male deputy delivered supper, which consisted of a bologna sandwich, potato chips, applesauce, and a small chocolate chip cookie. The sandwich bread was stale. There was mustard smeared on half the sandwich. But Connor was hungry enough that he ate every crumb. Eating also gave him something to do. Wishing he had a toothbrush, he swished water around in his mouth. The door opened again. It was the same deputy. Connor grabbed the empty food tray from the cot and gave it to him. The deputy handed Connor an orange jumpsuit and white flip-flops.

"You have a visitor," the deputy said.

"Who is it?"

"I don't know. Do you want to see them?"

"Yes," Connor quickly replied. "Do I have to change clothes first?"

"No. Follow me."

Connor tried to steady himself as he followed the deputy toward the booking area. He didn't want to break down and sob when he saw Reg but suspected that he might. They entered a medium-size room with six plastic tables surrounded by four chairs each. It could have been the fellowship room for a small church. The space was empty except for a man and a woman at one of the tables. It was Lyle and Sarah Hamilton. One of the plastic chairs had been removed so Lyle could park his wheelchair. Tears suddenly streamed down Connor's cheeks. He didn't break down, he simply cried. Lyle rubbed his right eye with his hand. Sarah, a serious look on her face, showed no emotion.

Connor sat across from Lyle. "Thanks for coming," he said. "How did you get permission to see me?"

"An old fishing buddy with connections in the sheriff's department cleared it," Lyle said. "He's a praying guy and knew why we wanted to come."

Connor faced Sarah. "What do you think?" he asked her.

"That you're in a spiritual battle and need all the reinforcements heaven has available."

"I'm not sure how to make that happen."

"We're here to help," Sarah replied. "And don't feel like you have to explain anything to us. Lyle and I know you're innocent. The Lord clearly showed me before we received the news that you'd been arrested."

"How did—"

"Not now," Sarah said. "They only gave us fifteen minutes, and we want to use it wisely."

"Okay."

Sarah bowed her head and began to pray. Within seconds Connor felt the skin on his back and arms begin to tingle. He had no idea what that meant, but he accepted it as good. If prayer is a weapon, Sarah's words weren't bullets, they were artillery shells. When she paused, Lyle started praying. After being with the couple several times, Connor realized that Lyle was praying more powerfully and at a deeper level. His legs might be paralyzed, but his spirit was getting stronger. The confidence in their words started calming the storm inside Connor. Lyle stopped. There was silence for several moments. Then, taking a deep breath, Connor prayed. He started by asking for God's help. Snippets of verses from Psalms surfaced in his mind. King David had walked the path Connor found himself on. He repeated some of the phrases he'd heard Sarah and Lyle use. He stopped and opened his eyes.

"You already prayed that," Connor said.

"Do it," Sarah responded. "You need to own it too."

Connor closed his eyes and continued. When he stopped, Sarah prayed again. Followed by Lyle. A door opened.

"Time's up," a deputy announced.

"Amen," Lyle said.

"We're not going to stop until we see the victory," Sarah said earnestly. "No matter how long it takes."

"I hope it's not too long," Connor replied, then remembered how Sarah had been praying many months for Lyle. "But that's not up to me."

Lyle reached out and grabbed both of Connor's hands. The former electrician still had a powerful grip. "Remember, we're with you," he said.

On his way back to his cell, Connor no longer felt like crying. A woman at the booking center stopped Connor and the guard who was escorting him.

"Do you want to designate the visitors who can see you?" she asked. "We've been getting a lot of calls."

"No," Connor replied. "Surprise me."

CHAPTER 37

NOT ABLE TO CONCENTRATE ON HER WORK, LIZ left the office early. She was sitting in her living room when her phone vibrated. It was Elena.

"Where are you?" Elena asked. "I came to your office, and the receptionist won't tell me where you've gone."

"I left early. Why did you go to the office?"

"You know I don't trust cell phones. That's why I'm here. I'll wait for you."

"I'm not coming back today," Liz replied.

"I tried to call Tyson Nash, but I wasn't able to reach him."

"Did you leave him a message?"

"I'm not going to tell you anything else until we're face-to-face."

Liz didn't want to return to the office for Elena. But if there was something that might help Connor, even though she no longer represented him, she had to find out.

"I'm on my way," she said.

Fifteen minutes later, Liz sat across from Elena in the main conference room. The client was trembling with rage.

"Where's your cell phone?" Elena demanded.

"In my office."

Elena placed both hands on the table. "I promised to call Tyson. When he didn't answer either of his numbers, I decided to check with the corporate office in DC. They always know where he is and can page him. The woman I spoke with said he was no longer employed with the company and wouldn't give me a forwarding number or email address. When I asked why, she hung up on me. I called back and asked to speak to his supervisor, a man named Michael Claxton. He told me Tyson was terminated for cause when an auditor in the billing department discovered he was charging both me and Daughbert Technology for the same services on the same day. My bills indicated surveillance work targeting Daughbert; the bill to Daughbert was for surveillance work targeting me. Claxton apologized and told me they'd notified their professional liability insurance company of what happened." Elena paused. "I would never imagine that Tyson was secretly working for Matt's company! When I first met him, he promised me that no one would know about our relationship."

"'Relationship'?"

"Professional, of course. Tyson's company had performed work for Daughbert, but I contacted Tyson directly through the Fletchall website."

"Regardless, you have a claim against the Fletchall Group for breach of the duty owed to you as a client," Liz said. "The question would be damages beyond invasion of privacy."

"I told Claxton I'd decide later about suing them and demanded to know what was in Tyson's file about me. He refused."

"His lawyers would tell him to say that."

"How can they do that?" Elena's voice grew louder. "I have a right to know! Matt must have found out what I was doing and turned Tyson against me by offering him more money."

"How can you be sure it was Matt?" Liz asked in surprise.

"Who else could it be? Matt was sneaky. It would be just like him to come along behind me and switch things around. The fact that Anne called Tyson makes me suspect she was in on it with Matt."

"Do you want me to get in touch with the Fletchall Group as your attorney?"

"Not yet," Elena replied. "There's so much going on. I don't want to get sidetracked. But I had to tell you about this."

"I understand why you're upset."

Liz escorted Elena to the reception area. Unfortunately, nothing she'd learned from Elena helped Connor. But she didn't want to leave the new information alone. Picking up her cell phone, she called Neil Peterson.

"This is Liz Acosta," she said when he answered. "I know you didn't want to talk to me anymore, but there's something new I have to ask you about."

"No," Peterson started, but Liz continued anyway.

"It has to do with someone you talked to the morning Matt Thompson died. A man with a South African accent called you that morning. What can you tell me about him?"

There was a brief silence. Liz checked to make sure Peterson hadn't hung up on her.

"How do you know about this?" Peterson asked.

Liz took a deep breath and told him about Connor and the boy finding the cell phone in the woods and unlocking it.

"I've wondered about that several times since the day it happened," Peterson said. "The man who called wanted to know if I was in the office and whether he could come by for a meeting. He said he worked for a vendor hired by Winston who suggested he contact me directly. When I told him I was available, he hung up without scheduling an appointment."

"Did he tell you his name or the name of his company?"

"Not that I recall, but he called me 'mate' during the conversation. And I remember the accent."

"Have you heard of the Fletchall Group Limited?"

"It's a private investigation company. Is that who he worked for?"

"Maybe. Why are you familiar with them?"

"They were hired from time to time to provide services for us. Nothing I can tell you about."

"I understand."

"What was the name of the man who had the cell phone?" Peterson asked.

Liz quickly decided the possible benefit of revealing information outweighed refusing to do so. "Does the name Tyson Nash sound familiar?"

"No. I only met one of their employees. It wasn't him."

"Would interacting with the Fletchall Group have been the responsibility of Matt Thompson or Winston Boone?"

"Definitely Winston.".

No one else came to visit Connor. He changed into the orange jumpsuit. One of the male deputies took his civilian clothes and stuffed them into a clear plastic bag. The jumpsuit was too small. The bottom of the legs barely reached Connor's ankles, and the arms stopped above his wrists. The shoes were much like the slides he wore when he went to the beach. Connor was allowed to keep his socks. He passed the time by pacing and doing push-ups.

When in college, Connor and some of his buddies had participated in a challenge to perform ten thousand push-ups in a single month. That worked out to over three hundred push-ups per day. At the time, Connor was too busy and only lasted a couple of days. Meeting the goal now would be easy, at least from an available-time standpoint. Before lying down for the night, Connor did five sets of fifty push-ups each. The last set was especially tough, but he pressed through. Suddenly, most of the lights turned off. Hoping the physical exercise would help him relax enough to sleep, Connor lay on one of the bottom bunks and closed his eyes.

═══════════

When he awoke, he wasn't sure how much time had passed. The lights were still dimmed. He'd slept soundly without dreaming. He waited for the arrival of whatever emotions or thoughts might appear. Not surprisingly, the realization of where he was and why he was there demanded first place in line. Connor prayed for the grace he needed for the day and hoped it wouldn't be solely spent in the jail cell. Rolling out of the cot, he washed his hands and face in the tiny sink. Dropping down, he performed his first set of fifty push-ups. Connor's arms were sore from the exertion of the previous night, but his muscles loosened as he continued. He was hungry. There were no sounds in the hallway, and he realized that he'd not heard anything except his own breathing and movements since arriving in the cell. He must be in a part of the jail significantly separated from the other prisoners. A crazy thought shot through his mind that he wasn't really in the jail. He was in a fake location like a movie set. He dropped down and performed another fifty push-ups. The door opened, and a deputy he'd not seen yet entered with a plastic tray of food.

"Breakfast," the man announced, handing the tray to Connor. "What time is it?"

"Five forty-five in the morning," the man replied. "We start early."

"Will I be allowed out of my cell today? Is there an exercise area?"

"Maybe, although it looks like you're getting plenty of exercise already."

Connor hadn't considered that he was subject to twenty-four-hour surveillance. He quickly glanced around the cell but didn't see a camera. The man closed the door.

Sitting on a different bunk than the one where he'd slept, Connor methodically ate every bite of scrambled eggs, two pieces of white toast streaked with margarine, two sausage links, and two pieces of orange cut in quarters. He nibbled on the orange slices until every bit of fruit was pried from the peel. The black liquid in an insulated paper cup barely qualified as coffee, but he drank it anyway.

"Lord, thank you for breakfast," he said when he placed the tray beside him on the cot. "What's next?"

Not expecting an answer, Connor was surprised when he had the strong impression that he should lie down again. He was wide awake and doubted he'd be able to go back to sleep. Obeying, he stretched out on his sleeping bunk and closed his eyes.

===

After a fitful night during which she worried about Connor and how he was being treated at the jail, Liz arrived early at the office. A few minutes later, she heard footsteps in the hallway. Checking, she saw that the light in Harold's office was on.

"What brings you in so early?" Harold asked.

"Couldn't sleep."

"Understandable. I know you're worried about Connor. I spent some time last night thinking about him too."

"What were your thoughts?"

"Trying to sort out why they arrested him." Harold paused. "And what I'd be doing if we were representing him."

"You want to help him, don't you?"

"Maybe, but I'm not going to put my answer on the record."

"I talked with Neil Peterson," she said.

"I thought he cut ties with you."

Liz told her boss about the conversation related to the Fletchall Group and Tyson Nash.

"It's likely Nash was the man in the video Connor took on his phone," Harold said. "Did you tell Elena what Peterson said?"

"Not yet. Would that qualify as information that doesn't have to be disclosed immediately to a client? She might react imprudently and yell at Winston Boone for usurping her private investigator."

"It sounds like the Fletchall Group had a relationship with Daughbert Technology that predated anything Elena set up. I think it's okay to hold off for a short while. Are you going to try to visit Connor at the jail today?"

"Yes."

"I'll pull a couple of strings to make it happen even if you're not on his approved list. That way you can plead your case of caring about what happens to him in person."

"Thanks."

"Go," Harold said, shooing her out of his office.

A couple of hours later, Becky buzzed Liz. "Reg Bullock is here. He doesn't have an appointment but says it has to do with Connor Grantham. Mr. Bullock goes to the church—"

"I'll see him."

As soon as he entered the reception area, Liz recognized the man's face. He extended his right hand. In his left hand was a laptop.

"Thanks for seeing me," Reg said. "There's something I'd like to show you."

Liz led him to the conference room and closed the door. "Before you say anything else, I need to advise you that this law firm no longer represents Connor," she said. "Mr. Pollard and I had to withdraw due to a conflict of interest with another client."

"Connor told me. Are you still interested in seeing what I have?"

Liz hesitated for a moment. "Yes."

Reg placed the laptop on the table and turned it on. "This is a surveillance video showing the area near the lodge kitchen at Burnt Pine Tree," he said. "It's outside at the meat smokers."

"Connor showed Harold and me a video he'd received from Andy McNamara yesterday morning. Is this the same one? He told us that he wasn't near the smokers on the day of Matt's death and at any rate wasn't wearing the clothes he's pictured in on that day. He mentioned that you were going to check some stored footage."

Reg pulled up a video file and opened it. "Yes, this is the same video. I was unsuccessful in finding the original we wanted to compare because the files had been damaged. But if you'll bear with me, I'd like you to see it again. I won't comment until after you've watched it."

Liz sat down in front of the laptop. The scene was exactly as she remembered. The date corresponded to the day of Matt's death, and there was no doubt that Connor appeared in the frame toward the end of the recording.

"Now we'll back it up a little and I'm going to stop it toward the end."

As Liz watched, the back corner of the lodge appeared along with the smokers.

"That's Raul," Reg said when the cook appeared.

"Right."

Raul loaded wood into the smoker and then left. There was a long section of nothing except the smoker. Connor moved into the picture. Reg stopped the video.

"Do you see the bush that's beside Connor's leg?" Reg asked, pointing at the phone.

"Yes."

"That's a winged euonymus or burning bush. We planted several of them around the lodge. That's a small one put in the ground last year. Do you see how red the leaves are?"

The bush was about a foot tall and covered in tiny bright red leaves.

"Yes."

"Those leaves turned red at least a month before the day Matt Thompson died. Because we had a hot summer, the burning bushes turned color earlier than normal. I remember because I talked about it with the head maintenance guy. Once the leaves turn, they don't stay on long."

Liz stared at the image. Based on the camera angle pointing downward toward the smokers, there weren't any complete trees in the picture, only a few trunks.

"And look at the ground," Reg continued. "Only a few leaves have fallen from the trees. This is the very beginning of fall. It's not from the Daughbert Technology weekend. Somebody doctored the date of the video, and the police need to know about it."

"I want to believe your interpretation," Liz said slowly. "But how can you be so precise about the dates?"

"I spend a lot of time in the woods, especially the Burnt Pine Tree property. I believe what I'm telling you is true."

"Could I have a copy of this to show Raul?"

"Absolutely. I think this could clear Connor."

"We don't know what other evidence the police have," Liz said. "But we could hire someone to forensically evaluate the video to determine if there's been tampering."

"Do it. I'll pay for it. I'm a client of the firm. Harold has performed work for me in the past."

After Reg left, Liz watched the video again and decided to contact the company in San Diego. She also researched the burning bush plant. An argument could certainly be made that the environmental evidence in the images conflicted with the date on the recording. But it would take an expert witness to explain it in a persuasive way. A lay opinion from Reg Bullock, who was one of Connor's supporters, wouldn't cut it. And there was still one more opinion she needed to obtain. Leaving the office, she drove to Manuel's Taqueria.

CHAPTER 38

CONNOR REMAINED ON THE COT AS THE WEIGHT OF God's presence, of heavenly glory, settled upon him. This time, he didn't wonder if he was on the verge of a heart attack. Rather, he positioned his heart to receive encouragement and strength. He was in a jail cell, not the sanctuary of Rock Community Church, but if God was with him, the difference in location became unimportant. All that mattered was the awareness of the Lord's divine covering.

He'd closed his eyes when the experience began. Comfort, power, and peace washed over him. A long period passed; Connor considered opening his eyes but hesitated out of concern the Lord might leave. He did so anyway. Nothing changed. Connor smiled. God's reality transcended the function of his eyelids. Thankfulness rose from deep inside him. He spoke it out. The glory didn't lift. He continued to express his appreciation to the Lord. The passage of time was irrelevant. Connor had no place to go and couldn't leave the cell if he'd wanted to. Illogical as it might seem, he didn't want to be anywhere else.

The door to the cell opened. The male guard who'd brought his breakfast entered. He had another food tray in his hand. Instead of a sandwich, there were three chicken tenders, a scoop of mashed potatoes, a piece of corn bread, and some kind of cobbler for dessert.

"Here's your lunch," the man said. "And we received word from the courthouse that your bond has been set at one million dollars."

"Thanks," Connor replied.

The man left. Connor took a deep breath. The strong sense of God's presence in the cell was gone, but the impact on Connor remained. He felt an extraordinary peace. The verse about a peace that passes understanding from Paul's writings came to his mind.

Connor nodded to himself and said out loud, "That's what he meant."

Before he ate his meal, Connor offered up a simple prayer asking the Lord to do what needed to be done next, whatever that might be.

===

Manuel wasn't perched on a stool in his usual spot near the cash register.

"Where's Manuel?" Liz asked the young woman who served as waitress and cashier.

"Fishing," she replied.

"Is Raul here?" she asked.

"He'll be the one who prepares your tamales."

"I'd like to talk to him before he does that."

The woman disappeared into the kitchen. A few moments later Raul, who was wearing a white apron, came out.

Liz greeted him. "Do you remember when I asked you about the preacher who'd come to Burnt Pine Tree with Mr. Bullock?" she asked.

"Yes."

"I'd like to show you a video and ask if it's the same one the police questioned you about."

Liz pulled up the video on her phone and played it. Raul nodded.

"That's me putting wood in the smoker," the chef said. "And there's the preacher."

"It doesn't look like you were outside when he showed up. Is that right?"

"I can't say for sure. I could have been on the other side of a smoker splitting wood. We liked to use smaller pieces."

"How long ago was this taken? Is the date running on the top of the video correct or could it possibly have been earlier in the fall?"

Raul furrowed his brow for a moment and pointed at the screen. "That's a big pile of wood beside the smoker. We only did that toward the end of summer so we could be ready for the fall and winter hunting seasons. I don't believe there was that much wood left on the stack at the time the video was taken."

"How sure are you about that?"

"Positive," Raul replied. "Taking care of the wood pile for the smokers was part of my regular job."

"What about the red bush and the absence of leaves on the ground? Does that help date the video?"

"I don't know about bushes. And we always raked leaves and twigs away from the smokers to cut down the chance of a fire in the woods. They were never allowed to pile up in that area."

"Okay, thanks," Liz said. "Did you tell any of this to the police?"

"About taking care of the wood for the smoker? Yes."

"No, about how the stack of wood is larger or smaller depending on the time of the year."

Raul shook his head. "No. They didn't ask me."

Later, while Liz ate her tamales, she considered Raul's opinion and decided it made sense. And no one could argue that he had a bias toward anything except the truth. Upon her return to the office, she went into Harold's office and told him about the meetings with Reg and Raul.

"I want to make it clear that Mr. Bullock came to see me," Liz said. "I didn't contact him."

"I picked up on that. And you only went to the Mexican restaurant because you were hungry and need to maintain a good working relationship with the folks who work there."

Harold stopped. Liz waited.

"And you want my help in getting this information to the sheriff's department for them to consider and pass along to the GBI," Harold continued.

"It's in Elena's best interest that suspicion about the circumstances of Matt's death end so the insurance company will have to pay. And like you said this morning, a part of you wants to help Connor if possible."

"Liz, you are getting more persuasive by the hour." Harold grinned. "I'll call the sheriff and suggest someone from his office contact Reg Bullock and the former cook at Burnt Pine Tree."

"Thanks."

"And when you meet with Connor you can let him know."

"What's a good time to go to the jail?"

"Before the end of the day. They informed me at the jail that he's not placed any restrictions on visitors."

———

After lunch, Connor returned to his cot. The season of *kavod* was over, though. He spent the next few hours praying, but not for himself, and doing push-ups. Praying for others in the midst of a time of intense personal need was liberating and kept him from self-focus. He'd just logged his three hundredth push-up when the cell door opened. Expecting supper, he stood up. Instead of handing him a tray of food, the guard handed him the bag containing the clothes Connor was wearing when he was arrested.

"Your bond has been posted," the guard said. "Get dressed. I'll be back in a few minutes."

The door shut. Connor stared for a second at the bag before slipping off the orange jumpsuit and putting on his regular clothes. He washed his face in the sink and sat on the edge of his cot. He looked forward to a hot shower and the chance to brush his teeth. But no place on earth had so profoundly impacted him over a twenty-four-hour period as the jail cell. Then he realized it wasn't the place but the God who inhabited the place that made the difference. He'd learned so much in such a brief time. From Lyle and Sarah. And from God himself.

The guard returned and led him to an area where Connor was given paperwork notifying him when he would have to appear in court to enter a plea to the charges against him. The practical problems that had faded in the cell returned. The guard opened a door to a waiting area where Reg Bullock waited. Reg stepped forward and hugged him.

"I'm a bit stale," Connor said.

"I don't care," Reg replied.

"I can't thank you and the others enough," Connor started.

"Hey, we were ready to pledge a lot more."

Stepping outside, Connor blinked in the bright sunlight. "I'll never think about jail the same way," he said as they walked to Reg's truck.

"I'm sure that's true." Reg glanced at him with a puzzled look on his face.

"Do I still have a job at the church?"

"You've been suspended, not terminated. That's the best I could do given the circumstances."

"Okay."

They got in the vehicle. "I was going to wait until I took you home, but I'm going to tell you this now," Reg said without starting the engine. "I've already shared it with Liz Acosta."

"Liz isn't helping me."

"She's working for me."

"I don't understand."

"That's not the important part."

Reg explained what he'd figured out about the video. "Liz is going to have the images analyzed to see how it was altered."

"And someone should talk to the cook who smoked the meats," Connor replied. "He might remember that day."

"Yes, Raul is a solid guy. I heard he bought into a restaurant on the east side of town."

When they pulled onto the street where Connor lived there were several unfamiliar cars parked in front of his house.

"What's going on?" Connor asked.

Reg parked behind a sedan with deeply tinted windows. Before they got out, two men came out the front door. One of them was carrying a hunting rifle. Connor exited the car and walked rapidly over to them.

"Who are you and what are you doing inside my house?" he demanded.

"The agent in charge is inside," one of the men replied.

Connor entered the house. There was someone in the kitchen

and two men in the living room. The more muscular of the men stepped toward him.

"Hold it right there," he said.

"I'm Connor Grantham, and this is my house."

The other man handed Connor a sheet of paper. "I'm Agent Flannery with the GBI. This is a search warrant for your residence."

"Why are you confiscating my rifle?"

"Potential evidence. Wait outside until we're finished."

Connor wanted to argue but knew it was pointless. He left and stood next to Reg in the yard.

"What are they looking for?" Reg asked.

Connor glanced down at the search warrant. It identified "evidence related to the death of Matt Thompson, including, but not limited to, drugs, documents, and firearms." He showed the paper to Reg.

"What's the caliber of your rifle?" Reg asked.

"It's a Browning X-Bolt 308."

"Matt's group was using Winchester 308 ammo on the day of the hunt," he said.

Connor pressed his lips together. A couple of minutes later Agent Flannery emerged and came over to them. He held up a pill bottle in a clear baggie.

"Is this yours?" he asked Connor. "We found it in the medicine cabinet in your bathroom."

There was no label on the bottle. The agent handed the baggie to Connor, who saw some pills in the bottom of the plastic bottle. They looked like the fentanyl pill he'd seen on the floor of Elena's guest bedroom, but he couldn't be sure without closer inspection and the opportunity to scan the pills with his phone.

"That's not mine," he said. "I don't take any prescription medication on a regular basis."

"Can you explain why it was in your medicine cabinet?"

Connor started to speak but shut his mouth. The agent waited for a moment, then turned away. Five minutes later the officers were gone. Connor and Reg entered the house. It was a wreck with drawers opened and contents spilled onto the floor. Connor went into his bedroom and bathroom. The medicine cabinet door was open. His toothpaste, mouthwash, and extra razor were where he normally left them.

"Reg, I'm not sure what to say," he started. "I've never seen that pill bottle—"

"Given what I believe, there's no need to explain. I don't want you to say anything in case I'm asked later about our conversations."

"Okay."

"Do you want any help straightening up?"

"No, no. I'll do it."

Connor glanced over at the nightstand where he'd been charging his cell phone before he was arrested. It was gone.

"They took my phone," he said.

"I'll bring you an extra one I have for the business," Reg replied. "Give me thirty minutes."

"Thanks."

Reg left. Connor took a quick shower, shaved, and put on clean clothes. He was picking up in the living room when there was a knock on his door. He glanced through the sidelight. It was Liz.

CHAPTER 39

WHEN SHE ARRIVED AT THE JAIL, LIZ WAS INFORMED that Connor had posted bail. She drove directly to his house and rehearsed several opening lines. But seeing him standing in the foyer of his house, words left her. She stepped forward and wrapped her arms around him. After a couple of seconds, she felt his arms around her. They stood in silence until he released her. Liz held on a moment longer.

"I'm glad you're out of jail," she said. "May I come in?"

"I think you already did."

Connor stepped aside and Liz entered the living room. Her mouth dropped open.

Connor spoke. "The GBI searched my house. They were still here when Reg brought me home from the jail. The agents took my hunting rifle, cell phone, and a bottle of pills in an unmarked container found in my medicine cabinet. The agent in charge showed me the pills. I'm afraid they were fentanyl."

"Oh no."

"Do you think they'll issue another arrest warrant for me?" he asked.

"Yes, if it turns out to be fentanyl."

"Someone planted the pills in my house while I was in jail. I open that cabinet every morning. There's not much in it."

Liz shook her head in bewilderment. "You need a lawyer."

"I need someone who can rescue me from the pit I've been thrown into. This is more about an investigation than lawyering."

"You're right." Liz glanced again around the living room. "Let me help you put your house back together."

They were working when Reg returned and gave Connor a cell phone. They talked briefly. It touched Liz when she saw how much the businessman cared for Connor.

"I've already forwarded the video you showed me to a lab in California for analysis," she said to Reg. "They should have an answer within a day or so."

"Can you and Harold help find Connor a lawyer?"

"I don't have those connections, so you may want to ask Harold. He's sympathetic to Connor's situation."

"That's my next task," Reg said, turning to Connor. "I'll let you know."

Reg left. They finished straightening up the living room.

"I'll take care of my room later," Connor said. "I'm hungry but don't want to go to a public place to eat."

"I understand. We could fix something at my place."

Connor was silent for a moment. "If I show up, it might upset Sam and Bev Devon," he said.

"She's been a huge supporter."

"But a lot has changed over the past twenty-four hours."

"Let's see what you have."

"My pantry isn't in the best shape. I was planning a trip to the grocery store before the arrest."

Connor's cupboard was very bare. The only options were

sandwiches and some frozen chicken and venison in his freezer. He had a decent collection of spices, and a couple of onions.

"I'm not tackling deer meat," Liz said as they stood in front of the refrigerator. "How about pollo a la plancha? But you don't have any black beans or rice."

"After what I've eaten recently, that sounds wonderful by itself."

Connor cut up the onions while the chicken thawed under cold running water. After that it was a one-person operation. Connor sat at the kitchen table while Liz cooked the meal. He told her about his experiences in jail.

"If I'd not had the dream about the waterfall, I wouldn't know what to think about this," she said. "But it sounds amazing."

"Jail is going to change the rest of my life for reasons no one would suspect." Connor added in a softer voice, "And thanks again for greeting me the way you did. It meant a lot."

Liz had her back to him as she sautéed the chicken. "You mean a lot to me," she said without facing him.

They ate in the backyard. Connor prayed before the meal and thanked God for her in such a sweet way that it made Liz teary. While they ate, she was impressed with how at peace he seemed. They talked about the food and Connor's garden. After the meal, they cleaned the dishes together. Connor didn't have a dishwasher in the older home.

"I don't want to leave," Liz said when they finished. "But I know I have to."

"I'd like to see you again," Connor replied. "I'm suspended from my duties at the church, so I don't have any place to go. If Reg calls about a lawyer, I'll follow up with that. Maybe we could drive over to Fannin County for dinner."

"I've never been there. Oh, I forgot to tell you that Elena wanted to visit you at the jail. She was going to tell you that she doesn't believe you're guilty of anything."

"That's good to know, but I don't think it's smart for me to meet or talk with Elena unless you or someone else is there."

"Do you want me to set up a meeting?"

"Only if she requests it and you can fit it into your schedule. No one except you and Reg has the number for my new cell phone. I'm going to keep it that way for a few days. Being off the grid is probably going to be best for now."

Liz wanted Connor to kiss her before she left, but he didn't. He simply walked her to the door and thanked her again for coming. Driving home, she thought about movie scenes in which two people passionately embrace and kiss right before bombs are about to drop on their heads. The depictions never rang true to her, and she knew they didn't reflect real life.

Shortly after arriving at her apartment, her phone vibrated. It was Elena.

═══════════

Connor was exhausted. He straightened up his bedroom without finding anything else missing. After putting on his pajamas, he lay down in his bed, which was much more comfortable than the lower bunk in the jail cell. But the lower bunk would always have a special place in his heart. He quickly fell asleep.

In the middle of the night, he suddenly woke up to a light flashing across the far wall of his bedroom. Connor slipped out of bed and, staying close to the floor, made his way to the window where the light originated. The light disappeared. Connor peeked over the edge of the windowsill. There was a streetlight near the corner of his lot. He thought he saw a figure running through the far edge of the area the light illuminated. Connor checked the doors of the house to make sure they were locked. Returning to bed, he lay awake for some time before sleep overcame him again.

═══════

On Saturday, Connor stayed around the house and worked in the backyard. He and Liz touched base a couple of times, and Michelle sent him a text message that a group of supporters at church were going to pray for him the following morning and asked if he wanted to be present. He replied:

No, but tell everyone how much I appreciate them standing with me.

═══════

Sunday was a cold, rainy day. Not wanting to hike, Connor took his Jeep out for a long ride on muddy roads. Twice, he had to use the winch on the front of the vehicle to pull the Jeep out of a ditch. In a lot of ways, the ride was a metaphor for his life. He was thankful for any winch the Lord provided. After eating a midafternoon lunch in a neighboring town, he returned home, thankful for the day's solitude.

═══════

At 6:15 a.m. on Monday, he received a text message from Liz:

I'm meeting Elena at the coffee shop in forty-five

> minutes. She heard you were out of jail and wants
> you to be there.

Connor didn't want to leave his house, much less be seen in public with Elena Thompson. He typed a brief reply:

> No

Liz's reply arrived in a few seconds:

> I had to ask.

Connor fixed a pot of coffee. Sitting in the living room, he wasn't sure what to do. Without the need to prepare a Sunday sermon or take care of any other ministerial duties, his time was unencumbered by responsibilities. He scrolled through the list of books he wanted to read on his tablet. Nothing piqued his interest. Checking the weather, he saw it was going to be a partly cloudy day with lower temperatures than usual for this time of year. A few hours in the woods seemed like the best option. But before he did that, he wanted to call Lyle and Sarah Hamilton and tell them what happened in the jail cell. He waited until he could be sure Josh had left for school to do so. Lyle answered the phone.

"This is Connor. I'm using a phone Reg Bullock lent me after the police confiscated mine."

"We heard you made bail," Lyle said. "How are you doing?"

"That's what I want to talk about. Is Sarah available?"

"Yes, I'll get her."

Liz arrived at the coffee shop before Elena. She ordered a latte and sat at a small table in a corner. There was only one other couple present. Elena rushed through the door. She brushed a strand of hair from her eyes and came over to her.

"Are you going to order a coffee?" Liz asked.

"Yeah, I need one," she replied. "Some kind of strong espresso."

Liz watched as the barista made the coffee. Elena returned to the table.

"Did you turn off your cell phone?" she asked.

"Yes."

"Why didn't Connor come?"

"He's not going out in public."

"Why not?" Elena rolled her eyes. "I don't care what the police think. He's not done anything wrong. I'm tempted to drive over to his house right now."

"Please don't," Liz said, hoping she didn't sound desperate. "Give him space."

"I don't know why he'd need space from me."

"He'll get in touch with you as soon as he feels it's right."

Glancing over her shoulder, Elena leaned in close and barely spoke above a whisper. "Connor didn't have anything to do with Matt's death, but I believe it may not have been an accident. Do you remember the pills Connor claimed he found in my guest room bath?"

"Yes."

"I had the odd-looking one analyzed and it turned out to be fentanyl. Someone was trying to kill me and make it look like an overdose."

"Why would someone want to kill you?" Liz asked in surprise.

"Because they were afraid I would figure out what they did!"

Elena replied. "Don't you see? Connor is innocent, but Anne and Winston Boone are guilty. They hired Tyson Nash to kill Matt and then come after me. Tyson is the one who planted the pills in my house for me to take. He knew what was going on with Matt because I told him everything."

"Elena, you've got so much spinning around inside your head."

"Anne called Tyson's phone the day Matt died. Don't you see?"

Liz paused. "I talked with Neil Peterson yesterday," she said. "He admitted calling Nash the morning of Matt's death at the specific direction of Winston Boone, who referred to Tyson as a 'vendor.'"

"Peterson was involved too!" Elena exclaimed.

"Not necessarily. He may not have known why Boone wanted him to call Nash, but he did so at his direction."

Elena spoke rapidly. "Once the police started investigating the cause of Matt's death, Anne and Boone implicated Connor. They were concerned about him because of the video he took of the big deer. You know, the video that proved Tyson was on the Burnt Pine Tree property."

"Connor never confirmed it was Tyson."

"But I believe it's him."

Liz wasn't going to disagree with Elena. "We need to let the police conduct the investigation," she said.

"But they're doing a terrible job! I want you to pass along what I've figured out. Will you do that? I want them focusing on what might actually be true."

"Yes."

Elena sat back in her seat. "Good. What does this mean for the life insurance? I know Anne and Boone will go to jail and won't receive anything. But you told me I'd still be able to collect the double indemnity amount even if Matt was murdered, correct?"

"Yes, under the language in the policy, but we'll sort through all that once the truth comes out from the police investigation."

"Whatever you need to do, do it now!" Elena demanded. "Connor and I are in danger. And so are you if anyone finds out that you know the truth."

<hr>

Connor told Lyle and Sarah about his God encounter in the jail cell. The couple then prayed with him. Shortly after the call ended, there was a knock on his front door. It was Liz. She looked frazzled.

"Come in," Connor said.

"Elena," Liz began. "She's all over—"

"Inside or out?" Connor cut in.

"Uh, inside. It's too chilly for this Florida girl."

They sat in the living room. Connor listened to Liz relate what Elena told her at the coffee shop.

"As much as I don't want to believe that Matt was murdered, some of what Elena said makes sense," Connor said. "And I may have had an intruder snooping around the house Friday night."

Connor told her about the light shining in his bedroom and the figure he saw running away from the house.

"That makes me nervous," Liz replied. "Elena told me all three of us may be in danger."

Connor was quiet for a moment. "It's just as plausible that Elena was working either alone or with Winston Boone and Tyson Nash to have Matt killed so they could collect the life insurance money. She's known about the video I took from the beginning. And Anne Thompson also called Nash shortly before Matt died. That points to her."

"I have no idea," Liz sighed. "But someone needs to track down Tyson Nash and question him. That's not something we can do. Lawyers with two years of experience and ministers aren't usually expert crime solvers."

"Agreed."

Connor stretched his legs out in front of him. "I may go for a hike today."

"Are you sure it's a good idea for you to be alone in the woods?"

"That's my element. I'm more comfortable there than any-place else."

"Promise that you'll call me when you get home."

"Will do."

It was late in the afternoon, and Liz hadn't heard from Connor. He'd not responded to four phone calls and six text messages, each one more panicked than the last.

Becky buzzed her phone. "Detective Norman from the sheriff's department is here to see you."

Liz's heart dropped. The only reason why the detective might want to see her was that something terrible had happened to Connor. She made her way to the reception area. The detective had his back to her.

"You want to see me?" Liz asked, her voice trembling.

"In private," the detective replied.

Fighting back tears, Liz led the way to the conference room. Before the door closed, she spoke. "It has to do with Connor Grantham, doesn't it?"

"Partly. I know your firm isn't representing him, but I wanted to let you know what's happened as a courtesy. It also has to do with Elena Thompson. May I sit down?"

"Of course," Liz said, biting her lower lip.

Norman looked directly into Liz's eyes. "It's ultimately up to the GBI, but I believe the murder charge against Reverend Grantham is going to be dropped."

"What?" Liz blurted out in shock. "Is Connor okay? I thought you were here to tell me that something horrible happened to him."

"I stopped by his house, but he wasn't there. That's when I decided to swing by here. Why do you think he's in danger?"

Liz rapidly told the detective everything she'd heard from Elena and Connor. Norman remained impassive.

"Elena wanted me to let you know all this because she's worried about her safety, and ours," Liz said as she finished.

"I believe part of what she told you is true. Much of it isn't. A primary suspect in the death of Matt Thompson is Tyson Nash, who was taken into custody in Atlanta a couple of hours ago. In his pocket were tickets to Qatar, which doesn't have an extradition treaty with the United States." The detective paused. "The other suspect is Elena Thompson. A patrol car is on the way to her house at this time to bring her in for questioning. Will this firm be representing her in any criminal case?"

Liz scrambled to organize her thoughts. "That's up to her and Mr. Pollard," she said. "He's out of the office for the rest of the day."

"Let us know as soon as possible."

"Can you tell me the reason why the charges against Connor are going to be dropped?"

"That occurs when the evidence points clearly in another direction."

"Can you tell me anything more specific?"

ROBERT WHITLOW

The detective stood and cleared his throat. "I'd better be going. But the truth will come out eventually, either through criminal discovery if you represent Mrs. Thompson, or in the newspaper if you don't."

Liz walked Norman to the reception area, then quickly returned to her office to check her cell phone. Still nothing from Connor. Without any confidence that it would elicit a response, she sent another text:

> Detective Norman came to my office. He believes
> all charges against you will be dropped!! Call me!!
> Now!!

The message didn't confirm delivery. Frantic, Liz couldn't stay at work any longer. She drove to Connor's house. Both of his vehicles were parked out front. She ran up the sidewalk, rang the doorbell, and pounded the door. Her heart was beating out of her chest. The door opened. It was Connor. He was wearing a jacket, hiking boots, and a ball cap. Liz didn't know whether to scream at him or embrace him.

"Where have you been and why didn't you call or text me?!" she demanded.

Connor stared at her wide-eyed. "I was going to. I got a late start and didn't have service with Reg's phone when I was in the woods. The battery died while I was on the hike. I didn't have the right charger, and on the way home stopped by the store to get one. I just plugged it in. I'm sorry you were worried."

"Worried?!" Liz responded and then burst into tears.

Connor reached out to put his hand on her shoulder. She turned away. It took her several seconds to speak.

"Detective Norman just left my office," she managed. "They've arrested Tyson Nash in Atlanta."

"Good."

"Norman believes all charges against you are going to be dropped. And they're taking Elena in for questioning."

Connor's face registered shock. He held out his hand again. This time Liz took it, and he led her into the living room. They sat down on the couch, and Liz told him about the meeting with Detective Norman. Liz stopped as her tears returned.

"A lawyer is not supposed to get emotionally involved in a case," she said. "Looks like I failed miserably."

Connor put his right arm around her shoulders. Liz leaned against him.

"Enough of this," Liz said, sniffling. "I guess that's all the pressure being released."

"For both of us."

Liz looked up at him. Connor leaned over and kissed her wet cheek, then kissed her lips. They parted after a few moments.

"Will you do that again?" Liz asked. "I wasn't expecting it and really want to enjoy it."

Connor smiled and moved closer to her.

CHAPTER 40

THE FOLLOWING DAY'S EDITION OF THE BRYSON newspaper set a record for number of copies sold. Liz was in her office when Becky excitedly brought her a copy.

"This is so wonderful," Becky exclaimed.

Articles about the case covered the first page. There was no factual information beyond what Detective Norman had told Liz, but her favorite line was: "Both the GBI and the District Attorney's Office confirmed that all charges against local minister Connor Grantham have been dismissed. He is no longer a person of interest in the investigation." Liz was reading the articles a second time when Harold came into her office. He, too, had a copy of the newspaper.

"Have you heard anything from Elena Thompson?" he asked.

"No texts, no emails, no calls."

"That's because she hired a lawyer in Atlanta named Kit Cook to represent her. I just got off the phone with the sheriff. He let me know."

"What do you know about Ms. Cook?"

"She's one of the top criminal defense lawyers in the state. Very aggressive. Very smart."

"Did the sheriff tell you anything else about the investigation?"

"Maybe," Harold responded with a slight smile. "Are you interested?"

"Don't tease me."

"Okay. It seems Detective Norman figured out the same thing about the date on the surveillance video of Connor outside the lodge at Burnt Pine Tree that Reg Bullock suspected. Without involving the GBI, he had the video analyzed and the results came back that it had been altered. In the meantime, the GBI independently ordered Connor's arrest, in part because of a call from Elena to Agent Flannery informing him that Connor gave Matt some fentanyl on the day of the hunt and did the same to her. She claimed there was a stash of street-manufactured fentanyl at Connor's house."

Liz's mouth dropped open.

Harold continued. "While the GBI was waiting for issuance of a search warrant, Norman initiated video surveillance of Connor's house and captured images of a break-in. The intruder was wearing the same type of toboggan hat as the man in the video Connor took with his cell phone on the day Matt died."

"Tyson Nash."

"Seems so. Anyway, the sheriff believes Elena is now going to try to link Nash as the hit man to Winston Boone or Matt's ex-wife, not her."

"Which is the story she tried to sell to me the other day at the coffee shop."

"Once that happens, it's going to come down to whether Nash or Elena caves in and offers to testify against the other in return for some kind of plea bargain that won't result in a life sentence or worse."

"Elena will try to get out of it."

"Possibly. She's so unpredictable. But she's no longer going to be a client of this firm. Send her a withdrawal letter and refund any of the retainer that remains."

"Gladly." Liz hesitated. "How much of this can I tell Connor?"

"None of it. But you can reassure him that what the newspaper printed today about him is as solid as the stone tablets for the Ten Commandments."

"I may not use that analogy."

"You should. I think it fits."

———

Connor called Reg. "I know I'm still suspended from my duties, but do I have to stay away from the church?" he asked.

"What do you have in mind? It's going to be a few days before the board can get together and decide next steps."

"Talk to Michelle and stare at the mountains through the windows in the office."

"I can't see any harm in that. But it's too soon to predict how the board is going to vote on your reinstatement as pastor. There are some folks who think it's time to move on because of the baggage on your record that's unacceptable. Personally, I think that's garbage. The criminal charges were dismissed because you're innocent. You're the same man you were before this mess started."

"Not true," Connor replied.

"What do you mean?"

"This has profoundly affected my relationship with God. I'm not sure what it's going to be like, but if I return to Rock Community Church, the congregation is getting a new pastor."

"That makes me curious enough to give you a second chance."

"Thanks for the vote of confidence," Connor answered.

"Hey, I've prayed more over the past few weeks than in most years."

"Prayer is one of the subjects that is going to receive a lot more attention if I return to the pulpit."

"Head on over to the church," Reg said. "If someone sees you and complains, I'll deal with it."

―――――――――

When Connor walked into the office suite, Michelle was sitting with her back to him and facing her computer monitor.

"Excuse me," he said. "I don't have an appointment but need to see a pastor with expertise in emotional and spiritual recovery from false accusations."

Michelle spun around in her chair. "Connor!"

"Yes, it's me."

Tears appeared in Michelle's eyes. She didn't try to wipe them away as they rolled down her cheeks.

"I've been sick with worry. And when I heard the news that you'd been cleared—" She stopped as more tears flowed.

"I'm still suspended from my duties, so I'm here as a visitor."

"If they don't beg you to come back, there is going to be a revolt!"

"Don't lead a rebellion. I'm trusting the Lord to sort it out. That's what Sarah Hamilton is praying."

Michelle grabbed a handful of tissues from a box on her desk and blew her nose. "This has been so hard," she said, shaking her head. "And I don't even have the right to say that because you're the one who's suffered. But it made me realize how much I appreciate and respect you. You have so much integrity."

"Thank you, thank you," Connor said with smile. "Hopefully, we'll know something soon about my status at the church."

"I may not lead a revolt, but the members of the board are going to hear from a lot of people who have very strong positive feelings about bringing you back."

"Let the voice of the people be heard."

Connor was silent for a moment. "Do you remember the afternoon I went into the sanctuary and encountered the glory of the Lord?" he asked.

"Yes."

"The same thing, only better, happened the night I spent in jail."

Michelle's eyes widened. "That's like something from the Bible."

"And I believe one of the things I'm supposed to do is encourage people to expect God to meet with them just as powerfully. It will be different for each of us but uniquely personal and wonderful."

"I have chill bumps." Michelle rubbed her arms. "That's always a sign for me that something spiritual is going on."

As soon as Liz arrived home, she saw Bev Devon hurrying from the house toward her. Liz waited for her.

"Have you talked to Connor?" Bev asked in an anxious voice.

"Yes."

"How is he doing?"

"Amazingly well considering what he's been through."

"Oh, I'm so relieved." Bev sighed. "When Sam and I heard that he'd been put in jail and charged with murder, we didn't know what to think or feel. Actually, that was more me than Sam. He told me

Connor hadn't done anything wrong, and the truth would come out. Then he fixed himself a bowl of ice cream."

"I could use a bowl of ice cream right now."

"Come over and have one," Bev said brightly. "Sam makes me buy all kinds of flavors. Sometimes our freezer looks like we should open an ice cream parlor."

An hour later, and after sampling three different flavors of ice cream, Liz returned to her apartment. Sitting in the living room, she realized that a great weight had lifted from her shoulders. And it wasn't just the fact that Connor was cleared of wrongdoing. It was related to the firm's representation of Elena Thompson. Involvement with Elena had caused an invisible burden to rest on Liz's soul. She'd been carrying it so long that she'd gotten used to the feeling. Now that it was gone, she could live free of the oppressive load.

"I'm glad that's over," she said out loud, and then realized her words were a prayer. "Amen."

CHAPTER 41

SIX MONTHS LATER

IT WAS A WARM, EARLY SPRING TUESDAY. LIZ WAS eating lunch outside at Manuel's Taqueria.

"And I'd like to order four tamales to go," she said to the restaurant owner.

"Great." Manuel nodded. "There's nothing wrong with eating tamales, rice, and beans twice a day. A lot of people do it."

"They're for my boyfriend's supper." Liz smiled.

"Do you have an air fryer?" Manuel asked.

"Yes."

"Use that, not the microwave. And don't overcook them. They're a forgiving dish, but you can abuse them."

"I would never want to abuse one of your tamales."

Liz returned to the office. As soon as she passed Jessica's door, the assistant called out. "Come in here. I have big news."

"What is it?"

"Tyson Nash has reached a plea bargain with the district attorney and is going to testify against Elena Thompson. He agreed to a thirty-five-year sentence. The case against her is going to trial in a couple of months."

"I'll stay away from the courthouse when that happens."

"Do you think Connor Grantham will be called to testify?"

Harold and Liz had discussed that likelihood with Connor.

"Yes, their efforts to frame him are a big part of the conspiracy to cover up the murder once it couldn't be labeled an accident."

"How do you think Connor will handle it?"

"Harold and I told him the best approach will be to tell what happened to him and not try to explain it. I'm sure the DA will prep him."

That evening, Connor and Liz were eating dinner together.

"Are you sure you don't want one of these tamales?" he asked.

"I had my daily quota at lunch. This salad is perfect for me," Liz said. "You should sprinkle more hot sauce on the tamales. That will bring out the full flavor."

"My mouth can't tolerate the heat like yours does. I'm not a fire-breathing preacher."

Connor took a long drink of water.

"Have you finished your sermon for Sunday?" Liz asked.

"Almost."

"What are you going to talk about?"

"My mother's death. It's time for me to take the next step from grief toward healing. Everyone who'll be sitting in the sanctuary has suffered a loss and needs to know the God of comfort. I invited my father."

"Really?" Liz asked in surprise. "What did he say?"

"That he'll try to make it. I'm not sure if it's a maybe or an indirect turndown. But I had to ask him. He likes you, and I mentioned that we could eat lunch together."

"I hope he shows up. If so, my goal is to make him laugh."

Connor cut into his final tamale. "Would you like to go on a hike this Saturday?" he asked.

"Where?"

"Can it be a surprise?"

"Is it going to be strenuous?"

"Nothing you can't handle. And there's no rain in the forecast."

———————

Saturday morning Connor packed up the Jeep. On the way to Liz's apartment, he passed the road that led to the Hamilton home. Lyle, Josh, and Connor had gone skeet shooting three times. Josh was a natural and loved it. Lyle had regained partial feeling in his legs, and his treating neurosurgeon held out hope that he might eventually walk with assistance. The doctor's explanation was that the nerves in Lyle's back weren't as badly damaged as first thought. Connor leaned toward a creative miracle.

Sarah was in the midst of cancer treatment with the resulting hair loss and all the other side effects of chemo and radiation. But the more battered her body, the more radiant her spirit. Connor held her in awe. Her prayer that she'd live to see Josh married had turned into a promise from the Lord, a new concept to Connor. Whenever Sarah came to mind, Connor stopped what he was doing and prayed for her. He did so today.

Arriving at Liz's apartment, he knocked on the door. It was a cool morning but would warm up considerably as the day wore on. Connor was wearing hiking shorts and a short-sleeved shirt. Liz had on a jacket and long pants.

"Aren't you going to get cold?" she asked when she saw him.

"Not at the pace we're going to walk. You know how quickly the body heats up on a hike."

"Just a minute while I change," she said, disappearing.

Connor waited in the kitchen. He saw what she'd prepared for their lunch. There were a variety of cold cuts and cheeses. The food for the day was going to be a mixture of charcuterie board and high-end deli. He sampled a piece of smoked salmon.

"Don't touch that," Liz commanded. "It has to be paired with the right cheese."

Connor popped it into his mouth. "Delicious," he said. "All I ate at the house was a bagel."

Liz had changed into clothes similar to what Connor had on. Her hair was in a ponytail.

"New shoes?" Connor asked.

"Yeah, they're supposed to be better on rock."

"How do you know we're going to be scrambling over rocks?"

"Just in case."

They took off. Liz propped her feet on the dash of the vehicle. The topic of Elena and the trial was taboo when they were on a personal outing. They turned onto a gravel road that after a mile transitioned to dirt followed by dirt plus ruts. Liz grabbed the handle near the passenger door as the Jeep lurched from side to side.

"Why are these roads always so rough?" she asked.

"So only the determined can reap the reward that awaits."

They stopped at a place where the road was so narrow the vehicle couldn't squeeze through and got out.

"I'm thinking about getting a puppy," Connor said as he slung the daypack onto his shoulders. "One that will enjoy being in the woods."

"What kind?"

"German wirehaired pointer."

"That's specific."

"I had one in the past. I recently found a breeder in Virginia. Do you like dogs?"

"Who doesn't love a puppy? Can we take him to the beach?"

"Yes."

Instead of starting off down the path, Connor leaned against the Jeep. Liz glanced over at him.

"Is something bothering you?" he asked.

"It's hard to hide anything from you," Liz said with a deep sigh. "Yes. I know we agreed not to bring up the subject on days like this, but I've been thinking about Elena, which makes me both sad and angry. I no longer feel responsible for her, and what she did was horrible. But she's still a person, and I know she's in torment."

"Today you're on the sad side of your feelings?"

"Yeah, I guess so."

And right there, Connor offered up a short prayer for Elena.

"Amen," he said.

"Amen," Liz said with a small smile. "That helped."

Liz walked beside Connor until the track narrowed to single-person width. They wound their way through hardwoods whose limbs were vibrant with new leaves. After about thirty minutes they crossed a tiny rivulet of water.

"That's only here because of the rain we've had over the past week," Connor said. "It comes from a wet-weather spring about fifty yards through the trees."

"You've been there?"

"Yes."

"I've never seen water coming directly from the ground."

"You will today."

Connor turned right. The way was blocked by spindly under-brush that he pushed aside with his hands and arms so she could follow. They entered a tiny moss-covered clearing. Small rocks were scattered across the ground. In between some of the rock crevices water seemed to magically appear.

"That's amazing," Liz said.

She reached down and touched the cool water.

"Eventually, a few molecules of that water will reach the Atlantic Ocean," Connor said.

Connor used his hands to carve out a tiny pool, then used his purifier to capture Liz a drink.

"I never get tired of this," she said as she swallowed the refresh-ing liquid.

They stayed by the spring for several minutes.

"Ready?" Connor asked.

"To go home?"

"No," he said with a grin. "The main attraction is up ahead."

Back on the trail, they began to climb. There weren't any switch-backs. They took it slow and steady. When Liz heard Connor breathing heavily it made her feel better about the strain on her lungs. They broke out of the trees onto a boulder field.

"Are we crossing that?" she asked, catching her breath.

"Yes. You were right to wear your rock shoes. It's not technical, but I don't want you to sprain an ankle."

"Remember, your legs are longer than mine by half a mile."

"And you're nimbler than me with better balance."

Connor led the way. Liz followed his lead but had to modify where she positioned her feet. They'd crossed about a hundred yards when Connor suddenly turned sharply up the hill and stopped. Liz joined him.

Connor pointed and said, "Does that look familiar? You saw it one morning on Facetime."

Liz tilted her head to the side. "It's the two trees growing from the same trunk."

Connor turned around and faced the valley below. "And this is where I come when I want to see Bryson and Etowah County."

Liz followed his gaze. The town was laid out before them.

"Is that the church?" she asked.

"Yep. And can you make out the courthouse to the left?"

Liz identified the roof. After a few moments she turned around to look again at the trees. She stepped forward and ran her fingers across the rippled gray bark. Extending her arms, she rested a hand against each massive trunk.

"Do you know why I brought you here?" Connor asked.

The joke Liz was going to make about eating smoked salmon and cheese suddenly died on her tongue when she saw the look on Connor's face.

"Tell me," she replied.

"I believe you and I are like those two trunks," Connor said. "And the Bible says two shall become one. Liz, I love you with my whole heart and want to spend the rest of my life on this earth joined together with you."

Liz leaned in to him. They embraced and kissed. When they parted, Connor reached in his pocket and took out a tiny box.

"Yes!" Liz said before he opened it.

Dropping to one knee, Connor asked her to marry him, and

she repeated her yes with a huge smile on her face. The diamond glistened in the sun as Connor slipped it onto her finger.

Standing side by side with the unity tree behind them, Liz joined her hand with his.

"Two becoming one," she said. "I like that."

ACKNOWLEDGMENTS

WRITING A NOVEL IS BOTH SOLITARY AND COLLABorative. When I'm sitting in front of my computer it's just me and the characters. I like that interaction. Once I finish the first draft of a story, other people enter the imaginary world. For *Double Indemnity*, Becky Monds, Jacob Whitlow, and Deborah Wiseman provided the collaborative component. I like that interaction too. I've been writing since 1996, and the longer I write, the more I appreciate the input of others. This is a better book because of their suggestions. I also want to thank my wife, Kathy, who helps shepherd my time and wholeheartedly supports what I'm doing.

DISCUSSION QUESTIONS

1. What were your first impressions of Elena? How did your perceptions of her change over the course of the novel? What do you think motivated her actions?

2. Had you ever heard of the double indemnity clause before? What purpose do you think it serves? How much did that clause play in to the motives for killing Matt?

3. We get to see Connor and Liz's relationship from their first meeting to their engagement. Would you have paired the two of them together if you were a matchmaking member of Connor's church? Why or why not? Why do you think their relationship works?

4. Sarah is an incredible woman of faith. What impact did her faith have on Connor? And what impact did it have on you as a reader?

5. Connor had some really incredible encounters with God in the church and the jail cell. How did they change Connor? Have you ever had encounters like that? If so, how did they change you?

6. At the beginning of the novel, Connor seemed to be led mostly by his head. He looked for answers in books and preferred quiet time in his study. How did he change over the course of the novel? Do you think there is a place for both head and heart clergy members?
7. After Connor is reinstated at the church, what changes do you think there will be in his ministry? How will the congregation respond?
8. Imagine it's ten years after the close of the book. What are Connor and Liz doing? What do their lives look like?

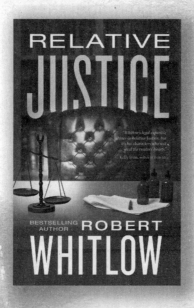

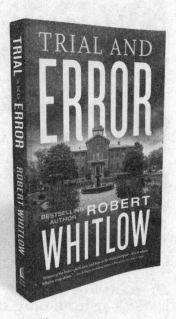

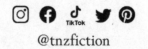

ABOUT THE AUTHOR

Photo by David Whitlow,
Two Cents Photography

ROBERT WHITLOW IS THE BESTSELLING author of legal novels set in the South and winner of the Christy Award for Contemporary Fiction for *The Trial*. He received his JD with honors from the University of Georgia School of Law where he served on the staff of the *Georgia Law Review*.

robertwhitlow.com
Twitter: @whitlowwriter
Facebook: @robertwhitlowbooks